PRAISE FOR THE NOVELS OF THE CHOSEN ONES

CHAINS OF FIRE

"The best of the series so far . . . unique—and edge-of-seat thrilling."
—Romance Reviews Today

"The urgency of plot ratchets up the emotional drama, giving the story an exhilarating edge." —*Romantic Times* (4½ stars)

CHAINS OF ICE

"High-stakes action and high-adrenaline adventure provide the literary fuel for the latest addictive addition to Dodd's scorchingly sensual the Chosen Ones series." —*Chicago Tribune*

STORM OF SHADOWS

"Christina Dodd has a knack for tense, heart-pounding action with a dash of quirky humor." —Errant Dreams Reviews

"A well-rounded cast, an exciting story line, and a romance that's as sweet as it is steamy. This book offers something for everyone who enjoys paranormal romance and is a must read for fans of the series." —Darque Reviews

"A riveting new series . . . The action and romance are hot! I have no idea what is next in this series, but . . . the suspense is killing me." —The Romance Readers Connection

"Fabulous urban romantic fantasy . . . a stupendous thriller."
—*Midwest Book Review*

STORM OF VISIONS

"The taut, suspenseful plot, intriguing characters, and a smooth, natural style show that Dodd has earned her place on the bestseller list." —*Publishers Weekly*

"Ms. Dodd plunges readers into a fast-paced tale with intriguing paranormal elements and treats them to a deliciously steamy romance that's sure to grab the reader's attention . . . suspenseful, packed with danger-filled action, and never slows as the story unfolds." —Darque Reviews

"Definitely hooked me . . . quirky, unusual, fun, tense, surprising, sexy, and wild!" —Errant Dreams Reviews

continued . . .

NOVELS BY CHRISTINA DODD

Danger in a Red Dress
Thigh High
Tongue in Chic
Trouble in High Heels
In Bed with the Duke
Taken by the Prince

THE SCARLET DECEPTION SERIES

Secrets of Bella Terra

THE DARKNESS CHOSEN SERIES

Scent of Darkness
Touch of Darkness
Into the Shadow
Into the Flame

THE CHOSEN ONES SERIES

Storm of Visions
Storm of Shadows
Chains of Ice
Chains of Fire

CHRISTINA DODD

REVENGE at BELLA TERRA

A SCARLET DECEPTION NOVEL

A SIGNET SELECT BOOK

SIGNET SELECT
Published by New American Library, a division of
Penguin Group (USA) Inc., 375 Hudson Street,
New York, New York 10014, USA

Penguin Group (Canada), 90 Eglinton Avenue East, Suite 700, Toronto,
Ontario M4P 2Y3, Canada (a division of Pearson Penguin Canada Inc.)
Penguin Books Ltd., 80 Strand, London WC2R 0RL, England
Penguin Ireland, 25 St. Stephen's Green, Dublin 2,
Ireland (a division of Penguin Books Ltd.)
Penguin Group (Australia), 250 Camberwell Road, Camberwell, Victoria 3124,
Australia (a division of Pearson Australia Group Pty. Ltd.)
Penguin Books India Pvt. Ltd., 11 Community Centre, Panchsheel Park,
New Delhi - 110 017, India
Penguin Group (NZ), 67 Apollo Drive, Rosedale, Auckland 0632,
New Zealand (a division of Pearson New Zealand Ltd.)
Penguin Books (South Africa) (Pty.) Ltd., 24 Sturdee Avenue,
Rosebank, Johannesburg 2196, South Africa

Penguin Books Ltd., Registered Offices:
80 Strand, London WC2R 0RL, England

First published by Signet, an imprint of New American Library,
a division of Penguin Group (USA) Inc.

First Printing, September 2011
10 9 8 7 6 5 4 3 2 1

For Lillian Gilmore,
ninety-six years young,
who knew me before I was born,
who lived next door and tells me stories about me when I
was a toddler,
who welcomed my husband and children into her
constantly expanding family,
who helped us when we were in need,
who remembers everyone's birthday, everybody's name,
and everyone who is dear to her.
Thank you for showing us how to live.
When it comes to kindness, attitude and love,
you're the gold standard.

And to Lillian's daughter,
Marilyn Johnson.
We miss you.

ACKNOWLEDGMENTS

Leslie Gelbman, Kara Welsh, and Kerry Donovan, my appreciation for your constant support. The covers for the Scarlet Deception series are absolutely fabulous; thank you to NAL's art department, led by Anthony Ramondo. To Rick Pascocello, head of marketing, and the publicity department with my special people, Craig Burke and Jodi Rosoff, thank you. My thanks to the production department, and of course, a special thank-you to the spectacular Penguin sales department: Norman Lidofsky, Don Redpath, Sharon Gamboa, Don Rieck, and Trish Weyenberg. You are the best!

Thank you to Ted Seghesio for so generously taking the time to answer my questions about the winery in spring, to David Messerli for steering the questions in the right direction, to Peter and Cathy Seghesio for guiding us in the nuances of wine tasting, to Jim Neumiller for kindly demonstrating to this city girl the rudiments of growing grapes. Last but not least, thank you to everyone in the Seghesio Family Vineyards tasting room for their hospitality and knowledge.

Chapter 1

Eli Di Luca walked into his grandmother's nineteenth-century farmhouse in the foothills above Bella Valley, carrying a case of wine, handpicked for a loving family celebration.

Every light in the house was on, the television was blaring, and six women were standing in the front room holding bottles of water and shouting at the big screen hung on the wall. "Catch it!" they yelled. "Catch it! Catch it! *Catchitcatchitcatchit!*"

He stopped. He stared.

Nonna's nurse, Olivia Kelly, so wide-eyed she always looked slightly astonished, stood apart from the group.

"Australian football?" he asked.

Olivia nodded shyly.

What an odd girl she was, part of the group, yet apart.

She reminded him of him.

The football player must have *caughtitcaughtitcaughtit*, because the other women high-fived one another, then saw him and waved cheerful greetings.

They were fascinating company.

His grandmother, his Nonna, was a young eighty years, stylish, cheerful, and so alive she frightened him with her energy. He'd never seen anything slow her down until almost three weeks ago, when she'd been attacked in her own home. This woman who had raised him, who had tamed the wild fourteen-year-old he had been when he returned from Chile, had been injured in a slow-boiling vendetta that had its roots deep in the past.

For years Eli had dwelled always on the brink of savagery; savagery was bred into him, and in his youth, during those six years when all the world was bleak and lonely, only savagery had kept him alive.

The assault on his grandmother had almost taken him over the edge. If she had been killed . . . the consequences would have made him a fugitive once more, for he would have hunted down the culprit and destroyed him slowly, broken bone by broken bone, until all that was left was consciousness, pain, and understanding of the wrong he had committed.

But Nonna had survived without permanent damage. Her arm was in a cast and she'd suffered a concussion, but she was home now, safe.

And so was Eli . . . for the moment.

In a normal voice, as if she hadn't just been jumping up and down, Nonna said, "Hello, dear, how was your trip?"

"Interesting." To put it mildly.

"I love San Francisco. I love the St. Francis. I wish I could have gone with you!" Nonna's eyes shone.

The venerable St. Francis hotel had survived the 1906 earthquake, World War I and World War II and all the wars after, the roaring twenties and the Depression, protests and prosperity and recession. The loud, joyful, boisterous winegrowers' tasting and auction had also left the hotel unscathed.

If only Eli could say the same of himself.

The memory of meeting the Italian Tamosso Conte during the event and hearing his outrageous business proposal haunted Eli's mind and heart.

The plan was absurd, insulting, and . . . tempting beyond all belief.

"Everyone missed you," he told Nonna. "Everybody asked about you, and asked why I had no beautiful, fascinating lady on my arm."

She laughed out loud. "You need to find a beautiful, fascinating lady to be your wife. Like Rafe did!"

His brother's recent marriage had put a sparkle in his grandmother's eyes and, he feared, would lead to a frenzy of attempted matchmaking.

Matchmaking was the one thing he did not need.

Taking advantage of the break in the action, Nonna's bodyguard, Bao Le, moved to the window and looked out. Diminutive, tough, and suspicious, she worked for Rafe, for his security firm, and from the beginning she had taken her job seriously. But a few weeks of caring for Nonna had turned the tables, because Nonna cared for everyone, and now Bao was part of their family.

It always happened. Eli was used to it.

Walking in, he shifted the box of wine to one hip and kissed Nonna's cheek. "How do you feel? How's the arm?"

"I feel fine. The cast is so much trouble, but not as much as this damned walker." Nonna pushed petulantly at the chrome cage around her. "I am thoroughly tired of it."

Olivia appeared immediately at her side. "The doctor said another couple of weeks, and if there have been no complications from your concussion, you can ditch the walker."

"I know. I know. The sooner, the better. But I've complained enough." Nonna patted Eli's cheek. "Did you get a lot of kudos for your wines at the dinner?"

"Pretty much."

Glowing with pride, Nonna looked around at her friends and relatives. "That's my boy!"

Brooke laughed. "There, Nonna—you sounded just like an Italian grandmother."

"And why shouldn't she?" Brooke's mom, Kathy Petersson, also stood with the help of a walker, but she was younger, so much younger than Nonna, in her fifties, Eli would guess. With her straight black hair, striking blue eyes, and curvaceous figure, she was an attractive woman. But she suffered from rheumatoid arthritis: It had taken the spring from her step, forced her from her position in the U.S. Air Force and into retirement in Bella Terra. But nothing tamed her fierce, fighting spirit. Now, with Brooke's marriage to Eli's brother Rafe, she had gone from Di Luca family friend to honored relative, and from the glow that lit her eyes, Eli suspected she hoped to be a grandmother herself soon.

You two will make beautiful babies together.

He wanted to flinch at the memory of those words.

Who the hell did Tamosso Conte think he was?

Eli answered his own question.

Conte thought—no, knew—he was the man who held all the trumps. But Nonna knew so many people, both here in Bella Valley and back in Italy. Perhaps Eli could shuffle the cards in his favor.

"Have you ever heard of an Italian gentleman named Tamosso Conte?" he asked.

Nonna's brow knitted. "I don't think so. Why?"

"I met him at the auction."

"I know him!" Francesca Pastore was fifty years old, a movie star, the most beautiful woman in Italy, a land renowned for its beautiful women—and she was Rafe's mother. "He is from Milan, a leather merchant, a self-made man, very rich, very powerful." She smiled. "Very charming."

Eli couldn't believe she was so indulgent to the man he found so direct and despicable. "He's short."

5

Francesca ran an amused gaze up and down Eli's six-foot-four-inch frame. "Is that how you think women measure charm, Eli Di Luca? If so, you are in for a sad surprise."

"Lately I've had all the sad surprises I can stand," Eli said. An understatement.

"Tamossa has been married, what? Five times, I think. He loves women. That's part of his magic." Francesca ran her hand through her long auburn hair. "You should try showing your love for the women, Eli. Nothing interests a female as much as a man who finds her fascinating."

He gave Francesca a lazy smile, bending all his charisma on her. "For a man like me, to be surrounded by women is a pleasure none other can surpass."

"Very good," Francesca purred, and fluttered her lashes.

Brooke applauded. "Wow. Impressive, Eli. I've always said you Di Luca men have raised the art of flirtation to new heights." She was pretty, smart, and talented, the head concierge of his family's Bella Terra resort (although in her determination to get away from Rafe, she had resigned . . . That hadn't worked out as she had planned). Because Brooke was also the first bride for one of the three Di Luca brothers . . . although if Tamosso Conte had his way, not the last.

Still smiling, giving not a hint of his inner turmoil, Eli asked, "This Tamosso Conte—have you ever met his daughter?"

"His daughter?" Francesca lifted her perfectly

arched brows. "He has been married many times, but he has no children."

Eli knew she was wrong. He'd seen the photo Tamosso had proffered.

The girl—she didn't look old enough to be called a woman—sat at a cluttered desk smiling at the camera. Her blond hair was twisted on top of her head, held up with a sharpened pencil, and careless wisps fell artlessly around her cheeks. She cradled her chin in her fist—a very determined chin, by the look of it—and peered right at the camera through big brown eyes. She was, as pictured, very pretty.

And all Eli had been able to think was . . . Photoshop.

Because her father had sagging jowls and a droopy nose, and he wasn't just short—he sported a workingman's build, with a barrel chest, broad shoulders, and a rotund gut. With genetics like that, the girl was doomed.

Eli supposed he shouldn't be so shallow . . . and maybe when he met her, no matter what she looked like, he'd like her.

Maybe when he married her, he'd worship her.

Maybe when pigs could fly, all the chicken would taste like bacon.

"You okay, honey?" Nonna asked. "You look a little ill."

She saw too much, so he moved the wine box in his arms as if he were growing tired of the weight, and looked around. "Where's Rafe? Where's the bridegroom?"

"He's in the kitchen." Brooke smirked at him. "Cooking."

Eli smirked back at her. "Training him right, hm?"

"He complained about the shouting, said that our voices were so high we gave him a headache, but I said if he thought that was going to get him out of sex tonight, he—"

Eli's sweet little eighty-year-old grandmother, the one who never swore, shouted, "Shit! Did you see that?" She pointed toward the screen.

The women started shouting again.

Eli backed out of the room and headed down the hall for the kitchen. He passed the dining room, passed the one bathroom in the house—when the extended Di Luca family got together, that made for some desperate moments of pounding and pleading—and went into the brightly lit and recently renovated kitchen.

Rafe was layering slices of eggplant with pasta, cheese, and Nonna's marinara sauce.

Noah was putting chicken fillets on a cooling rack, and that was placed on a cookie sheet that would catch any loose breading, and spraying them with cooking oil.

Both of his brothers had their sleeves rolled up and kitchen towels tucked into their belts. Both wore frowns of concentration.

"Does anyone besides me see the irony of having the women in the living room watching sports while the men cook dinner?" Eli put the case down on the counter and pulled out the first three bottles of wine.

"Shut up and put on your apron." Noah was the youngest of Gavino's sons, handsome, charming, and urbane, the manager of the Bella Terra resort and, to all appearances, the most well-adjusted. That was possibly the truth . . . although it didn't say much.

Eli walked over to him and peered over his shoulder. "What are you doing, man?"

"Rafe is making eggplant Parmesan casserole and I'm making chicken Parmesan."

"That's not how you make chicken Parmesan," Eli said. "And—eggplant Parmesan *casserole*? What's wrong with this picture?"

His two brothers turned on him. In unison, they asked, "Do you want to fry the chicken and the eggplant?"

There was only one right answer. "No."

"Then pour for us and get to work." Rafe was a military hero who now owned his own security firm. He gave orders well.

Briefly Eli toyed with the idea of taking wine to the ladies first, but decided he wasn't that much of a gentleman. So he uncorked three different Di Luca varietals, chosen to please each brother's palate, and while he did Noah said, "I don't mind cooking, and besides, I couldn't sit in there and listen to Nonna talk about some guy's tushie anymore."

Eli nodded. He could understand that. He poured the wine, put the glasses at his brothers' elbows, and said, "I've got to get the champagne. For, you know, the wedding toast." He bumped his shoulder against Rafe's.

"Pretty cool, huh?" Rafe stopped layering the casserole and turned. They bumped chests and hugged; then he did the same with Noah.

Eli supposed they should be civilized and have a wine toast, but they were guys, and somehow the body slam expressed their glee so much better.

After years of never making it work, Rafe and Brooke had finally tied the knot in a runaway marriage to Reno.

Nonna and Kathy wanted a real ceremony in a church, but all Eli could think was—thank God Rafe and Brooke hadn't waited. Thank God they had snatched at happiness while they could. There had been too much pain in the Di Luca brothers' lives; it was good to, at last, see one of them find happiness.

Thanks to Tamosso Conte, Eli had a chance for happiness, too, as good a chance as any person who ever tied the knot.

If that was cynical, so be it. He had planned to say "I do" someday.

He had simply never planned to walk down the aisle for money.

"I am proposing a marriage of convenience. Yes. A marriage between two people based on property values arranged between the prospective groom and the bride's father with an eye to a successful union that provides for the bearing and raising of offspring."

"You want me to marry your daughter?"

"I've researched you, Eli Di Luca, and you are Italian, from a good family, a responsible winemaker. You trusted a

friend. Your accountant stole your money and fled to South America. Now you're desperate to save your winery. So if you can convince my daughter to wed you, we have a deal. I'll pay your debts. You give me grandchildren."

"Grandchildren? With a woman I've never met? I don't even know her name."

"Chloë Robinson. My daughter's name is Chloë Robinson."

Now Eli had a decision to make, and he had to make it . . . soon.

Chapter 2

Noah finished spraying the chicken and opened the oven. He waved his hand inside. "Damn it! I forgot to turn it on."

His brothers chortled.

"Like you guys could do any better." Noah shut the oven and flipped the temp to four hundred.

"I turned *mine* on." Rafe indicated Nonna's much-loved second oven.

"If God had meant me to cook he wouldn't have made me the manager of a resort with a five-star restaurant," Noah snapped.

"That's not helping you now." Eli headed back down the hall to the front door, and as he passed the front room, the women were groaning—apparently a football player had bruised his tushie.

Kathy was offering to rub it for him.

He shook his head, walked out onto the wide, white-painted front porch, and stopped to take in the view.

Nonna's house sat on the crest of a hillside, and dated from the late nineteenth century, when Ippolito Di Luca arrived in central California, bought land all around long, narrow Bella Valley, and planted his first acres with the grapes he had brought from the old country. Nonna said Ippolito, a legendary vintner, had nursed his cuttings through the sea voyage from Italy, and within ten years his winemaking talents allowed him to buy this piece of ground. Here he had built this stylish farmhouse with tall ceilings, narrow windows, and ornate trim. Here he had brought his bride. Here they had started the Di Luca dynasty.

Of course, she had brought land and vineyards as her dowry.

So really, this marriage of convenience Eli was contemplating was nothing new. It was practically a family tradition.

Except, of course, the first Di Luca bride knew all the facts. Stories about Allegra Di Luca said that she took pride in providing her share of the income, that she ran the home and the farm while Ippolito created his wines. Would Chloë Robinson be that kind of help to Eli?

Who the hell knew?

"Grandchildren? What if I don't like her?"

13

"How could you not like her? She's American, like you. She's pretty. She's young. Twenty-three."

"For God's sake, man, I'm thirty-four. Too old for her."

"She needs a mature man, one to make her decisions for her."

"Your American daughter is going to let someone make her decisions for her? What does she say about this marriage of convenience?"

"Nothing. She knows nothing. And I would take it badly if you told her."

"I wouldn't dream of it."

"She's stubborn. She rejects every husband I offer her, so you'll have to be crafty. It won't be easy. She's smart, like me, and she has become . . . suspicious."

"Imagine that."

"She graduated in the top of her class at Rice University in Houston. She wrote a book. Only twenty-one years old when her first book was published, only twenty-two when it was optioned for a movie."

"How are her teeth?"

"Good. Strong, white. Also, she's a virgin."

"Don't be ridiculous. She's twenty-three and . . . Wait. How would you know?"

"I had her investigated, of course."

For the first time, Eli had felt sympathy for the poor kid. Her traditional Italian father was brokering a deal to marry her off. He didn't get the joke when Eli asked about her teeth as if she were a horse he was considering for purchase. And Tamosso had investigated her love life.

"A powerful man like you, you want a wife unsullied by another man's touch."

Not really. What Eli wanted was to pick his own wife, make sure she was calm, quiet, attractive, desired the same things he did, was willing to support him in his endeavors. . . .

He'd said all that once to Nonna. She'd suggested he buy a yellow Lab.

Women. They stuck together.

But he wanted a helpmate; he sure as hell didn't need a young prima donna with a career that took her into the limelight.

If only he were willing to ask his family for help.

But when he had taken control of Di Luca Wines, he had sworn he would create a place for himself in this world, in Bella Valley. He had vowed he would elevate the family fortunes—and to his great pride, he had been doing just that.

He had no modesty about his gift for creating wines that sang on the tongue. The gift was God-given, but he had gone to school, worked hard, learned how to cultivate his senses and when to trust his instincts. He was good at what he did. He won awards. His wines always rated at the top of the lists. He was everything Nonna (and Tamosso Conte) believed—one of the world's finest vintners.

Until his accountant, his *friend* Owen Slovak, had fled to South America, leaving Eli to discover that the bank account was clean and the taxes were in arrears.

If Eli didn't lay hands on a small fortune soon, the IRS was going to foreclose on the winery.

What a fool he had been to trust anyone outside of his family. To trust anyone at all . . .

So why not ask his family for help? They would give it willingly and without mockery.

But he couldn't stand to look in their faces and know he had failed them.

He could not bear to know he had broken his own vow.

Eli gazed at the silver ribbon of the Bella River that wound through the verdant bottomlands, at the plum orchards where falling blossoms swirled like pink snow on the wind, at the grapevines that dug their roots into the tough, shallow soil that rimmed the basin.

From here, he could make out the resort that had carried the family through Prohibition and the Depression and lifted them on a tidal wave of prosperity from the twentieth century and into the twenty-first. The main building was nestled among luxuriant landscaping and the vineyards that he tended so carefully. The town surrounded it, taking sustenance from the tourists and their dollars. North and south, east and west, the long valley was embraced by richly wooded mountains.

His brothers thought Eli loved nothing and no one, but that wasn't true. Here was the place his heart called home.

He descended the steep steps to the drive and to his

truck, a powerful extended-cab F-250 with a Power Stroke diesel engine, a six-speed manual transmission, and massive tires with tread that chewed up the ground.

He drove it, so Noah said, like an old lady.

Nonna objected, saying she was an old lady and she drove her '67 Mustang convertible faster than Eli drove his F-250.

Eli didn't care what they said. He knew what he had under the hood, and he knew he could go anywhere in his truck. If he had to, he could climb a sequoia.

As he pulled the case of champagne out of the backseat, he saw Bao watching him from the window, saw Nonna and Brooke join her and wave enthusiastically. He showed them a bottle and smiled when they stood at attention.

Yes, everyone was ready to celebrate.

This would be a great day . . . if only he weren't keeping things from his family. If he knew which move to make.

The phone rang in his pocket.

He put the case back in the truck, checked the phone number, and winced.

It was Conte.

Eli's moment of decision had arrived.

Chapter 3

"I want an answer." Conte's Italian accent sounded heavier, more *Godfather*-esque, on the phone.

The answer was yes, of course. Yes. Eli agreed to Conte's deal. He had only to say it. Say it!

But Conte had lost his patience. "I had not thought you would be so obstinate about what is really a simple plan. Perhaps I have picked the wrong man. I have an alternative choice, of course. I'll make him an offer."

"Wait! No, I . . . want to be sure of the terms." Eli drew a breath. "You said we would sign a contract and the terms would be clear. I'm to court your daughter, marry her, and you will pay my debt."

"That's right."

"All of my debt."

"The tax bills the accountant did not pay, the penalties, and the interest, and the United States government will no longer be threatening to foreclose on your winery. Plus I'll pay whatever bills your accountant left unpaid when he fled to South America. I'll put you back on your feet, Eli Di Luca, although I will ask that you not trust anyone so blindly ever again. Not even for my grandchildren would I bail you out again."

"I can promise I'll never put that much trust in anyone ever again. Despite evidence to the contrary, I'm not the trusting sort." Eli remembered the photo of Chloë, then recalled Conte's heavy features. She was an author, ambitious, flighty, probably nuts. She'd have a muse . . . hopefully the muse didn't want to sleep in the bed between them.

He smiled acidly at his own joke.

Yes, he was receiving the money, but he was binding himself to a woman of unknown character. He was shelling out, too. "When the debt is paid, I'll once more be in complete control of Di Luca Wines."

"I don't want your winery." Conte seemed to mean it.

Nevertheless, Eli would examine every word of the contract. "How do I convince your daughter that she loves me?"

"I don't care. You're a handsome young man. I suggest you feign love for her."

"You don't care if I actually love her?" Not that he would, but Conte seemed to dote on her.

"A man who loves a woman is weak." Conte's voice was sharply bitter. "Besides, do *you* want to love? I would have thought not—after all, your parents were grand lovers, and look what happened when your mother discovered your father was having an affair."

The guy was ice-cold in his analysis of Eli's past, Eli's family, Eli's prospects.

And he was right. Eli might as well marry this Chloë Robinson. With his parents as an example, he knew he had as good a chance for happiness here as anyone who wed. "No. I don't want to love. But I don't intend to have a broken marriage, either."

"Then make sure she has no reason to stray. She's only a woman, Eli Di Luca, and you're a smart man. Treat her like one of your wines, and your marriage will be solid."

Good advice from a man who had been married so many times.

"All right. It's a deal. Have your lawyer contact my lawyer. I assume you know who that is?" Since he knew everything else, Eli meant.

"The contracts are already in his office."

"You bastard." Conte had never had any doubt he would accept.

"He'll look them over today. You can sign them tomorrow." Conte's businesslike tone changed. "Enjoy your family celebration. They are one of the reasons you won the chance to marry my daughter, Eli Di Luca. Your family . . . they are good people."

"Yes." Eli glanced up at the window again.

Nonna stood watching him, wearing a worried expression.

He pantomimed exasperation and sent her a reassuring smile. "My family and I will do everything to make your daughter one of us."

"Chloë," Conte said. "Her name is Chloë."

"I know."

"Say it."

Conte was right. This resistance to using her name, as if that would make her real . . . it was stupid. "Chloë. We'll make Chloë part of our family."

"Thank you, Eli Di Luca. You're a man of honor, and I am glad to give my daughter into your keeping."

Eli shut his phone and stood for a moment breathing. Just breathing.

Good. That was done. Now all he had to do was court the girl.

Not a problem. He knew how to make a woman happy, and this woman was young, easily dazzled, without subtlety. He would turn her head with his attentions.

How very simple this courtship would be.

Picking up the case of champagne, he went around the house again and in the back door. He was pretty proud of how natural he looked and sounded as he stacked the champagne in the refrigerator and said, "Our Italian ancestors—the male ones, anyway— would be horrified at how pussy-whipped we are."

Noah slid the chicken breasts into the now-hot oven. Turning back to face the kitchen, he said, "Pussy-whipped? You want to talk pussy-whipped? Rafe's trying to convince Brooke they shouldn't drive *back* to Reno and get a divorce."

"That's truer than you know." Clearly Rafe was torn between amusement and terror. "Every once in a while I look at her and she has that I'm-bolting-now expression. Scares me to death."

"I always thought if you two got together, it would be because *she* hog-tied *you*." Eli could hardly contain his amusement.

"No such luck. She doesn't trust me yet. There's too much water under the bridge or over the dam or wherever the hell the water goes." Stepping back from the casserole, Rafe examined it. "Does that look right to you?"

"It'll be great," Noah said.

Rafe opened the second oven and thrust the pan inside, then turned back to his brothers. "Listen—you guys are no spring chickens. You need to get married before you're too old to get it up."

Noah laughed.

Eli did not.

Both brothers looked at him in concern.

"I was kidding," Rafe said, "but if you're really having trouble getting it up, there are pills that help. Not that I would personally know . . ."

"Eli *is* the oldest," Noah said. "Once a guy passes thirty, they say the angle of the dangle points toward the toes. Not that I would personally know . . ."

Eli and Rafe smacked the back of their kid brother's head, one after the other.

Noah just laughed. He was twenty-eight.

Eli said, "I'll marry someday"—*possibly sooner than*

you think—"but I swear it won't be because I stepped in a big gooshy pile of love."

"You make it sound like a cow patty." Rafe leaned against the counter, picked up his wine, and sipped with a smile.

"Call it like you see it." Eli found himself repeating Conte's mantra. "A man who loves a woman is weak."

"Then why get married at all?" Noah picked up the tongs, leaned into his oven, and turned the chicken tenders.

"Family. Children." Eli was preparing them, trying to ease their shock at the upcoming events. "I can marry and keep a wife happy. She doesn't need to know—"

"—that you're dead inside?" Noah didn't know the truth, not the whole truth, but he was right.

Still, Eli had his reasons. "Have you looked at our father? And our mothers? And the relentless drama and the anguish and screaming and the blood? Dead inside beats the constant, clawing need for overwhelming passion and excitement. Give me a quiet life with a good, obedient woman and I'll be happy."

"Obedient?" Noah snorted. "Where will you get this chick? Tell me you're not going to mail-order a bride from Russia."

With Chloë in mind, Eli said, "No. I think an Italian girl would be good, though."

Rafe turned his glass around and around in his hand. "You've got a point about the quiet life, and keeping an upper hand and all that, but it's too late for me. I've been bribing and cajoling Brooke every step of the way. You got anything you want to tell us, Eli?"

"Yeah." Eli hoisted the case with the rest of the red wine. "I need to take this into the dining room."

"Set the table while you're in there!" Noah called.

Eli accepted the task. It kept him out of Rafe's way until something came along to distract him. Because Rafe was watching Eli as if he heard more than Eli was saying. That was the trouble with having a brother who was in security. He paid attention.

Eli didn't mind setting the table. It wasn't as if this were the first time. One of his earliest memories was of proudly helping Nonna polish the heavy silver the first Di Luca bride had brought as part of her dowry. Together he and Nonna had spread a red linen Christmas tablecloth over the battered walnut surface. She displayed the fragile white glass plates behind glass doors, and every Christmas she used them, one at each place, telling him how his great-great-grandmother Adele had collected them during the Depression from soap boxes.

His little mind hadn't understood that at all, but it didn't matter, because at Christmas the whole family was together, Nonno and Nonna, his great-aunts and uncles and cousins, and his daddy and mommy were not fighting, and all was right with his world.

In that memory, he must have been three, because after that . . . after that, his mother was in prison and he had a baby brother and a new stepmother, and his father still paid no attention to Eli. Gavino paid attention to his family only when it somehow profited him.

Now Eli opened the drawers in the cabinets that stretched the length of one wall, the cabinets that had been hand-built in the forties by his great-grandfather, and found the blue linen tablecloth with its border of yellow and red morning glories. On his last trip to Italy, he'd picked it out for Nonna, knowing she'd love the colors and treasure the gift because it came from him.

Nonna had that way about her, appreciating every little thing anybody did for her. That was why the house overflowed with everything from a priceless watercolor painted by the once-starving artist Nonna had befriended, to a pile of shiny rocks given to her by her eager grandsons.

Yet one thing was missing: a priceless old bottle of wine, and more than anyone in the family, Eli wanted that bottle. It was not only his heritage; that wine held the taste of the past and held the secrets of their future . . . or perhaps the contents were vinegar.

But if Eli held that bottle, Tamosso Conte would hold no power over him.

Eli rubbed his forehead with both hands.

Foolish thoughts. The bottle had disappeared. It wasn't his to start with. He needed more than it would bring at auction.

And the mess he was in . . . it was all his. All his.

Chapter 4

"What's the matter, dear?" Nonna stood in the doorway, Olivia at her elbow, the other women behind them.

The game of Australian football was over, and they were staring—at him.

Desperation aided glib answers. "I was trying to decide which plates to use, Great-grandmother Adele's American Sweetheart or the ones from Target."

Clearly scandalized, Nonna said, "The good plates, of course. We're celebrating Rafe and Brooke's marriage!"

"But we have to hand-wash them." His question had been a ploy to distract her, but his despair was real. Hand-washing those plates took *hours*.

"I'll do it, Eli," Nonna said reprovingly.

"No, you won't, Nonna." Brooke shot Eli an angry glance. "You can't get your cast wet. *We'll* do it."

"You've been on your feet for too many hours." Francesca tucked her hand into Nonna's arm.

"I couldn't sit down. The game was too exciting!" Nonna's eyes sparkled as she remembered.

"I couldn't either, and I'm pooped." Kathy pushed her walker up the hallway toward the kitchen. "Come and sit down with me."

Great. Now Eli felt like a heel for inadvertently suggesting his grandmother should wash dishes.

Brooke came in and pushed on his shoulder. "A man's place is in the kitchen. Let the girls set the table."

Bao joined her.

Eli lingered, but Brooke knew her way around Nonna's house—she'd been visiting since junior high—and Bao had been with Nonna as her bodyguard from the first week after the attack. These two moved efficiently to set each place with the perfection Nonna demanded.

So Eli collected Nonna's cut-crystal champagne flutes and headed into the kitchen.

Francesca was quizzically looking in the oven at the eggplant Parmesan casserole.

Kathy was painfully lowering herself into a chair.

Nonna still stood, almost bouncing on her toes. Company always energized her. "Eli! What kind of champagne did you bring?"

"Just for you, some Frank Family rouge." Nonna loved her pink champagne.

"You're a good grandson." She put out her arm and hugged him. "Thank God I'm off the pain pills."

"We'll make sure you don't drink too much." Eli laughed at her moue. Nonna knew her wines, but she was a taster—she sipped, nothing more, taking pleasure in the flavors, not the intoxication that followed.

She started to pull the vegetables out of the refrigerator for the salad. Rafe gently bumped her out of the way and took over.

Olivia assembled the vinegar and olive oil for the dressing.

Rafe took the loaf of whole-wheat sourdough, sliced it in half, drizzled it with olive oil, and mashed roasted garlic on top.

Noah started a huge pot of water boiling for the pasta.

"What am I supposed to do?" Nonna asked. "I feel like an old lady standing here while everyone else works."

"You've done for us our whole lives," Rafe said. "Let us do for you now."

"You know us, Nonna," Noah said. "As soon as that cast is off, we'll be over here cajoling you to bake us your special chocolate-chip cookies."

Everyone paused for a moment of reverent silence.

Bao walked in. "She makes good chocolate-chip cookies?"

Brooke followed on her heels. "The best chocolate-chip cookies in the world."

Eli and Noah nodded in unison.

Rafe extended his arm to his new wife and hugged her. "When they're warm from the oven . . ." he said.

Nonna beamed at them. "All right. You've buttered me up. I'll sit down and let you wait on me."

"But now we all want cookies," Kathy said wryly.

"And I cannot have them." Francesca slid her palms down her slim waist. "I have an audition coming up."

"You look beautiful, Mom, just like always." Rafe smiled at her.

She smiled back.

Their rocky relationship seemed to have smoothed out, at least for the moment.

Eli popped the cork on the first bottle of champagne, poured the flutes full, and tapped on the crystal with a spoon. "Who wants a glass of the bubbly instead?"

The champagne toasts lasted only until the food was on the table; then the Di Lucas got down to the serious business of pouring good red wine with their meal. Bao and Olivia sat with the family, were a part of the family, as was anyone who ever dined at Nonna's. Rafe and Brooke held hands under the table. Noah teased them about sitting in a gooshy pile of love.

When the main course was over, and Brooke carried out the cheese and fruit plate Kathy had assembled at her shop, and the boisterous laughter had been replaced by quiet conversation, Eli took the plunge. "I'm going to have a visitor staying with me."

Silence fell, a silence so profound and astonished he knew his chances of passing this off as a casual announcement were doomed.

"Who is your guest?" Nonna asked politely.

"A young writer who's made quite a splash with her first book—"

"So it's a girl?" Brooke asked.

"Yes, I met her father at the winemakers' dinner, and he asked—"

"Is she pretty?" Francesca asked.

"Her picture is very nice, and she wants privacy to—"

"So you haven't met her yet?" Kathy asked.

The women were interrogating him.

His brothers were letting them.

But Rafe and Noah looked as interested as the others.

Even Olivia, for all her silence, appeared fascinated.

Cornered by a pack of curious relatives, Eli said, "I haven't met her, but what's the big deal? I can have a visitor if I want."

"You *can*." Rafe placed an array of cheese and fruit on Brooke's plate. "You just never *do*."

"You built that new, big house on the hill with four bedrooms, a pool table, and a huge living room. Who have you ever had stay with you? *Who?*" Noah asked.

Eli was sorry his brothers had joined the conversation. "Someone could stay with me if they wanted."

"Most people wait for an invitation." Rafe slid a grape into Brooke's mouth and smiled.

She blushed.

Wow. Sexual games, right here at the table. Eli wanted to give them a hard time.

But Noah wasn't finished rattling Eli's cage. "You won't even pave the first half mile of driveway. It's a washboard. I won't drive my car up there; I'd tear the mufflers off!"

"I suppose we could all casually drop by some night and announce we're having a party." Kathy sounded thoughtful.

"I'd pay to see his face if we did." Noah grinned at her. She grinned back.

"Quiet," Nonna ordered, then turned back to Eli. "What's her name?"

"Chloë Robinson."

"We read her!" Bao looked between Nonna and Olivia. "What was that book called?"

"We listened to the audiobook while Nonna was doing rehab," Olivia said.

"*Die Trying*. It was a good mystery. It distracted me from the pain," Nonna said.

"It kept me awake afterward, scared to death." Olivia turned to Eli. "Have *you* read her book?"

"Not yet, but it's a bestseller, so I'm sure it's—"

"You should read it before you meet her." Bao sounded bossy and authoritative, a woman who took command as needed.

He had no intention of reading *Die Trying* or whatever it was called. Bad enough he had to marry the girl, much less torture himself reading some female idea of scary suspense.

"Is she going to stay in the house with you?" Nonna asked.

"No. I'm putting her in the guest cottage." Eli hoped that would silence most of the curiosity.

After all, he wasn't giving up his privacy for a woman. Or her muse.

Not yet.

"As soon as you can, bring her to dinner," Nonna ordered. "I would love to meet my new favorite author."

Chapter 5

Chloë Robinson looked around at the quiet two-lane road that ran through a remote part of Bella Valley.

She looked at her bug-splattered blue Ford Focus.

She looked at the right front tire, so flat it was resting on the rim.

Damned tire.

Damned deadline.

Lately she blamed everything on her deadline, on being late with her book, on having second-book syndrome. She wouldn't have driven over the nail if she weren't distracted by her plot, by being halfway through a book that seemed slow and clunky, weighed down with too many expectations. Her first book had been written so easily, had been so much fun, and only when it hit the bestseller lists had Chloë realized that if she wanted a career writing books, she'd have to do it again. And again.

Yep. This was definitely the fault of her deadline.

And Eli Di Luca. It was his fault, too.

She sighed.

It was also her own fault. What kind of fool was she to stand in front of her father and proclaim that all she needed to finish this book was a quiet place to write?

She dragged her suitcases out of her trunk, stacked them beside the road, and found the spare, the jack, the tire iron.

Saying she needed a quiet place to write was just an excuse, and a stupid one, too. She didn't expect him to take her seriously.

But like a pudgy Italian whirlwind, he had come back with the invitation from Eli Di Luca to stay in a guest cottage on his California estate and finish her book.

Papa said Di Luca was a fan.

Papa obviously thought his daughter was a gullible idiot.

She dug the spare out of the trunk and rolled it over onto the dusty shoulder of the road.

One quick trip to the Internet showed her what she already knew—Eli Di Luca was a successful, handsome Italian, exactly the kind of guy her father had been flinging at her.

On the road, a car slowed and stopped.

She tensed, stood, tried to look tall and tough.

A guy, who did *not* look tall and tough, called, "Looks like you know what you're doing!"

"I do." She did. Because eight years ago, when she'd taken driver's training, her instructor had made her change a tire. She hadn't done it since. She didn't know if she could loosen the lug nuts or get the jack to work right. But only a fool would ask a strange man for help. . . .

Not that he was offering. "Do you need me to call someone for you?"

"No, I already called." Her smile was more a baring of her teeth.

The garage had said they were busy and it would be two hours. The bastards.

She said, "I figured while I was waiting, I might as well give it a try."

"Power on!" He rolled up his window and drove away.

"Yeah, thanks." She read the directions in the trunk about how to assemble the jack, and did it . . . on the third try.

She wished she were back in Texas, where some man would stop, swagger over, and tell her to rest her pretty self while he changed her tire. She'd do it, too.

Okay. If she'd had this flat while driving through west Texas, home of tarantulas and dust storms, she would have waited a long time before she even saw a man. But other than Mr. Power On, it wasn't as if they were coming out of the woodwork in California, either.

Men had their place in the world.

Taking out the garbage.

Opening jars.

Fixing flats.

The irony of having a flat tire here, within two miles of her goal, did not escape her.

What other reason—except being late on her deadline—could explain that kind of bad luck?

The deadline. Second-book syndrome.

And her father.

God help her. She loved him. She really did. He was a great guy. But her mother had warned her: When it came to women, he was a Neanderthal. He thought a woman should be married and producing children, particularly if that woman was his daughter and the children she would bear would be his grandchildren.

He was proud of her. He adored her. But they wanted different goals.

He wanted grandchildren to make up for all the years he'd missed of her life.

She intended to live the life she had worked so hard to make for herself. She did not want a husband he had bribed, begged, or blackmailed to marry her.

She read the directions about how to place the jack, read them three times, knelt in the gravel, and maneuvered it into place. Taking a breath, she started to raise the car.

The way things were going, she'd be lucky if the damned car didn't slide on this gravel, fall off the damned jack, and crush her damned hands and at least one damned foot.

Hey! But at least if her fingers were broken, she wouldn't have to finish the damned book!

That's the way, Robinson. Look on the bright side.

When her father had given her a plane ticket from Austin to Santa Rosa, she debated telling him no, she wouldn't go. But she had experience with his matchmaking schemes. He never gave up, and if she didn't go to California, somehow Eli Di Luca would find his way to her.

Besides, right now, as Texas simmered under a blistering spring heat, California sounded pretty good. So she'd decided to go . . . but on her own terms.

She'd packed her car and started across country, determined to have an adventure. She'd driven across west Texas, the most godforsaken, desolate stretch of land in the world. She had traversed the deserts of New Mexico and Arizona, gawked at the magnificence of the Grand Canyon, driven through Los Angeles, where the freeway never ended, and onward to the coastline, where she had walked in the sand, played in the ocean, and locked her keys in the car.

That had been embarrassing.

After calling a locksmith and retrieving her keys, she'd stopped in Hollywood at a spa and, um, done something impulsive.

She touched her hair gingerly.

Very impulsive and possibly ill considered.

She'd driven into the Sierra Nevada mountains, through the mighty sequoias and into Yosemite National Park, where she had cried at the epic majesty of that glacial valley. She'd veered into the Central Valley, and found spots as hot and flat and bare as Texas. No tarantulas, though. No sagebrush, either. Just miles and miles of farmland as far as the eye could see. But when she drove into the wine country, the scenery changed. The valleys were narrow and long, the highway crowded. Grapes grew everywhere, beside the road, up on the hillsides. And every five hundred yards was another sign for another winery.

When her GPS instructed her to turn off and take the pass over the mountains and into Bella Valley . . . she'd almost died of terror.

She was from Texas, from the hill country. Not from the let's-drive-on-a-narrow-winding-vertical-road-and-scare-the-pants-off-her country.

That road had scared the pants off her. Going up. Going down. And then . . . she'd come around a sharp corner and there it was, Bella Valley, spread before her like some flashback to early California, when people were scarce and the land drowsed under a loving sun. Wide oaks dotted the golden hills. Orchards and vineyards rode the rise and fall of every fold in the earth. In the distance a town, Bella Terra, nestled beside a silver river that wound in wide loops through the bottomlands.

She didn't care about Eli Di Luca, but right then and there, she fell in love with his home.

She had almost called her father to tell him. But there was no point in encouraging him any further.

Anyway, she didn't dare call him right now. He had *not* been happy about his baby girl driving two thousand miles by herself. He had predicted dire happenings. Like this flat tire.

She stepped back and looked.

Okay. The tire was off the ground.

Should she have loosened the lug nuts first?

Crap. Yes. She should have.

She lowered the jack again, and when the weight of the car held the tire in place, she pulled the handle off the jack—good thing the instructions told her it acted as the tire iron, too—and wrestled with the lug nuts.

How was she supposed to loosen them when some guy with an air compressor had tightened them?

She bounced on the tire iron.

If her father knew about this flat tire, he'd call Eli Di Luca, who'd come to the rescue.

She wouldn't mind if a Texan called her "little lady" and patronized her while he fixed her tire. Having one of Papa's suitors rescue her would be seriously annoying.

No matter how much of a pain in the ass she found her father and his plans, she was still glad he was in her life. But between his machinations and her becoming a successful author, she had grown skittish about *dating*. She never knew whether the guy was going to talk about how he wanted to settle down and raise a large family or whether he was going to earnestly tell her he had a great plot for a book, and suggest she write it for him and they'd split the profits. And inform her that if they skipped the New York publishing house and published it themselves online, they'd make millions and billions of dollars and get to keep it all themselves.

In the end, she didn't know which was worse: the guy who lunged at her with the intent of impregnating a rich man's daughter, or the guy who bored her silly explaining every detail of his story.

Hm. Her father should look for a guy who had a plot idea and also wanted to marry money. She would go out with him; he'd talk about his book until she was in a coma; then he could have his way with her at his leisure.

She grinned and carefully stacked the lug nuts in a pile, then went to work with the jack again.

And no matter how much people who thought they could write when they had never tried annoyed her, she loved talking with other authors, published and unpublished, the ones who put their butts in their chairs day after day and *wrote*. If not for their knowledge and assistance, she would not have realized she was suffering from the well-documented second-book syndrome. According to authors who wrote lots of books, there was only one cure—to finish the book and start another. And another.

So she would. Because she was tougher than she looked.

She had gotten the car off the ground again, hadn't she?

She tugged the flat off, carried it to the trunk, put it in.

She put the spare on. Tightened the lug nuts. Lowered the jack.

She had changed the tire! She had changed the tire!

Lifting her arms over her head, she did the victory dance.

She was a goddess! A goddess!

. . . Of course, that was when a winery tour bus full of people drove past, staring as if she were crazed.

She lowered her arms.

Damned deadline.

Chapter 6

"Someone's coming up your drive." Royson Ryan straightened up and looked toward the dust cloud on top of the ridge.

"Son of a bitch." Eli glanced at the horizon. "Now? I'm busy."

Roy and Eli were at the bottom of Gunfighter Ridge, at the end of a row of grapevines, repairing the drip irrigation lines—except when the coyotes were thirsty. The creatures were smart; they chewed through the plastic, got their drink, and wandered off, leaving precious California water to gush through the break until the pressure dropped and Roy or Eli or one of the hands hurried to fix it.

"Maybe it's that girl. The one you were waiting for." Roy gloated.

Damn it. Roy hadn't been at dinner with Eli's family. He hadn't had to be. Gossip slid through this valley on a greased track. The cashiers in Safeway knew Eli was expecting a girl who would stay with him. The Luna Grande cocktail waitresses knew he was putting fresh flowers in the cottage every day. Every time he saw them, his brothers gave him a ration of shit over the fact that she was supposed to be here two weeks ago and she hadn't put in an appearance.

He was pissed because he didn't want her there, and more pissed because he needed her to show up or the IRS would put a lien on his land.

He had spent his adult life making sure he was never forced to choose between the frying pan and the fire—and now here he was, trying to figure out the precise moment to jump.

No matter. He'd learned early not to let anyone see him in pain, not even someone he'd known as long as he'd known Royson. Wiping all expression from his face, he said, "I'll go and chase whoever it is off my land," and started up the hill.

Royson snickered.

Damn it. Eli would have fired him in a New York minute, except that Royson was the best foreman in any winery in the country, maybe in five countries, with a gut feeling at any given time about what the grapes needed, a sure instinct of where and what to plant, and an uncanny knowledge of what each season would bring.

So Eli would pretend he didn't hear the snickering.

The climb to his house was steep, through rows of vines that zigzagged up the hill. The bud break had occurred early, in late February, and the leaves had unfurled to soak up the sun. At the same time they had the fresh, bright, spring green color of new growth. He saw no sign of grapes yet, but he knew they were waiting just out of sight, ready to sag below the leaves, small and green, tightly bunched. . . .

It was odd, but every year until he saw that first bunch of tiny grapes he didn't truly believe the cycle had begun again. He needed to know that the earth, the sun, the wind, and the rain would collaborate again to create that most precious of miracles: a rich, heavy, fully ripened fruit.

He could take it, mash it, start the process that turned it from juice to wine, delicate or hearty, fruity or spicy, glorious in all its incarnations. He was a master at creating wines.

But only God could create the grape.

Every year, until Eli saw God's hand at work, he lived on the edge of fear that this year it wouldn't happen, and Eli would again be nothing, a pawn in the hands of fate.

The incline became abruptly steeper, and his house came into view, the house he had so carefully designed. His architect would dispute that, say *he* designed the sprawling, copper-colored adobe home. But Eli had known what he wanted: an Italian villa nestled into the hillside, cool and restful, on three levels, and with a view of the valley. The orange tile roof softly glowed, and the wide eaves protected the interior from the California sun. On the main level—the second story—the wide veranda ran the length of the house and overlooked the same valley as at Nonna's, but from a different angle.

He had allowed an interior decorator to work closely with him to pick out the furniture, insisting on comfort first, with a lack of fuss and frills. He wanted his home to be welcoming, restful, and *his*.

As he crested the ridge, he saw the car, a blue Ford Focus, parked in front of the cottage. A blonde was lifting bags out of the trunk, but from a distance it didn't look like Chloë Robinson. She was shorter than he thought she would be, maybe five-five. And thinner. Bony. "Geez, girl, eat a burger," he muttered.

She had dust on her clothes.

Her complexion was pale, and as he neared, he saw she wore not a speck of makeup. Freckles dotted her nose. Her lips were lightly pink, as if she'd been biting them. And her hair—it was white-blond, straight and short, sticking up all around her head like a dandelion puff waving in the breeze. As she turned to face him, he saw that two pomegranate red strands sprang from her left temple and grew long enough to cup her cheek, and a sparkling blue stud was stuck through the upper part of her right ear.

Juvenile. So juvenile. Surely this wasn't Chloë.

But the face was right: cheeks sweetly rounded, big brown eyes, and a warm smile. Her picture hadn't lied. She was very attractive.

She was two weeks late with no explanation, her father was bribing him to marry her, and she looked younger than he'd expected, which made Eli feel like an even worse cad and bigger lecher.

And she was smiling? She had *guts.*

He stopped six feet away. Planted his feet. And demanded, "What happened to your hair?"

The smile disappeared. Temper flared in her eyes. "What happened to your *face*?"

She had the slightest traces of a slow Southern accent. She looked like the fragile type of woman who dissolved at a single cross word.

Apparently he'd read her wrong.

He rubbed his cheek. "My face? What's wrong with it?"

Taking his arm, she pushed him over to her car and pointed at his reflection in the side-view mirror.

Okay. She had a point. He wore jeans and rubber boots caked with dirt; a denim shirt soaked in sweat, sunscreen, and grease; and his oldest hat. He had grease smeared up one side of his nose and over his forehead; the hair that had escaped from under his hat had been styled with thick, rich, black mud.

This was not the way he'd planned their meeting. He'd planned to dress nicely, comb his hair, and, most of all, bathe.

Damn the woman. They weren't even married and

already she was making him worry about the way he looked.

He turned to see her carrying two of her bags up onto the small stoop of the cottage. She inserted a key into the lock—he'd sent the key to her, along with a stern admonition that it was for the cottage door only and not to try the house—and opened the door. At her first glimpse inside, she gave an exclamation of surprise and pleasure . . . and he almost smiled.

He'd spared no expense in the cottage, using a studio floor plan from the Bella Terra resort. Because he wanted to live alone, but he wanted his guests to be comfortable. Not that he ever invited any guests, but he knew someday he would be called on to house the overflow from a family event . . . like his marriage to Chloë.

She disappeared inside.

He picked up her big suitcase.

He gasped.

The son of a bitch was heavy. Very heavy. The airlines would charge extra for this one. Good thing she drove. He lugged it up the steps onto the porch. He toed off his boots, then walked through the door and found Chloë looking around the generous, lush living space with a sitting area, a fireplace, and a queen-size bed.

He had had a desk brought in, French provincial in a high-gloss black finish with hand-painted gold accents on the edges of its top, apron, and drawers and down the gracefully curved legs. He'd draped one of

Nonna's antique lace shawls over the top and, in anticipation of Chloë's arrival, he'd sprinkled the surface with fresh rose petals *every damned day*. Now he was glad, because with the antique mother-of-pearl lamp and the bouquet of pink roses in the Tiffany crystal vase, her work area looked romantic and writerly.

With awesome patience, he put the suitcase against the wall. "What's in there?"

"Research books." She examined the tiny kitchen, opened the fully stocked utility drawers, checked out the microwave, the oven, the refrigerator, the sink. "My mom and I call that the suitcase of death."

"I survived."

"You do look healthy enough."

It didn't sound like a compliment.

She headed into the warmly decorated bathroom complete with a shower, soaking tub, and heated towel bar, and came out nodding enthusiastically. "This is fabulous. It's comfortable. It's roomy. My God. This is better than I could have ever imagined. Thank you for allowing me to stay here. Thank you!" Walking to the French doors, she flung them open and stepped onto the deck.

He followed, wanting to see her see the view.

She paced toward the railing, grasped it with both hands, and leaned forward, sunshine on her face, lips softly open, eyes wide.

On this side of the cottage, the ground dropped away, lending the illusion that the deck hovered in midair. The panorama cut across Bella Valley rather than down its length, over the lazy loops of river that wound through orchards and vineyards. Here and there, a farmhouse dotted the landscape, but from this deck's view, the town might not have existed. On the other side of the valley, the hills rose, terraced with vines, and behind them the mountains stood densely wooded, cool and shadowy.

"Amazing," she whispered. She sniffed the air, turned to him, and grinned. "It's so perfect it looks like a cheap painting. How you must love living up here!"

"I do." And he liked that she appreciated what he had and was vocal about telling him.

She turned back to the vista. "How much of it is yours?"

"The view is all mine."

She chuckled softly.

He might as well tell her. As a Di Luca bride, she had the right to know. "What with marriages and mergers, the Di Lucas own their share of the valley. Bella Terra resort is ours and sits on the street downtown, with seventy acres of grapes stretching behind it into the hills. The rest of the winery land is in parcels here and there, scattered across the landscape and up into the hills. Altogether I manage about four hundred twenty acres."

She whistled softly. "Those *are* valuable holdings."

A lot of women had thought so. A lot of women had tried to convince him that marriage without a prenup would prove his love. A lot of women had miscalculated . . . for he hadn't loved any of them.

Now Chloë's voice changed, became speculative. "I'll bet your ancestors did anything necessary to get this land and hold it."

Startled at the direction of her thinking, he asked, "Why do you want to know?"

"I'm a writer. I like to know what people do, and why."

He thought of all the years and all the threats to the Di Luca dominion, and thought, too, how close he teetered to losing everything his family had fought to possess. "You're right. My ancestors did whatever it took to keep their land."

"How about you? What would *you* do to keep your land?"

He stared at her profile. The breeze ruffled her sheared head and carried a hint of spicy, feminine scent to his nose. The sun kissed her pale complexion and made the rusty freckles that decorated her nose and cheeks glow. Her gaze was steady, her lips faintly smiling.

Did she know about the trouble he was in? The contract he'd signed? Was she acting on a suspicion, or was she clueless?

Regardless of what she knew or suspected, he saw no point in lying. Any one of his acquaintances would bust that story wide-open. "If there was a threat, I'd protect my family first, then my land, because . . . what's mine is mine."

"So it's not about the money?"

"I don't value the money for money's sake, but for what it gives me."

"What's that?"

"Security."

She waited as if expecting him to say more. She looked at him, saw he was through speaking, laughed, and nodded. "I've always thought that people who say money doesn't buy happiness have never been without."

He had, he thought, passed some kind of test.

She pushed the conversation back on track. "Is all your acreage planted in grapes?"

"We've got a few old orchards around Nonna's house, but yes, four hundred and ten acres are vineyards, mostly red, mostly zinfandel and Sangiovese, with some other varieties mixed in. We even grow a few whites." He knew pride rang in his voice.

"Are whites more difficult than reds?"

"I create unique wines. Whites are more difficult to make worthy of note."

"I understand. But I like cabernet," she said mildly.

"I do, too, but they grow better in the next valley over, so when I make cab, I buy those grapes." She wasn't looking at the view now; she was looking at him, eyes sharply attentive, and he realized he'd started telling her about his family, his lands, his expertise, trying to get her attention, strutting like a peacock.

It was all very well for him to tell himself he wasn't interested in anything but her dowry.

Apparently his biological directive said otherwise.

Perhaps Conte had seen something in him Eli had not recognized. Maybe like a grape Eli had reached the peak of maturity, and it was time for him to marry and reproduce.

What a mental image.

But whatever magic made him want to follow her around seeking the source of that warm, female scent . . . it seemed to have no effect on her. She wasn't staring up at him adoringly. She had returned her gaze to the vista, her eyes narrowed on the horizon as if she were deep in thought.

Then, turning on her heel, she walked inside. "Thank you for allowing me to use your cottage. I'm sure I can finish my book here." She laughed over her shoulder. "Or not. You should worry that I won't finish so I can stay right here!"

She looked so pleased, so enthused, so pretty . . . and so oblivious about the ignominious contract that had led her here that Eli grunted in ill-tempered dismay. He followed her in, veered away, and headed toward the front door.

"Wait!" She ran after him, grabbed his arm, and yanked him to a halt.

He glared down at her.

She stared up at him. "Look. You don't have to be so pissy."

"Pissy?" *Pissy?* He was not pissy.

"It's okay." She patted his arm comfortingly. "I know what my father's up to."

Chapter 7

Eli considered Chloë. Considered what to say. His first thought—*You know I've committed to a marriage of convenience with you?*—was promptly rejected.

Don't admit to anything!

"You know what your father's up to?" he repeated warily.

"You don't have to feel self-conscious. Papa wants me to get married. He makes no bones about it. So he parades young men in front of me like it was breeding day for his prize mare." She grinned, but painfully, as if someone had given her a wedgie and she was trying to be a good sport about it.

She didn't know about the contract. Eli relaxed.

"Don't worry about it," she said. "I'm not interested in you."

He tensed. *That* was blunt. And surprisingly exasperating.

Chloë stood with her feet planted firmly on the hardwood floor, crossed her arms, and looked him right in the eyes. "I've got a job. I've got ambitions. I've got a deadline. I've got a mother who warned me about my father and his schemes before I even met him, and she's been right about everything except . . . well, he's cooler than she led me to believe."

Apparently when Conte talked to Eli, he had left out a few pertinent details about his relationship with Chloë. "When did you meet your father?" Eli asked.

"Last year. No, the year before. My parents never married."

Eli hadn't thought to ask Conte why his daughter was an American. Now he discovered he was sharply curious. "Your father abandoned your mother?" Conte didn't seem the type to dump his daughter, no matter what he thought of the mother.

"No! Not at all. My mother worked for my father. They had an affair. . . . Well, you've met him, right?"

"Yes, I've met him." On one of the darkest days of his life.

"So you know he's overbearing and pushy and an Italian mogul down to his bones. He believes he should always get his way, and my mother knew that was no way to raise a child. So when she discovered she was pregnant, she left without telling him."

"Pardon me, but that seems . . ." He hesitated. Chloë seemed fond of her mother—and that woman was going to be his mother-in-law.

"Like a shabby way for her to treat him." Chloë nodded. "Yes, she and I have had words about that."

"She supported you well?"

"Very well. My mom is from Boston. Both her parents are alive. She had a degree when she worked for my father, returned to the States, got a position in the Italian department at the University of Texas in Austin, became a tenured professor. I was never without."

"Except you didn't have a father."

"I didn't feel the lack. Not at the time. But the things Papa said when he found out about me . . . He was so mad. And hurt, I think. But my mother still thinks she made the right decision, and knowing him as I now do, I have to at least partly agree." The desk caught her eye. She wandered close and with one finger gently touched one of the rose petals scattered over the lace. "You know he's got money?"

"I figured." An understatement.

"Lots of money. He's always at work, he's got guards all over his estate, and if anyone knew I was his daughter, I'd be kidnapped and worse. But he's been married so many times and had so many hugely public affairs, everyone assumed I was his girlfriend. We let them. It was easier. Safer." As Eli eyed her, she said, "It's not like I resemble him."

"True." Eli didn't have a lot of good opinions about parents; his own had been such shits. But he knew most people had reasons, good ones, to love their parents, and he still really didn't understand Chloë's situation. "After all those years of silence, why did your mother suddenly tell you about your father?"

"I asked her."

"Why didn't you ask sooner? I mean, didn't you have curiosity before you were—"

"Twenty-one. I did ask, but she always acted like"— Chloë thrust her hand through her hair, then looked at her palm as if the length surprised her—"like talking about him pained her. The first few times, I didn't insist. Finally I did. I think she loved him, but didn't trust him. That's got to suck."

"Yes." He remembered his mother and the pain that had driven her from one despair to another.

Then he remembered what he intended for Chloë: a loveless marriage with no chance of reprieve.

But she *would* trust him, and *never* know he felt nothing for her. That was best for them both.

"These roses look fresh. Why do you think the petals fell off?" Picking up the lace shawl, she shook it over the black-and-gilt trash can.

As he watched incredulously, rose petals fluttered down, then disappeared from sight. He'd personally plucked those rose petals—and she'd dumped them?

She folded the shawl and put it on the shelf in the closet.

She didn't like the lace shawl? He'd never met a woman who didn't like lace.

Opening her duffel bag, she rummaged inside. "Anyway, that's the story of my parents. I took a semester off, went to Italy, met Papa, finished my book while living on his estate, got published, graduated, and once that happened—boom! He decided I'd lived my life and needed to get married. He wants grandchildren."

Eli knew that all too well. "Do you not like children?"

She turned, clutching a human skull. "Not the point, Eli Di Luca. The point is I'm twenty-three and have no desire to be married, much less married for a piece of my father's fortune. *And* I realize this is an odd concept—but I'd like to fall in love."

"Any candidates?" He hadn't thought so, but just because her father offered her to him didn't mean she was free.

"No."

"And is that skull real?"

"Yes." She lovingly placed it on the left-hand corner of the desk facing the chair.

There its empty eye sockets would stare at her and its eternal grin would give her cheer. Or something like that.

"No boyfriends?" he asked.

"I've had a few, of course. But now it's complicated. You know what I mean." She waved a hand toward the open French door. "You've got money. I'm sure women come after you with hot schemes for your fortune."

"It's happened," he admitted. "But how can guys chase you for your father's fortune if they don't know Conte is your father?"

"You are *such* a chauvinist." She stomped back to her bag, pulled out two bronze candleholders, and stomped back to the desk. "First—they chase me for *my* money. I did pretty well with the book, you know."

He winced. "You're right. I am a chauvinist, and I should know better. My grandmother would slap me upside the head for being so stupid as to assume you were courted only for your father's fortune."

"*Thank* you." Chloë placed the candleholders on either side of the skull.

Each candleholder was ten inches tall, a squat dragon with its head back and its mouth open, ready to hold a taper.

He hadn't thought to ask Conte whether his daughter was a witch. The matter had somehow slipped his mind.

"Are you going to hold a magic ceremony?" he asked politely.

"No, but I find when I write about murder, it's good to have the props where I can see them." She removed the crystal vase filled with roses to the bedside, and returned with two bloodred candles and her laptop. She arranged everything, stepped back, contemplated her modifications, and nodded approvingly. Turning back to him, she said, "What Papa does with the guys he sics on me is tell them I used to be his girlfriend, that he's very fond of me and wants me to have a family, and he's going to leave me one percent of his fortune."

"Good God. One percent is . . ." Eli's research had

placed Conte's fortune at anywhere between five billion and ten billion dollars.

"One percent is enough to send them racing to my side to pledge their devotion." Chloë laughed, a light sprinkling of amusement. "I haven't had the heart to tell Papa a good part of their interest is their belief that for one percent, I must be really great in bed."

"You're lucky you haven't been kidnapped anyway." A horrible thought.

She thought, and nodded. "I hadn't considered that. But you're right."

"There's electronic security here in the cottage." He showed her the number pad by the door, gave her the code, showed her the emergency button by the bed. "When you're inside, set the alarm."

"I will."

"Don't forget."

"I promise." She laughed into his face. "I'm twenty-three, not twelve, and you're fifty, not a hundred."

"I'm thirty-four!" And he realized he'd been suckered.

"But you act so old," she mocked.

He didn't know what to say, how to respond. His brothers teased him, of course, but women . . . didn't.

Sometimes they analyzed him.

According to one of his lovers, the woman with the psychology degree, he suffered from "communication problems," "control issues," and "a lack of emotional availability." That was fine with him. Emotional unavailability saved him a lot of time and heartache.

But unless they were related to him, women from the age of ten to the age of a hundred reacted as if he were attractive and dangerous, as if he frightened and enthralled them. "You, um, think of me like your elderly uncle?"

"Nope. Not an uncle. Not one of my relations. But for sure someone's great-grandfather!" Her brown eyes sparkled with amber lights.

Just as he thought. He *was* too old for her. "I've got to go back to work."

"Me, too." She sighed mightily, as if the prospect were hard and onerous.

"I thought you liked to write."

"I do. Beats having a real job," she said.

Was she joking? He thought she must be, because her sparkle faded and something that looked like misery turned her eyes a muddy brown.

Good. Life was serious. She needed to learn that.

He touched his hat, then walked out the door.

As he strode down the hill, through the vineyard, and back to work on the broken water lines, he thought about her. About his future bride.

She had a temper.

She was too open, too willing to share personal information. She was frivolous. She laughed easily, teased by the slightest provocation.

She didn't realize how swiftly life could become a desert of hopelessness where love was nothing but a memory and all your future stretched before you, barren and forlorn.

Not that he ever wanted her to know. He would protect her from that, at least.

Among the fresh new leaves on the vines, something caught his eye: a cluster of tiny round berries hanging low on the trellis. He stopped, knelt, cradled them tenderly in his cupped palm, this sign of good luck. He looked up toward the cottage.

Perhaps this meeting with Chloë had been fortuitous after all.

Chapter 8

Chloë flung herself backward on the bed, wrapped her arms over her face, and blocked out the world for a long, long minute.

But she couldn't block out the memory of Eli Di Luca's horrified face, and his deep voice demanding, *What did you do to your hair?*

Let's see. When she'd driven through L.A. and seen the billboard for the Alibi Spa, she walked into their trendy salon on a whim and told them she wanted something completely different. The hairdresser admired the length—past her shoulders—and the pale color, and suggested the streaks of pomegranate red.

But that wasn't enough for her. When she demanded he cut it all off, he had stood like a deer in the headlights.

Guys, even gay guys, had such a *thing* about long hair. But she'd insisted, and he'd reluctantly used his razor until, for the first time in her life, she was sheared like a lamb—and glad of it.

Chloë was tired of caring for her hair. She was tired of being Chloë, who couldn't get her second book done. She wanted to be the new Chloë, wild and free, someone who wasn't afraid of anything, specifically not of the blank page.

What did you do to your hair?

She'd come out of the beauty shop feeling empowered.

Then she had second thoughts. Had her dash away from her problems and across the country led her to an impulsive, ill-thought-out act? Which was not necessarily a bad thing, just not . . . well considered.

Not that she didn't like the haircut. She actually did. And she wasn't sorry. The people in the salon said she looked like a pixie, and personally she thought all she needed was pointy ears and she could be one of the extras in *Lord of the Rings*.

So she'd been kind of wavering back and forth between terror that she'd made an impulsive, hideous mistake and pleasure that she'd been so bold and decisive . . . until Eli had seen her, looked horrified, and asked the fatal question.

He was good-looking, too, nothing like the college guys she'd known, but mature, serious, covered with mud and reeking of virility.

Not that she cared.

What did you do to your hair?

63

When Eli asked Chloë about her hair in that accusing tone, as if he had every right to question her . . . he was lucky she didn't have an ax handy or he would have had to run for his life.

She crawled off the bed, grabbed her phone from the bedside table, and walked out onto the deck.

Good thing she and Eli had agreed they were incompatible.

He wouldn't have to look at her.

She wouldn't have to smell him.

The jerk.

She dialed her mother's number.

Out here, the breeze puffed into her face and the view caught her by surprise again. She contemplated the valley, the winding river, and grass and trees and vineyards. It reminded her of her father's estate in Italy . . . but not really. After the endless freeway that was southern California, this felt newer, fresher, more open, refreshingly rural yet not remote.

She could live here forever—although she was pretty sure Eli Di Luca would mightily object to her infinite occupation of his cottage.

The phone rang. Her mother picked up.

"Hi, Mom, I got here at last."

She listened to her mother's sigh of relief. "It's a long drive, isn't it, honey?"

"Whoo, boy."

"Any problems?"

"Not till I got here and met Eli Di Luca. You were wrong about him."

"He's not your dad's next candidate for your husband?" Her mother's voice developed a lilt.

"I would say not. He's good-looking—a prime marital candidate—but what a crank!" Although that was not strictly true. He was critical, a guy who thought he was superior because he had a penis and could pee at a picnic. For sure he didn't approve of her. "I finally told him I knew that Papa was setting us up and that it was no big deal; Papa did it all the time and I'm not desperate. Then he seemed to loosen up a little."

Lauren's laugh warmed her. "I'll bet that took him aback."

"I think so. But he took me aback, too. After the way Papa described Eli Di Luca as this big, buff winemaker, I didn't even think it was him for the first few minutes. He came out of the vineyard covered in mud. I didn't expect that; I figured he was a hired hand or something. Do winemakers usually work in the grapes?"

"Dear, what I don't know about winemaking could fill a large book. Now, wine *drinking* . . ."

Chloë chuckled.

Her mom continued. "How is this place? Is it comfortable? Can you work there?"

"It's gorgeous, Mom, so much more than I expected. I'll take a picture of the view and send it to you."

"But can you work there?"

Chloë heard that note in Lauren's voice, the one that said she was worried about her daughter.

Truth to tell, Chloë was worried herself.

But she put a reassuring note in her voice. "I can

work here. I wish you could have been here to see Di Luca's face when I put out my skull."

"I can imagine. That thing gives me the creeps."

"Him, too, I would guess. Best gift Papa ever gave me."

Her mom got quiet. She usually did when Chloë talked too much about her father. Telling Chloë about him had been difficult for her, and she always acted oddly about him, not as if she hated him, exactly, but as if the memory of him hurt her.

For all Conte's weird insistence that Chloë marry as soon as possible, she loved the old guy. How could she not? He was so thrilled at her mere existence. Who else would ever believe her to be a miracle of love?

"Mom, I need to unpack and go to work." Briefly Chloë toyed with telling her about her hair, then decided against it.

It was *her* hair. She'd live through the good choices and the bad choices. She half smiled. In fact, with her writing schedule, no one would see her for so long. It would grow out before she saw sunshine again.

Chapter 9

Eli stood outside looking at the cottage.

Chloë had been in there for days. Weeks. He'd seen nothing of her except a light that burned far into the night. He'd heard nothing from her except once, when he sat on his own deck, he'd thought he heard a cry of rage and frustration.

Or maybe it was an injured vulture falling to its death over the vineyard.

Her father wanted to know how his courtship was going.

His grandmother was bugging him to bring her to dinner.

More to the point, he needed the money he'd get from marrying her.

Needs drove him. He responded to those needs.

When he married that young woman he would never cheat on her. Certainly she would never know he didn't love her. She'd be happy. He'd make sure of it.

But if she never came out . . . he would have to go in.

Climbing the stairs to the porch, he knocked on the cottage door.

Immediately she flung it open.

The smell of a burned *something* gusted out the door.

"Is there a fire?" Alarmed, he pushed his way inside.

"I put frozen lasagna in the oven and forgot about it." She sounded exasperated, as if that should be only too obvious.

He looked around.

The air was hazy with smoke. The blinds were shut. The only light came from the desk lamp.

The bed was unmade. She'd hung a bra on her chair. Books filled with paper sticky notes were piled beside the desk and open on top of the desk. One e-reader was flung on the sheets; another was propped against the desk lamp. The trash can overflowed. The place looked like hell.

Chloë looked like hell. She wore some kind of green plaid flannel pants with an elastic waist and a green top. Her fluff-ball hair drooped. She was pale as death, and she glared through bloodshot eyes. *"What?"*

He didn't know where to start. "Is the maid from the resort not coming up to clean?"

"Once a week. She was here"—Chloë ruffled her hair—"yesterday, I think."

He looked around. *The poor maid.* "Why are the blinds closed?"

"The view's too good. It distracts me." Again that snappish, impatient tone.

"How's the book going?" It seemed like a pertinent question.

Until she burst out, "Fine! Just fine! Writing a book is easy, isn't it? All you have to do is put your fingers on the keys and type out your dreams. Anybody can do it. Right?"

"I couldn't."

She flung out an arm like he'd just made an obvious point. *"Thank* you!"

Things were not going well, he surmised.

"Did my mother call you?" Chloë asked suspiciously.

"No." Possibly Chloë's intensity, her angst, her anguish provided an opportunity he could manipulate to his advantage. With a persuasive ability he hadn't known he possessed, he said, "You need a break. Why don't you come with me and I'll buy you some lunch?"

"I have to work. I'm late on my deadline." She sounded petty and disagreeable.

He was not, he realized, going to take no for an answer. "Lunch. Then I'll show you around Bella Valley."

"I don't want to be shown around Bella Valley." And cranky. She sounded cranky.

"A lot of Italian, Chinese, and Mexican immigrants settled here, mingled with the Americans, native and otherwise."

"Shut the door when you go." She started back toward the desk and her open computer.

He continued. "The early days were rife with carnage, murders."

She paused, her hand on the back of the chair.

"*Unsolved* murders. When Prohibition took effect, the violence escalated. The economy collapsed two years later. Life was desperate. The cops were called revenuers. Half of them were corrupt." Walking to the French doors, he flung them wide. Light poured into the room. A draft between the open front door and the deck sucked away the smoke. "The revenuers destroyed the breweries, the liquor distilleries. The river ran red with wine."

She stared at him with an arrested expression.

He was starting to enjoy enticing her with brutality and death. "Men who had been perfectly respectable vintners were suddenly criminals. They went to prison. Their families were fatherless."

Slowly she said, "I thought all the crime during Prohibition was in New York and Chicago. Back east."

"Think again. According to federal law, during Prohibition every family could make two hundred gallons of their own 'nonintoxicating juice' for personal use. Who do you think raised the grapes? We did. The Italians in California."

"Whoa."

"We had our moonshine, too, mostly brandy, but . . . Come with me. Bring your notebook. I'll show you the water tower I recently acquired."

"A water tower?" She edged closer. "Why should I care about a water tower?"

"I bought that water tower because it's sitting in the middle of a vineyard planted with Alicante Bouschet grapes, grapes that were planted in the early nineteen twenties." Clearly she didn't understand, so he continued. "When Prohibition went into effect, the wine producers in this valley—people who had been very successful—became nothing more than grape growers. But the kind of delicate wine grapes grown in Bella Valley couldn't make the train journey east, where the Italian families were waiting to manufacture their own . . . nonintoxicating juices. So the wine producers ripped out the delicate grapes and replaced them with grapes like the Alicante Bouschet varietal because they were hearty and could be shipped back east without spoiling."

"I still don't understand why I should care about your water tower."

"The older vines produce mature grapes. I wanted to try my hand at producing Alicante Bouschet, so when this vineyard came up for sale, I bought it. It's passed through a lot of hands in the last ninety years, so I checked to see who had owned the vineyard and planted the grapes in the early twenties. I laughed when I discovered a man named Massimo Bruno had owned that vineyard."

She looked him up and down. "*You* laughed?"

"You don't have to sound incredulous. I laugh . . . when something is funny."

"Of course," she said politely. "I didn't mean to imply you were humorless."

She made him sound as if he *were* humorless. That wasn't true. There just wasn't much that was funny in this world.

"Who's Massimo Bruno?" Chloë shuffled through the piles on her desk until she found a ragged spiral notebook and a pen.

Nothing funny in this world except perhaps the thought of him romancing a pretty girl by tantalizing her with murderous mysteries. God forbid his brothers ever found out. "Massimo Bruno produced the most famous, most expensive wines ever produced in California. They were known for their subtlety, their smoky undertones, their ability to age well . . . and it didn't hurt that in 1930, Massimo disappeared without a trace. Because wines are like diamonds—if they have a dramatic history, they're priceless."

Chloë cradled the notebook in her arm and started scribbling. "He disappeared? Where? Why?"

"He vanished before my grandmother was born, but Nonna says her mother didn't trust Massimo, said he was a thug."

Her eyes narrowed. He could almost see her mind racing.

Good. He had her hanging on his every word. "I decided to take down the old brick water tower before it fell down. I ordered my men to remove it brick by brick—"

"Why brick by brick?"

"I resell them. Old bricks bring a premium on the market."

"You don't miss a trick."

"I like to think of it as recycling."

For the first time today, she grinned and relaxed. "Nice spin."

"You should hear me give my 'Italian men make better lovers' speech. It's a guaranteed seller."

She chuckled, then saw him watching her—she was lovely, even in plaid flannel, even when she looked tired—and stopped.

He held her gaze.

Color climbed in her face. She looked down at her notebook.

At last, she had noticed him not as a landlord, not as her father's friend, not as a nuisance suitor, but as a man.

Good. Because he had definitely noticed her not as a wife to be acquired for her dowry, but as a woman he'd like to find naked in his bed on warm, dark night. Apparently he had a thing for green plaid flannel.

As if nothing had happened, he said, "My men started at the roof of the water tower to remove the brick veneer. While they were still within three feet of the top, part of the wall collapsed. They expected to see a water tank. Instead they saw the *lid* of a water tank, and on top of that, a couple of copper barrels and the glint of metal pipes. They backed off and called me. Because inside the water tower, there's a still."

"What?" Chloë stepped closer, eyes shining, irresistibly drawn by the story. "*What?* There was a still in the water tower? A still, like where they distill wine into brandy?"

"It's 1930 and it's Prohibition. Revenuers are using their axes on every barrel of liquor and wine they find. Can you think of a better place to hide it?"

"That's brilliant!" She ran to her desk and stuffed her computer case with the spiral notebook, five different-colored pens, and her MacBook Air. "You'll take me there?"

"After lunch."

"Okay, I'm ready."

He fought a smile. "I don't know a lot about fashion, but aren't those your pajamas?"

Looking down at herself, she said, "Shit!" grabbed an outfit from the closet, and ran into the bathroom.

When he heard the shower running, he went out on the deck and waited—and made his plans.

Chapter 10

Chloë came out of the bathroom dressed in what she considered appropriate field gear: faded jeans and a pink button-up shirt over a black, short-sleeved tee. Sitting down in the chair, she laced on a pair of low-rise hiking boots—they were new; she hoped she wasn't screwing up taking a chance on them—then checked her computer case again.

"You might add a hat," Eli advised from the door that led onto the deck. "You don't have much hair left, and what you have doesn't cover your lily-white neck."

The short hair/lily-white comment was clearly not a compliment, but she didn't care. After two interminable weeks of working and getting nowhere, she was going out into the world. The fresh air blowing through the cottage already seemed to be dispersing the cobwebs, and the sight of Eli Di Luca's dark silhouette against the light was oddly menacing. Or critical. Or something. All she knew was that her heart beat faster knowing he stood there.

Funny, considering that when she'd gotten here and gone to work on the book, she'd easily dismissed him from her mind.

"Ready?" He locked the French doors, then came to her and took her computer case. "We'll eat at the resort; then we'll drive out to the water tower."

"I can carry that," she offered, and halfheartedly tugged at the strap. She was from Texas; she knew how to let a man perform the little courtesies between a man and a woman. But somehow, that kind of relationship between the two of them made her uncomfortable, as if it moved them to a level of intimacy. Which was stupid when she considered the fact that he was lifting less than ten pounds.

"Humor me. My old-fashioned grandmother taught me my manners." He walked away from her. "Do you know how to set the alarm?" When she nodded, he walked out the door and down the steps.

When she joined him in the driveway, he said, "We'll need to take the truck. Your little car won't make it."

"Okay."

He looked surprised. Probably it wasn't politically correct for a guy to assume he had to drive, and California was all about being politically correct. But she didn't equate her femininity with a steering wheel.

His forest green extended-cab F-250 pickup had big, serviceable wheels and tires and a jacked suspension that lifted it so far off the ground she would need help to get in.

"*Nice* truck."

He raised his eyebrows at her.

"I'm from Texas," she said. "We know our trucks."

"I should have known." He gave her a hand up into the cab. When she was settled, he handed her the computer case, walked around, and climbed into the driver's seat.

The dashboard was dusty and he had a few paper coffee cups rolling around on the floorboard, but she supposed, after the condition of the cottage, she was in no position to criticize.

The winding road to Bella Terra involved a couple of switchbacks as they descended the ridge, then smoothed out as it joined the highway.

Eli's driving wasn't flashy, wasn't too slow. He drove skillfully; she didn't notice the curves. But that didn't surprise her; Eli seemed to be one of those men who occurred too seldom in life: a man capable of doing whatever he did with a deceptive ease.

Chloë rolled down the window, let the breeze blast tease her face, and watched the vineyards and wineries and fruit stands go by. They slid from one enclave of Bella Valley to another, the olive and oak trees casting dappled shade onto the two-lane road. The vines stretched in endless rows. Peach trees shed their blossoms as California's early spring scattered them across the landscape. Here and there a farmhouse or a barn stood on a small plot of grass, and wineries of various grandeurs beckoned invitingly. The air smelled new, as if the vines and trees and the earth itself breathed out the coming summer.

There was isolation here, and wilderness beckoning just over the hill, yet farmers worked the vineyards, and tourists drove the roads. Maybe in the summer Bella Valley would be hot and crowded, but right now, it was perfect, and it fit Eli Di Luca.

He belonged here.

She liked that she didn't feel as if she needed to entertain him. In fact, she thought she annoyed him so much he'd much prefer if she didn't talk. Of course, that brought up the question—why had he asked her out?

Probably her father had called and demanded an accounting.

Yes, that had to be it.

Although . . . Eli looked better than the first time she had seen him—he was clean and in jeans, a blue denim shirt, and work boots; he certainly hadn't gone out of his way to impress her.

Maybe he wasn't here at her father's behest.

Plus, she still suffered from that gut feeling he didn't like her, as if he'd been angry at her before he'd even set eyes on her.

Some guys were like that, she supposed . . . although usually not with her. Men tended to like her.

So. Nothing personal in this excursion. It was business, and that knowledge helped her forget that uncomfortable moment when he'd looked in her eyes and she'd suddenly remembered she was in her pj's, her bra hanging from a chair, and he smelled like warm spice and cool citrus, and tall guys with long legs and broad shoulders made her weak at the knees—among other places.

He slowed down to twenty-five as they entered the outskirts of town.

On her first spin through on her way to Eli's home, Chloë had noted that the town of Bella Terra was marvelously quaint, a place founded in the nineteenth century and relatively undiscovered until the 1980s, when the California wine industry was well on its way to its current prominence. Main Street was actually the main drag, where elaborate Victorian mansions that advertised themselves as bed-and-breakfasts sat arm in arm with ultramodern condos made up of tin roofs and jarring angles. The grocery stores and strip malls were located on the outskirts, but those outskirts weren't too far from the central town square. Posh art galleries, chic clothing stores, and wine-tasting rooms circled the park, and shoppers and tourists strolled and shopped and mingled with the locals.

As Eli parallel-parked the truck with an ease that made her envious, she said, "I keep looking at the bandstand and expecting to see a revival of *The Music Man*."

"That was last summer," he said, so deadpan she didn't know whether to believe him or not. He came around to her side, took her computer case and helped her out, then held on to her hand as he led her toward the Bella Terra resort. It felt funny to be towed through the streets behind him; he wasn't paying attention to her, yet he twined his fingers in hers, made sure she had room to walk, kept her close. As they stepped into the check-in area, he nodded in greeting as bellmen, desk clerks, and the concierge greeted him, and headed through the lobby as if he owned it.

She supposed, since it was his family's resort, he had the right.

In the Luna Grande Lounge, a guy of about fifty stood behind the bar, frowning over a printout spread from one end to the other. Behind him a glass-covered wall of wine storage rose two stories to the ceiling, and the tallest library ladder Chloë had ever seen traveled along a horizontal steel rod and allowed access to even the highest bottles . . . except that a quick scan proved that none of the cellars had any contents.

But then, the entire bar was empty, the chairs upside down on the tables; it looked like they were remodeling.

"Tom!" Eli said.

The guy looked up, surprised. "Eli!" His gaze shifted to look her over, and he noted their joined hands.

Self-conscious, she freed herself.

Eli let go of her easily.

"Is this the woman you're hiding in your cottage?" Tom asked.

"Sure." To Chloë's surprise, Eli sounded sanguine about the teasing. "Chloë, this is Tom Chan, one of my best friends and one of the world's foremost experts on wines. Tom, Chloë Robinson, famous author."

Tom reached across and shook her hand. "It's a pleasure to meet you, Chloë. Loved your book. I'm a mystery reader from way back, and you had me fooled clear to the end."

No matter how often she heard it, praise for her book warmed her, and she smiled at him.

Tom looked startled, then smiled back. "No *wonder* Eli invited you to live with him."

"She's not living with me," Eli said curtly. "She's living in the cottage."

"Right. That's what I meant. You two want to have lunch in here? We're not officially open yet after the incident a few weeks ago, but, Chloë, since you're a famous author, we'll let you bring your friend in here." Tom smirked at Eli.

Incident? "What happened?" she asked.

Tom glanced at Eli, and when it was clear he wasn't going to answer, he said, "We had a vandal break in and take out most of the wines on the wine wall. Dropped them from the top of the ladder. Wiped us out. Expensive bottles of wine. Priceless. Irreplaceable." Tom's eyes filled with tears.

"We caught the vandal. But the wines are gone." Not a muscle stirred in Eli's face, but she felt emotion vibrating through him.

A grief similar to Tom's? And anger . . . an anger that swirled with currents of violence and vengeance.

"You love your wines," she said.

He met her gaze, and his brown eyes kindled with the kind of slow-burning rage that would have made her afraid, if she had been the one to break those bottles. "Wine is the thread that connects me to the Di Lucas who came to this country, settled this land, and planted the grapes, to the Di Lucas in Italy who tended their vineyards. Wine is my heritage—and I take it badly when my heritage is threatened."

Chapter 11

Did Eli Di Luca harbor other emotions, other loves? A man who felt so strongly about his heritage must surely hate darkly, laugh loudly, love deeply.

Yet never had Chloë seen a sign of any great emotion in Eli. She was a pretty good observer of human behavior—what writer wasn't?—and she couldn't even imagine such a thing. He'd seemed to be a stoic, rather unfeeling guy. Now she realized . . . perhaps she was wrong. Perhaps when she looked at him, all she saw—all anyone saw—was a mask, a shell that covered and contained the real man.

And she wondered . . . What hid beneath that shell that he had so carefully constructed?

"Shall I call a waiter out of the restaurant?" Tom picked up the house phone.

"You do that," Eli said.

"Take any table you want." Tom gestured to the empty restaurant and joked, "None of them are reserved."

"By the window?" Eli didn't wait for her to answer, but took the chairs off the table with the best view of the carefully landscaped, lush garden, and held the back of one until she sat down. He sat opposite her, facing the door. In a low voice, he said, "The Chan family moved here not long after the Di Lucas arrived, working on the railroad as Chinese laborers. Then they settled down to work in the fields and orchards. They've always been ambitious and they worked hard. Not even the Chinese Exclusion Act kept them down."

She scrambled for her spiral notebook. This was good stuff.

Eli waited until she had it open and her pen poised. Then he continued. "The hard work paid off; the Chans own vineyards in Bella, Sonoma, and Napa valleys. Tom's brothers and nieces and cousins are doctors and lawyers and shop owners. Tom's considered kind of the loafer, because after he came back from the Gulf War, he didn't want to go after a law degree. All he wanted to do was consult on wines. Of course, restaurateurs come from all over the world to talk to him, but his mom doesn't get it. She still nags him to get the degree."

Thoughtlessly, Chloë said, "That sounds like my dad in reverse, nagging me to dump my career."

"And get married." Eli's voice was warm and deep.

"Yes." She'd already talked to Eli about it. Assured him he was safe. Why was she uncomfortable now?

Because he was looking at her differently than he had that first day. Because he'd held her hand in the street. Because he was a good-looking guy who'd seen her in her pajamas, and he'd noticed the bra on the chair. Because he smelled good enough that she wanted to sniff him like a fine glass of wine . . .

All of which added up to a resounding nothing . . . but she was still uncomfortable.

A plastic-covered three-sided ad for new menu items sat at the edge of the table. She picked it up and studied it.

Tom limped over with two glasses—she hadn't realized, but apparently he was disabled—and set them on the table. "Honey, there's no point in reading the tricorner," he said. "Note the wine stains. It's not current."

"I know. I can't help it. I'm a compulsive reader. Do you want me to recite the nutrients on the Cheerios box?" She grinned cheerfully at him.

"No, if you're going to seduce me with oat bran, we need to be alone." Tom pulled a bottle of wine from under his arm. "I had this one stashed under the bar, a nice Di Luca Arneis. Light, refreshing, perfect for lunch."

Chloë said, "I don't usually drink before, um, the evening. . . ."

The two men looked at her uncomprehendingly, as if she were speaking Latin.

"I can make an exception today." Apparently Bella Valley was much like her father's home in Italy: Wine was appropriate anytime.

Tom utilized the corkscrew with dexterity and speed, and poured her glass full. "This is one of Eli's best whites."

She'd learned to taste wine in Italy; she took a sip of the cool, pale wine and rolled it over her tongue. "Dry, full-bodied, with notes of apricots and . . . pears?"

Eli exchanged a glance with Tom, and both nodded as if pleased.

Tom poured for Eli. "I don't know if you know, Chloë, but Eli is an incredibly talented vintner, and although he can be difficult, he's a good guy all around."

"For God's sake, Tom." Eli glared at his friend.

"I'm just trying to help you out." Tom sounded hurt and righteous. "You're not getting any younger, you know. You need to get out and get yourself a good woman before you're so decrepit there's nothing of you worth getting."

Chloë sputtered with laughter.

"Drink your wine." Tom winked at her. "He looks better from behind an intoxicated haze."

"He looks good no matter what." She lifted her glass to Tom. "All the men in this bar are beauty and charm combined."

Tom perked up. "Let me get a chair and sit down."

"Go away, Tom." Eli sounded territorial.

Or maybe he thought of himself as her protective uncle.

"You know," Tom grumbled as he limped away, "you young guys just can't take the competition."

Eli solemnly met her gaze. "Tom and your father should get together."

"I like that they can both make us embarrassed."

"I think they embarrass themselves."

It didn't matter if Eli thought of himself as something like an uncle to her. She could never convince herself he was anything but a scrumptious man in denim.

She sipped again. Interesting.

Not the wine—the change in the dynamics in this relationship.

Just this morning, she would never have thought she could sit across a table from Eli Di Luca and feel breathless with anticipation, as if something great were about to happen.

The waiter who arrived was young and efficient, bringing water, menus, making suggestions for lunch. They ordered.

Chloë clicked her pen, clicked it again, clicked it again. She put the point to the paper, looked inquiringly at Eli. Anything to distract her from the weird vibrations in the room. "I don't know much about this area during Prohibition. Were there a lot of stills distilling brandy?"

"Lots. Prohibition wiped out many very prosperous families. Everyone was scrambling for money."

"Your family, too?"

His brown eyes held no warm highlights; they were almost black as he remembered a time before his time. "Most certainly. The Di Lucas stayed with grapes, but Prohibition and the revenuers' axes destroyed the family's prosperity. Our folks were tough and resourceful, so we opened this resort."

"Original thinking."

"The story goes that my great-great-great-grandmother, who was a young widow when Prohibition took effect, spearheaded the idea. Everyone thought she was crazy. Her sons fought her. But she said if we built a luxury place for the very wealthy—and even during the Depression, there were very wealthy people—they would come. She invited Rudolph Valentino for the grand opening, then told the San Francisco newspapers he was coming. The newspaper reporters arrived. Rudolph Valentino did not. But she had a reputation for irresistible charm. She gave them good food, good lodging, good music, probably slipped them a little nonalcoholic grape juice that she had fermented." He grinned.

My God. He *grinned*.

He had a bit of Great-great-great-grandmother's charm after all.

He continued. "They went back and wrote flattering stories about the resort. By the next year, Rudolph Valentino did stay. The Bella Terra resort catered to the wealthy from San Francisco, from burgeoning Holly-wood, and eventually the East Coast and around the world. Bella Terra became the vanguard of our resorts and the main family business for the next fifty years."

"Your family owns *more* resorts?" Now Chloë was really impressed.

"Two more, one in southern California and one on the coast of Washington, both run by more Di Lucas. My grandmother had only one son, my father, but generally speaking, Di Lucas breed like rabbits."

Do you have children? Do your brothers have children? Do we have to talk about breeding? "Is the winery more profitable or the resorts?"

"The resorts taken altogether make more, but in the eighties, the winery began to make a profit again. I started to take the reins when I was in college and took over completely when I was twenty-two."

So he'd been in charge for twelve years. No wonder he had that I'm-the-dude attitude. "Do you own any part of the resort?" she asked.

"The Di Luca family shares all profits on the family properties, with salaries given to those of us who work here."

"And you're not only the winemaker; you also direct the operations in the vineyard."

"Right. I make a good salary." He watched her with a half smile. "Is this research for your book or are you asking for another reason?"

She had, she realized, been quizzing him about his income as if she were vetting him as a prospective husband. She'd sounded as bad as her father, and she blushed—damned fair skin—and mumbled, "For the book."

But for all her embarrassment, she was satisfied once more that Eli wasn't entertaining her for her father's money.

He didn't need her father's money at all.

Chapter 12

To Chloë, the water tower didn't look like a water tower at all, more like the turret of a medieval castle rising from the middle of a vineyard filled with vines gnarled and bent like hunchbacked old women wringing their hands. The tower's round, orange brick skin reached three stories in the air, baking in the afternoon sun. Up by the octagon tin roof, a hole in the bricks gaped like a missing tooth, and, as Chloë watched, a pigeon flew out from beneath the eaves.

"Don't look up with your mouth open," Eli advised.

The comment gave her pause; *did* he have a sense of humor? Because it was the first inkling of one she'd seen.

"These vines are different from the ones around the cottage," she said.

"They're planted in the old way, not trained to grow flat on an espalier but left to grow naturally and trimmed into shape. They're not as easy to farm, but the older vines produce our best wines." Leaning over, he caressed the branches as he would a lover.

That was more like the Eli Di Luca she thought she knew, in love with his grapes.

A mechanical lift like the kind used to reach signs or electrical wires sat beside the tank, but this one had wheels and tires, and the tracks showed it had been driven into place.

"A cherry picker," Eli said. "So my guys can stand on the platform, disassemble the tower, stack the bricks, and lower them to the ground without breaking any. Once they realized what was in there, they came down as quickly as they could and called me."

"Do you think the water tower was built specifically to house the still?"

"Absolutely."

"Why put a water tower in the middle of a vineyard? Especially if you're going to use it to hide your still? Aren't there better places to hide it?"

"Think about it. A vineyard needs water, so a water tower makes sense. When you build it, it doesn't attract anyone's attention. Assemble a wooden tank, fill it with water, surround it with brick that extends ten feet over the top, add a roof and you've got a hidden room inside there." Eli pointed toward the roof.

"How ingenious." Chloë worked hard to think up

creative plots; this would never in a million years have occurred to her.

"Plus, this is a rural area *now*. Think what it was like in the thirties." He gestured toward the two-lane highway that ran straight through this, the flattest part of the valley. "Town is fifteen miles south, and in 1930 the population of the whole valley was maybe ten thousand."

She squinted her eyes and gazed across the valley, trying to see it as it had been eighty years ago. "I don't know a lot about stills, but don't they require a constant fire for several days before the liquor is ready?"

"That's right."

"Then how did Massimo pull that off? Wouldn't he have had to vent the smoke somewhere?"

"I don't know. I haven't been inside."

Outraged, she demanded, "You haven't gone in? How could you not?"

"It's a crime scene," he said patiently. "An old crime scene, it's true. But I called law enforcement—that's Bryan DuPey, the chief of police and a school friend. He said he'd put it on his schedule. Obviously not high on his schedule—it's been a week."

"Oh, no." She clutched her throat with both hands, realized Eli's proximity made her uneasy enough to overreact, and dropped them to her side. "This DuPey didn't forbid you to go up, did he?"

"No, he doesn't care as long as I don't put the still back into use. I've managed to refrain."

Another brief flash of a sense of humor. She thought.

"Come on. I'll take you up on the cherry picker," he said.

"Please, let's go up the way Massimo would have!" She looked around, spotted a narrow metal door set at ground level. "It's more atmospheric."

"Maybe we can find you another skull."

Humor and sarcasm. So Eli Di Luca was more than just a walking, talking wine expert and sex god.

"I should never have had that glass of wine with lunch," she said aloud.

"I suspect you'd want to go up the old way, glass of wine or not. Wait here. I've got a cooler with bottles of water on the backseat."

She watched as he strode away from her. She liked that long stride, the way his hips moved. Something about the way he walked brought two terms to her mind: "alpha male" and "good in bed." The way he leaped to care for her made her wonder what it would be like to lay her head on his shoulder. . . .

She'd been working too hard.

She needed to get out more.

She'd told her father a hundred times—she did not need a man.

She needed to remember that.

Eli came back carrying her computer case and an icy bottle of water.

She pressed the bottle to her forehead. "I badly need to hydrate."

With awesome patience, he took the bottle away

from her, opened the cap, and handed it back. "Hydration doesn't occur through the skin. Drink."

She drank.

"Okay now?" he asked.

"A lot better."

"Come on." Eli slung the case over his shoulder and opened the door. "Before we started demolition we didn't know what held the tower up, so we picked the lock and checked it out."

Chloë followed him into the cool, dim, basementlike cavity. The dampness made her shiver, and the smell of earth and wood rot rose thick in her nose.

The wooden tank was large, twenty feet in circumference, and rose a claustrophobic eight feet above her head, supported by impressive oak legs set symmetrically around the edge. An old wooden ladder hung from the edge of the tank, and she walked over and looked up. The ladder continued up in the narrow space between the wooden tank and the brick shell, and at the top she saw a dim light.

Putting his hand on the ladder, he rattled it and grimaced, then put his foot on the lowest rung. With his full weight, he swung back and forth. "All right, it'll hold us." He descended. "You first."

So if she fell, he would catch her? Or so he could check out her ass?

She didn't care why. It was of no importance to her.

She took another swig of water, put the bottle on the floor, and started climbing. The first eight feet felt odd, straight up in the air. Then she reached the side of the wooden water container and slipped into the space between that and the bricks. The fit was tight. The bricks were warm at her back. She grasped the rungs carefully; they were rough, a mass of splinters.

When she was about halfway up the side of the container, Eli called, "Doing okay?"

"Fine." She paused and glanced up toward the light, then down toward the shadows, trying to absorb the sensations, put them into words so she could later transfer those sensations to paper. She put her hand against the tank. The wood felt dry against her skin. "There's no water in it?"

"Not for a long time," he said.

She continued climbing.

"I estimated the tank was twelve feet high." He was right below her. "So you'll be at the top soon. If you need help, I'm right here."

She wanted to snort. She didn't need help; she clambered onto the flat top of the water tank on her hands and knees. The octagonal roof was ten feet above the floor. At every corner it connected to the wall, and that left vents all the way around between the brick and the metal. There subdued light leaked in; she could see the concentration of soot where the smoke had leaked out.

The best light entered through the small, high hole Eli's men had broken through the brick; it revealed a thick layer of dust and soot covering the wooden floor. The boards felt sticky to the touch, and as she stood, she wiped her palms on her pants. Directly beside her stood an imposing copper pot as tall as she was, and so wide she couldn't get her arms around it. Pipes ran from the top to two smaller copper containers.

The still.

As Eli poked his head into the chamber, she offered him her hand and echoed his offer: "If you need help, I'm right here."

He surprised her by taking it.

She needed to remember the man liked to hold hands.

He came to his feet far too close to her, looked down, and half smiled. "Is it everything you'd hoped?"

It took her a long moment of stupefaction before she realized he meant the still. "Yes, it's perfect." A pile of wood remained, half-rotted and waiting to be thrown into the metal fire pit beneath the still. "I've got to take pictures." She rummaged in her computer case for her camera, brought it out, took a photo of Eli standing before the largest tank.

"Look at that thing." Eli stared admiringly at the tank. "It's huge."

She looked at the camera screen to check the photo. Good. The flash had filled in lots of good detail.

She took a picture of the ceiling. Also good.

"The still must be seventy-five gallons," Eli said.

Stepping into the middle of the chamber, she took a photo of the side that had been hidden from her by the still. Her flash illuminated . . . something. She pulled the camera away from her face and looked.

Her breath caught. "Eli?" she whispered.

"If Massimo was distilling wine into brandy," Eli

said, "he must have been selling the proceeds all over the county."

"Eli?"

"I believe it, though." The copper monstrosity consumed his whole attention. "Prohibition made law-abiding citizens into criminals, and—"

"Eli!"

He turned to her. "What?"

She pointed a shaking finger across the room. "If you want to know anything about the still, perhaps you could ask him."

Chapter 13

The mummified remains of a man reclined on the floor across from the still. His skin was gray. The dirt of the last century and this one covered him like a blanket, like a camouflage.

Chloë pulled a thin LED flashlight out of her bag and pointed it at the body.

The corpse's head was propped up on a log, and even though his eyes were shut, the sunken sockets seemed to be staring at them, his face twisted in an expression of unending agony.

Eli glanced at Chloë; she was pale with shock, holding the camera clutched tight in one hand and the flashlight in the other.

Reaching out, Eli wrapped his arm around her to

tug her close, putting his hand on her head and nestling her against his chest.

Although she remained stiff in his arms, she let him hug her.

That told him a lot.

"He's been dead a long time." Her voice sounded detached, empty of emotion. "His clothes date from the nineteen twenties or thirties. Do you think it could be Massimo?"

"I suspect it is." Keeping an arm around her, he pulled out his cell phone and called 911.

The operator picked up.

He recognized her voice; it was Patricia Greene. He'd dated her in high school. "Hi, Pat, it's Eli Di Luca. Hey, I'm out here at the old brick water tower—"

"The one with the still?" she asked.

Everyone knew everything in this town. "That's the one. And it appears there's more to report crime-wise than a little old bootlegging."

"Did some kids spray-paint their names on the water tower?" Pat didn't sound nearly as upset as a righteous employee of the city should sound. "My daughter told me some of the eighth graders were talking about it. You know what kids that age are like."

"No, and thank God they didn't. We've got a body."

Pat's casual voice changed tone. "You're sure it's a body? There's no sign of life?"

"It's a very old body, Pat. I'm guessing he died

eighty years ago. But I promise you, it's murder."
Against his chest, he felt Chloë nod her head.

Pat's voice changed again, became official. "I'm
sending DuPey a message right now, and he'll be on
his way out in no time. Please stay on the scene. He's
going to want to question you."

"Will do," Eli said.

"Are you there alone?" Pat asked.

"I'm here with a friend." He could almost hear Patricia biting her lip, keeping the questions at bay.

At last she said, "Keep her there, too, please." *Her*.
Pat was fishing.

He let her get away with it. No point in doing otherwise. "Right. See you around." He hung up.

Slowly Chloë pulled away from Eli. "Before law enforcement gets here, can we . . . see if we can figure
anything out? Because once they arrive, they'll take
him away, and the way he's looking at us . . . I think he
wants justice."

Eli let her go, satisfied that she had let him comfort
her, that they'd taken a slow, easy step toward intimacy. "What makes you say that?"

"He's handcuffed. He's barefoot. His vest is unbuttoned, his shirt is open, and those black stains on his
shirt—I'll bet they're blood. His sleeves are pushed up,
shoved up, but he didn't do it." She slipped the camera
into her computer case.

"Why not?" Fascinating the way her mind worked.

"He's a dapper dresser." She paced toward the body.
"Look, off to the side. That's his hat."

"It might belong to one of the killers."

"Every man in those days wore a hat, and this one remains in good condition. So it had to be a quality brand, and nobody else would have left it here, at a crime scene. So it's Massimo's, maybe handmade for him." She glanced at Eli, eyebrows raised.

He nodded. "Keep talking. I'm with you."

"He's wearing suit pants. You can't tell me most men in the Depression could afford clothing like this." She knelt gingerly beside Massimo and shone her LED flashlight from Massimo's head to his toes. "No, even if he was in the mood to be casual, he would have neatly rolled up his shirtsleeves."

"You're observant."

She looked back at him. "Not usually. My mom said I always had my head in the clouds. True, but if something captures my attention, I can make some deductions. After all, I not only write mysteries; I've read a lot of them, too."

So. Eli had to get her attention, huh? He could do that. All he had to do was be more interesting than a long-dead corpse.

"Wait a minute." With a shrug to the waste of badly needed income, Eli pried a piece of pipe from the still and slammed it into the brick wall about a foot below the opening. The brittle mortar cracked along a long seam. Putting the pipe down, he leaned against the wall. Bricks clattered and shattered all the way to the ground, and a flood of sunlight brightened the enclosed space. He did it again, and again, until he'd brought the opening down to floor level and out as far as his arms could reach.

When he turned back to Chloë, she was watching him, eyes wide, and he by God had her attention.

But not for long.

In the distance, he heard the scream of sirens.

"If you want to examine him," he said, "do it fast."

She flicked off her flashlight and returned to her observation of the body. "Look at his expression, Eli; he was tortured. Look at the skin on his arms, here on his chest, on the bottoms of his feet. They're covered with little circles. They used cigarettes to burn him. And right there, there's one of the cigarettes they tossed on the floor."

"Really?" Eli walked over and picked it up. He examined it. "Hm." He put it in his pocket.

She used the handle of her flashlight to push Massimo's shirt up. "Here's the reason for the blood. A knife wound. Went in right below the ribs. He was probably already dying and this was the end. Poor guy." She dropped the shirt. "They killed him in the heat of summer, or he wouldn't have mummified like this."

Eli asked the obvious question. "But what did they kill him for?"

The sirens came closer.

"The still?" Chloë suggested.

"Why torture him? Why kill him? Blackmail, yes. If corrupt revenuers found him here, they could have demanded a portion of the profits. This"—Eli waved a hand at the body—"is different. They wanted some-thing, and he wouldn't, or couldn't, give it to them."

Again Eli had Chloë's attention.

"You said your great-grandmother thought Mas-simo was involved in crime that had nothing to do with liquor."

"That's right."

"But no one knows what."

"No one even knows if it's true." The sirens were so close to the water tower, Eli stuck his head out to make sure the police weren't driving among the vines.

Two cars bumped along the gravel access road, one after the other, lights spinning red and blue.

But Bryan DuPey had lived his whole life in Bella Valley. He knew better than to risk Eli's wrath by driv-ing into a vineyard.

He parked as close as he could, though, cut the si-ren, and got out on the driver's side. Some guy Eli didn't recognize got out on the passenger side.

One of DuPey's officers and the coroner exited the other car.

Eli turned back to Chloë. "They're here."

"I wish they hadn't been so fast." She stood and rubbed her hands on her pants, leaving black streaks behind. "I'd like to search Massimo's pockets."

"Go ahead."

She flinched. "I'm not quite thick-skinned enough."

"Points to you," Eli said. "No reason to, either. His executioners, whoever they were, ripped the lining out of his jacket. If there was ever anything in his pockets, it's gone now."

"So whatever they were looking for was small enough to be kept in his pockets."

DuPey shouted from below, "Hey, up there!"

"It could have been a key that led to something big." Leaning out, Eli hollered, "Take the cherry picker up." He turned back to Chloë. "The coroner is Mason Watson. Don't tell him you touched the body. He is a fanatic about a pristine crime scene."

"I won't," she promised. "I corresponded with a coroner about bodies and what affects them and how, and she told me to always, always stay back."

"You didn't go view an autopsy?"

"If I watch *NCIS* too close to bedtime, I have nightmares." She smiled painfully. With soot smeared across her cheek, dirty fingers, and that bright white upstanding hair, Chloë looked like a modern Dickens urchin.

Odd to see her not as a tool he would use to keep his vineyard, but as a woman who thrived on solving a riddle, who sought vengeance for a man long dead, who lived recklessly and with enjoyment.

When Eli put aside the resentment at having to marry her . . . he liked her. More than that, she stirred desire in him. Not the simple physical need, but possessiveness, too, and a shadowy fear.

She gazed at him from such clear, guileless eyes he wondered whether she saw beyond the Eli of everyday life, beneath the iron control he imposed on himself, and into his darkest depths.

Perhaps she was not a simple mystery writer after all.

Perhaps she was not merely his future wife.

Perhaps she was the one person against whom he couldn't defend himself.

Chapter 14

Chloë thought she and Eli had been, well, not enjoying themselves—discovering a body wasn't fun,
exactly—but finding common ground. They'd been
communicating with an ease she seldom was able to
savor with another person . . . especially not an available man.

But now he watched her so intently that she asked,
"Do you think it's stupid that someone who writes
about murder is too squeamish to view a simple proce-
dure?"

He shook himself like a dog shaking off rain. "Not
at all. The sight of an open, bleeding body is not a
nightmare easy to shake off." He sounded so normal,
but—

What an odd thing to say.

He was a vintner.

When had he seen an open, bleeding body?

With most people, Chloë would pose the question—
she loved to hear personal stories—and most people
confided in her.

With Eli Di Luca . . . she just didn't have the nerve.

Like an alarm, the mechanical beeping of the lift
started, loud and rhythmic.

She tore her gaze away from Eli's, moved away
from Massimo's body. By the time the men jumped off
the cherry picker onto the water tower, she stood off to
the side of the still, mouth dry, looking everywhere but
at Eli and wishing she had a drink from that water bottle she'd left below.

Four guys leaped through the hole Eli had created.

The guy in the lead was of medium height, wiry,
with thinning brown hair and tired eyes.

"Hi, DuPey." Eli introduced him: "Bryan DuPey,
this is my guest, Chloë Robinson. Chloë, DuPey is our
chief of police. We went to high school together."

DuPey shook her hand. "The good thing about my
being chief of police is that he doesn't call me Dopey
anymore. At least, not to my face."

"Not while you're carrying a gun," Eli said.

Another sign of humor.

DuPey looked harmless, but he summed up her and
the scene with one comprehensive glance. "Hey, Eli, I
hope your family isn't going to make a habit of finding
bodies."

Startled, Chloë glanced at Eli.

"That makes two of us." But he didn't offer any further explanation.

The patrolman who stepped up to Chloë was a little older than she was, probably twenty-eight, a little taller than her, probably five-foot-seven, handsome, and clad in a uniform so precisely ironed he made her feel as if she'd shown up for a formal party dressed like an electrician. But when Eli introduced her—"Finnegan Balfour"—Finnegan smiled as he shook her hand a little too long.

So even with her dandelion-puff hair, she knew she could still attract a man . . . or maybe he had a manuscript he wanted her to look at.

Man. When had she become such a cynic?

When she pulled her hand away, he smiled some more, tipped his hat, and headed toward the still. "Oowee!" He had a drawl Chloë couldn't quite place. "This is a *big* one."

The coroner was somewhere in his fifties. He wore jeans, a button-down shirt, spotless white running shoes, and a baseball cap, and he carried two bulging leather bags and looked at the body with an almost spooky gleam of joy in his hazel eyes. "Good to meet you," he said to Chloë, but she was pretty sure he would never recognize her unless she were stretched out on a slab in his morgue.

The last man stood back, silhouetted against the light, waiting to be introduced.

DuPey gestured him forward. "Chloë Robinson, this is Wyatt Vincent."

Wyatt joined them, a man of about forty, tall, well built, well dressed. He shook her hand. "Miss Robinson, I admire your work. I'm hoping for a new book soon."

She gave him her standard smile and answer. "Thank you. I'm hoping for that, too."

"Wyatt comes from a long line of police officers," DuPey said.

"The family is rotten with them." Wyatt's mouth quirked; he sounded self-deprecating, but to Chloë he seemed to be the kind of guy who got your attention and held it. He seemed sure of himself, yet his sandy hair, blue eyes, and light tan probably made him a good candidate for a stakeout. He looked as if he could blend in anywhere in the United States.

She'd bet he was good at anything he did.

Certainly DuPey sounded as if he admired him. "Wyatt was in the FBI for years, worked all over the country, then wanted to come back to California, so he brought a whole lot of knowledge about criminals and criminal behavior back to Sacramento and opened his own firm for consulting with police departments on how to sharpen their investigative skills and head off trouble before it happens. After our little problem last month, I called him in to help us brush up on procedures."

"Welcome to Bella Valley." Eli shook his hand.

"Thank you. I've been in the valley before. My family's lived in central California for . . . oh, I guess we moved here in the forties, must have been, from Chicago." He dipped his head to Eli. "Hope you don't mind that I tagged along. Sometimes I miss the actual work on the ground, and this sounded like an unusual case."

"His dad knew my dad," DuPey said, then told Chloë, "My dad was the chief of police here when we were kids."

"Did anybody disturb the body?" Mason asked.

"I walked over by him." Chloë figured she might as well confess; someone had clearly disturbed the dust and soot of the past eighty years, and it wasn't Eli; his feet were at least twice the size of hers.

"And knelt here." The coroner was observant. "Fascinated, were you?"

"I've never seen anything like this," she admitted. "Never even heard of something like this."

"Me neither," Finnegan said from behind the still, "and I'm originally from Kansas."

"What has that got to do with anything?" DuPey snapped.

Finnegan stuck his head out. "Kansas is dry by default, unless the county decides otherwise."

"Dry?" Chloë understood. She didn't think these Californians had a clue. "You mean . . . no liquor is sold there?"

He tipped his hat to her. "Yes, ma'am. I saw plenty of stills there, but no dried-up old corpses."

With an edge of irritation in his voice, DuPey asked, "What did we talk about, Finnegan?"

"Oh. That." Again Finnegan tipped his hat in Chloë's direction. "Pardon me, ma'am."

"For what?" she asked.

"We're supposed to call them bodies. It's more aesthetically pleasing." He winked at her. "If we use the right words, we won't get into trouble on TV when we report the crimes, and the ladies won't call and complain because we're insensitive."

She gave a laugh, which she quickly muffled.

DuPey looked not at all pleased.

Finnegan ducked behind the copper still again. Metal rattled.

DuPey said, "Finnegan, don't touch anything!"

"No, sir." Finnegan appeared again, saluted with a pipe elbow he'd somehow gleaned off the still, and vanished.

DuPey sighed as if discouraged, and his tired eyes grew even more tired.

Chloë walked over to the opposite side of the body and knelt. "Do you mind if I watch?"

"You're the author, right?" Mason asked.

"Yes." Did everyone in town know who she was?

"Yes," Eli answered as if she'd spoken out loud. "In this town, you can't say something in a Porta Potty on a south-side construction site that isn't reported in a north-end saloon within ten minutes."

"It's not that bad, Eli." DuPey sounded absentminded as he examined the still. "No one gives a damn about most of us. It's you Di Lucas with your celebrity aura who attract attention. And last month made all of you headline news again." Before Chloë could ask what had happened last month, DuPey added, "For all that this is old, this is a nice still."

"How old do you figure it is?" Eli asked.

DuPey whipped around. "How old do *you* figure it is, Eli?"

"If that guy over there built the still, then it's Prohibition for sure." Eli put his hands on his belt. "Why? You think I've been making brandy up here?"

DuPey took the lid off and sniffed. "No . . ."

Wyatt knelt beside Chloë. "I haven't seen anything like this since we caught the Twilight Slayer in Phoenix."

Chloë glanced at him. "You were involved in that case?"

"I had a hand in the solving of it," Wyatt said. "He captured women he thought were vampires, staked them out in the desert, and let them bake. When a body dies of dehydration and then shrivels, that mummified look comes on fast. 'Twasn't pretty."

She observed as Mason took pictures, then carefully moved the clothes aside to view the injuries. "So I was right? Whoever killed this guy did it in the heat of summer. They handcuffed him, tortured him, killed him, left him to dry."

"Good deductions," Mason said.

"Why do you say 'they'?" Wyatt asked. "Could be one killer."

Chloë knew she was being tested. She didn't care; right or wrong, this was information she could somehow put to use in a book—preferably in her current book. The horror of finding a body had faded, to be replaced by an endless realm of plot possibilities that bubbled in her mind. "Possible. But he built a still up here where no one could catch him, and from the amount of soot on the roof where the smoke vented, on the walls and on the floor, he used it for a long time. So he was smart. He's well dressed, so he was prosperous. He would have made sure no one could sneak up on him, so he worked some kind of early warning system and probably some booby traps."

"You'd make a good investigator," Wyatt said.

"Indeed. Very good, Miss Robinson." Mason pointed at the corpse's hands. "Observe that the skin on his knuckles was scarred, so he knew how to fight."

A thump brought Chloë's head around, and the boards behind her shook.

Eli was down on one knee, his hands pressed to the floor. "Be careful. There's an uneven place on the floor."

"You fell?" She couldn't believe it. He didn't seem the type to ever make a misstep. "Are you okay?"

"Fine." Standing, he grimaced at his filthy hands. "Only my dignity is hurt." Pulling his handkerchief out of his pocket, he wiped his palms and grimaced again as the big square of white cotton turned black. "Chloë, you look pale. Is the heat up here getting to you again?"

She got the message, sighed, and stood. "Yes. I hate to leave, but I was a little faint before, and I need to go lie down."

"Probably a lady like you is suffering from delayed shock at discovering the body, too," Finnegan said.

Against all evidence, Mason and Wyatt nodded solemnly.

These superior men set her teeth on edge.

But before she could contradict them, Eli put his hand under her elbow and pulled her to her feet. "I'll take you home," he said.

That made the law enforcement men exchange grins, which irritated her even more.

But not as much as Eli; his face turned to granite and in a goaded voice he said, "As a favor to her father, I'm allowing Miss Robinson to stay in the cottage to finish her book. I'd appreciate it if you'd remember that."

Mason and Wyatt sobered and leaned over the body again.

Finnegan disappeared behind the still.

DuPey said, "I'll walk you to your truck. I need to question you both about your find here. Just a formality. I'm pretty sure you didn't commit the murder."

"Yeah, thanks," Eli said.

They descended in the cherry picker together—Eli let Chloë handle the controls while DuPey stood tight-lipped and white-knuckled—and when they got to the ground, he started asking his questions. By the time they got to Eli's truck, they'd covered why they'd come and how they'd discovered the body.

Eli helped Chloë into the truck, then turned to DuPey. "You were acting funny in there. Has someone used that still recently?"

"Not recently. But I expected to see a little more corrosion in there." DuPey shrugged. "I'd have a lab check the still and date the last time it processed liquor, but it's such an old crime scene that I can't justify the expense."

"So I can have it removed?" Eli dug into his cooler and handed Chloë a cold water; then, while they were damp, he wiped his hands again.

DuPey took a bottle as well, drained it, and handed it back. "Yep. Mason'll take the body to the morgue and do his thing, but if it's Massimo, as we all suspect, there'll be no way to know. According to the stories, he had no family and no children, so no DNA."

"Poor guy. No family to mourn when he disappeared. No gravestone with his name." Chloë's heart ached.

Eli glanced up at her. "If what Nonna says is true, he chose his life and by all rights had no reason to expect anything else." He headed around the truck and got in.

"He doesn't care now," DuPey said.

"No, I suppose not," she said, more to herself than to them. "But I bet in those last moments of his life, he wanted vengeance."

Eli started the truck.

DuPey waved them off.

As soon as Eli put the F-250 in gear, executed a three-point turn, and started up the bumpy gravel road toward Bella Terra, Chloë twisted to face him. "So tell me, Eli—what did you pick up off the floor of the water tower?"

Chapter 15

Eli made her wait until they reached the cottage to answer her question, and by the time they got there, she was hopping up and down with frustration. Because he hadn't fallen down by accident, any more than he had believed she was overcome with horror at the scene in the water tower. He had discovered something, something related to Massimo and the crime, and she wanted to know *what*.

He showed her his hands. The filth of that floor hung in the creases and under his fingernails, and he used that as an excuse to make her punch in the security code.

All the while he was grinning. Teasing her, as if he were almost human.

As soon as they were inside, she kicked the door shut, grabbed his shirt, and in the low, guttural, threatening voice of a demon, said, "Tell me all."

He set her aside as if she were a *girl*. "Do you have a mesh strainer?"

"A mesh strainer. You want a mesh strainer?" Her voice rose.

He tapped her nose—he had her total attention and he was playing it for all he was worth.

"You are really frustrating." She rubbed her nose, knowing he had smeared soot on it, and tagged along as he went into the kitchen.

He found the strainer, put it in the sink. Reaching into his pocket, he brought out his now-grimy handkerchief, laid it in the strainer, and carefully spread it across the mesh.

Gobs of sticky soot and filthy wood splinters filled the handkerchief. He turned on the sprayer. "It's going to take a minute to wash the dirt away. In the meantime, look at this." Reaching into his other pocket, he pulled out the cigarette butt he'd removed and handed it to her.

It was grimy, too, old and disgusting, and she stared at it, trying to figure out why he would pick up and keep a cigarette used to burn Massimo. That was macabre. Unless . . . "This thing has a filter on it," she said.

"No cigarette without one could survive up there so long."

"When did they start making filtered cigarettes?"

"I don't know, but I doubt it was during the Depression."

She pulled out her computer, put it on the counter and opened it, and searched for the answer. "Filters on cigarettes were specialty items until the 1950s, because there weren't a lot of machines that could make them." She picked up the butt and examined it again. "Brand is . . . Kent? Looks like. Kent started using a filter in 1952. So someone was up in that place in the fifties or later? With Massimo's dead body? Doing what?"

"Might have been using the still. DuPey seemed uneasy about that."

"With a dead body watching? That's cold."

"So was the torture." He turned off the water. "Where's your flashlight?"

She pulled it out of the case and handed it to him.

He flicked it on and pointed into the strainer in the sink. "There. Look."

Something glinted. Sparkled. A small cut stone. She bent toward the sink. She took a long breath, trying to quiet the sudden thunder of her heart.

Handing her the flashlight, he picked up the stone and placed it in his still-grimy palm.

It sparkled like a diamond against a black velvet setting.

"No . . ." she whispered. "It can't be."

"It's a gem. Maybe a diamond?"

"Yes. Maybe a diamond." She shone the flashlight, and the stone gathered the light, blazed with sparks of blue and red and . . . "About a half carat. It looks pink. A pink diamond?"

"Let's find out. Let's use it to cut some glass." He turned toward the window.

"Not the window! Let me get my travel mirror." She hurried into the bathroom and returned with the round, cheap mirror she kept in her makeup case. Putting it on the counter, she gestured to him to proceed.

She watched, breathless, as Eli used the edge to cut through the glass.

"I don't suppose that's a conclusive test, is it?" Her voice quavered with excitement.

"I don't suppose. But if this *is* a diamond"—he placed the gem in his palm again—"it would explain what the torturers were looking for. Why someone in the fifties took a chance and returned to the scene of the crime."

"Yes . . ." She couldn't take her eyes off the stone. "But you picked it up off the floor. Was it unseen on the floor for eighty years?" Without drawing a breath, she answered her own question. "Yes, of course. If it had been seen, it wouldn't have been there. How did it go unnoticed, especially if someone was up there?"

"I didn't see it right away. Neither did you."

She nodded in agreement.

"At one point, when the tower was full of water, the wood was probably damp and soft." Eli rolled the stone around with his thumb. "We know a thick layer of soot and dirt covered everything. This was buried, and its sharp edges kept taking it deeper."

"Right. It wasn't until you knocked out the wall and let the light in that we even had a chance to spot the, er . . ." She found herself unable to say the word. Knowing what it was, knowing it was in her cottage, made her nervous, as if villains lurked outside waiting to torture her as they had tortured Massimo.

"Our biggest stroke of luck was the coroner. Mason wears running shoes, and when he stepped on the stone, it clung to the tread and came up in a clod of dirt. The clod dropped and I saw the diamond flash." Eli seemed unworried, more interested in the mystery than in any danger.

"So the diamond gave us the clue we needed. I told you Massimo wanted revenge!"

Eli looked at her as if she were nuts.

The man had no imagination. "Okay, maybe it was pure chance. But the other is a better story!"

"You're the writer." It did not sound like a compliment. "Anyway, I pretended to trip, picked up the stone before someone else saw it, and figured we'd better get out of there."

"I knew you were faking."

"I hope the others aren't as suspicious as you." He put the diamond onto a plate, set it aside, and used the dish soap to really scrub his hands. "Especially not DuPey. I've known him since high school."

She dismissed that with an airy wave of the hand. "He thinks you're an upstanding citizen. He as good as said so."

"Yeah. I've got him fooled." Eli sounded amused.

"So Massimo disappeared in 1930?" Chloë took her computer to her desk, typed in "pink diamond," "robbery," and "1930." This search took a little longer, and required some digging on her part, but finally she said, "I had to have Google translate this old news story from Dutch, so it's a little sketchy, but I think this is it." She read, "'Amsterdam, December twenty-sixth, 1929. On Christmas Day, a Vermeer titled *View of the Harbor* was stolen from the Rijksmuseum by a talented team of burglars. The carefully planned robbery bears the hallmark of other thefts in Italy and France. Vermeer, noted for his work with light, was one of the finest painters of the Dutch Golden Age.'"

"What has that got to do with our diamond?" Eli used paper towels to dry his hands.

Chloë held up one finger. "'Amsterdam, December twenty-seventh, 1929. A cache of prized pink diamonds vanished from a shipment on its way to be set in platinum for the Duchess of Wheatley. The diamonds range in size from a half carat to the proposed diamond centerpiece, a six-point-eight-carat pink diamond, the Beating Heart, with an inclusion that, when viewed through a jeweler's loupe, looks like a red heart that appears to pulse."

"My God. Massimo had *guts*." Eli's tone was reverent.

"I assume he stole the painting on commission for an art collector, then used the police's distraction with the theft to take the diamonds undetected."

"It's possible he had done it before."

"But this time someone caught on."

"Probably the guys he stole the diamonds from."

"Security had to be hands-on and pretty harsh in those days." Eli leaned over the counter toward her. "Did anyone ever find the pink diamonds?"

She shook her head. "I don't think so. I'll do more searching, but so far I've turned up nothing. So where did Massimo hide them?"

Eli stood frowning at the crumpled paper towel he held, and something about his silence got her attention.

"Eli? Do *you* know where he hid the diamonds?" she asked.

"What?" He looked up. "No. I . . . No. But I think it's time you met my grandmother."

"You think she'll have information we can use?" Chloë asked eagerly.

"Nonna read your book and she's been nagging to meet you. But I've taken enough of your time today." He tossed the paper towel, picked up the diamond, carried it to the desk, and stuck it in the skull in the gap between the two front teeth. "There. It should be safe there. After all, no one knows we have it. Now, get some work done." He walked to the door. "I'll pick you up for lunch tomorrow."

Chapter 16

Eli came home early to take Chloë to lunch. Stupid thing to do; a guy never showed up early for a date. But he'd been up at dawn to go over the schedule with Royson and he'd seen her light burning. He'd almost dropped by then to see if everything was all right.

He was sure it was. She'd set the security system yesterday when he left. But the idea that some guy with designs on her father's money would take her from him made him antsy. She was lucky she hadn't been abducted before.

He was lucky she hadn't been abducted before.

Not that he had the guts to hold himself up as a worthy suitor; calling it a marriage of convenience was like calling a Massimo a gem redistributor. Eli knew himself to be an opportunist, plain and simple.

But at least he was sensible. He could make her happy.

For all his self-lecture, he found himself standing on her porch an hour early. He knocked on her door.

It gave beneath his knuckles.

It was open.

No!

He thrust the door open. The place looked better than the day before; she'd picked up. But no one was here.

His kernel of worry blossomed.

He checked the bathroom, the deck. Her computer was open on the desk; it was still warm.

She hadn't been gone long. Had someone taken her? Or had she gone off on her own?

Walking out on the front porch, he looked around. Saw her footprints on the grass leading out toward the vineyards and followed them.

And there she was, on the grass between the tall rows of vines, flat on her back, with her arms and legs outstretched and her eyes staring skyward. "Chloë!" he shouted, and took two sprinting steps toward her.

She rolled onto her side and looked at him. In a normal voice, she said, "What?"

He stopped. Felt foolish. Snapped, "What are you doing?"

"I'm listening." She rolled onto her back and flung her arms out.

"To what?"

"To the vines talking to one another."

Had she fallen and hit her head?

Had someone *hit* her on the head?

He took another few steps toward her.

She was dressed in navy gym shorts, a loose button-down white shirt tied at the waist, and battered running shoes. She glistened with a light sweat. She looked comfortable. Boneless. Complacent.

"Are you all right?" he asked.

"I'm fine."

He waited for more, but she stared up at the sky as if enthralled.

He glanced up.

Some blue. Some clouds. The usual.

"Do you want to go inside now and, um, get ready?"

She dug her phone out of her pocket and looked at the time. "No. But if you're going to stand there and interrupt me . . . go away. Either that or lie down here and be quiet."

He looked down the rows. Nothing but tall vines rich with leaves, grass on the ground, a glimpse of the valley. He looked up the row. Her cottage stood there, and behind it, the lawn stretched up to the wide expanse of his house. Everything seemed very normal except . . . for no reason he could see, Chloë was stretched out flat on the ground.

He should turn back, go to the house, call Nonna and cancel lunch, and return to work and leave Chloë to her silliness.

But he was supposed to be courting her. So maybe some silliness was in order. And besides . . . besides, something about the way she listened stirred a memory buried in the depths of childhood, of a time when he sat among the vines without fear, secure in the fact that he would be safe . . . in this place.

Feeling odd and awkward, he walked over and sat down beside her.

Without looking at him, she made room.

He leaned back, arms at his sides, legs straight.

He looked at her, waiting for something, but she didn't speak. Didn't seem to pay any attention to him. Just gazed at the sky . . .

It was so quiet here. Quiet except for the rattle of leaves as the breeze brushed them.

She was right: It did sound like the vines were talking in some foreign tongue that he could almost understand. He wanted to tell Chloë she was right . . . but it really was so quiet.

The California sun had heated the ground all morning, and, crushed beneath his body, the grass gave up its summer scent, fresh and green. The blades tickled his bare neck and the palms of his hands, and beneath them, he felt the earth breathe. . . . Well, that was silly enough right there, and he almost got up and went back to the house.

For God's sake, he was a grown man. What if Royson came along and saw him? What would Eli say? *I was listening to the earth breathe?*

Not that he cared what Royson thought, but he hated when people had any reason to gossip about him. His mother's family had trained him—it was always better to remain in the background, quiet and unnoticed. Then he had a better chance of getting away. . . .

He stiffened.

God, what a revelation. He thought he'd put his mother's family far behind, and yet they still influenced him so much.

Eli looked at Chloë again.

Her eyes were half-closed. She appeared to be dozing . . . or listening with all her might.

The tops of the leaves were over his head and hedged the sky with parallel lines of deep green. The wispy clouds slid in fluid stripes across the pale blue, mixing and re-forming like dancers in some modern ballet. And all the while, the grape leaves on the trellis shimmered on the periphery of his vision; the earth rotated beneath him and wheeled through the universe, chasing its date with destiny. . . .

He couldn't remember the last time he'd felt like this.

He couldn't remember the last time he'd lain beside a woman, content to be shoulder to shoulder without planning his next move: seduction, sex, then up and on to something else: work, family, TV, anything in his life that was not her, whoever she was.

Here, now, with Chloë, he just . . . was. At peace.

And he didn't even like her.

Actually, no, that was wrong. It wasn't that he didn't like her. It was that he didn't like being forced to marry her.

It would be better if he didn't rush into a marriage

of heat and passion. Even the warmth of the sun wasn't enough to melt the frozen center at the pit of his belly when he remembered his mother and the anguish and jealousy that poisoned her life. And his.

He'd established to his satisfaction that Chloë was not in any way like his mother. Except for those few moments when he'd seen her give in to despair over her book, she seemed remarkably cheerful and stable—at least for a writer. And she brought every advantage with her. Eli guessed his father-in-law was going to be a pain in the ass, but once the dowry was paid and the winery out of debt, Eli would put Conte in his place.

Altogether she was a good choice as a wife. She had a career, so she wouldn't unduly interfere in Eli's life. She was pretty enough to stir his libido. In fact, now, from the depths of his relaxation, he recalled a dream he'd had last night . . . of Chloë beneath him while he—

He sensed movement beside him.

His eyes sprang open.

When had they closed?

Chloë was leaning on her elbow, studying his face. When he looked at her, startled and tense, she smiled. "I've never seen you relaxed before. You're very handsome when you're not frowning."

Frowning? He had frowned at her?

Of course he had. "Spring and summer are our busy times in the vineyard," he said stiffly.

"I've noticed. I've seen you leave in the morning and come home late at night. You're busy all the time."

"Aren't you supposed to be? Busy writing?"

"There's more to writing than typing. You took me to the water tower. Now the shape of my plot is changing. I came out here to walk. And think."

"Did you settle the problem?"

"I think so." She smiled again. "Maybe. Probably."

Had he thought she was pretty *enough*? Right now, looking down at him, a half smile on her lips, she was more than pretty. She was beautiful: pale skin with red freckles sprinkled across her upturned nose, eyes the color of amber, college-girl blond hair that looked like an angel's halo around her head, and those two strands of hell's fiery red at her temple.

She was heaven and hell, guilt and temptation.

Her legs were long, bare. The camp shirt wasn't buttoned very far; he could see the beginning of the pale swell of her breasts.

Leaning her head close to his face, she breathed in as if testing his scent.

And when she did, he breathed her in. Like a glass of fine wine, she had scents he could identify: orange blossoms, cinnamon, a hint of vanilla. But beneath those surface aromas another scent note tantalized him. . . . It was Chloë, and her own female fragrance twined around his senses, enticing him, branding him with yearning.

Slowly, she leaned closer and layered her lips to his.

Damn it. He should be making the first move. He should be in charge.

But the sun shone and the clouds billowed, and Chloë was kissing him. He liked the way she kissed, not passionately, not aggressively, a slow exploration with lips soft, yet closed.

It was nice.

It was not enough.

He opened his mouth under hers, tasted her . . . and she sprang back as if he'd used a cattle prod.

Their eyes met; he'd kissed a lot of women, all of them willing.

He'd never viewed consternation before . . . but he did now.

She rolled away.

He caught her and rolled her back.

Now she was flat on her back and he was leaning over her, holding her lightly, his hand on her waist.

Eyes wide, cheeks pink, she looked as if she wanted to take flight.

"It was just a kiss." He kept his voice low and slow. "Wasn't it?"

"Just a kiss." Clearly he made her nervous. She was talking too fast. "But, um, you know, it's time to get ready to go to your grandmother's."

As she spoke, he watched her lips. Pouty, full, with a natural pink tint. A long throat that begged to be caressed. And from this angle, he could see more of her left breast . . . she hadn't known he would join her. She hadn't left off the bra or unbuttoned the shirt for his benefit.

He returned his gaze to hers.

How lucky that he had arrived so early to check on her. "I am ready," he said.

Her eyes dilated. In alarm? Or passion? "I'm . . . not."

"Getting ready won't take long. You'll see." Placing just his fingertips on her breastbone, he slid and touched, little by little pushing the shirt aside.

Her heartbeat increased; he felt it under his hand. Goose bumps rose on her skin.

She licked her lips. "I don't think you ought to . . ."

He cupped her breast, small and tender.

Her voice caught in her throat.

He ran his thumb around the nipple. It sprang up like a new bud; so she was tentative, not afraid.

"Eli, we don't have this kind of relationship." But she put her hand on his shoulder . . . and she whispered his name.

"We do now." Leaning over, he kissed her the way she deserved to be kissed, putting his interest, his passion, his pleasure into her mouth.

She was still wary.

But he breathed with her, allowed her to taste him, taught her what it was to kiss a man who worshiped a woman's body. He fed her back all her wonder in the day, offered his very real gratitude for showing him what pleasure there was in a moment of peace stretched out in the grass in the sun.

It wasn't enough. Of course not. Not for him.

He wanted, really wanted, to run his palm up her thigh, glide his fingers under the loose hem of her shorts, touch her, caress her, find out whether she was wet and make her wetter.

That was too fast, too soon.

He prided himself on his control, on his slow seductions.

And she was going to be his wife. No need to rush things.

But he *wanted*.

And as the kiss became more than just an appetizer before the feast . . . he could sense she wanted, too. The taste of her fascination changed, became blind desire. She opened her mouth and let him feast. Her arms slid around his shoulders. She lifted her body to his.

He kissed her now with the steady, driving rhythm of intercourse, using his tongue to demonstrate his need.

He dropped his knee between her legs—it wasn't as good as the touch of his hand; at least, not for him— but when he pressed his thigh against her, her eyes sprang open. She gasped and shuddered, on the edge of orgasm.

Then color swept her face.

Too fast. Too soon.

If she tumbled over the edge, if she came here, now, in the sunshine, embraced by a man she barely knew merely because he kissed well, she would be mortified, and everything he'd gained with her would be swept away.

Worse, if he didn't stop, if she came, he would humiliate himself in a way he hadn't since his first date.

Where was his discipline?

He dragged himself back, allowed her room to

move, forced himself away from the worst of the temptation.

"Gotta go shower. Get dressed. Put on makeup." Her voice started low, got stronger.

"I know." He did know.

He hated to let this moment go.

But he must. For her sake.

For his own, too.

He was not like his mother.

He didn't let passion rule him.

He would never allow emotion to ruin his life.

So he smiled at Chloë as if his balls weren't aching. With leisurely care, he removed his hand from her breast. He buttoned two of the buttons on her shirt—cover that temptation!—and gave her a warm, close-mouthed kiss. "You go on. I'll call Nonna and tell her we're going to be late." He pulled his phone out of his pocket and, as if he were totally relaxed, he asked, "Can you be ready in a half hour?"

Chapter 17

The road to Eli grandmother's house wound through the vineyards, past wineries, past orchards that cast hypnotic dappled shadows on the pavement, rising and falling . . . and rising.

A beautiful drive.

Chloë should be enjoying this break from work.

But in all her life, she had never before been nervous about meeting a man's family. She didn't really have reason to be nervous now.

But somehow those kisses in the vineyard had changed everything.

Not that she hadn't been kissed before. She had. And by some pretty good kissers. If she'd been asked before, she would have said she liked to kiss.

Eli was in a whole different class. He didn't seem to understand that kisses were supposed to be pleasant interludes: not serious, not mind-altering, not an experience to make the earth shake and the heavens tremble.

How had he done that? How had he brought her to the verge of orgasm with . . . kissing? He knew it, too. When she remembered the way he'd looked at her, all dark, smoldering sensuality, as if he were ready to jump her right there in the vineyard . . . well. She was so embarrassed she could die.

Which meant she should not be sitting in his truck, hands folded in her lap, both sandaled feet firmly on the floor mat, one foot crushing a paper cup, while she gazed out the front window and tried to think of something to break the silence. Something that did not include, *Take me back; I don't want to meet your grandmother; it feels like a commitment and it shouldn't.*

Eli apparently felt no such compunction to speak; he drove in silence and with the same negligent efficiency he had used yesterday.

How could today feel so different?

The smoldering sensuality had disappeared . . . well, except she didn't trust that. Yesterday she hadn't realized he smoldered at all. Now she suspected him of constantly smoldering and concealing it so well she never even smelled the telltale smoke.

He was like Clark Kent, looking exactly like Superman, yet no one suspected what powers he concealed. . . .

"Not too much farther," he said, and glanced at her. "I like the dress. You surprised me."

She smoothed the skirt of her brightly flowered sarong dress. "Why?"

"You don't seem to be the type to wear a dress."

"What type do I seem to be?" she asked frostily.

His mouth quirked. "Unpredictable—"

You're a fine one to talk.

"—so I suppose I should have expected the dress."

"I'm going to meet your *grandmother*. I can't wear a grass-stained shirt!"

"Nonna wouldn't care."

She narrowed her eyes at him. "I was taught to have respect for my elders."

"When you talk, I don't usually feel the Southern influence or hear a Texas accent. But I heard it that time." He smiled.

He was smiling more often, as if he were becoming more human . . . as if their intimacy had softened him.

Not intimacy. Just a kiss or two, and his touch on her breast . . . *Don't think of that.* "So tell me about your grandmother."

"She's smart, she's funny, she's a great cook, and she raised me." Brief. To the point. Not exactly friendly.

"Sounds like a nice lady." Actually, Chloë now knew a lot about his grandmother and a lot about him. Last night she had surrendered to curiosity and looked him up online.

She'd discovered plenty about Di Luca Wines. Their Web site was beautifully designed, a charming stroll through the vineyard, winery, and tasting room, and the family bio had shown a photo of the three Di Luca brothers with their movie-star-gorgeous father and their graciously smiling grandmother. Everything about the Web site invited the viewer to wander through Bella Valley and taste the wines—everything until she reached Eli's bio.

That was dry as dust, a mere recitation of the schools he had attended, the awards he had won, his dedication to making great wines. His photo was worse; he looked like a romance hero facing a firing squad, his back against the wall: handsome yet resistant to publicity.

Then she'd found the other stuff, the nasty stuff, about his beauty-queen mother stabbing his movie-star father and going to jail. Those headlines were thirty years old, but big and easy to find. It hadn't been so easy to figure out what happened to Eli afterward, but she'd finally decided he lived with his grandfather and grandmother until his mother got out of prison, and then went to live with her.

But he didn't give his mom any credit for raising him, which brought Chloë back to that sense that everything about him shouted, *Private!* and *Dark secrets!*

So what was she doing talking to him, listening to him, kissing him? She didn't need those kinds of complications in her life. She had a book to write.

"Your light was on early this morning," he said.

"I worked late, fell asleep, and woke early with more stuff in my brain."

They turned off the main road and onto a long, paved drive lined with gracious, wide-branched oak trees and dark green rhododendrons.

"So the writing is going well?" he asked.

"Seeing the water tower yesterday, and the still, and the body, wrenched my mind out of the rut it was in and sent it careening in a new direction. I worked out my plot, got stuck again, went for a walk, and figured out the whole thing." *I got kissed in the vineyard.* "The field trip yesterday was exactly what I needed. Thank you." Good. Smooth finish.

"Talking to Nonna will give you more grist for the mill. She's a natural storyteller, she never forgets anything, and she loves to share the history of Bella Valley."

An old-fashioned white farmhouse with a tall porch and Craftsman-style detailing came into view, then disappeared behind the bend, then was back again. It wasn't huge, nothing like Eli's behemoth house on his very own hill, but it exuded comfort, a home that had absorbed the dust of a hundred and twenty years, seen storms and droughts, and had settled in to become an extension of the land.

Eli parked the giant truck in the wide turnaround off to the side.

"What a great house." Rather than wait for him to come and help her, Chloë opened the door and slid down and out onto the ground.

As an evasive maneuver, it sucked, because as she mounted the stairs, he was there with his hand under her arm. "This is the Di Luca family home," he said. "We leave, but this place calls us back."

She turned and looked. At the flower beds that were planted with brilliant reds and yellows and cool whites. At the dark-leaved trees hanging heavy with oranges. And beyond, at the long, sweet sweep of the valley, where, in the afternoon sun, the colors faded from sharp green to a misty blue. "I can see why. This valley is beautiful, warm, welcoming, a community. Yet there's room to stretch and grow."

He looked at her sharply. "Yes. That's it. Exactly." Capturing her chin, he lifted her face to his and examined it, murmuring, "How is it possible that you understand so well?"

Flustered, she backed away. "It's obvious that . . ."

He followed, put his arm around her waist.

"I mean, every person who comes here must feel the magic of the place. . . ."

He leaned close. His gaze captured her, commanded her, examined her, learned her . . . and at the same time, she felt the distance between them.

He wanted to kiss her.

He wanted to hold her at bay.

He was too private. He was too deep. She'd been in his company less than eight full hours, but beneath the face he presented to the world she sensed a soul that was bleak and pain-swept.

Retreat! But fascination held her in place.

She felt his breath on her lips. Her eyes fluttered closed.

And the front door flew open and an elderly woman called, "Come in, children!"

Chloë stumbled backward, face flaming.

Calmly Eli turned to face his grandmother. "Nonna. You got your cast off!"

"This morning." Stepping out onto the porch, she flexed her elbow. "Good as new."

She was like a small bird, thin and lively. Her big brown eyes observed and approved. She darted forward to kiss Eli and accept his hug, then held out her hands to Chloë. "Welcome, dear girl! I'm Sarah Di Luca, Eli's grandmother."

"How do you do?" Chloë could barely slip the words in.

"I've been nagging Eli to bring you over. I hope you don't mind, but you are my newest favorite author, and I'm so excited to have you in my home." Sarah smiled, open and kind, gracious and warm, everything that her grandson was not. Taking Chloë's arm, she led her into the house. "I have a delicious lunch prepared, but I warn you, you'll have to sing for your supper. I want to know everything about how you plot your marvelous books!"

Chapter 18

"My mother hated Massimo." Sarah led the way through the afternoon warmth toward the arbor on the side lawn. "She said he was a gangster. But he was famous around Bella Valley. I heard he was not handsome, but it was the Depression—tough times—and he had money and spent it lavishly. He made wine, good wine. He gave gifts."

Chloë walked with Sarah's hand on her arm.

Eli paced behind them.

Lunch had been, as promised, delicious, eaten at the kitchen table with two of Sarah's employees, Olivia and Bao. All three were fans of Chloë's book, and they peppered her with questions and made her feel proud that her writing had connected so well with her readers.

Eli had eaten, but said little. Chloë thought he was not antisocial.

Probably he was sitting there smoldering with sexuality. You'd think it would give him indigestion.

When they were finished eating, Eli had suggested that he and Chloë take Sarah for a walk. They left Bao and Olivia cleaning the kitchen and, with Eli carrying a small basket, they headed out across the yard.

As they walked, Sarah told Massimo's story.

"Massimo had no family," Sarah said, "not in the Old Country, not here. He used to disappear for months at a time. He'd slip out of town, then quietly return. I remember my father saying Massimo had the luck of the devil. Then my mother would say it was because he had made a deal with the devil, and everyone knows the devil is not to be trusted." Sarah turned to Chloë and said apologetically, "Massimo had disappeared by the time I was born, so for me this is all simply memories of conversations."

They reached the arbor, white painted and covered with twisting and graceful wisteria vines. There Sarah and Chloë took seats on the Adirondack chairs overlooking the garden. Eli placed the basket on the table between them. He pulled out a small bottle of his own Miele cabernet port and opened it, then poured it into three tiny crystal wineglasses. He put a plate of chocolate-chip cookies between them, then watched with a faint smile as Chloë helped herself to one and took a bite.

"Oh, my God. These are the best chocolate-chip

cookies I've ever had." She took another bite. "Oh, my God."

"It gets better," Sarah said. "Try it with the port."

Chloë glanced at them; they were scrutinizing her as if the anticipation of her pleasure heightened their own.

Chloë took a sip of the port, and another bite of cookie.

She closed her eyes as the flavors sang in her mouth, the blend of dense, dark chocolate, black walnuts, and rich dough paired with a port so potent that she tasted a concentration of berry preserves, orange, and spices.

In a whisper, Sarah said, "She savors her food and wine like an Italian."

"I know." Eli sounded as if he were smoldering again.

But when Chloë's eyes sprang open, he picked up his glass and wandered away toward an artfully placed Greek marble column. He looked tough and capable in his jeans—they fit his legs and rear as if they'd been tailored for him—and his black T-shirt.

"Eli is a very handsome young man," Sarah said.

Sure she'd been caught staring, Chloë glanced at Sarah in embarrassment.

But Sarah was watching him fondly, as if her observation had been nothing more than any proud grandmother would make. And maybe it was.

But somehow, Chloë didn't think so.

Sarah was smart, and she'd seen that almost-kiss on the porch.

Sarah patted Chloë's hand to get her attention. "But

I was telling you about Massimo. Even my mother admitted his wine tasted like the promise of heaven."

Chloë listened, enthralled, as Sarah's voice rose and fell with the tenor of her tale, and Chloë's fingers itched to take notes, to transcribe this tale into a story to be read and shared.

"When he gave the gift of a bottle," Sarah said, "it was treasured, brought out for only the most important of occasions, shared with only the best of friends. He would make one barrel to be given to the sons of the valley on the day of their births, to be opened on their twenty-first birthdays."

"Not the daughters?" Chloë nibbled on another cookie.

Sarah laughed. "There was nothing politically correct about the times, and certainly nothing politically correct about Massimo."

"It would be too much to expect." Chloë took another sip of port.

"I suppose you could say Massimo received justice. In 1930, his luck ran out. The revenuers finally caught up with him. They smashed his wine barrels with their axes. They should have put him in jail, but, because it was Massimo, they weren't able to prove the wine was his. However, after they left, he managed to salvage enough wine for one bottle. One bottle only of Massimo's last barrel." For the first time, Sarah seemed to lose her pleasure in telling the tale. The sparkle in her eyes faded; her voice lost its lilt. "That bottle started the trouble, the trouble that has never gone away."

Chloë leaned forward. "What trouble?"

"On the day my husband, Anthony Di Luca, was born, another son was born across the valley. Massimo rightly gave the bottle to Anthony, saying that because he was born first, he deserved the bottle. To the infant Joseph Bianchin, he gave a silver rattle. Massimo disappeared not long after. But in the Old Country and in this country, the Bianchins were always proud, arrogant bullies. They said that because Massimo liked them best, *they* should have the bottle."

Chloë remembered the body in the water tower, and put the cookie down. "Is it possible the Bianchins killed Massimo?" She thought Eli was too far away to hear the question, but he turned as if listening to his grandmother's answer.

"I never heard a hint of the possibility. The Bianchins, especially Joseph, are capable of murder, but they were always cowards, fighting only if the odds were overwhelmingly in their favor, or hiring thugs to remove those who displeased them." Sarah's lip curled in scorn. "Massimo was tough and smart . . . and dangerous. They didn't complain in front of him, much less dare to raise a hand against him."

Eli nodded as if in agreement, then leaned against one of the pillars and observed them from beneath heavy-lidded eyes.

"Anthony and I married on his twenty-first birthday, and, of course, that was Joseph's birthday, too." Sarah's smile trembled, and faded. "The Bianchins crashed our reception with guns and knives and destroyed everything."

"Oh, no," Chloë breathed, and covered her mouth in horror.

"They tried to kill Anthony," Sarah said.

Chloë's horror grew.

"But Massimo's bottle was still safely hidden, so in that they failed." Sarah lifted her chin in defiance.

"How horrible for you! What an awful end to your wedding day!" *How could anybody be cruel to this sweet woman?*

"It was a long time ago." But all too clearly, Sarah remembered—and she loathed. "Anthony survived, but he took his revenge every chance he got, by bringing out the bottle and showing it off to family and friends, knowing that across the valley Joseph was angry. I finally told him we had to drink it, to put the matter to rest, but he wouldn't, and after his death, when I went looking for it . . . it was gone."

"Gone where?" Chloë looked between Sarah and Eli.

"Gone," Sarah repeated. "Those last few years, Anthony suffered from dementia. He hid the bottle; I don't know where."

Eli strolled forward. "But Nonno was a winemaker, too. The bottle needed to be stored in the dark in a cool place. No matter how bad his mind got, he would never have forgotten that."

Sarah agreed.

"I'm almost afraid to ask—what's it worth?" Chloë tensed in anticipation.

"A bottle of so old and exalted a vintage, and with this history behind it, is worth tens of thousands," Eli said.

"Of dollars?" At once Chloë felt stupid. "Of course, dollars, but . . . tens of thousands of dollars for one bottle of wine? Who pays that much for an old bottle of wine?"

"In 1916, bottles of champagne from the Heidsieck vineyard in Champagne were shipped to the Russian Imperial family. The ship foundered off the coast of Finland and was lost until 1997 when divers discovered the wreck and over two hundred intact bottles of the champagne. They are now being sold to guests at the Ritz-Carlton hotel in Moscow for"—Eli paused dramatically—"two hundred and seventy-five thousand dollars."

Chloë clutched her heart.

"It's the incredible history and the age of the wine that accounts for the price," he reminded her.

Chloë had to protest. She had to. "I've had five-dollar bottles of wine that I thought were a waste of money."

Sarah started chuckling.

Eli tried to subdue a smile. "Some say that when it comes to wine, collectors have more money than sense. Of course, as a maker of fine wines, I would never say that."

Still incredulous, Chloë said, "I get spending huge

sums for a cool piece of art or a vintage dress or something, but once you open a bottle of wine that's so expensive—"

"The value is then nothing," Eli said.

"And after so long, isn't there a chance that the wine is bad?" Chloë asked.

"More than a chance," he agreed. "It almost certainly is vinegar or worse. But occasionally one of Massimo's wines still tasted like the promise of heaven."

Chloë tried to imagine it. Not that she hadn't enjoyed expensive wines—today at lunch, for example—but when she was buying, she preferred to keep the tab under ten dollars. Five was better.

That, she supposed, was still her college-girl mentality. "Is this bottle that Massimo gave to Anthony on the date of his birth . . . is it the last remaining bottle left on earth that was made by Massimo?"

"Not at all," Eli said. "One of his bottles will pop up now and then at auction."

"And be purchased for tens of thousands of dollars?" Chloë thought she sounded obsessed by the amount . . . but really. For a probably bad bottle of wine? What fool had that kind of money to waste?

A sliver of suspicion sliced into her mind. "Someone always buys them?"

"Yes. Someone always buys them. Most of his wines go for a good amount, but like gems"—he looked meaningfully into Chloë's eyes—"the history of a bottle adds value. In this case, where the story concerns a legendary winemaker who disappeared, a brutal rivalry between two families, and the attempted murder of my grandfather . . . the bottle is steeped in history and violence, making it all the more attractive for the potential buyer."

Right then, Chloë almost announced her suspicion of where the diamonds were hidden.

But Eli shook his head slowly. . . .

So he had had the same idea yesterday, when he suggested this field trip. That was Eli: intelligent and smoldering. What a great combination.

"Do you know, Sarah, was there a lot of crime at the time of Massimo's death?" Chloë asked. "You know . . . home invasions? Robberies? Anything like that?"

Sarah looked at Chloë as if she'd lost her mind. "I never heard about it if there was. Why, dear?"

"I think she's comparing those times to now, when we have Joseph Bianchin, who's still willing to do whatever it takes to get his undeserving mitts on the bottle." Picking up his grandmother's hand, Eli bowed his head as if paying homage.

Sarah put her hand on his head. "Eli, dear, I'm fine."

He lifted his head, and Chloë caught a glimpse of his expression: love, fear, anguish.

Something had happened to Sarah, and even the hint made Chloë sick with the echo of Eli's fear . . . and made her wonder once more at the depths he hid so well.

Sarah leaned back in her chair. "Why did Chloë need to hear this story?"

"Because we found Massimo's body yesterday," Eli told her.

"Massimo? Is dead?" Sarah touched her fingers to her temple. "Of course he's dead, but . . . are you sure the body you found is his?"

"As sure as we can be," he said. "Whatever he was doing caught up with him—he was tortured before he was killed."

"Tortured? No one would have tortured him about the wine!" Sarah frowned fiercely. "Half the time the revenuers were corrupt, but I never heard of them killing anyone."

Chloë started to speak.

Eli shook his head at her.

"So my mother was right." Sarah's eyes filled with tears. "Massimo should never have made a deal with the devil. The devil is not to be trusted."

Chapter 19

Eli looked helplessly at Chloë. He seemed bewildered by his grandmother's reaction.

"Why are you grief-stricken, Sarah?" Chloë gently asked. "If you never met Massimo, why do you care?"

Eli moved back to give Sarah space to speak.

"I was born into the Depression, and I vividly remember those years—the poverty, the struggle to survive, how everything was gray and hopeless. My father told stories, and in those stories, Massimo sounded like Robin Hood, disappearing to rob from the rich and bring back to us, the poor. Massimo made good wines when it was illegal. He was hope, and when he disappeared and I asked my father where he had gone, my father said he had taken his fortune and retired to the Old Country. There, in my mind, he was eternally alive." Sarah brushed a tear off her wrinkled cheek. "Now you say he was cruelly murdered. For me, it's the death of a legend."

The breeze whispered through the wisteria leaves and made the vine's purple blossoms twist and dance, and the first fading petals whirled in circles as they slowly descended to earth.

Sad and thoughtful, Sarah watched them. "But I'm a foolish old woman to mourn for a man who died before I was born."

"Not so foolish. Someone should mourn for that man. Why not you? And me?" Chloë shared a smile with Sarah, all the more painful for its poignancy.

"Thank you, dear. You're very sweet." Sarah stood. "Shall we go in?"

Chloë rose and began to collect the glasses and cookies and return them to the basket.

Sarah started toward the house.

Eli gave Chloë a meaningful glance and a push.

Chloë hurried after Sarah, took her arm, and walked with her.

Eli followed. Although he made no sound, Chloë knew he was close behind, watching them, listening to every word . . . and hanging back from his beloved grandmother's wrenching emotion.

Not that most guys liked tears. Chloë knew they didn't. But he was so openly affectionate to his grandmother, and so visibly afraid of her tears. It was as if he thought they were catching, and yet . . . she couldn't imagine him ever crying.

Of course, two days ago she couldn't imagine him ever smiling. But on rare occasions he did, and that made those occasions worth celebrating.

"Have you figured out why Massimo was tortured?" Sarah asked.

Chloë waited for Eli to answer, and when he didn't, she said, "Not yet."

"Or who did it?" Sarah pressed Chloë's hand.

"I wish we knew." That was completely honest, anyway.

"I wonder if it had something to do with Anthony's bottle of wine," Sarah said.

Chloë would almost bet on it. Again her suspicions trembled on the tip of her tongue, but she swallowed them and asked, "Can I see the wine cellar?"

Sarah laughed a little shakily. "Of course. Everyone else has tried to find the bottle. You might as well take a stab at it." She glanced behind them. "Take her down, Eli, and be careful on the stairs. They're steep and narrow."

"Like these." Eli stepped up to hold her arm as they climbed the front porch steps, the three of them together. "We've got to replace them, Nonna."

"Rafe has already said he's going to do it," Sarah said.

"Let me know when and I'll come to help." A few beats, and Eli said, "I thought Rafe and Brooke were leaving for Sweden soon?"

Sarah stopped in front of her door. "They've postponed their trip."

"Really?" As if astonished, Eli shook his head slightly. "Why?"

"I don't know," Sarah said.

But Chloë didn't believe it. Not the way Sarah's eyes were twinkling.

They walked through the hallway straight back to the kitchen. There Bao and Olivia were chatting quietly as they finished the luncheon cleanup.

Olivia took one look at Sarah's puffy eyes. "How about a nap?"

Sarah sighed and said to Chloë, "When you are eighty, dear, do try to remain healthy, or all of a sudden your life is not your own." But she kissed Chloë's cheek, and Eli's, and, with Olivia at her side, she started toward her bedroom at the front of the house.

Chloë watched until she was out of sight. "What happened to her?"

"Joseph Bianchin sent a man to attack her here in the house. She received a broken arm and a concussion."

"You're joking." Chloë turned to him in a fury. "The baby who got the rattle? The rat who pillaged your grandparents' wedding reception and tried to kill your grandfather? He's still alive and after the elusive bottle?"

Eli put a comforting hand on Chloë's shoulder. "Nonna's fine, but for the moment we're keeping Olivia around to care for her, and Bao to protect her."

Bao leaned against the counter, wiping her hands on a dish towel. "Bianchin broadcast enough information about that bottle to bring every repeat offender in the Western states down on our heads, and yet for the last few weeks there's been no sign of anyone on the property. I can't decide what it means, but I am uneasy every minute."

Chloë looked at her in a different light and realized . . . the young woman was smiling, relaxed, but she moved with the economy of motion and the intent directness of a martial artist, and that constant pacing from window to window . . . She wasn't nervous. She wasn't watching the flowers bloom. Bao was guarding Sarah and her home.

What had started out yesterday as a fun excursion to see a historic still became abruptly real and perilous. "Is Joseph Bianchin in jail for his crime?"

"We caught the guy he hired, but Bianchin covered his tracks too well for us to get him." Eli clearly despised the old man. "But he as good as told Nonna he was guilty, and for that, my brother Noah gave him reason to be afraid. Bianchin's left town, and the fervor has died down . . . it seems. . . ."

"It's too good to be true," Bao said dourly.

"Honestly?" Chloë didn't believe the mystery couldn't be solved. "No one can find this bottle of wine?"

"I've searched, too." Bao gestured around the kitchen.

"We'll go down in the cellar and you can try. Maybe a fresh pair of eyes will see what we can't." Eli opened the narrow wooden door next to the counter. "The stairway is truly steep, so let me go first."

The stairway was nothing but treads and risers strung together and painted white, and Chloë followed him down into the cool darkness, clutching the banister and wishing it weren't quite so precipitous.

Windows at ground level provided feeble illumination: The cellar was a generously sized room, twenty by thirty, with a high ceiling and rough cement walls. It smelled earthy and rich, like an orchard where the fruit ripened in the sun.

Eli reached the bottom and flipped a switch, and a fluorescent fixture flared to life. "This is nothing but an old basement dug when they built the house. The Di Lucas have used it to store their vegetables and their wine for a hundred and twenty years."

"No matter how they look, every cellar feels the same, doesn't it?" She walked over to the wall, pressed her hand against the chilly concrete, and felt the weight of the earth pressing back.

Most of the long wall was covered by a wine rack: well made, but rustic and unfinished. Bottles old and new filled the slots, and that accounted for the scent of fruit; wine had an intoxicating odor of its own. Dust coated the floor, and, as Chloë watched, more dust sifted down from the ceiling. She looked up, wanting to see a wine bottle dangling up there by the pipes; there was nothing but sturdy oak beams and looping electric cables.

"It has appeared basically the same ever since I can remember, except now a precious bottle of wine has gone missing, and that makes me actually scrutinize it.

We—my brothers and I—have tapped on the walls. We've searched in the window wells. We've tried to slide the wine rack aside in hopes there is a hidden cubbyhole. We've dusted every bottle and read the label and the markings." He shook his head. "But I'm not in an Agatha Christie novel, and whatever secrets this cellar holds . . . it keeps."

They were alone, with no one to hear their conversation, and finally Chloë was able to voice her suspicions. "You think Massimo hid the Beating Heart in your grandfather's bottle of wine, don't you?"

He shot the question right back at her. "Don't you?"

"If what we read and surmise is correct, he made a habit of stealing valuables, probably on commission, and then picked up a few jewels on the side and smuggled them back into the United States. In 1930, it couldn't have been difficult. Charles Lindbergh crossed the Atlantic in what?" She couldn't remember.

"Nineteen twenty-seven," Eli said.

"So Massimo was making the crossing on a ship. There were customs, but no X-rays. A clever thief could hide jewels in his shoes or the lining of his suitcase, or he could swallow them. He'd come back to his home in Bella Valley, bottle his wine with the gems inside, and give them as gifts to newborn sons with the expectation that the wine would be put away out of sight until the child's twenty-first birthday." She pressed her hand a little harder against the wall, giving birth to the half-formed thoughts in her mind. "When an appropriate amount of time had passed, he retrieved the bottles and replaced them with bottles without jewels. The families got what they expected—a good bottle of wine for the birth of their sons—and Massimo escaped suspicion until he was able to sell the gems."

"Foolproof," Eli said. "Except when it wasn't."

"Somebody somewhere figured out he was the diamond thief. Somebody caught him and tortured him to death trying to find out where he'd hidden the gems." The cellar grew suddenly colder. "But he didn't confess."

Without pause, Eli followed her logic. "Because if he had confessed, there would have been a wave of crime as the men who wanted those diamonds acquired every bottle of Massimo's wine by whatever means necessary."

"Massimo was your grandmother's Robin Hood to the very end—and Joseph Bianchin is a troll." Chloë had never even met the man and she hated his guts.

"The question is—why now? Why after all these years is Joseph Bianchin after that bottle of wine?" Eli met her eyes across the width of the cellar. "Because he's an old man and this is his last chance?"

"Or because he figured out there were diamonds in the bottle?" The cellar air was cool in her lungs, and she felt so alive she was almost sparkling.

"We know he collects Massimo's wines and has for years."

"So *he's* the one with more money than sense," she said.

Eli half smiled, and nodded. "Yes, he's the one. As I

said, he's old. He's eighty-one. He's had some health problems. So let's assume when he gets a bottle, he drinks it."

"In one bottle, he found a stash of diamonds. Not the big diamond. But diamonds of enough value to pique his interest." Eli and Chloë knocked ideas back and forth like tennis balls, and with such a grim subject, she hated to say she was having fun . . . but she was.

"More important—they were pink diamonds, and those are rare enough to give him the lead he needs," Eli added.

"Sure. If I can do the research and find out about the Beating Heart, so could he—and he did. Once he figured out the way Massimo worked and what was probably in Massimo's last bottle of wine—the bottle of wine Massimo gave to the Di Lucas as a baby gift—Bianchin wanted it." She waved her arms in emphasis. "He'll stop at nothing to get it!" She felt like Sherlock Holmes. Or maybe Watson, since she really couldn't imagine Eli playing the supporting role.

"I think we've got it." He sounded quietly appreciative, and looked at her as if he thought she were a miracle.

The only other person who had ever looked at her that way was her father. To him, as his only child, she was.

Down here in the cellar, when she was alone with Eli, the atmosphere swirled with currents of mystery and desire, and she didn't know whether to fling herself at him or run away.

She settled for a joke. "Have I got chocolate-chip cookie crumbs on my face?"

He smiled, slow and warm, catching her gaze with his . . . and she couldn't look away. "You look beautiful, and I was thinking . . . having my own private mystery writer to figure out all the angles is an immense amount of help."

"Not if I can't help you find the bottle of wine." But his compliment pleased her a little too much.

He paced toward her. "I thought when you came to Bella Terra you'd be a moody, spoiled princess whose muse needed her own room."

Chloë laughed nervously and backed toward the stairs. "No. No muse. The bitch never sticks around when I need her."

"Instead you're strong and smart." He stalked after her. "You smell like ripe berries and warm spice."

She laughed again, all too aware that they were alone, her halter dress was short, and his brown eyes flattered and desired. "Isn't that the way you describe wine?"

"Yes, and I want to drink you in. Chloë . . ."

"You guys!" Olivia called down the stairs. "Nonna wants to see you before you leave."

The mood broke.

For one moment, Chloë saw naked frustration on his face.

He looked down, took a breath, looked up. "All right, we'll be right up!" he called. In a voice both calm and reasonable, he said, "It's probably for the best. It was getting a little heated in here."

"We can't have that. Bad for the wine." Bad for her, too, to get so involved with a man she barely knew, a man who made her back away from that danger he projected.

But she was still bitterly disappointed to leave that heated moment.

She started up the stairs.

The trouble was . . . she'd begun to be more interested in the enigmatic Eli Di Luca than in the baffling bottle of wine.

Behind that calm facade, what secrets did he hide?

Chapter 20

Eli watched Chloë climb the cellar stairs ahead of him.

He liked this sundress. It bared her back and arms, displaying long, sleek muscles and a lithe, catlike movement that made him want to pet her. Her legs were good, too, really good, and in that skirt and from this angle, he could see a lot of them.

He really, really did like this sundress.

He probably should feel ashamed of himself for leering at an unsuspecting woman. In normal circumstances, he was sure he would.

But these were not normal circumstances. He was going to marry Chloë.

Besides, she wasn't what he expected. When Conte

had proposed the deal, Eli had thought he'd be stuck with a girl without personality or wisdom, someone whose primary ambition in life was to perch on the back of a Jaguar convertible while Eli drove her through the center of town during the annual Wine Crush Parade.

Instead, she drove a blue Ford Focus.

'Nuff said.

Olivia waited for them in the kitchen. "She insisted on staying awake to say good-bye."

"We'll get in and get out, I promise. Thanks, Olivia!" Chloë flashed a happy smile and hurried down the hall.

Okay. There was that, too.

Chloë adored his grandmother.

With every new moment, Chloë created layers of interest in him. First she was fascinated by his tales of early Bella Valley. It was as if she felt his passion for this place. Then she mourned over Massimo as if he were a relative, and thirsted to avenge his death. Then she showed the complexity of her mind as she puzzled through the mystery of why Massimo was murdered.

Tamosso Conte was right: His daughter was smart. And while Eli knew a lot of guys didn't admire a woman with brains, Eli had lived with and admired his grandmother—and she was the smartest woman he knew.

"Children, come in." Nonna waved them into her bedroom.

Chloë rushed to the bedside.

He followed.

Nonna was propped up on her pillows, and Chloë leaned in to hug her. "Thank you for sharing so much of your family's history with me. I've enjoyed every minute of today."

"You will come back to visit?" Nonna put her hands on Chloë's cheeks and smiled into her face.

"I would love to, and I'll bring you the first copy of my next book. If not for you and Eli, I'm afraid I would never have had the inspiration to finish it. As it is now, I can honestly say second-book syndrome is non-sense." Over her shoulder, Chloë flashed him a mischievous smile.

"I'll hold you to that promise," Nonna said.

Yes, Chloë adored Nonna, and Nonna returned her affection.

Not that Nonna was ever critical, but she could spot a phony a mile away, and through every moment of lunch and their talk afterward, she had been listening to Chloë as if weighing the young woman's words . . . and now she genuinely liked her.

As he moved to Nonna's side, Chloë patted his shoulder. "Sarah, you have a fabulous, caring grandson. You must be so proud."

"I am proud of all my grandsons." Nonna took Eli's hand. "I think this one is going to turn out all right."

As Eli leaned over and kissed her cheek, she murmured, "Promise you'll bring her back."

"I promise."

This marriage of convenience, as Conte so quaintly

called it, was exactly that—convenient. Eli didn't have time to find a wife; he'd had one delivered to him on a platter.

But conscience jabbed him, cold and sharp. It wasn't *right*.

He could not do this. He couldn't marry Chloë for money.

He couldn't stand the thought of what his grandmother would say if she knew.

No matter how much he tried to ignore them, his own morals wouldn't allow it.

Yet he had no choice. . . .

But he did.

He could take the route his pride had refused—he could tell his brothers the truth. He would tell them he got too busy and trusted the wrong man.

Noah would point out that he'd been saying for years that Eli tried to do too much.

Rafe would agree, and add that he'd told Eli to leave the growing of the grapes to Royson and concentrate on his winemaking.

They would both ask—in suggestive tones—whether Eli was trying to compensate for some small deficiency.

When he told them about the loss of the cash and the staggering debts he owed, they would give him a bad time. They might even be pissed. But they were his brothers. They wouldn't judge him harshly. Together they'd get an equity loan on the resort. Probably Noah and Rafe would liquidate some of their personal holdings. Financial juggling like that would take some time, but he would make this work without Conte's proposed marriage of convenience.

He didn't even have to wonder why he'd had such a change of heart.

He could see the reasons right here in this old-fashioned bedroom.

Chloë was smart and funny. She made him feel warm, admired, part of a family, at home. Together with his grandmother, she alleviated the loneliness that had plagued him his whole life.

And who knew? If Chloë continued living in his cottage, and they saw each other occasionally, maybe . . .

His phone rang. Pulling it from his pocket, he saw the number—and frowned.

His accountant.

His *new* accountant, Val Mowbray, the one who hadn't given him one good piece of news since she'd taken over the mess left by Eli's treacherous buddy Owen Slovak.

"Let me get this," he said to Nonna and Chloë, and headed out onto the front porch as fast as he could go. "What is it?" he asked Val.

He didn't actually ask. He snapped.

Val didn't snap back, but as always, she was brisk and efficient. "I just got a certified notice from the IRS. At noon on Monday, unless paid in full, they're putting a lien on the winery."

"What?" Eli leaped down the steps and walked into the yard, trying to put more distance between this news and the two women in the bedroom . . . as if that would shelter them from the truth. "How? Why? You said—"

"I know what I said. It's the IRS. There are protocols. They're skipping steps. I've never seen them move so quickly. I mean . . . they're part of the government!"

Eli's outrage heated to two thousand degrees. "Can't you do anything?"

"I called. I talked. And talked. And talked. I've been talking for seven hours, on and off."

"Why off?"

"Because they kept disconnecting me." Eli could almost see Val putting air quotes around "disconnecting." "I got nowhere. I couldn't figure it out, because I've never seen anything like this drive to seize your lands. Finally I called my friend in the Washington office and asked him to check into it."

Eli thought he already knew, but he said harshly, "Tell me."

"He wouldn't exactly tell me what was going on— couldn't because he didn't exactly know, I think—but I gather someone with contacts in high places is putting pressure on them to take the land ASAP."

Familiar rage engulfed Eli. "Joseph Bianchin."

"I don't know." Val sounded as frustrated as he felt. "I've never actually seen the IRS bend to outside pressure. If it's him, he must have some nasty goods on someone with power."

"That sounds exactly right." Noah should have killed the old bastard instead of running him out of town.

As he always did, Eli pushed his fury down, hid it away, gained control. "Is there nothing we can do?"

"Hand them a check before Monday."

"Five days. And part of that a weekend." No time to tell his brothers. No time to marshal their financial forces. "All right. I'll take care of it."

"What are you going to do?" Val asked.

The screen door slammed.

Chloë—beautiful, smiling, euphoric—came out the door and clattered down the stairs.

Eli watched her, the pit of his belly cold as ice. "I'm going to get the money to pay them off."

Chapter 21

Chloë bubbled over with enthusiasm. "I had such a good time today. Thank you for taking me to meet your grandmother!"

Eli nodded and drove.

"She's amazing. You must be awfully proud of her."

"I am."

"What a story she told—about Massimo and your grandfather's bottle of wine and Joseph Bianchin. . . . He sounds like a nasty old villain. Someone should tell him it's not politically correct to tie virgins to the railroad tracks. I mean, does he have a mustache that he curls?" She grinned spitefully.

"No."

"I suppose that would be too good to be true. But someone needs to take him down."

"Agreed."

"We can do it. All we have to do is find that bottle of wine. I'll bet those diamonds are in there. It certainly sounds like he believes it, too, or he wouldn't have hired someone to attack your grandmother. Don't you think so?"

"I said so, didn't I?"

She froze. He'd snapped at her.

Not that that was so different; he'd been pretty much an ass the first time she'd met him. But after the last couple of days, she wasn't expecting it. She'd grown used to being herself, saying what she thought without fearing his mockery or his scorn. And after their time in Nonna's cellar, his impatience felt like sandpaper on her skin. "Are you okay?" She tried to remember when he'd grown quiet. "Was the phone call bad news?"

She thought for a moment that he was going to ignore her, pretend she hadn't spoken. Then in a milder tone, he said, "Just accounting stuff. Math always puts me in a vile mood."

She relaxed a little. "I know what you mean. The first year after I published my book, I had to pay self-employment taxes. Holy smokes. I'm still in shock."

"Beats being without a job." He was still terse, but his irritation seemed to have eased.

He was good-looking, charming when he wished to

be, so obviously he could have had his choice of room-mates. But he lived alone as a matter of choice. So here was a man who cherished his solitude.

So did she, and sometimes silence healed life's little wounds.

She had been chattering a lot, and probably loudly, with excitement.

"I know. I have friends who have been out of college a year who still live with their parents and work at TechLand. I mean, I love both my parents, but I don't want to live with either one of them." As they turned off the highway, she glanced out the window and resolved to give him his moment of quiet.

But Eli really seemed to have recovered. "I've met your father," he said. "Interesting guy. You don't look like him at all."

"I know. But we did the DNA. I'm all his." She was still being cautious.

"I never doubted that. And I'm glad you don't look like him." Eli shot a warm, smiling glance at her. "What's your mother like?"

"Really smart. *Really* smart. She's always right, even when she's not."

He laughed briefly, as if Chloë had caught him by surprise.

"She's sharp-tongued," Chloë continued. "She doesn't suffer fools lightly. I assure you, the worst thing I could do while growing up was to deliberately play dumb. With just a few words, she'd rip the skin off my hide."

"Was she a good mother?"

"Really good. She taught me a lot—not to put up with bullies, to read contracts before I signed them, to think things through." Chloë meant to be brief. But he was listening so well, as if he were really interested. "She taught me other stuff, too, stuff she didn't mean to teach me."

"What kind of things?"

"Some things she does I don't like, and I don't want to do them. I'm not always going to be suspicious and look for the hidden motives in anything and everything. Sure, it saves her from making a fool of herself, but it also makes her suspicious of anything and everything." Chloë turned back to him, wanting him to really hear her. "I don't want to live like that."

"She's not trusting."

"She would say she's being wise."

"She thinks you're *too* trusting?"

"Yes, but I think that's better than being too cynical."

He hesitated. "Yes."

In the normal run of conversation, Chloë would now ask him about his mother. That was the polite thing to do—talk a little, ask a lot.

But as they bounced up his gravel driveway, Eli changed again, looked like he had the first time she'd met him, stony faced and angry, and he appeared to be watching for something.

The way he glanced from side to side made her start glancing around, too.

"What are you looking for?" she finally asked.

"Nothing." A pause. "Someone's been up here."

He made it sound sinister. "UPS? I ordered a jeweler's loupe."

"No, I know what their tire tracks look like."

He knew what their tire tracks looked like? He watched for stuff like that? Why?

She wanted to ask, but he was concentrating, driving as if he expected to have to turn around quickly and get out of here. As if he scented danger on the air . . .

The hair stood up on the back of her neck.

They got closer to the house, reached the asphalt part of the drive. The ride smoothed out. Still he was watching. He pulled up in front of her cottage, stopped the car, and said, "Wait here."

He walked slowly to her cottage, glancing at the ground, then all around, then at the ground again.

The sun beat down on the truck. It was too hot in here, too dry and still. And the way he was acting . . .

Her breath grew short. She tried to see what he was seeing. But the stretch of lawn around his house was green and lush. His house stood like the prow of a ship, surveying the valley. Her cottage looked small and cozy. . . .

What did he see? What did he suspect?

He looked at the steps as he climbed onto her porch. He checked the cottage's security pad, then opened the door and walked in. He was gone long enough to raise her anxiety level to red.

Finally, he stepped out on the porch and gestured her in.

She flung herself out of the truck. As soon as she got

close, she asked, "What? What is it?" But she asked quietly, somehow afraid that some evil, invisible entity would hear her.

His voice was quiet, too, pitched to a level below his usual rumble. "They're gone now, left the property, but someone's been inside the cottage."

Dread grabbed her by the throat and squeezed. "The diamond! Is it gone?"

His mouth was a straight, tight line. "Not at all. We were very wise. We hid it in plain sight, and whoever was in there discounted its importance."

She nodded, relieved and yet . . . How did he know this stuff? How did he know how to look at the ground and tell someone had been there? When had he learned that rare kind of skill, that caution, and so much about human nature?

Like ominous clouds, his dark secrets loomed on the horizon again. "We need to call the cops," she said.

"And tell them what? Someone sneaked in without tripping the alarm and didn't steal anything? You met DuPey. I went to high school with him. But he bungled the investigation of Nonna's attacker, and if it hadn't been for Rafe and Brooke, I don't know what would have happened. Plus we have Finnegan Balfour."

Chloë remembered the big-eyed, smiling boy from Kansas. "He's a nice guy," she offered.

"But not the sharpest crayon in the box." Eli grimaced. "Wyatt Vincent might be able to figure something out, but I'd hate to tell a guy like that, who worked for the FBI and is a consultant to police forces across the country, that I knew someone broke in because of the way the leaves are bent on the grass."

"Yes. True. I get it. But . . . we can't *not* tell the police."

"We will. Let's get some evidence first. My brother Rafe owns a security firm. He can set up an array of cameras, connect them to my Wi-Fi network, and if the guy comes back—and I imagine he will—we'll know who it is."

"What do we do in the meantime? I'm not staying here."

He held the door open, inviting her in. "Gather up whatever you need to work and move into my place."

She looked up the ridge and across the wide swath of lawn to his house. "That's not going to be safe."

"I have better security." As if embarrassed, he said, "I never thought anybody would break in here when the obviously much more expensive house was right there."

He made sense.

Gesturing toward the lawn and walk, he said, "The tracks go here, not there. You're the one they fear. You're the one who can figure out where the diamonds are."

"Me? Don't be ridiculous. Why would anyone think that I—" She stopped. They, whoever *they* were, thought she could solve the mystery because she was a mystery writer. Her own small fame had revealed her.

"Did you have your notebook with you at Nonna's?" he asked.

"No. It's here." She dived toward her desk, suddenly frantic to see that it really *was* here.

It was, red and ragged, spirals twisted out of shape, open to the spot with her notes taken at the water tower and afterward. In large sprawling letters at the bottom, she'd written, *DIAMOND!!!!*, in all caps. And in small caps, PINK and VALUABLE.

She put her hands to her forehead. "If anyone was in doubt about what we were doing, they're not now."

He joined her and looked down at the notebook. "Would you know if someone looked at this?"

She tried frantically to remember whether the notebook had been open or closed. "I left it open."

"To this page?"

"I don't know."

"The only person who could have slipped through the alarm on this cottage was a professional. How would you have known your belongings weren't safe here? God!" He paced away from her. "I am sorry. This is my fault."

She hurried after him. "No, it's not! In the right hands, any security system can be cracked. I know this stuff." She tried to smile. "I'm a mystery writer."

"My house should be secure." He went to the closet, pulled out her suitcase of death, opened it on the bed. "Don't worry. I know you need privacy, but you work in my office." He opened her drawers, pulled out her underwear, threw it in the case. "I'll be working, too, mostly in the vineyard and at the winery. I won't bother you, I promise, and I wouldn't feel comfortable leaving you alone unless I know you're safe."

"Okay." She wasn't going to argue with that. When she thought of someone in her cottage, looking at her things, reading her notes, handling her books . . . it made her stomach hurt.

More important, she would feel safe in Eli's house, under Eli's protection.

She never doubted that Eli was one of those guys who guarded what was his.

His house was his, and in some indefinable way she had begun to believe . . . that she was his, too.

Going to the bed, she pushed him aside and started packing her books.

Chapter 22

Chloë climbed to the main level of Eli's house, put her bags down, and looked around.

The tall, massive great room consisted of the living room and the kitchen, a vast space looking east through a wall of windows across the valley. The decorative touches were spare; the furniture was sparse: an extra-long tan recliner, a wide, comfortable-looking couch upholstered in sage, a coffee table created from a single polished slab of wood cut from the length of a glorious old tree, two swooping copper arc lamps, and a modern area rug that covered the swept granite floor. One huge golden painting of a long stairway leading up to a hidden garden hung over the fireplace. The kitchen sported all stainless-steel appliances, a basalt countertop bare of canisters, knives, or utensils, a backsplash of gleaming green glass tiles, and handcrafted wood cabinets stained a deep cherry.

It was perfect. Understated. Very Eli.

She should be comfortable here, yet somewhere, someone was watching them. Watching her.

Why?

Eli came puffing up the stairs, carrying the Suitcase of Death with its load of heavy books. He set it down and leaned against the wall, holding his chest and gasping as if he were having a heart attack.

She ignored his dramatics. "I've been thinking—do you suppose my father has offered me up to someone besides you?"

"What?"

"Someone came here looking for something. They broke into the cottage and didn't take anything, and the diamond was sitting right there. Do you suppose it's some Mafia-type jerk my father came up with for me to marry?"

Eli made a show of wiping the nonexistent sweat off his forehead. "It's possible. But you thought I was the designated jerk, didn't you?"

At this point, she wouldn't have thought anything could make her laugh. But this did. "If it's you, you're taking your own sweet time about it. Most of the guys figure a meal, a couple hours of romancing, a quick horizontal tango, and it's off to the church."

He actually looked offended. "Maybe I'm smarter than they are."

"Maybe so," she said soothingly. "For sure you're a better kisser."

"I think I've been insulted."

She chortled. "No, I didn't mean it like that." She chewed on her theory some more. "I have to admit, Papa's previously never come up with anyone dangerous. It could have just been a run-of-the-mill break-in."

She had talked herself into feeling better until he said, "Run-of-the-mill burglars do not make sure everything looks the same as when he broke in. We know someone murdered Massimo. Someone attacked my grandmother. And the diamonds are still missing. Money moves people to violence. Stay with me so I can keep you safe." He looked bleakly serious and as if he wanted an answer.

"Yes. I will."

"Thank you." He had gotten his way, and now he gestured around at the great room. "What do you think?"

"If it had been me, I would have found some framed mirrors, and added some art prints, and maybe some glass art . . . but that would have been gilding the lily." She walked to the windows. "Because your designer was right. The focus is here."

"My designer was an idiot. I'm the one who put the brakes on the froufrou."

That was so Eli that she laughed again. "You're a lucky man to have a heritage that included these lands and this view."

He lingered by the door, giving her space and time

to settle in. Settle down. "Don't you have a heritage, too?"

"A couple of them." She faced him. "Texas and Italy, and two parents warring about who I am and what part of me is theirs, and it's all too late. Because I'm myself, and if all were right in the world, at this point in their lives, they would have each other rather than an eternal sad war over what might have been."

"When they separated, they missed out on their time together."

"My mother says she did the right thing, because my father's been married five times since they were together and he would have given her nothing but heartache. But she's never found anyone to replace him, so I think it's a tragedy."

"I think you're right." His voice deepened and grew sad.

Why should she care whether he agreed with her? When it came to her parents, it wasn't important what she thought and most definitely not what he thought. But his like-mindedness gave her comfort.

"Where should I work?" She picked up her computer case and her bag of office supplies.

"I'm going to put you upstairs. Sorry, but I wasn't prepared for this, and it's the only desk in the house. And this time of the year I'm gone most of the time, so we'll not be in each other's way. Come on." He led her up to the top level. "This is my aerie."

His large office seemed more cluttered than the living room, more lived-in. A dusty black marble-topped desk faced the windows where another view spread out before them—and from this height, it was even more magnificent than the one below. The wide, short file cabinet sat behind the desk with a multifunction printer perched on top. A door went out on the small deck, and there an iron chair and small round iron table beckoned.

Walking to the desk, he picked up piles of papers and stacked them on the floor. "I wasn't planning for guests," he said.

His excuse made her feel better, eased that discomfort she felt whenever she remembered the clutter he'd seen yesterday in her work area.

"You can do whatever you want, but try not to mess up the piles," he said. "I know you don't believe me, but there's a method to my madness."

Bookshelves lined the large room, magnificent bookshelves that reached all the way to the twelve-foot ceiling. Books filled them. Books and bookends made of marble and alabaster, heavy stone bookends carved to resemble grapes or wine bottles.

Eli saw her looking at them and ran his hand over one of the shelves. "The carpenter who made the cabinets in the kitchen and the bathrooms created these for me. We recycled the redwood from the massive old barrels used to store wine in the early twentieth century."

"They're gorgeous." She pulled out a book and looked at it.

Like Beast offering Beauty her heart's desire, he said, "You can read whatever you like."

She flipped through a book on the French wine country, put it back, pulled another book off the shelves, a book on the theories of trellising grapes. She suspiciously examined the rest of the titles . . . all tomes on viniculture, winemaking, and wine history.

"Do you ever read for pleasure?" she asked.

His eyebrows went up as if he were startled, as if the idea had never occurred to him.

In exasperation, she asked, "Do you ever do anything for pleasure?"

When he looked at her, his brown eyes amber with light, she wished she hadn't asked.

Time to change the subject. "You've got some great books here."

"Thank you. Someday when I'm retired, I'll get to read them all."

"Do you have an e-reader, too?" Because her book was definitely not on these shelves.

"No. Nor will I ever have one. I want paper."

Silly to feel hurt. Millions of people had never read her book, and hundreds of thousands more would never go see the movie. Wasn't he curious about her and her writing? If he had written a book, she'd be interested enough to read it—she glanced again at the shelves—unless it was about how to recognize the noble rot on Riesling grapes.

Okay. He would probably publish his book on viniculture and she would probably not read it. But at least she'd buy it!

"I'm a writer," she said mildly. "I don't care how

you read, as long as you read. Can I scoot some of your books aside so I can put out my books?"

"My home is yours. Do whatever you like."

"I know. Just don't disturb the piles." She got the skull out of the bag of office supplies and placed it on the desk facing the chair. Carefully, she pulled a tissue out of the bag and, on top of the stone surface, she spread it open to reveal the diamond. With a flourish, she placed it once more between its grinning front teeth. "I'm set!"

"I'm off to pull something out of the freezer for dinner. Steak okay, or do you not eat red meat?"

She looked at him as if he were crazy. "I'm from Texas."

"I'm sure there are vegetarians in Texas."

"I'm sure there are smokers in California, too, but they don't brag about it."

"Steak and salad. Come down when you're ready." He ran down the stairs, one of those half smiles on his face.

"Not too much longer," she told the place where he had been standing, "and I'll teach you how to smile a whole smile."

With a towel from the bathroom, she wiped the dust off the desktop and the one-foot-tall marble figurine of some Roman god reveling in debauchery. The attached plaque identified him as Bacchus, the god of wine.

So even in art, Eli stuck with his theme.

Sitting down in the chair, she played with the adjustments until her feet touched the floor. She looked in the drawers. Lots of pencils, pens, pads. A stapler and a staple remover. The kind of stuff she expected to see in a home office. One drawer was full of computer programs. The other drawer, the desk's file cabinet, was locked, probably filled with tax stuff. When she opened the belly drawer, she expected to see his keyboard.

Instead, there was a small stack of envelopes, all from the same foreign postmark. From Chile.

And at the bottom of the stack, a piece of paper had been crumpled up, then smoothed out, then crumpled up, then smoothed out . . . The scent of tobacco clung to the letter. The paper itself looked worn, as if he wanted to throw it away and couldn't.

Slowly, wanting to know what drove him, recklessly needing to know his secrets, she pulled it out from beneath the envelopes and started to read.

Chapter 23

Eli knew Chloë trusted him.

She trusted him partly because he'd won her trust, partly because she refused to be as cynical as her mother.

If she only knew . . .

No time for regrets.

He had to close this deal.

He had to make her marry him as quickly as possible. He had a plan. It should work.

First step: Get her into the house with him. Scare her a little about bad guys chasing her. Make himself look like the one man who could save her.

Check.

Embarrassing as hell to act like a thirteen-year-old

boy trying to impress a girl, but he didn't have time to plan something clever, and anyway—it looked like this was working.

Because she trusted him.

Second step: Feed her, give her wine, finish the seduction he'd started before he'd had an attack of conscience.

Third step: Tell the kind of lie he had never told in his life.

He was going to tell her he loved her. If he had to. And if it took more wine and more sexual persuasion to convince her, he'd do it. He'd do whatever he had to do to save his winery.

Fourth step: Convince her to go through with the ceremony and actually marry him. Thanks to Conte and his schemes, she was wary. But Eli had thought he had time to carry off this seduction, and that had turned out to be an advantage. She believed he wasn't one of her suitors, or at least, one who didn't give a damn about marrying her.

After that, it was a short drive to the Santa Rosa airport, a short flight to Reno, a quick wedding, and home again to collect his payment from her father.

It would work. It had to. Failure was not an option.

He heard her coming downstairs. Poured the first glasses of wine, picked them up, turned with a smile to offer her one—and saw her standing on the bottom step, Abuela's crumpled letter clutched in her hand. "Eli, what's this?"

"What are you doing with that?" He put the glasses

on the counter with controlled force. "Did you read that?"

"I did. I didn't mean to, but the foreign postmarks got my attention, and this . . ." She lifted one of the sheets. "It was crumpled up, so I noticed it. Then I saw the shaky old handwriting and I thought . . . I guess I thought it was something from your grandmother. And it is, but from your other grandmother. Your mother's mother. In Chile."

"I know who she is. I know where she's from. You shouldn't have read it. You invaded my privacy." He wanted to shout at her, to stomp like an infuriated child.

"I know. I'm sorry, but, Eli, why would you ignore a plea like this?" Chloë's eyes were worried, her delivery fast and anxious. "She's an old woman. She wants to see you one last time before she dies."

Chloë didn't understand. She could never understand. "I will not see her."

"How can you say that?" She lifted the letter and read, "'It's been too many years since I last beheld your face, my most beloved of grandsons, and in the deep cold of a mountain winter when I know I'll not see another autumn, I would beg that you come to me and allow me to make amends for the—'"

"I know what it says." Striding to Chloë, he snatched it out of her hands and crumpled it up. Again.

"You've done that before. You always spread it out again. She wrote it six months ago and you haven't thrown it away yet. No matter what she did to you, no matter what you say about not wanting to see her, you can't let it go." Chloë *sounded* sensible. She *looked* bewildered and almost hurt by his cruelty.

He didn't care. "I *can* let it go." Going to the brushed stainless-steel trash can, he lifted the lid and tossed it inside. *Threw* it inside.

But the scent of Abuela's little cigar clung to his skin, and he washed his hand once. Twice. "I can't let go of the anger. Never. For what that woman did to me, she deserves to burn in hell."

"It sounds as if that may be happening sooner rather than later. She's an old lady." Chloë gestured widely. "She's dying!"

"Maybe. Or lying. She does that with unparalleled skill. She's had enough practice."

"Eli, if you really, really believed that, you wouldn't have kept the letter."

"I kept the letter to remind me of how much I hated . . . hated . . ." Loathing bound him in its cruel shackles, and he could hardly get his breath.

"Why?" Chloë spoke softly, pleading for an explanation. "What happened in Chile that you can never forgive or forget?"

He wanted to scream.

He wanted to cry.

He wanted to fling himself on the floor in the kind of tantrum he had never in his life thrown.

He couldn't do that.

He couldn't be like . . . them. Like her.

Like his mother, Valentina.

Everything faded to black, the vortex of rage spinning, tightening on him. His focus narrowed to one point, to Chloë's face, to calm himself. And for the first time in his life, he began to tell his story.

"My first memory is setting the table with Nonna for Christmas." Toddling around the table, trying to do everything right, to make his Nonna happy. "I broke a glass, and I cowered away from her. I remember I was so surprised when she hugged me and swept it up with no reproaches. Later, I heard her speaking to my father the way a biblical mother would speak to a son who reveled in the pleasures of Sodom and Gomorrah. I was surprised that she dared, but I knew it would make no difference. It wasn't my father who made me cower. It was my mother. She had a temper that at the slightest provocation rampaged out of control."

"Your mother . . . hurt you? Abused you?"

"You wanted to hear this. Now listen." He waited until Chloë sat down on a counter stool and folded her hands in her lap. "My second memory is hearing my father scream when my mother stabbed him." He paused, watching her, cynical and sneering. "You know about that, right? That my mother stabbed my father?"

"I read about it. On the Internet. Yes." She glanced down.

Good. She was embarrassed. "Because you thought you had the right to know my secrets."

She looked up again, looked at him as if he puzzled her. "Because I was curious about you. I like you, but you're . . . not easy to know."

"Of course. That makes snooping all right."

Chloë's feet hit the floor, and her eyes flashed. "When my father sold me to you as a guest, did you check my Web site? Read an excerpt, try to figure out why someone like me would write a murder mystery? I know you, Eli—you knew what my father was up to and you at least looked at my photo to see if I was the ugliest dog in the world."

"What . . . your father . . . was up to?" he repeated. For a moment, he thought she knew the awful truth.

"Matchmaking. Remember?" Now *she* mocked *him*. "We talked about that on my first day here, and we said we didn't have to freak out because my father had a thing about getting me married. And I wasn't freaked-out, but I'll bet you were, as fond as you are of your privacy and your cool emotions. You checked me out, too. Didn't you?"

"Yes." He'd give her this point—because he'd checked her out by holding her photo in his fingers and listening to her father propose marriage on her behalf.

"All right then." She subsided back onto the stool. "I know your mother stabbed your father because she found out he was in love with Francesca Pastore."

Eli snorted. "He wasn't in love with Francesca. But he was screwing her. Probably she was pregnant." Eli loved his brother. And he had come to terms with the lovely Francesca's role in his life. But when he remembered that terrifying night, he lived it all again. "I was asleep. I woke up to that scream—sometimes at night,

I still hear it in my dreams—and her shrieking at him. Lights. Sirens. People taking photos, lots of them, and yelling questions at my parents and at the police. I crept out of bed and watched men and women in uniform take both my parents away, my father on a gurney and my mother with her hands cuffed behind her. She saw me watching from the top of the stairs and shouted that I should stay there; she'd return for me. I remained frozen in place, thinking that if I moved before she returned, she'd hurt me as she had hurt my father." For a moment, that little boy and his fear were alive in Eli. "The chaos slowly cleared. The servants left. No one called child services. The next day, Nonna found me there, still in my pajamas, afraid to move. She brought me to her home."

"Oh . . . Eli." Chloë offered her palm to him.

"No. You wanted to know about Abuela. Let me tell you." *And don't say anything. Don't touch me. Don't show sympathy.*

Chloë withdrew her hand, clutched the sides of the seat instead, as if she feared she would fall off.

"I lived with Nonna for five years, until my mother got out of prison. Five years of normal life. Of swinging in the yard, eating Nonna's cookies, going to school, riding my bike. Relatively normal, anyway. There was always my father falling in and out of love and begetting sons and abandoning them, but to me that was normal, too." Chloë ought to know what she was getting into, he supposed, although a smart woman would be running the other way. "During that five years, whenever Nonna took me to see my mother, Valentina was behind bars and the old fear of her faded."

"Was she insane?" Chloë didn't sound mean; she sounded anxious.

"No. Impetuous. Spoiled. Very intelligent and yet, about life . . . she was a fool." As he would never be. "She was a beauty queen at sixteen. She married my father at seventeen. She was a mother at eighteen."

"She was a child!" Chloë's knuckles turned white against the seat.

"Yes, and by the time she was twenty-one, the man she loved had discarded her, and all her bright promise was destroyed." Eli could be bitter on her behalf; she was, after all, his mother.

"How old was your father when he seduced her?"

"I don't know . . . twenty-five."

"What a lecher." Chloë spit the word.

"Every day of his life," Eli said, then thought of the eleven years that separated him from Chloë and felt ill.

Small comfort, but at least she wasn't a teenager. At least she'd lived a little. At least she knew who she was and what she wanted. He wasn't like his father. Or his mother. He had spent his life patterning himself after Nonna and Nonno—not in their open lovingness; he couldn't do that—but in their morals and the way they treated everyone, with respect and kindness.

Now Eli was betraying their example and their teachings. He knew that.

But he wouldn't survive without the winery. He cherished the vineyards, growing green and strong, and exalted in the wines, subtle, lavish, and scented. The vineyards and the winery united him with his brothers, with Nonno and Nonna, with all the generations of Di Lucas who settled in this rich valley and strove so hard to be Americans, to be prosperous, to always, always be a family. He could never let them get too close to him: Nonna, his brothers, not even his ancestors. He was too stunted by the old pain and the bitter loneliness. But he could show his love by holding their lands and their wealth in trust for them.

He would do what he had to do. He would deceive Chloë. He would marry Chloë.

For without the winery, he was like a vine without water . . . without the winery, he would wither and die.

Chapter 24

Chloë slid off the stool, moving stealthily, as if afraid a sudden movement would make Eli attack. "I'm hungry," she said softly. "Do you mind if I make the salad?"

He was not feral. No matter what she said, no matter what she did, no matter how black his anger or how bleak his world, he would not harm her. "In my opinion, there's nothing as attractive as a woman working in the kitchen." When she stuck her tongue out at him, he felt almost normal.

But nothing about this was normal. Because he couldn't shut up. Chloë herself had pried open Pandora's box. Maybe he was making her uncomfortable, but she would have to deal with the consequences.

Not fair. Chloë had started this stupid, self-pitying rant, yes.

But although Eli despised himself for buckling, he knew he had been living under too much pressure.

His accountant, a man he had called a friend, had robbed him and done everything to destroy him, and then run without conscience or a word of explanation.

That had left him vulnerable to Conte's blackmail and led him to his inexorable decision to dupe Chloë into a relationship based on lies and deceit, and his own guilt added even more pressure.

Most of all, the dam of so many years had weakened, and all the pent-up pain and anguish came pouring out.

He had tried to forget.

He never could.

Now he was stripping himself bare, all because Chloë had found that damned smelly letter and read it. She had read his private letter.

Damn her. She deserved everything she heard here.

Chloë found his big wooden bowl. "Do you have a salad spinner?"

"In the lazy-Susan cabinet in the corner."

She got it out. Pulled vegetables out of the crisper. Looked up inquiringly.

"I'm not making excuses for my mother. She was selfish to the bone, cared for nothing and no one but herself and the humiliation my father visited on her. But she said he cheated on her while she was pregnant, and knowing my father as I do, I believe her. Because he was bone selfish, too, and has never loved anything but himself." In a weird way, Eli still grieved for his mother and the wasted opportunities of her life.

Chloë tore romaine leaves, rinsed them, and spun them dry.

"The everyday routine of my life with Nonna made me forget that danger lurked so close." Eli turned his back to her. "I was eight when my mother got out of prison. She came to get me at school, waving to me as if she were glad to see me. She looked so pretty. She was smiling. I got in the car with her. I didn't think anything about it. I didn't realize I would almost die so many times before I saw my home again."

The spinner stopped. "She kidnapped you?"

He didn't turn, didn't want to see her aghast eyes. "My father was no good as a parent, so my grandparents had custody of me. My mother hated everything to do with my father, including his parents, and she saw me as an instrument of revenge."

"But she was your mother!"

Now he faced Chloë.

She looked as shocked as he had imagined.

Silly woman, to imagine all parents were like hers. "You mean—she was my mother, so she must love me?" He mocked Chloë's secure childhood. Just a little. Just because he envied her, not because he would ever want anything different for her. He liked the woman her upbringing had shaped. "My mother knew if she took me, it would wound my grandparents, who had cared for me so well that I never felt the lack of her presence." He would have been happier if he didn't understand his mother so well. "She dragged me onto a private airplane and we flew to Chile. When I cried for Nonna, she told me I would never see her again."

Chloë muttered something, something that sounded like, "What a bitch." She went back to spinning the lettuce, and glanced up apologetically. "Sorry. I . . . She just lost my sympathy."

"The Silva family compound sat deep in the Andes." Eli paused, remembering his first glimpse of those beautiful mountains, jagged like blades. Before his time among them was done, they would cut the heart out of a lonely boy. "My mother's father was dead. Her mother—the woman who wrote the letter—"

"Abuela," Chloë reminded him.

As if he didn't remember her name. "Yes. Abuela was a survivor. She steered the family through revolutions, financial setbacks, scandals. She was ruthless, and I was nothing but a tool to be sharpened for later use. I was deposited in the dormitory for the boy cousins. The first night I cried myself to sleep. When my cousins got through with me, I never cried again."

Chloë shot him a dark glance. "Why?"

"Do you know what a blanket party is?"

She shook her head.

"It's when guys get together and cover another guy with a blanket so he can't strike back, and they pound him to death with clubs."

"Your *cousins* had a blanket party for you? When you were *eight*?"

He walked away from Chloë, from her pity and her concern, and looked out the window, where the setting sun painted the valley in rose and gold. "I was a foreigner. I was little. I was skinny. I was whiny. And my Spanish was indifferent."

Chloë made no noise, asked no questions, but he felt the weight of her interest as she waited for the rest of his story.

"'Only the tough survive.' That was Abuela's motto. And I did survive." Looking back, he felt sorry for the stupid kid he had been. "Broken ribs. Broken collarbone. Broken cheek. Cracked kneecap. Abuela was angry. She didn't like spending so much money to fix me, so she forbade my cousins to ever cover me in a blanket and beat me up again. After that, they didn't use a blanket. But I learned to fight against any odds, and eventually, *they* were afraid of *me*. Of course," he said reflectively, "I haven't slept all the way through the night since."

"That explains those bedroom eyes." Chloë inspected him. "Where was your mother? I know you said she didn't care about you, but she didn't take you there to get you killed. Did she?"

"My mother had her own problems. Abuela wouldn't let *her* leave, either. She said my mother had done enough damage with her flightiness. I assume she meant the mistake of marrying my father." He pressed on the glass. It felt cool under his palms, and yet nothing could cool his anger at having to tell this story.

"Madre had been home about a year when Abuela presented her with a man who would take her as his wife."

"Your grandmother arranged her marriage?"

As your father has arranged yours. "Abuela arranged her marriage to a powerful, wealthy man. Madre married him, too. I told you. For Abuela, her children and grandchildren were to be sacrificed for the good of the family. I suspect when Madre eloped with my father, she derailed Abuela's plans. But only temporarily—when she returned to Chile, she was still a beautiful woman, and so she married."

"For the good of the family," Chloë repeated.

"Yes. About a year later, she was killed along with her husband in a politically motivated shooting."

"She left you alone with your cousins, your grandmother?"

"How could she leave me alone? She had never been there for me." The light outside was fading.

Better. That was better. As the light grew dim in here, as he could no longer see Chloë's indignant, shocked, pitying face, the words flowed more easily.

"Eli, about your parents. I didn't realize—"

"No. You didn't. Your parents aren't together. They aren't married. Yet they both love you." Bitterly he envied her that. "Neither of my parents loved me, but when I was in Bella Valley, I didn't need them, because I had Nonno and Nonna." He stopped, struggled to slow the flow of words, to filter his feelings so Chloë didn't see him raw and bleeding . . . and despise him.

But the words kept coming, fast as bullets, tearing out of him as if they had been pent up inside for too long, waiting for her to listen to them. "All the cold nights, all the long days, the memory of home kept me from despair. At first, I thought if I asked often enough, I could convince Abuela I truly wanted to go home. Then I thought if I was a good boy and worked hard at school, she would let me go. Finally, I made my fatal mistake. I told my uncle, who was the vintner at the family winery, how to blend his wine. And it won awards."

"How did you know how to blend wines?"

He tapped his nose. "I inherited the knack."

Chloë made the next, correct leap in logic. "You proved you had worth."

"Exactly. I was smart and I made good wine. I no longer had the potential to be useful. I *was* useful."

As if she suddenly remembered what she was doing, Chloë went back into action. She shuffled through his cupboards, found red wine vinegar and extra virgin olive oil, found a container, and started blending the dressing. "Did they continue to mistreat you?" She located a whisk, and she beat something in a bowl as if she were trying to kill it.

"No, no. No one dared. Not anymore. Abuela would have had a blanket party all her own. No, I slept in the dormitory with the other grandsons, ate well, dressed warmly." He set his jaw and smiled at his own defiance. "Which is why, the first time I ran away, I survived. Even in the summer, night in the Andes is very cold."

"The first time you ran away?" Chloë had found the cutting board and the knives, and she chopped vegetables—radishes, celery—at the speed of light. "How many times did you run away?"

"How many times does it take to learn to track a rabbit through the snow? How many times does it take to learn to start a fire with wet wood? How many times does it take to learn to build a snow cave and survive a storm? How many times does it take to learn not to leave a trace of your passing?"

"You ran away . . . so often?" The knife slowed. "How much time did you spend out there?"

"I ran away unsuccessfully three times. The first time they caught me in a week. The second time, they brought out the dogs and got me within three days. The third time . . . it took me a long time before I went out again. I was determined to evade them. So I waited until I got everything right. I drugged the dogs and went out into a snowstorm, and I was gone for eight months, without contact with a single soul, surviving because I had no choice. It was either that or return to the family compound, and I would rather die." *Then and now.* "The head of the drug cartel discovered me unconscious. He fed me, thawed me out."

"Did he force you to run drugs for him?" she asked in horror.

"No." Eli hadn't thought he would ever tell this story and chuckle, but he chuckled now. "He returned me to the family compound. Frankly, I think he was afraid of Abuela."

Chloë stood holding a jar of capers, and finally she asked, "How did you come home? Home to Bella Valley?"

"Turns out I was doing it all wrong. I'd run into the wilderness. I couldn't get home that way, and sooner or later I was going to die—which would have been easier than living."

"Oh, Eli." Chloë abandoned the salad, started to come to him, to comfort him.

"No!" he said harshly. "If you want to hear the rest, stay where you are. I can't bear your sympathy."

She stopped. Looked hurt. Nodded jerkily.

He could do this.

He was almost finished.

"One day, a Chilean actor visited, and I resemble my father enough that he recognized me. I asked him to help me. He looked so scared. . . . I thought he was going to wet himself. He said no. I asked him to pass a message to my father. He was backing up and he said, 'If I told anyone Gavino Di Luca's kid was being held against his will, it would create an international scandal and your *abuela* would flay me.' He meant it, too, but he made me think. The way out was to find a reporter who would listen to me, paparazzi who would make money off asking what had happened to Gavino's son."

Chloë stood there, holding a tomato to her chest as if she couldn't move until he finished the story. "How old were you when you figured this out?"

"Fourteen."

"Did it work?"

"Like a dream. I ran away. My family looked in the wrong direction—they looked for me in the mountains." When he thought about his uncles and his cousins stumbling around in the snow, it made his heart glad. "I went to the capital, stalked a reporter, reminded him of the stabbing eleven years before, that my mother went to prison and, when she got out, she abducted me. That was juicy right there. But I told him my father hadn't seen me in the last six years, that I needed to get back to him, that there would be a touching reunion of father and son for him to photograph." When Eli remembered his own dramatic performance, he wanted to cringe . . . but it had done the job. "The reporter was smart. He recognized a story that would make him a fortune. My father recognized a story that would put him before the news cameras. I didn't care that they both made hay off of my adversity."

"In that case, the bitter was balanced by the sweet."

"Nicely put." There. He'd told Chloë everything. He'd said it all aloud and he was still standing. "There were a lot of pictures—I had to squat a bit, because by the time I was fourteen, I towered over my father and he didn't like that. But after the media circus was over, and six years in exile, I got to come *home*. Home to Nonna. Home to Bella Valley. Home to the Di Luca winery."

Chloë looked around the great room as if seeing it with different eyes.

There was only one hateful memory left to expunge.

"The last thing I saw as I sat on the jet to come home was Abuela standing on the tarmac watching me. Until the plane lifted off, I wasn't sure she wasn't going to exert her influence to force me to disembark." Saying the words raised the specter of that moment. . . .

Abuela, tall, stick-thin, dressed in perpetual mourning, her hands folded before her, her dark, dark eyes staring at the window of the airplane where he sat. The family whispered she was a witch. Unable to look away from her accusing stare, Eli believed it—and he was afraid.

He tore himself out of the memory, paced toward Chloë, and said, "And you want me to reconcile with that woman."

Chapter 25

Chloë had wondered about the dark, hidden places in Eli's soul. Now she saw them revealed to the light, and she ached for the boy he had been, and the man he was now. Abandoning the knives, she walked across the living room. "Eli, maybe your *abuela* did what she had to do to keep her family safe and prosperous, and maybe it was wrong, but in that letter, she recalls the time you spent together and the lessons she taught you."

He held up a hand.

Chloë stopped well back from him.

His eyes were almost black with rage and pain, his voice guttural with resentment. "She was the daughter of a winemaker. She knew the process. Once she realized I had a gift, she personally made sure I learned everything she had to teach."

"So you shared something, the two of you."

"For her profit!"

When Chloë looked around his home and Bella Valley, he seemed to have everything a man could want . . . and yet he had wounds she had never in her life imagined.

Home meant everything to this man. It was a sanctuary. A refuge.

And yet even here, he couldn't hide from his memories.

He couldn't hide from himself.

She tried again. "That letter—it wasn't groveling, but she wants to see you. She says there's no one else."

"My uncles, my cousins—they're there, I assure you. But she always liked to be alone. Isolated from the rest of the family, coming out only to reign over the meals or pass judgment on any transgression."

"She says she's sick."

"I don't believe her."

"Believe her or not—it's like Joseph Bianchin suddenly wanting your grandfather's bottle of wine. Why now, after so many years? We think he found some diamonds in another bottle." Chloë waved an arm. "Why is Abuela asking to speak to you now? She has a reason; she's an old lady, so it's probably not a reason you want to consider. She's probably looking at the end of her life and thinking she wants to make contact with the grandson who has made her proud."

"You don't know her at all."

"No, I don't. But I know an unhappy fourteen-year-old boy didn't know her, either. You're not a child anymore. She can't hold you hostage again."

"Don't you understand? I spent my childhood flinging myself against the walls of my prison, and she built those walls with her own hands."

"She's asking for a reconciliation. Maybe now you're not ready to reconcile with her, but this isn't a timetable you can control. If she dies and the day comes when you realize there were things that should have been said . . . there's no second chance." Chloë kept her voice low and soft, like a tamer soothing a lion poised for attack. "This is your opportunity to put your childhood in perspective, to forgive and forget. Once you do that, it's over at last."

"My childhood was over the day I landed in Chile."

Very slowly, very carefully, she reached out her hand and placed it on his chest.

He flinched. His heart was racing.

Softly she said, "I think your memories hold you in bondage. Cut the bonds. Let it go."

"You don't understand what you're asking. You don't understand. And I don't want you to. I never want you to know what it is to have the ones who should love you betray you." His eyes closed, and he whispered, "No one should ever know that pain."

Chloë couldn't stand it. She moved in close, slid her arms around his waist, hugged him tightly. "I won't betray you."

The lion pounced. He lifted her in his arms. He looked into her eyes, and his eyes glowed as if lit by a hot ember. "I keep myself under control for a reason. I am *like* them. Like *them*. Like my mother. Like my uncles. Like my cousins. Wild. Undisciplined. You ask me to remember those dark days when I lived on the edge of a vortex of despair and pain, and the memories drive me to madness."

She stared into his face.

He was breathing hard, his nostrils flaring. "If you don't run away *now*, I won't answer for the consequences."

But he clutched her tightly around her waist. Her feet dangled. His body flamed against hers.

She made her decision. Wrapping her legs around him, she said, "I want to see the wild man. I want to see you out of control."

He flung back his head as if she'd stabbed him in the gut. He took a rasping breath.

She could almost see his battle with the beast within.

When he lowered his head, he had lost the fight.

He strode to the couch, dropped onto it. With her straddling his lap, he unfastened the halter on her dress, pushed it off her shoulders and down her arms, baring her breasts to the fading light and the chilly air . . . and his mouth. Lifting her, he licked, he suckled, and he nibbled until she was gasping as he had earlier. The way he used his teeth against her nipple, the clever route his tongue took to ease the sting, and then that deep, rhythmic sucking . . . it brought her up on her knees, clutching his hair and holding him there. And there.

When he lifted his head and looked up at her, she kissed him, hard and long, thrusting her tongue into his mouth, a blatant imitation of his own seductive kisses . . . was that just this morning?

He kissed her back, but not with the focus he'd used this morning.

She discovered why. With his hands on her thighs, he pushed her skirt up, slid his fingers under her panties. He opened her, then used his thumb on her clit as if he had the right to touch her whenever and wherever he wished.

Breaking off the kiss with a moan, she flung her head back and rocked against him. He slid his finger inside her. . . .

No! Too much. Too soon. Too intimate.

Why? She had been loving the wildness of him. Why change her mind now?

Because this felt like ownership.

She wasn't ready. Not for that. Catching his wrist, she pushed him away.

He didn't fight. He did as she wished, pulling out of her—then, using both hands, he ripped the delicate lace at the side of her panties. They dropped around one knee, leaving her exposed to the cool air . . . and to him.

He stayed between her legs and toppled her onto her back. With his hands holding her thighs, he lifted her and put his mouth on her, and all the skill and passion he had shown in kissing, he put to use in other ways. He utilized his lips, his tongue, his teeth, licking her clit, probing inside her, then sucking until she screamed and fought not in denial but in ecstasy.

He wouldn't stop. The pleasure went on and on. The climax rose and fell in intensity. Every nerve in her body quivered with the shock of ongoing pleasure, and it wasn't until she collapsed in a boneless heap that he pulled away.

She watched through half-closed eyes as he stood and unbuckled his belt, opened his pants, and pushed them down. She heard the sound of foil tearing, saw him don the condom, then put one knee on the couch, lean over her, and—

"No!" Outrage brought her up on her elbows. "No, sir! You take off your shirt. You take off your pants. Take them off now!" Because she was sitting here with her dress pulled down and pulled up, exposed everywhere except at her waist, which was not an erogenous zone . . . at least, not until he proved to her it was. But she had never seen him with more than his collar button undone, and she damned well deserved a look at the man-candy. She would have it.

He visibly seethed with frustration; then with a low curse, he stripped off his pants and threw them across the coffee table. He started unbuttoning his shirt, got all but the middle button undone, and ripped it loose as he tore out of the shirt.

She wanted to laugh except . . . "You're gorgeous," she whispered.

He was thinner than she'd realized, his skin stretched across his ribs and belly with no padding to lessen the impact of his sculpted muscles. His shoulders and arms were bulkier than she had imagined, a testament to brute force produced not by lifting weights but by shoveling, moving pipe, living the life of a grape grower. She knew his legs were long, but hadn't realized his thighs would be so carved and strong.

She knew he was a man, but hadn't realized his erection would rise and strain, threaten and seduce, promise and entice.

He stood and let her look . . . for a moment.

But when she reached behind her to unzip her dress, he leaned in and kissed her upthrust breasts, the hollow of her throat, behind her ear, her lips. . . .

She didn't remember *how* to run a zipper.

The heat that burned in him burned in her, too, and she radiated want, need. Sliding her hands around his waist, she lifted one knee in invitation.

Her offer severed the last slender thread that bound him to civilization; he pushed her into the cushions, sank down on her, holding her with his weight. He wrapped his elbows under her knees, opened her, and unerringly found the entrance to her body.

He pushed. And pushed.

She was wet and trembling.

The condom was lubricated.

But the fit was tight. She gasped, and gasped, and tears sprang to her eyes.

He held himself still, shuddering. His expression, when she saw it, was that of a trapped beast, savage and angry, but his hands were gentle as he stroked her inner thighs. "Damn it. You should have told me. You're a virgin."

Chapter 26

Eli could not fucking believe it.

Chloë was a virgin.

"Technically, I *was* a virgin." Her voice was normal. Almost normal. But he heard the telltale quaver.

He'd hurt her.

Of course he had.

He'd lost control. He'd come at her like a Cossack run amok. He'd kissed her breasts because he couldn't resist, gone down on her, kissed her lips to imprint himself on her. He'd been a totally selfish bastard, and when he felt her . . . her maidenhead break inside her . . .

Who the hell called it a maidenhead?

Who the hell had one anymore? She lived in modern-day America, she was twenty-three years old, she'd gone to high school and to college . . . and when they were finished, he was going to be asking some questions. But first . . .

If he had any decency at all, he would pull out. Give her another round of pleasure. Restrain himself.

He couldn't do it. He had to have her.

Wrapping one arm around her and using the other to control their descent, he rolled off the couch.

He helped her sit up on him, tried to sound soothing, and managed only to sound desperate as he said, "Take me, then. Make yourself happy."

Her eyes were wide, startled, looking down at him as if he were the first man and she were the first woman and they were doing this for the first time in the history of the universe. . . .

He had to stop thinking stuff like that, or she'd be on her back again.

"What about you?" she asked.

"I'll be happy no matter what."

They were stretched between the couch and the coffee table. She had her legs folded beneath her.

As if puzzled, she pushed her hands through her fluff-ball hair; then, in a flurry of motion, she reached behind her and unzipped her dress. She twisted as she pulled it off her head. She tossed it toward his pants.

Her breasts, rosy and firm, thrust forward, then up, then bounced.

He was buried inside her, the heat of her enfolded him, her body gripped him, and if she didn't start humping soon, he was going to die of frustration. Or come for no more reason than that he was inside her and growing harder by the second. He *was* harder, but she seemed more at ease, as if the hurt had subsided. Experimentally, she leaned forward, lifted herself, then pressed down again, then lifted herself.

She paused, as if that wasn't quite right.

He thought it was *great*. But he held himself motionless in an agony of need.

With a look of concentration, she gripped the coffee table in one hand and the couch with the other and used them for leverage. Up and down, up and down, straight up and straight down, a half smile growing on her face as she found the pace.

He wanted to let her do it all, to find the place where only pleasure existed. But as she thrust onto him a little more, as she rubbed her clitoris against him, as the ripples of bliss started inside her and spread throughout her body, as her faint smile disappeared and she moaned, and that entirely feminine expression of blossoming glory took her, it broke him.

He thrust back at her, answered her motion with his own, seeking pleasure, giving pleasure, Eli and Chloë blending until he couldn't tell where one left off and the other began.

He wanted to possess. He wanted to own. He wanted to be on top, direct the motion, the rhythm, give and not be given to.

But he'd trapped himself between the table and couch, and all he could do was grip the table leg on one side, the foot of the couch on the other, try to crush them in his fists, and follow Chloë's lead.

Instinct and desire directed her. Her motion grew faster and faster.

His balls grew tighter and tighter. He was barely holding himself back.

With a cry, she thrust hard, grinding herself on him, her inner muscles clutching his cock as she climaxed.

About damned time.

He arched beneath her, his body caught in a spasm as he came so hard and so fast he thought his heart would burst. Like a kid having his first girl, he groaned. Caught himself in disbelief. Groaned again, in rapture so intense it truly did feel like the first time.

Then she collapsed on him, overwhelmed, gasping for breath, laughing and crying.

He wrapped his arms around her, stroked her hair with hands that trembled—what had she done to him?—and, driven by some primal directive he scarcely recognized, he said, "That's it. You've got to marry me. Tonight."

Chapter 27

Chloë laughed huskily and kissed his nipple. "Eli. You're sweet."

"No." He grasped her arms, half lifted her so she would look into his face. "I'm not kidding. We've got to get married. Tonight." He spoke, frantically, urgently, as if he meant it.

"Eli, that's not necessary. Yes, I was a virgin, but I knew what I was doing." She patted his shoulder, trying to calm him.

"You know the worst part of me, and still you let me . . ." His chest heaved as if he struggled to carry a heavy burden up a long, dark road.

She wanted to put some space between them, give him time to return to his right mind.

But it wasn't that easy. She was sitting on him, naked. He was stretched out beneath her—long, muscled, beautiful as only a man who worked for his living could be. "Eli, you didn't force yourself on me. I mean, obviously. You have no reason to feel guilty. I knew what I was doing." She tried a joke. "I knew what went where, didn't I?"

Predictably, he didn't laugh. He didn't even seem to hear her. Sweat popped out on his forehead. "We can go to Reno now, marry, and get home tonight."

She should have been annoyed. She *was* annoyed. But he was suffering for reasons she couldn't fully comprehend. "As romantic as that sounds, no."

"You love me."

Propelled by shock, she sat all the way up. "That is so not true." Her voice had gone into the highest possible octave, and she attempted to bring it down. "Eli, you've slept with other women. You didn't love them."

"No, but I was a typical guy who didn't equate love with sex. You . . . waited. It means something that you gave yourself to *me*." He sounded like he wanted to believe that. . . .

No. He sounded as if he did believe that.

But men were supposed to be logical. So she would attempt to be logical. "I slept with you because you shared yourself with me, showed me you're a man of deep feelings, a man who had suffered, not like most guys, because you've got a hangnail or something, but for good reasons."

She already recognized his stubborn look, and he was wearing it now.

"Eli, I managed to get through my teenage years without having sex. It happens. So now I'm twenty-three years old, which means I know how to wait, plus I've got a smidgen of intelligence. I recognized that we have shared interests and we've now shared experiences and here's the good part." She smiled brightly. "I know how to seize the day."

"As do I." He sat up. "But what happened between us wasn't seizing the day. That phrase indicates a deliberate choice was made. What we did wasn't a choice. It was a force of nature."

His words rang a little too true for comfort.

They hadn't enjoyed sex; they'd survived a cataclysm.

He continued. "Nothing you've said has changed anything. You love me." He looked deep into her eyes. "Don't you?"

She found she couldn't look away.

He was confusing her. He wasn't right. She knew he wasn't, and yet . . .

What was it about this man that made her yield, and yield eagerly?

She was pretty enough, and as far as she could tell, most high school and college guys would do it with a troll. So while she hadn't spent her whole life getting hit on, she'd had plenty of opportunities to dance the bump. Once her father started playing chess with her life, guys even more eager had stepped onto the stage of her life.

She had been interested in sex; she hadn't been interested in the guys.

Now Eli had come along, they hadn't yet spent a total of twenty-four hours in each other's company, and so far she thought he was basically a stodgy, stuck-up man with intimacy issues . . . and yet here they were, chest-to-chest, face-to-face. His breath touched her lips, his eyes gazed insistently into hers, and he was still inside her, the two of them so intimately touching that they were one.

He thought she was in love with him.

She wasn't. She couldn't be.

But his gaze hypnotized her, and his palms settled on her shoulders, warm and supportive.

"We barely know each other," she whispered.

"I know you." His fingers massaged up and down her arms. "And you know me better than any other human being on earth knows me."

"Yes. I do." She was good for him. When she had first met him, he'd been closed as tightly as a clamshell. Now the shadows over him were lightening—and she gave herself the credit. If she stayed with him . . . would he heal from the wounds of his childhood? Would he open himself to love? "We don't need to get married merely because we know each other."

"I need to marry you." He spoke definitively. "Call me old-fashioned, but I need to bind you in every way possible. I need to know you'll be here with me tomorrow and forever."

Old-fashioned? Yes, that probably defined Eli Di Luca. She compromised. "Let's wait a few days. Think about it."

Beneath her, his legs tightened. He lifted his hands from her shoulders and, with his palms embracing her chin, he caressed her cheeks with his thumbs. "I can't wait a few days. I don't need to think about it. I didn't expect this to happen, but I can't in all honor touch you again until we're married, and I can't be with you and not touch you. You've seduced me, Chloë, and all I want is to taste you, be inside you, make love to you in every way possible. You've got to marry me. I'd rather be lost in the Andes in the deep snow than bear this kind of suffering."

Inside her, he was stirring, hardening, even while his fingertips slid down to trace her nipples. The excitement of making love for the first time reignited. She breathed deeply, thrusting her breasts more deeply into his cupped hands.

"Yes," he murmured. His eyes grew darker, his gaze more intense.

Inside, she flexed, not because she meant to, but because she had to.

He flinched. His breathing grew deeper. His gaze smoldered. "Please. Chloë. I can't be strong if I don't have you. We were meant to be together. Please. Marry me. Live with me. I want you desperately. I need you . . . desperately."

His words coaxed. His touch seduced.

She wasn't thinking right. She knew she wasn't.

But maybe he knew something she had barely realized. Maybe she did love him. Maybe that was why she went to bed last night and dreamed, not of the diamond, but of him. Maybe that was why she woke up this morning as excited as a child on Christmas morning. Maybe that was why his kisses stirred her and his pain made her ache for him.

Maybe that was why they were together now, intimately joined and desperately in need, and she felt . . . oh, she felt as if she were made anew. Torn between the desire to giggle and a blossoming horror, she said, "My God. I do love you!"

"Yes." His eyes fluttered closed as if in relief, then opened again, and now the chocolate brown of his eyes was warm, happy.

In love. In *love*. No matter where she put the accent, she couldn't quite believe it.

"So you'll marry me? Now? Tonight?" His urgency lit a similar fire in her.

She'd been trying to be logical and now . . . now she was considering . . . she was considering marriage.

"Don't hyperventilate," he said.

"No. I won't." Although she was feeling light-headed.

She had never done anything really stupid in her whole life. But then, she'd never fallen in love before.

A woman in love must be the definition of stupid.

She took a last long breath . . . and took the plunge. "Yes. I'll marry you now. Tonight."

He kissed her, and kissed her, and before it was over, wine magazines were shoved off the coffee table and she was flat on her back on top of the cool, polished wood while he showed her again how much he wanted her.

When they were finished, she hid a smile in his shoulder. "About the wedding . . . I ask only one thing."

He had the good sense to sound suspicious. "What's that?"

"I want Elvis to marry us."

"Elvis? You mean . . . an Elvis impersonator justice of the peace?"

"I think that would be great."

"No." Eli sounded grim. "Absolutely not. Marriage is a serious business."

Chapter 28

The Elvis impersonator justice of the peace worked overtime to marry Eli and Chloë.

They used Eli's grandfather's wedding ring. It was so big Chloë had to make a fist to keep it on her left hand.

As soon as the ceremony was over, Eli drove them back to the Reno airport—they'd had the rental car less than three hours—to catch a flight back to Santa Rosa, and Eli drove to his house.

He drove to their home.

Other than "I do," he scarcely spoke a word during the entire trip. It was as if he'd said everything possible earlier and now he had nothing left.

Yet he held Chloë's hand as if he couldn't bear to let

her go, and that was enough. Because she didn't care whether he spoke. Once the ceremony was over, she didn't have anything to say either.

She'd never done anything so stupid in her life.

The phrase echoed over and over in her brain. She didn't have a doubt that marrying Eli in such a hurry was stupid. Yet she couldn't scrape up any regret. Something was keeping her unrepentant, some emotion that was growing stronger by the second.

He pulled to a stop in front of the house, and came around to help her out of his truck.

He looked as if he were in shock, drawn and pale beneath the tan.

Good. That made two of them.

When she stepped onto the chrome side rail, he swept her off her feet and into his arms.

Startled, she laughed and clutched his neck.

He stood holding her, looking down at her as if . . . as if he held his life's desire.

His expression was so intense it made her heart beat faster. Blushing, she lowered her lashes. And all the while, she was thinking, *This is my wedding night. My wedding night.*

She was trying to convince herself she had done this. Married him. She'd never done anything so stupid in her life. She must be in love.

His arms tightened, and he headed for the house.

"I can walk," she said.

"I did everything backward. I'm going to get *this* right." He ran with her up the stairs—it was interesting and a little unsettling to realize how strong he was—and put her down only to put his key in the lock and open the door. Picking her up, he carried her across the threshold. He shut the door with his foot, lowered her to the ground, pushed her against the wall, and gave her one of his patented kisses, lips to lips, tongues seeking, breath shared. When she was clinging to his shoulders, he pulled back. His eyes were almost black again, and hot, and she remembered what to do—wrap her legs around his waist so he could carry her to the couch and . . .

He said, "We can't do that."

"What?" What was he talking about?

"You just . . . I'd hurt you again." His voice was rough, a rasp on her fragile feelings. "We'll have to wait."

"What?" she repeated.

"I've got to . . . I've got business to attend to."

She stared at him, bemused and disbelieving. "At three in the morning?"

He drew a long breath. "International market."

"You sell wines to the international market?" She knew she sounded incredulous. She *was* incredulous.

But why would he lie?

For that matter, after that impassioned speech about wanting her, why would he refuse to make love to her? "You skunk," she said.

"Skunk?" He half laughed. "Skunk. As insults go, that's . . . cute."

"I can be more explicit."

228

"No." He kissed her again. "No." He kissed her as if he couldn't resist.

This time when he pulled away, she clung to the collar of his shirt. "Eli . . . even skunks need love."

His eyes were wild, desperate. Taking her hands away, he held them and said, "For the love of God, Chloë, let me . . . I need to leave you alone. Just for tonight. I can wait one night."

"Is this a test?"

"One night."

"What about *me*?"

"Be sensible." He wasn't being patronizing. He was pleading. "If we . . . do anything . . . more, you'd be too sore."

True. "I don't care," she said.

"Then we'd have to wait again, longer next time, and . . ." He tore himself away from her, crossed the room toward the stairs as if the hounds of hell chased him.

She collapsed against the wall and watched him, resentful . . . and appreciative. The man could be a butt model . . . for all the good it did her.

When he turned around and came back, she straightened up. "Changed your mind?"

"You haven't moved in yet. The master suite is this way." He hovered just out of her reach, and indicated a hallway that led off the living room. "Which suitcase do you want? Show me and I'll bring it." He acted like she had the plague.

She pointed.

He grabbed it and headed toward the hall.

She stalked after him.

The master bedroom was almost monkish in its asceticism.

She was not feeling monkish. She was feeling tired. And grumpy. And horny.

"Do whatever you need to. . . ." He faded toward the door.

"I'm thinking of a bedspread with big flowers and lots of ruffles," she announced.

He stopped. Looked concerned. Saw her giving him the evil eye. He disappeared out the door.

She flounced into the bathroom. She took a shower and put on her most boring pajamas. She climbed into the low California-king-size bed and pulled up the covers. She decided to sulk—and fell right to sleep.

She woke up once when a warm, male body pulled her close. But the next morning, when she opened her eyes, he was gone.

Chapter 29

Chloë worked in the office all day without pause, revising her manuscript, writing a new scene, understanding her protagonists for the first time, why Gabriel was so tortured, why Hannah was so withdrawn, what had instigated the terrible chain of events that brought Hannah to the attention of a ruthless murderer. . . .

When the phone rang, Chloë stared at it, shaken from her creative frenzy and for a moment not even sure what the sound meant.

But it was Eli's phone, and she didn't think she ought to answer it. She might be his wife—but who knew that? Except her. And him. And after last night's chaste experience, she wasn't sure that he hadn't changed his mind.

Besides, she didn't have time to answer it. Her fingers tingled with the words waiting to be written.

The answering machine clicked on. The caller started leaving a message. "Eli, it is Tamosso Conte and I wanted to know if you—"

Even before he gave his name, she recognized the voice. Snatching up the phone, she said, "Papa? What are you doing calling me here?"

Her father stopped right in the middle of a word. "Chloë?"

He sounded so surprised that at once she felt stupid. "Or were you calling Eli?"

"Eli. Yes, I was calling Eli." Papa sounded off balance. "*Cara*, you surprised me. I didn't expect you to answer his office phone. That was foolish of me. . . ."

She tried to think of something to fill the awkward pause, but she'd been writing so much she had no words left for conversation.

At last he asked suspiciously, "You *are* working there, aren't you?"

"Yes, I'm working."

"Is he nearby?"

"No, he left this morning"—before she got up—"and I haven't seen him since." She hadn't heard from him either.

Short honeymoon.

She glanced down at herself. Good thing, she supposed, because when the book woke her up she had made her coffee, hustled upstairs without a shower, and started writing while still in last night's pajamas.

She was a disgrace to Southern womanhood.

"What time is it there?" she asked.

"There?" Papa sounded bewildered.

"What time is it in Italy? It must be the middle of the night."

"Yes. It's the middle of the night in Italy. Beautiful Italy . . ." Abruptly he changed the subject. "How's your book?"

"Good!" She could answer that honestly enough. "You were right. Coming here has helped me a lot."

"I am the papa," he said with authority. "I am always right."

She could *hear* him preening. "The trouble is, you believe that."

"Why would I not? It's the truth. I should perhaps call Eli on his cell phone."

"Because you're, um, business associates?"

"That's right."

"How can you be business associates? You're a leather merchant."

"I import things, you know?"

"You import Eli's wines to Italy?"

"Yes, and soon you'll be seeing Milan's best leather goods sold in Bella Terra's gift shop." He sounded remarkably pleased with himself.

"Oh." She hadn't believed it before. She'd thought her father's story about how he and Eli worked together was all a bunch of hooey. Knowing her papa, they might be doing business only because Papa had researched Eli, decided he was a suitable husband, and approached him with some kind of offer Eli couldn't resist.

Eli Di Luca, let me import your wines to Italy. I'll make your family famous in their homeland. And by the way, here's my eligible daughter.

Oh, yes. That kind of plot sounded exactly like Papa.

Wouldn't he be surprised when he found out it had worked?

She grimaced.

Surprised . . . and obnoxious.

Which would make her mother madder, which would make Papa even more obnoxious. It was a vicious circle, one that revolved around Chloë and her mother's decision to keep her a secret from her father, and while refusing to exchange a word, they scored off each other. The childish way they acted made Chloë wonder whether she could convince Eli they should keep their marriage a secret until after their second child was born. Because once her parents started fighting about Chloë's wedding, it might very well end only in bloody death and destruction.

"About Eli—do you like him?" Papa sounded sly and wicked.

"I like him. He's the best choice of a husband you've found so far." She held her breath, waiting to see whether her father would admit to his nefarious schemes.

"Ha! You are too smart for me!" Papa's voice deepened and became positively jovial.

Chloë wanted to blurt out the news. *Your scheme worked. We're married!*

No. He'd tell the world. Somehow, even if he had to hold a press conference, he would get the news to her mother. Chloë *had* to hold herself back.

She realized there was an expectant pause in the conversation and hurried to fill the gap. "I'll tell Eli you called."

"You do that. *Arrivederci, mia figlia bella.*"

"*Arrivederci, mio papa.*"

After they hung up, Chloë tapped a pencil on the desk. What business did her father and her husband have together? Was Eli really selling wine to Italy? The night before, had Eli abandoned her to talk to her father?

That was a lowering thought.

But she didn't have any time to verify Eli's relationship with her father.

She needed to write, and she needed to do it *now*.

Moments of inspiration had to be utilized when they occurred.

Chapter 30

"I don't know how you did it, but congratulations. You saved the winery." Val Mowbray handed Eli the IRS confirmation of payments received. "Whoever is after you will be fried when he finds out, because the IRS can't touch you now."

"Good." Eli was so angry—at Joseph Bianchin and at himself—his lips felt stiff. "Pay off the rest of the debt ASAP. I'll want the receipts this afternoon."

"You bet." Val offered her hand. "You're back in business with barely a hitch."

Eli shook her hand, left her office, and walked down Bella Terra's main street.

He should have felt a huge weight off his chest.

Instead he felt guilty. So guilty.

And that made him furious.

Last night, when he demanded Chloë marry him, he hadn't been thinking about the winery. He hadn't been thinking at all. He'd been in some kind of primitive claiming mode. She was his, and he would take her.

Like that was better.

He ran up the stairs to Bella Terra's police station.

No matter how he looked at it, no matter how he figured it, he had used Chloë without a thought to what she wanted, to what she needed.

Even if he somehow managed to justify last night as an act of primal possession, he had still managed to remember to fax Conte a copy of the marriage certificate and collect on their bet. So after all these years and all his struggles, the facts stared him right in the face; he was like his Silva relatives, like Abuela, playing every angle, selfish to the bone.

But he resolved that he would be a good husband to Chloë. It wouldn't be hard; all through last night and all through the morning, he'd had to fight the desire to rush to her side and make love to her the right way . . . slowly, with control, until she was out of her mind with need, passion . . . love.

She loved him.

He had planned for that. Worked for it. Why it was a surprise, he couldn't quite comprehend. Why it was a delight . . . He knew damned well why it was a delight.

He'd told her his secrets, all except one, the one he would have to live with—the memory still made him shudder at the weakness he'd shown her—and still she'd given herself to him. He'd done a lousy job of loving her—and still she wanted him.

She loved him in spite of himself, and he didn't expect that. He had never imagined any woman would crack the shell he'd built around himself and, once inside, like him despite the frailty she discovered.

He would feel better, he thought, if he confessed his crime to Chloë. She was a logical woman. Surely she'd understand.

If she didn't . . . well, here he was, continuing his plan to make her happy by involving her in solving the mystery of Massimo Bruno.

Most women wanted jewelery. Chloë wanted murder.

The air in the police station was different: musty, thick, full of frustration and anger and justice served in spite of itself. The place had that 1930s ambience: linoleum floors, glass partitions, the hallway of doom that led to the holding cells, and a big, scarred, wooden countertop with a bored cop waiting to help you.

Luckily for Eli, he knew the cop. "Hey, Terry, did you draw the short straw?"

Terry Gonzales was fifty, overweight, cynical, funny, and the smartest man Eli had ever met.

Right now, he looked half-asleep, but then, he always did. When the time was right, he could move with frightening speed. "I broke up a fight at the Marinos' bar last night," he said. "At the Beaver Inn. They say I caused unnecessary damage to their fine establishment."

The two men looked at each other.

The Marinos' bar was so *not* a fine establishment.

"So until the dispute is settled, I have to do office duty. How can I help you?"

"Is DuPey around?"

"No, he's ignoring his paperwork to show the hotshit FBI guy around town."

"Who's the hot-shit FBI . . . Oh, you mean Wyatt Vincent?"

"That's the one. He's here to tone us up so we're prepared for big-time crime." Terry's delivery was always deadpan.

But Eli thought it was especially so now. "You don't approve."

"I've been a cop here for thirty years. You know how it is with us old guys. We don't like change."

"You're so full of it." Terry kept abreast of all the new developments, but he always played down his abilities. He'd once told Eli that in law enforcement, it was better to be underestimated. Kept a man alive.

"It's a job requirement," Terry said. "Anything else I can help you with?"

Eli thought for a moment. "Is anyone here who examined that crime scene in the water tower?"

Terry's smile was the definition of a shit-eating grin. "There's Finnegan Balfour. He's in the patrol room having coffee. You want me to call him up?"

"No. Absolutely not." Eli remembered the kid from

Kansas, the one who knew his way around a still, and asked, "Why did DuPey hire him, anyway? He seems to be . . ."

"Worthless? Inept? Bumbling? Lazy? A yokel?"

"Yes. So he really is—"

"Worthless? Inept? Bumbling? Lazy? A yokel? Oh, yeah. He's DuPey's wife's nephew. He was a cop in Kansas, got into trouble back there, and in exchange for expunging his record, he had to promise to get out of town." Terry leaned his bulky elbows on the counter. "You know DuPey. He's a pretty good police chief, but we all know who's in charge at his house, and it sure as hell ain't him. The kid is even living in their basement."

Remembering that Finnegan had developed a crush on Chloë in record time, Eli asked, "What'd Finnegan get in trouble for?"

"Let's just say his moral standards are a little skewed." Terry smirked and shook his head. "Don't worry. He's not dangerous. Just one of the dumbest sons a' bitches I've ever met."

"Guess not. He's managed to land himself a cushy job at the Bella Terra Police Department, he can't get fired, and he's living with his relatives." Eli watched as Terry thought about it.

"Damn. I hate that you're right." The policeman heaved a heavy sigh.

"How about Mason?" Eli asked. "Is he in?"

"Dr. Death? He's in his office, chortling over some new crapometer the Sacramento Police Department is letting him borrow. I'm telling you, there's something wrong with a guy who deliberately chooses to cut up a corpse. But I remember when he was a kid. He was the one who loved dissecting the owl pellets." Terry buzzed Eli through the gate. "Come on back."

Eli walked through and headed for the offices, then stopped and returned to the front desk. "Terry, if a woman is married for her money and doesn't know she was married for her money, what do you think would happen if she found out?"

"Her husband could never sleep safe again. Why? You broke and looking for a rich wife?" Terry guffawed, deep in his chest.

"Not anymore," Eli answered.

Terry stopped laughing.

Eli walked to Mason's office.

Chapter 31

Mason was leaning over a machine that vaguely resembled an overhead projector, except with blinking lights and a myriad of gauges. He glanced up, and although Eli had never before visited him at work, Mason accepted his presence without a blink. "Come and look at this."

Eli entered the small, cluttered office crammed with leather-bound books and smelling of dust and something funky, like old socks.

Since Mason was the coroner, Eli hoped he was right—old socks seemed like the best possible option. "What do you have there?" He hovered off to the side in case the machine really was a crapometer and Mason wanted him to look at some crap.

"This machine analyzes trace amounts of drugs in dried blood or in corpses who have been dead a very long time." Mason ran his hand through his thinning hair.

"The corpse who has been dead a very long time—that's the body we found in the water tower?" Eli edged closer.

"Yep. I've found out all kinds of stuff about him. He was starving and dehydrated, but also"—Mason turned to Eli, eyes manically bright—"he was given a huge dose of a laxative to empty his bowels."

Eli stepped back again. "Why?"

"I'm not a detective or with the FBI, although Wyatt says I would be a good addition to the force." Mason sounded smug. "But I surmise whoever our corpse's killers were believed he'd swallowed something of value and they wanted it to come out."

"Why didn't they just cut him open?" That seemed easier.

"Maybe they were scared off by someone poking around the water tower." Mason shrugged. "Maybe they were squeamish."

"Squeamish? They stabbed him."

"Digging around in someone's intestinal tract after something is not the same as a quick in-and-out." Mason beamed with pride. "Autopsy is not for the weak at heart!"

"Or for the weak of stomach." All too obviously, Mason enjoyed his job. "What did you decide? Do you think the body is Massimo Bruno?"

"No doubt in my mind. It took forever, but I found a photo of him in our archives." Mason went to his desk and pulled a small, fragile black-and-white photograph from the out-box.

Eli took it by the edges and stared at a gentle-looking older gentleman. "He doesn't look like a gangster. He looks like he should be growing peaches."

"One thing police work teaches us: Appearances are deceptive. Now look at this comparison." Mason brought a scan of the photo up on his computer, and next to it he added the photo of the mummified head.

Eli leaned forward. The hooked nose, the broad forehead, even his glowering expression . . . the resemblance was striking. "Would you send that to my e-mail?"

"Sure." Mason found Eli in his address book and hit SEND. "Going to show your mystery-writer girlfriend?"

"She's not my girlfriend." Eli wasn't kidding about that. "Did you find out anything else pertinent to the case? Anything else I should know?"

From the door, DuPey said, "You don't need to know anything at all. Damn it, Eli, why use the police force to help you court that girl? Just use your famous Di Luca charm and she'll fall into your hands like ripe fruit."

Hm. Apparently DuPey was still bitter about Eli's brief hookup with his now-wife while in high school. Eli hadn't known DuPey was sweet on Karina . . . truthfully, he wouldn't have cared, either. High school was just high school, and only DuPey had taken his romantic relationships seriously.

But DuPey's father had been the chief of police before him, the biggest bully the county had ever seen, and whenever something went down at the high school DuPey, scrawny DuPey, had caught the brunt of his father's displeasure. But DuPey never squealed on anyone to his dad. At the time, if Eli hadn't been so wrapped up in his own misery, he would have admired DuPey for his steadfast courage.

Instead, he had tamed his inner beast with a liberal application of girls attracted to a handsome, anguished, rich Di Luca brother.

"I'm interested, too, DuPey," he said, "and believe me, so's my grandmother. It's not every day the most famous disappearance in Bella Valley is solved."

Wyatt slid past DuPey and into the office. "He's right, DuPey. Everyone does seem to be obsessed by this Massimo guy. The older people want to know who killed him, and the younger people want to know how many of his bottles are out there, if their grandparents have one, and how much it's worth. Fascinating case. Fascinating response." He turned back to face DuPey. "It's such a minor crime and such a big fuss . . . it shows that you really have kept a good lid on crime in this area." He had that kind of take-charge personality that marked him in Eli's mind as a guy who could never have stayed with the FBI. Owning his own company was probably inevitable, and having the kind of company where he consulted on law enforcement improvement gave him a natural edge in the world.

Bringing him in to consult was probably the smartest decision DuPey ever made.

"I admit, the last few months have been a shock, with two murders, a couple of attempted murders, vandalism that destroyed hundreds of thousands of dollars' worth of merchandise, and now a still in the water tower and a mummified body." DuPey came in and collapsed in Mason's chair. He looked tired again, and when Finnegan poked his head in the door and cleared his throat, DuPey groaned.

"How's Miss Robinson doing?" Finnegan shuffled his feet and asked shyly, "Did she have any nightmares from finding the body?"

Mason chortled like a monkey. "Her? Are you kidding? That woman is too smart for that kind of missish reaction. By God, Di Luca, she was asking all the right questions and making all the right conclusions. She even told me Massimo's killer had been looking for something, and asked if I thought Massimo might have been given a laxative."

Finnegan lurched backward in horror. "She asked about that?"

"Yes!" Mason said. "She's simply brilliant. If she had a stronger stomach, she would have been a great coroner."

Wyatt's blue eyes danced with amusement. "But then we'd be missing a great mystery writer. Right, Di Luca?"

Eli nodded. "DuPey, how's the tune-up of the department going?"

"Good," Wyatt answered for him. "DuPey's a great people manager, and he utilizes every possible method to keep crime down in Bella Valley."

"Including keeping my officers busy . . . even if they are related to my wife." DuPey looked meaningfully at Finnegan.

Wyatt watched with amusement as Finnegan faded back toward the patrol room, and shook his head. "I understand why you're stuck with that boy, but damn. What a loser."

"That's not all." DuPey rubbed his face with his hands.

Wyatt turned to Eli. "All I can do here is show DuPey what can be done once a crime is committed. Trust me, sometimes when I consult in a police department, I have to start from the ground up—organize the department, tell them how to do the day-to-day operations." He clapped his hand on DuPey's shoulder. "But DuPey's like me. Police work is in his blood."

"No way around it," DuPey agreed, and got to his feet. "Eli, no offense, but you don't need a preview of the case before I break it to the press. So give my regards to Miss Robinson, tell her I'm glad to hear she's as good at solving real crimes as she is at creating her own, and we'll see you later." DuPey pushed Eli toward the door.

Eli followed him past the offices, past the desk where Terry was talking to Finnegan, and into the tiny lobby. "So, DuPey, since when did you look forward to talking to the press?"

"I don't. But Wyatt really knows his stuff, and he thinks we can get some great press off solving the Massimo disappearance. He might be a grandstander, but in this case, he's right—funding's being cut in law enforcement on every level, so when we get a case that'll catch the attention of the public, we need to milk it for every drop of positive attention." DuPey's droopy, bloodhound eyes were red rimmed. "Me, I'm more worried about the guys who are still alive getting their asses into trouble."

Eli glanced up and saw Finnegan talking to Terry. "And keeping your wife's nephew busy?"

"He's an idiot." DuPey made the pronouncement with a finality that made Eli grin. "How's your grandmother? Is she completely recovered?"

"Nonna's doing well. We're keeping security at the home ranch and she's got a nurse with her at all times."

"Glad to hear it. No sign of Massimo's wine?"

"No, and your beloved mystery writer, Chloë Robinson, took a shot at searching for it, too." Although she wasn't Chloë Robinson anymore. Chloë Di Luca . . . Tonight he'd remind her to change her driver's license. Tonight he'd remind her why she had married him. Tonight . . .

"She couldn't find it, huh?" DuPey grimaced in disappointment. "If we could locate that bottle, I'm pretty sure this itchy feeling on my scalp would go away."

"Lice?" Eli asked.

DuPey smacked him on the arm. "Instinct. It's like someone is watching and waiting for his moment to spring."

"Bianchin."

"Yes. No. I don't know. There's more to it than that." DuPey rubbed his hand across the back of his neck. "I keep thinking this is bigger than we could ever imagine."

Chapter 32

Eli couldn't help but agree. But he didn't need DuPey poking around and finding out about those pink diamonds. Once the police got involved, Eli and Chloë had no chance of keeping the matter quiet, and if one valuable bottle of wine could bring thugs to Bella Valley, he couldn't imagine what would happen when they discovered priceless jewels were involved. "I think what's going on is a hangover from the trouble Joseph Bianchin started when he decided he wanted Nonno's bottle of wine."

"But why did he decide he wanted it now? That's the question."

"He's old. He can't wait much longer." Eli put a note of amusement in his voice.

DuPey nodded sheepishly. "There is that. Yeah, I'm probably just getting jumpy."

"I can't blame you. Ever since I saw that body in my water tower, I've been a little jumpy myself." Eli checked his watch. "Okay, I'm out of here. Go catch the bad guys and make our streets safe once more."

"Bite me," DuPey said, and disappeared into the back.

Eli raised his hand in farewell to Terry—Finnegan was still yammering, and Terry looked close to an explosion—and headed out the door and toward Bella Terra's town square.

Penny's Bookstore had been in business for twenty-three years. Penny knew what he liked; she ordered books on wine growing and he bought them. But she was upstairs with some of the valley's early tourists, so he strode over to mystery and suspense and took a look.

He found it almost at once: *Die Trying* by Chloë Robinson.

The cover was simple, striking: a white mask with a drop of blood on the corner, set on a black background.

Eli picked it up, looked at Chloë's photo on the back, flipped through the pages.

Wyatt Vincent obviously knew his way around a murder, so the fact that he liked Chloë's novel meant it was well researched, well written. Nonna read voraciously, and she had loved it. Finnegan was an idiot, and he'd read it.

Apparently what she wrote appealed to everyone.

And while Eli did occasionally read fiction, reading Chloë's book seemed . . . he didn't know . . . as if he were surrendering to Conte's schemes.

Which was dumb. He and Chloë *were* married. He *had* surrendered. He might as well read it—

Penny, sixty-five, brisk, and a saleswoman from her head to her toes, appeared at his elbow. "Eli, how's it going?"

"Good. How's business?"

"Slow. It'll pick up next weekend."

He lifted his brows in inquiry.

"It's Grape Blossom Fest. Eli, you've lived here all your life. How can you not remember?"

"It's dumb," he said.

"It brings the tourists," Penny countered. She looked at the book in his hands. "Ohhh. I heard you had a houseguest. Going to dip your toes into her novel?"

That sounded suggestive to Eli, and he was sure Penny had meant it just that way. Damn it. He couldn't buy this book here. That would start another round at the Let's Gossip about Eli Di Luca Fest. "I wanted to see what she looked like before she cut her hair," he said, and put the book back on the shelf.

Penny picked it up and looked at the author photo. "She cut her hair? Why?"

"Because she's a woman," he said, and glanced at his watch. "I've got another couple of stops to make, so I'll be on my way."

"Wait! I've found an antique book written by a winemaker in New York State."

"I'll get it next time I'm in." He lifted his hand in farewell and headed toward the resort.

Two more stops, and he could go home. Home to Chloë, working in his office, her hair a bright dandelion puff, her face mobile and expressive, her smile inviting, her tits . . .

No. He couldn't think of that: the perfect size to fit in his palm, the way she turned warm and pliant when he rubbed his thumbs in slow circles around her nipples. *No!* He needed to concentrate on her hair, her face, her smile. And her words.

Everyone who met her thought she was intelligent and perceptive. Certainly everyone on the police force admired her. His grandmother thought the world of her.

When Eli wasn't mad at her for looking through his private papers, he thought she was smart, too. And he hated that, because she made him think he ought to call Abuela.

All his life he'd seen that women like Nonna and maybe Chloë saw things differently than he did. They didn't seem to see the black-and-white. For them the whole world was painted in soft shades of gray, or maybe even in color. With women, who knew?

And Chloë wasn't right about Abuela exactly. He wouldn't go that far. But the stuff she'd said had merit.

She wants to see you. She says there's no one else. And, *You shared something, the two of you.*

They had indeed. Long nights of lessons. Her blunt impatience with any confusion. That stern, wrinkled face with those big, dark eyes staring at him, and her sharp, thin voice saying, *Don't tell me you can't. You're my hope for this family. You will do it.*

Abuela had not been kind, and she had been determined to keep him in the Silva family. What was hers, she kept. . . . Hmm.

He might have gotten that from her.

But through long evenings spent in her suite of rooms, she'd taught him about wines. Not merely taught him— she had seared her knowledge of wines into his memory as if graven in stone. She knew things no other teacher had taught him, and as he created his Di Luca wines, he'd put her knowledge to work time and again.

He walked through the Bella Terra lobby, ignoring the greetings, and into the Luna Grande Lounge.

The bar was empty; Tom Chan was nowhere in sight.

Eli pulled out his phone and looked at the screen.

Last night, he'd programmed in Abuela's number.

He didn't know what he was thinking, or why he'd done it. It had been a stupid impulse, like this one to give her a call.

But in his head, he heard Chloë's voice.

She says she's sick. She's probably looking at the end of her life and thinking she wants to make contact with the grandson who has made her proud.

He touched the screen and watched it dial. Country code, phone number. He could make this call and . . .

And say what?

You controlled my life for six long years and made every day a living hell?

The phone was ringing.

I can't sleep through the night, because I'm waiting for my cousins to beat me with a bat? Women have told me I'm emotionally damaged, and since I can't love the woman who loves me, I guess they're right?

"Hello?" It was her. Abuela.

His fingers went cold. He recognized the tobacco-roughened voice.

How could he ever forget?

He cut the connection and put the phone back in his pocket.

No. He would not speak to her. Not now. Not ever.

Irritated at himself for imagining Abuela needed him, he checked the time.

Where was Tom? Where was Victor?

He heard them talking as they crossed the lobby, his friend who tended the bar and Victor, newly anointed as the lead concierge for Bella Terra.

Distractions, both of them, and he was glad to see them walk through the door. He said, "I've called on you two because I need something put together, something very special for me, and I know you both have the skills and the know-how to do this in a hurry. I wouldn't trust this to anyone else."

Chapter 33

When someone rapped on the office door, Chloë jumped and gasped, grabbed the arms of the chair, and stared, wide-eyed, at Eli.

He'd pulled her out of a murder scene in Maine, and her heart raced in alarm.

"Sorry." Eli looked almost as surprised as she felt, and gestured behind him. "I made noise when I was coming up the stairs."

"It's okay. I was scared. Hannah realized her patient had been murdered and she had been set up as the perp." Chloë leaped to her feet. "I've got to go to the bathroom." Not the most romantic thing to say to your new husband, but she'd been sitting at that desk for hours without a break, and now that he'd interrupted her she realized . . . she really had to go.

While she was washing her hands, she looked at herself in the mirror.

Hair standing up on *half* of her head.

No makeup.

Still in her pajamas.

He was truly getting to see her at her worst.

She walked out, barefoot and feeling like a bumpkin.

He, of course, looked the same as always, in jeans, shirt, work boots, and a darkly handsome austerity. He said, "So, seeing the water tower, the still, and the body helped you with your writing."

"It's added a historical edge to the story that . . . Never mind." She glanced at the bookshelf. He didn't care about her writing. He didn't read fiction.

No wonder he seldom smiled. When he woke up in the morning, he had nothing to look forward to all day long except real life . . . although the way he was looking at her right now, all smoky-watchful, told her he was pretty pleased with his life.

She ought to point out that she looked like hell.

No, she ought to keep her mouth shut.

"I've got something for you," he said.

"About time," she breathed.

"No, not that." He strolled across the office, his gait reminding her he was dangerous, a man of depths and secrets. Delving into his pocket, he pulled out a Tiffany blue box tied with their signature white satin bow.

Her breath caught.

He went down on one knee, slid the bow off the box, opened it, and brought out another, smaller black velvet box.

"Oh," she whispered.

He popped that box, showed her the black satin interior with Tiffany & Co. embossed on the top part of the inner satin cover . . . and the glittering rings within.

The platinum wedding band was set with white diamonds separated by platinum crosses. Beautiful . . . but Chloë had trouble focusing on the band. It was the engagement ring, and the size and color of the center stone, that commanded all her attention.

"It's a one-point-seven-two-carat pink diamond," he said. "Set with two white diamonds on the side. I thought it was beautiful and symbolic of our courtship."

Tears rose in her eyes. Silly tears . . . why should his gesture affect her like this?

"Courtship?" She half laughed. "Is that what we're calling it now?"

But the fact was—they were already married. He didn't have to do this. And yet here he was, this strong and wonderful man, on his knee before her, fulfilling her girlhood dream of the perfect man at the perfect time with the perfect ring.

"Maybe for you it wasn't a courtship. I always knew what I wanted."

More tears in her eyes, and one that escaped. Hastily she wiped it away.

"Last time I proposed, I wasn't on my knees," he said.

"Last time you proposed, it wasn't a proposal." Her voice wobbled, and she steadied it. "It was a demand."

"Last time I proposed, I was angry at myself for being so precipitous. Now I want to ask you—would you spend the rest of your life with me?" He looked so serious, as if her answer mattered . . . as if he loved her.

She knew he didn't. He'd never said the words, and if he had, she wouldn't have believed him anyway. He was too damaged for love.

But she knew she was healing him, civilizing him, and maybe someday soon his soul would open and touch hers.

When she didn't reply right away, he took her hand. "We have a lot of talking to do, about what we want in our lives, but I swear I'll take care of you, Chloë. I'll support you in your writing. You've done so much for me, and I'll do everything in my power to make you happy."

"I would like to spend the rest of my life with you"— she stroked her fingers through the dark warmth of his hair, and her voice was wobbling again—"and I promise to take care of you, too, and do everything in my power to make you happy."

"Thank you." He pressed a kiss on her fingers, and his voice vibrated a little, too. "Thank you." He cleared his throat. "Listen, Tiffany's was really nice about the rings and told me to bring you back so you could pick out the one *you* want. Because if you want a different ring, I'm fine with that."

"No! I can't imagine a better choice than this set." She grinned. "I'll get a pink highlight in my hair to match."

He surprised her when he grinned back. "You do that." Taking the diamond-encrusted wedding band out of the box, he brought it to the end of her finger. "You're sure this is the one?"

"I'm sure."

He slowly placed it on her finger.

The cool metal warmed quickly as she flexed her hand.

"Is it the right size?" he asked.

"It seems perfect."

"I measured your finger last night while you were asleep," he said smugly.

"Of course you did." She couldn't imagine Eli leaving anything so important to chance.

Next he plucked the engagement ring from its nest and slowly slid it on next to the wedding band. The pink diamond's emerald cut flashed with glorious color. Its clarity was like looking into a deep, sunlit pool in a fantasy world. "It's the most beautiful thing I've ever seen," she whispered.

"Not even close." He stood and took her in his arms, and held her as if she were more precious than any diamond. "Would you like to go out tonight?" he asked, his voice slow and warm and deep.

No. I want you to show me a reason to stay in. "If you like."

"I thought we'd go down to the resort and celebrate." He smiled crookedly down at her.

Smile at me like that, and I'll go anywhere and do anything. "I guess this all means the marriage is still on?"

She expected him to laugh, not kiss her until she remembered, in slow, meticulous detail, every moment of last evening . . . or at least the part leading up to their leaving for Reno.

"The marriage is definitely still on." He sounded almost hoarse, as if the effort of keeping himself in check were wearing on his resolve. "It will never be over."

"Then why don't we stay in?" she whispered.

"Let me take you out to dinner. Let me do one thing right."

"You're obsessed with doing one thing right. You need to realize—you definitely do one thing right." She rubbed her hand down his spine.

He looked down at her, all dark-eyed smoky passion, and stroked her hair off her forehead. "You're a miracle," he said.

She didn't feel like a miracle. She felt like a woman driven by frustration and uncertainty, and the need for a shower.

He acted like a man who desperately wanted her . . . but what did she know? Apparently nothing.

Taking her by the shoulders, he turned her toward the door. "Go put on some clothes. Put on something pretty . . . like your dress yesterday. I promise you'll enjoy the evening."

*   *   *

When Eli and Chloë walked into the Luna Grande Lounge, she came to a halt.

A long, white cloth–covered table was set with eleven old-fashioned blue-and-white plates and heavy silverware and filled with people: Nonna, Olivia, Bao, and a lot of people she didn't recognize. As inquiring faces turned their way, she asked, "Eli?"

"I invited my family."

"What's up, Eli?" A handsome man—he had to be Eli's brother—lounged at the far end of the table. "What's making you suddenly social?"

"I'd like you all to meet Chloë." Taking her hand, Eli lifted it and showed her rings to the room. "My wife."

Chapter 34

The roar that went up from Eli's family and friends made Chloë catch her breath and take a step back.

They were on their feet, all of them, rushing in an incredulous tidal wave to shake Eli's hand and hug her, or hug them both, and all of them were laughing and talking at once.

Eli pulled Chloë in close, and in that quiet way of his, he said, "Calm down. Calm down! You're scaring Chloë."

Still laughing, the crowd backed off a little.

Eli introduced them.

Nonna, of course, pink cheeked and smiling, with Olivia off to her side and Bao standing back, arms crossed, watching the whole group and everything around it.

Eli's brother Rafe and his new wife, Brooke—they were pleased, yet at the same time, so involved with each other they saw Eli's marriage as a logical extension of their own love story.

Francesca Pastore, easily recognizable as one of the most beautiful women in the world, and Kathy Petersson, former air force officer, now forced by rheumatoid arthritis to use a walker. Proud mothers-in-law of Rafe and Brooke, both loved the excitement.

Francesca demanded to see the ring, appraised it with a shrewd eye, and in her exotically accented voice said to Eli, "Spectacular, *caro*. I never expected to see such a gesture from you. It must be love."

Eli laughed softly. "The stones are beautiful, but nothing to compare with my wife."

Francesca tapped him on the cheek and turned to accept a flute of champagne from Tom Chan.

Noah, the youngest Di Luca brother and blessed with the family's good looks and charm, hugged Chloë hard, kissed the top of her head, and said, "I don't know what you see in my oldest brother, but if you really want to tie yourself to that old man—well, welcome to the family."

Tom Chan grinned broadly, poured champagne for everyone, and proclaimed himself the matchmaker who brought them together.

Victor Ruíz, the resort's concierge, stood in the door

diverting the resort's guests by explaining it was a private party.

And it *was* a party.

Eli placed Chloë at the head of the table and sat at her right hand. The champagne and then the wine flowed as one course followed another, and when the dessert appeared—chocolate mousse with fresh-peeled mandarin orange slices soaked in Grand Marnier— Chloë stood. "I have to use the ladies' room."

"So do I," Nonna said promptly.

Bao and Olivia rose at once.

"Me, too." With Francesca's assistance, Kathy laboriously got to her feet.

Brooke jumped up. "I thought we'd never go."

Eli looked at his brothers. "Why do they go together?"

"They're like gazelles—they travel in packs," Noah answered.

"Stuff it, Noah." Brooke tucked her hand into her mother's arm and helped her navigate her way through the lobby and into the restroom.

Like the rest of the resort, the ladies' room was clean and beautifully designed, with cream marble countertops, fired blue ceramic sinks, blue art-glass lighting, and a long row of stalls. French vanilla potpourri lightly scented the air, and in a small waiting room elegant stools sat in front of lighted makeup mirrors.

As if they were synchronized, the women entered the stalls, left the stalls, and washed their hands, then rushed into the waiting room. There, where the light was the best, they demanded to see Chloë's rings.

She held out her hand first to Brooke, then Kathy, then Francesca, then Nonna, then Olivia. Even Bao, the tough bodyguard, seemed impressed with the gems that sparkled for joy.

Francesca examined them the longest. "A very impressive array. A man who gives jewelry like that is trying to tell a woman something."

"That he loves her," Olivia said solemnly.

"I don't think so," Chloë said, then clapped her hand over her mouth. She must have been tipsy or she wouldn't have admitted it out loud. But it was too late; she couldn't pull it back. "Eli isn't in love with me. Not yet. But he has potential"—she smiled as laughter rippled through the bathroom—"and I have great hopes."

"Chloë, I can't help but think Eli must love you," Brooke said. "I can't imagine another reason he would marry you."

"Honey!" Kathy said in horror.

Brooke rolled her eyes in embarrassment. "I didn't mean it like it sounded. I meant—he's such a loner. I never imagined he'd actually get married unless he found someone appropriate, his age, who knew the wine business and Bella Valley and would be the perfect helpmate when it came to promoting his wines. You, Chloë—you're beautiful, you're charming, you're young, you're intelligent, you have your own career—you're the antithesis of the woman I thought he would marry. So *I* believe you've captured his heart."

Nonna looked from one to another and smiled fondly.

"I hope you're right." Chloë caressed her rings and thought how nice it would be to think he loved her.

"Well, really," Brooke said to the group. "What other reason would he have for marrying her?"

Abruptly, Chloë's lighthearted sense of intoxication vanished. What other reason could Eli have for marrying her?

Chapter 35

What other reason?

He'd insisted on the wedding because they'd had sex and his sense of honor demanded they make it official.

When she thought about it like that, the whole state of affairs seemed outrageous, this party surreal, and a very real alarm caught her by the throat.

What other reason could he have for marrying her?

Chloë started to speak, to speculate.

The door of the bathroom burst open and a group of three women rushed in. One of them headed right into a stall. The other two halted at the sight of the Di Luca party.

An attractive brunette of about thirty-five saw them,

her eyes lit up, and she said, "Brooke Petersson! I heard you got married, and to Rafe Di Luca of all people. Is it true?"

"Yes, Karina, it's true." Brooke took on a militant posture. "It's Brooke Di Luca now."

"It's about time!" Karina swept in and hugged Brooke. "After all those years of him leaving you and you hanging around Bella Terra waiting and waiting, I imagine this must be a huge relief."

Caught in a bruising embrace, Brooke looked over Karina's shoulder at Chloë with an I-want-to-kill-her expression clear on her face.

Chloë didn't blame her. After thirty seconds in Karina's company, Chloë had her number. This Karina, whoever she was, was not someone well liked; nor was she someone to be trusted. She was one of those women who loved to slip the knife right between the ribs.

Karina was married, of course. She wore a nice ring, not too big, not too small, but it was the only moderate thing about her. She talked too loud and too fast. Her clothes were expensive and worn too tight, as if she didn't want to admit to the encroaching weight gain. In Bella Terra's casual resort atmosphere, her overly plucked brows and exotic eye makeup were too dramatic.

In an aside, the careless kind important people give to the elderly, she tossed out, "Hello, Mrs. Di Luca, hello, Mrs. Petersson."

Both women stiffened at her dismissive tone.

But Karina had chosen the wrong opponents.

"Karina, it's good to see you." Kathy leaned on her walker and smiled in a direct way that made Chloë recall Kathy's military background. "I was talking to the Di Luca women about my shop and how many people are using me to create fruit and cheese platters for their parties. How did *your* party go last week?"

Karina took a quick, embarrassed breath. "The party was good, and you did such lovely platters. I'll be by tomorrow to pay you for my last extravaganza!"

Kathy inclined her head. "I'd appreciate that. I'd hate to think you couldn't afford to pay your bills."

Wow. Score one for Kathy.

With a smile that verged on a smirk, Nonna moved smoothly into the conversation. "Karina, I'd like you to meet the newest member of our family, Eli's new bride, Chloë Di Luca."

Karina's jaw dropped, actually dropped open.

The woman coming out of the stall froze in her tracks. She darted an alarmed glance at Karina and whispered, "Oh, my God."

The other woman hid a smile behind her hand.

Chloë didn't know what was going on, but she knew Nonna had used her as ammunition against Karina. Not that Chloë objected—but Nonna was a sweetheart, which meant Karina really, really made her cranky.

Karina snapped her mouth shut. "Eli Di Luca got married?" Her gaze slid up and down Chloë as if Chloë were a well-traveled road. "To, um—"

"Chloë is a *New York Times* bestselling author of a marvelous mystery." Nonna took Chloë's hand and squeezed it. "Eli's been helping her with her research for her next one and here we are, with a new member to the Di Luca family!"

"Well," Karina said brightly. "Isn't that nice!"

The women behind Karina leaned on each other and laughed silently.

"I can see you two in the mirror," Karina snapped.

They both froze and sobered.

"Let me see the ring." Karina snatched Chloë's hand in a strong grip. "How cute. A pink sapphire!"

Francesca started to say something.

Chloë shook her head. "Yes." She smiled brightly at Karina. "It's a pink sapphire."

"And the other stones are . . . ?"

"Diamonds, of course." Chloë put on her shocked face. "You don't imagine Eli would settle for anything else?"

Even those lesser diamonds were enough to make this Karina person turn pea green with envy. "Of course not. Not Eli. He is quite a, uh . . . well. He's a Di Luca. I'd love to know how you caught him."

"It was no secret," Nonna chirped. "She wasn't even trying."

At the killer expression on Karina's face, Chloë edged toward the door. The other women in the Di Luca party followed and stood outside in the lobby, as wide-eyed as if they'd narrowly escaped torture and death.

"Who was *that*?" Chloë asked.

"Sorry, dear, we should have introduced you," Nonna said.

"No." Chloë shook her head. "Definitely you shouldn't have. She's got such an attitude!"

"She's Karina DuPey." For a pleasant woman, Brooke could sneer quite effectively.

"The wife of the police chief? Oh. Well. In the South, when we talk about a woman like her, we always say, 'Bless her heart,' because of the clothing and the makeup." Chloë looked at the group with a limpid gaze. "Also, it's less direct than calling her a bitch."

They laughed and started slowly back to the Luna Grande.

"I've known that girl for twenty-three years, and she's always been overly impressed with her position in this town." Kathy's mouth was puckered as if she'd bitten into a lemon.

"I take it Eli used to date Karina?" Chloë asked.

"Right you are," Brooke said.

"His taste has improved," Francesca drawled.

"Right again," Chloë said.

"I think she convinced herself he hadn't married because he was in love with her." Nonna couldn't have sounded more sure.

"So much for that fond delusion," Brooke said cheerfully.

In the Luna Grande, the men seemed to have multiplied, and Chloë realized why Karina DuPey was in the ladies' room—it looked like a police convention in here.

Police Chief Bryan DuPey was there in his rumpled uniform, looking more relaxed, but still weary and worn.

Chloë had met his wife. Now she knew why.

Wyatt Vincent wore a tan suit and a white shirt, and his midnight tie was loosened around his neck. He held a glass of wine and wore a genial expression, and when his blue eyes met Chloë's, he lifted his glass in a toast. "Here's the bride," he announced.

Finnegan Balfour turned sadly to face her. "I was hopin' I'd be the one to charm you," he said.

"You do charm me," she said flirtatiously, but when he moved closer, she slipped away to Eli's side.

For all that he was handsome, Finnegan was a little odd. His uniform was perfectly ironed and so precisely creased, he didn't seem like a real cop; he seemed like an actor playing a cop on an old TV sitcom, and he watched her closely, as if he knew her better than she knew herself.

Eli put his arm around her, drew her close, and turned her to face a large, middle-aged, Hispanic officer. "I don't think you've met Terry Gonzales."

The officer had hands the size of trash-can lids; her hand disappeared in his, but he shook it gently and in a deadpan voice said, "If this boy ever gives you trouble, you let me know."

She thanked him; then as they turned away, she whispered to Eli, "All Terry needed to do was call me 'little lady' and I would have thought I was back in Texas."

Eli grinned. "I've known Terry for years. He's a good guy. Come and meet our lone female in uniform."

Robin Webster was about Chloë's age. She was pretty. She filled out her uniform well. And in her eyes

Chloë saw a cynicism so raw it hurt to see. Something had happened to Robin that sent her into law enforcement, and it hadn't been good.

"With all of you here, I have to wonder what's up?" Chloë asked her. "Did the criminals take the night off?"

"Wyatt threw a party to thank the Bella Terra Police Department for our patronage. We dined in the private room off the restaurant, and when we finished, we were waiting in the lobby for the wives and we heard your good news." Robin was polite, if not enthusiastic. "Congratulations."

"Thank you. We're very happy." Chloë didn't know why she felt the need to tell Robin they were happy; maybe it was that cynicism that spoke so loudly.

"And please, let me assure you." Robin smiled tightly. "There are officers on the beat, and I'm going back to the department as soon as I can leave here. I've had nothing to drink; you're still safe from crime."

"I didn't mean . . ." Clearly, Chloë had misspoken. "I'm sorry if I gave offense. It was a bad joke."

"No offense taken." Robin gave way to Mason Watson. "Here's the coroner to offer his congratulations."

"She's a good cop," Eli said in Chloë's ear. "But known to be a little touchy."

The coroner clapped Eli on the shoulder hard; he'd had a little too much to drink, and he spoke a little too loudly. "I never thought you'd convince any girl to take you off the market. And you got that rare treasure, an intelligent woman. Good job, Eli!"

Nearby, Nonna sighed loudly.

"Mason, your social skills suck," Eli said.

"What?" The gleam in Mason's eyes dimmed. "What did I say?"

"Nothing anyone's concerned about," Chloë said soothingly.

DuPey nudged Mason out of the way and shook Eli's hand, then shook Chloë's, then shook Eli's again. "I certainly want to make sure I offer my congratulations, too. I've been hoping for this for years."

Chloë construed that to mean that his wife had been holding Eli up as the man she should have married.

Mason shoved back at DuPey and, putting both his hands on Chloë's shoulders, he leaned into her. "Just be careful. In my business, they always say corpses come in threes. So far this spring, I've had two on my slab. Make sure you're not the third one."

"I'll do my best," Chloë promised, and stepped away from his high-octane whiskey breath.

Eli signaled his brothers.

But Mason babbled on. "I'm just saying that because the Di Luca brides seem to have a way of getting in trouble. First Nonna, then Brooke . . . They lived through it. But the third time's a charm!"

"Come on, Mason." Noah took him by one arm. "Let's arrange for a hotel room for you."

"Good idea." Rafe took his other arm. "Come on. We'll hand you over to Victor and he'll put you to bed."

As they led Mason away, he told them earnestly, "I don't care what they say around town. You guys are really nice."

They got him into the lobby, where Victor took charge.

As they returned to the Luna Grande, Eli nodded his thanks.

Karina walked in, the other wives hot on her tail. "I see you all have heard Eli and Zoe's *really* good news," Karina announced. "Bryan, have you seen Zoe's ring?"

"Chloë," Brooke corrected.

Karina blinked at her as if confused. "Right. Chloë. Such a big stone. And pink!"

"Pink?" Terry frowned in confusion. "Do they even make pink diamonds?"

"I can't imagine Eli Di Luca is going to give his bride a fake." DuPey was positively jovial.

"It's a pink sapphire," Karina corrected. "That's just as good as a diamond. Really!"

DuPey caught his wife around the waist and squeezed.

She turned to him in surprise, but something about the way he looked at her made her shut her mouth.

He spoke to the group. "I want to thank Wyatt for inviting us to such a great gathering. It's been a pleasure working with him, and I know we've all learned a lot."

Wyatt nodded and put down his glass. "It has been a pleasure working with the Bella Terra Police Department."

"We need to leave these good people to finish their dessert and coffee, and go to work now"—DuPey nodded at Robin, then at the others—"or prepare for work when the shifts are up." He lifted a hand to Eli and pushed Karina ahead of him and out the door.

The rest of the force followed, waving and calling their good-byes.

The silence that followed was profound.

Finally Noah asked, "Does she still have the hots for you, Eli?"

"Impossible," Rafe said.

The two brothers guffawed.

"Yes, except . . ." Francesca frowned. "Women like that—they're dangerous in their way. Chloë should be cautious around her."

Francesca projected a knowledge of human nature that Chloë respected. She asked, "For how long?"

"Forever," Francesca said.

Chapter 36

The evening had been cheerful and loud, full of good food and fine wines, and many toasts to the newly married couple. Eli was pleased to see Chloë join easily with his family, and after her first moment of surprise, she seemed touched that he had thought of and arranged for the party.

The ring had been a resounding success, with Rafe smacking him on the back of the head for his extravagance and grumbling that Brooke would want one next, and Brooke smacking him on the back of the head and telling him that if she wanted one, she would buy it herself.

But while on the surface all seemed cheerful, Eli was aware of unhappy rumblings among the Di Lucas. His brothers and his grandmother were suspicious, and not in a good way. Which led him to wonder when he had become the kind of man who would generate those kinds of suspicions.

When the dessert plates had been removed and the port consumed, Nonna started to rise, then sank back in her chair with a laugh. "I think a little fresh air is in order. I broke my own rule. Eli, I toasted your marriage a little too often with your wonderful wine."

Ever the nurse, Olivia came to her feet. "I'll get you some water."

"Dear, don't bother yourself," Nonna said.

"Dehydration is the leading cause of falls in the elderly," Olivia replied.

"Then I'm all right, because I'm not elderly." Nonna sounded a little firmer than usual, even annoyed.

Olivia sank back into her chair, pink cheeked.

"Eli, would you walk with me?" Nonna asked.

"Of course." Eli stood at once and went to her side.

"Shall I come along, too? Sadly, I would probably benefit from some fresh air, too." Chloë was rosy cheeked and smiling.

But Noah came to his feet. "You stay and enjoy yourself with the girls. I'll come along. I'm the only one who's gone up against Bianchin and won, so I'll be able to protect Eli if someone attacks."

That brought a jeer from Rafe and Bao, but as Nonna, Noah, and Eli went out the door, the party settled back into its former exuberance.

Nonna walked toward the back of the hotel, where

lighted paths led to the private cottages and the guests were few. As soon as they were alone, she stopped, looked around, then faced Eli. "What in the hell do you think you're doing?"

He didn't ever remember her using that tone of voice with him. "What do you mean?"

"Why did you marry that girl?" she asked.

A chill went up his spine. "Because she and I . . . got involved."

"No. *No.* You have friends, but hold them at arm's length. You have family, but never tell us what you're thinking. You invited this girl to your house. You never invite anyone, not even me."

Eli realized he might have hurt her feelings.

Her eyes sparkled with ire. "In less than three weeks, you're married? Are you trying to tell me you fell in love in three weeks?"

Eli had never believed his grandmother would see beyond her joy at having another grandson married, much less that she would be angry. He didn't know what to say. "We have a lot in common."

Noah moved to stand at Nonna's right shoulder. "What is wrong, Eli? I heard rumors—"

"What kind of rumors?" Eli asked.

"Rumors that the winery is in trouble," Noah said.

Eli couldn't believe this—and he sure as hell wasn't going to take it from his youngest brother. "I got married. People do it all the time."

"Not you," Noah said. "I like Chloë, and she doesn't deserve being used for whatever damned reason you're using her. Look, I'm a businessman. I run the Bella Terra resort, and I run it well. Once I heard the rumor about the winery, I started thinking, and let's face it, your accountant left town a little abruptly."

"This is none of your business," Eli said stiffly. "I've treated Chloë with honor, as every woman deserves, and I'll be a good husband to her."

Two guests walked toward them.

Noah cleared his throat.

Eli and Nonna moved aside, smiled stiffly, nodded.

The guests stared curiously as they passed.

When they were out of earshot, Nonna returned to the attack. "Don't try that innocent act with me, Eli. I'm your grandmother. I raised you. I know how to tell when you're lying, and you're lying right now." Her eyes were snapping. "Is Noah right? Did you marry her for money?"

Eli couldn't keep eye contact.

When he looked away, Noah said, "My God, Eli!" He ran his fingers through his hair, paced away, paced back. "I'm your *brother*. You think I wouldn't have helped you out? Is it really money? Because, bestselling author or not, I can't believe Chloë has enough to rescue Di Luca Wines if that's what needs to be done."

"Her father's wealthy," Eli said. "He offered me a deal."

"You married . . . You married . . ." Noah was stammering.

Noah never stammered.

"Didn't I teach you better than that, Eliseo? Did you

really marry this girl for her father's fortune?" Nonna sounded brokenhearted.

"I'll be a good husband to her," Eli repeated.

"As if that cures anything." Nonna touched her forehead as if to stop the ache within.

"Chloë thinks you love her," Noah said.

"How do you know that?" Eli recognized that he was getting defensive, but how could he help it? They were attacking him . . . and saying things he knew to be true. Things he had hoped to hide.

"Just look at her!" Nonna gestured back toward the hotel. "She sparkles for you. When she finds out, what do you think is going to happen? Do you think she will forgive such a bitter betrayal?"

"She won't find out."

"You're a fool, Eli Di Luca," Nonna said.

Noah shook his head in disbelief. "It's bound to come out sooner or later."

Even as the guilt rose in him, Eli tried to explain again. "I respect her. I like her. Marriages have been built on less."

"Not *our* marriages. We are Di Lucas," Noah said.

"I gave up my family to marry your grandfather. My mother cried the day of the wedding. After that, I saw her only when my grandfather was out of town. But Nonno and I—we *loved*, and it was worth the pain and loss, although to this day . . . I miss my mother." Nonna put her hand on Eli's arm. "What's going to fill in the gaps in Chloë's life when she discovers you love your wines more than you love her?"

Eli wanted to jerk away, to free himself from these reproaches and go back to his belief that he could make things right for Chloë. "I have a responsibility to the family to be the best vintner there is and make a success of the winery."

"I never taught you to believe such a thing," Nonna said. "Never."

"No." He thought of Abuela, old, stern, smoking her little cigars. "It wasn't you."

"Look, Eli, I know you had a tough time in Chile. You stalk around here like some wounded prima donna, but you aren't the only Di Luca who ever suffered." Noah knew what he was talking about. "Stop with the anguish, already, and suck it up."

"I don't act like a wounded prima . . ." Eli stopped and thought. "That's not even the right gender."

"You suffer in a silence so loud it's deafening. Grow up," Noah said in palpable disgust. "Just grow up."

The two of them squared off.

"Boys," Nonna said softly and firmly. "That's enough."

She didn't use that tone very often, and both of them backed away.

"Eli, I want you to know how disappointed I am in you." Nonna shook her finger at him. "Marriage is a blessed sacrament and you used it for personal gain. I hope and pray somehow this union survives such a betrayal. But Noah's right. I remember when you came home from Chile, so distrustful, so silent, so turned in on yourself. I thought it was a bad idea to insist that you talk about your experiences. I thought living with your brothers and Nonno and me would show you the way to open yourself up. I think now I was wrong, and I'm sorry for you." She whisked a tear off her cheek. "But mostly I'm sorry for Chloë. If you're going to make this a real marriage, you're going to have to put Chloë first, and that means delving inside yourself for the emotions you hold so tightly in check. It means growing into the man you should have been before the cold and the loneliness stripped you of your humanity." Putting her arm around him, she hugged him tight. "I love you, dear, but if—when—Chloë finds out, she's going to say this is unforgivable. She'll be right. I hope you're prepared for that. I hope you know the right thing to do then."

She let him go and started toward the hotel.

Noah lingered for a second. "You're my older brother and I've always respected you. I wish you hadn't smashed that to bits. I'd rather think the world of you . . . than not." He caught up with Nonna and escorted her back inside.

Eli looked up at the stars and wondered if they were right and if Chloë would somehow discover the truth. Because he had been alone before and survived, but now, somehow, life without Chloë would be unbearable.

Chapter 37

"That was a wonderful party, Eli." In the bedroom, Chloë spun with her arms up in the air, her skirt lifting as she whirled. Collapsing on the bed, she smiled at the ceiling. "And this is a wonderful ring." She lifted her hand and stared at it. "I love it sooo much."

His wife was a little tipsy. Taking her ankle, he held it and slipped off her shoe. "I'm glad you liked the party and the ring."

"I can tell I'm going to like being married to you. Do you know why?"

"I'm not sure." He repeated the shoe removal process on her other foot and tossed the heels toward the closet.

"Good parties, *great* jewelry, and"—she popped up like a jack-in-the-box—"you!"

He put one knee on the bed beside her, pushed her back onto the mattress, looked into her eyes, and said, "Remember that. No matter what happens, remember that." Leaning his head to hers, he kissed her with all his skill and all his restraint, and then made slow, controlled, exquisite love to her until dawn tinted the sky.

Chloë sat at Eli's desk. She stared at the marble figurine of Bacchus, the god of wine, at his smiling, foolish face, and she breathed deeply.

She'd told herself the same thing for the past three days.

Eli's family knew about the wedding. They had known for three days. It was only a matter of time before her father found out, and then her mother would find out. If Chloë didn't tell her first, she'd be hurt. . . .

She had to tell her mother.

She had to tell her *now*.

She didn't want to.

As Chloë had explained to Eli, she loved her mother, but her mother's choice to be cynical and distrusting made Chloë dread her reaction to their hurried wedding. Frankly, her mother was going to spit hissy all over Texas.

But once this task was done, Chloë could call Papa and tell him, and as angry as her mother would be, Papa would be precisely that amount of thrilled.

No matter what, though, she wasn't giving Eli up.

He was her husband. She was keeping him until death did them part. She thought about the way he held her last night and every night. Although she wished he would stop being so careful with her. He acted as if she were made of crystal, easily shattered, and although she thrilled when he caressed her, when he created a world where only the two of them existed, twisting in the slow rise of passion, she missed that raw, untamed virility he'd let loose that first night. When she thought of him, of the courtship he'd so carefully constructed for her—it was those moments on the floor, trapped between the sofa and the coffee table, that made her toes curl.

Yes, she would keep him.

Picking up the phone at last, she called her mother.

"Hello, dear. I was just about to call." As always, her mother sounded happy to hear from her. "I've been thinking of you for the last three or four days."

"Have you?" It had happened before. Her mother always knew when something was up with Chloë.

"Is your book going well?" Lauren had that faintly anxious tone in her voice.

"Really well. Eli Di Luca took me around Bella Valley and shared the history with me, and I've been able to incorporate some of the ideas into the story." The best part, Chloë thought, was seeing the resemblance between the photo of Massimo alive and the corpse in the water tower. They'd solved the dusty mystery of Massimo's disappearance, and that thrilled her no end. Now if only they could trace his murderers . . .

"You've been spending a lot of time with Mr. Di Luca?" Lauren asked carefully.

"A lot of time, yes. I like him, Mom. He's a really interesting guy." Chloë was wildly aware that she sounded like a used-car salesman closing a deal.

A slight hang of hesitation, then warm amusement. "So your father finally found a suitor who's not a dud?"

"He's different from the usual guys. He's amazingly successful. He comes from money. His family is great, really supportive, and *normal*."

Another pause. "Why are you selling him to me?" The amusement was gone.

Chloë took the plunge. "We got married four days ago."

"What?" Chloë heard a thump as her mother's chair hit the wall. Lauren was on her feet. "No!"

Chloë came to her feet, too. "We really did."

"How? Why?"

Now came the tough part. "I fell in love." Chloë waited, expecting her mother to point out her foolishness.

Instead Lauren said, "I'm going to *kill* your father."

Reaching out to Bacchus, Chloë stroked the cool, heavy marble, trying to ground herself and calm her anxiety. "I already told you, Mom. Papa may have tried to convince Eli to court me, but Eli didn't go for it. For the first two weeks, the only time I saw Eli he was a total jerk. Then he came over and we started talking, and one thing led to another, and now . . ."

"Bullshit!" Chloë could imagine Lauren pacing her small office at the university. "I recognize your father's fine hand in this. He probably helped this Di Luca plot how to get under your skin."

Chloë strove for patience. "Mom, don't you think that's a little paranoid?"

"Just because I'm paranoid doesn't mean they're not after me. My God, Chloë, think!" Lauren shot words at Chloë. "First this Eli ignored you, disarmed you, told you that he didn't need your father's money. Then he showed you around and enticed you with mysteries and murders. He rescued you from something—from falling? From a fight? From some nonsense he'd set up? Then he gave you some sob story about his dark past."

Chloë clutched Bacchus so tightly, his uplifted cup cut into her palm.

"I'm spot-on, aren't I?" Her mother drove her point home. "He has a dark past, doesn't he?"

"He had a rough childhood," Chloë conceded.

"So he told you all about it. Then what? He seduced you?"

Chloë didn't answer. Couldn't. When her mother said it like that, it sounded so logical.

"Oh, Chloë," her mother said in despair. "Haven't I taught you better than this? Didn't I teach you to always question it when these guys start telling you what you want to hear?"

"Yes, Mom, but the fact is, two people can have a lot in common without money changing hands."

"Not when your father's involved. Look around. Think with your *brain*. I'll bet you'll find out fast enough that this Di Luca fellow needed money for some reason or another."

"He bought me a gorgeous ring." Looking down at the sparkling pink diamond, Chloë smiled, her heart lifting.

"An expensive ring?"

"Very expensive." She'd looked it up on the Tiffany Web site. *Very* expensive.

"Whose money did he use?"

Chloë lost her temper. "Mom, there's no reasoning with you."

"It was a guilt ring. Or a bribe."

"When you're over the shock, I'll talk to you again."

"I'm going to kill your father," Lauren repeated.

"I love you, Mom. Talk to you soon." Chloë hung up with a little more force than needed. Leaning her elbows on the desk, she glared at Bacchus.

Why did dealing with her mother always have to be so hard? Did she always have to rain on Chloë's parade? Chloë hadn't put these last few weeks together the way her mother had. Because it wasn't true. Eli hadn't collected money from her father from marrying her. The whole idea was absurd. He owned a winery. He was one of the most successful vintners in the world. He was part of a wealthy family. . . .

But a voice in her head taunted her. *You don't know anything about his finances. You haven't asked. He hasn't volunteered.*

He doesn't know anything about mine, either. Quite the reasonable response, she thought.

The voice was relentless. *You've got no responsibilities. If you fall on hard times, you've got only yourself to support. If he falls on hard times, he could lose everything. And you know the pride he feels for his wines.*

What could have gone wrong that he would need my father to bail him out?

Her gaze fell on the locked desk drawer.

Why don't you find out?

She was a mystery writer. She'd done her research; she knew how to open a simple lock. With her nail file and her credit card, she went to work.

Chapter 38

Eli drove up to the house and got out of his truck with a grimace. He needed a shower.

He'd spent the morning in the cellar blending wines. He'd spent the afternoon in the fields with Royson surveying the developing grapes, kneeling in the dirt, arguing about the pruning, getting grubby.

He'd enjoyed every minute.

If all went well, if the rain and the sun cooperated, this looked like a good year for the crop.

No, it looked like a great year for the crop.

For the first time since he could remember, he looked to the future with something besides dread. With Chloë beside him, he could handle anything. With Chloë beside him, he was the luckiest guy in the world.

He pulled a book out from under the seat—her book, *Die Trying*, the mystery that had made her famous. He'd managed to hunt it down at the grocery store and slip through self-checkout and buy it without anyone in town noticing. He hadn't read any of it yet—he really was too busy—but somehow owning a copy eased his guilt. And he would read it. He really would. Someday.

Running up the stairs to the main level of the house, he got out his key.

All he had to do was learn to live with this niggling fear that his grandmother and Noah were right, and that somehow, Chloë would discover the deal he'd made with her father.

She wouldn't. How could she? He wasn't going to tell her.

Conte sure as hell wasn't going to spill the beans.

Nonna and Noah had picked at him until he coughed up the information, but no matter what they thought of him and his reprehensible behavior, they were his family. They would never betray him.

And he was doing everything right with Chloë, treating her with fastidious care, never making the mistake he'd made the first night: losing his temper, using her with an impetuous lack of control. Every moment of their lovemaking, he had been so careful with her body and her passions, learning where to touch, how to kiss. . . . She was so responsive, so beautiful . . . she made him yearn. She made him live. . . .

He let himself into the house. Put the book down on

the table beside the door. Made his plans. Shower, shave, dinner, and then . . .

Chloë stood in the kitchen, head down, staring at something on the counter. On the breakfast bar, her skull grinned at him, the small pink diamond they had found stuck jauntily between its teeth.

"How are you doing?" He smiled, happy to see her waiting for him. "Did you get a lot of writing done today?"

Several things happened at once.

She looked up, her eyes as flat and desolate as the Mojave Desert.

She held up her hand to stop him, and her rings were gone from her finger.

And he noticed the suitcase of death, packed and sitting by the door.

He halted in his tracks. "What happened? What's wrong?" Stupidly, the truth never occurred to him. "Is your mother ill?"

"Not at all. I spoke with her today." Bitterly, Chloë said, "She's in prime form."

He should have relaxed. At least she hadn't talked to her father.

But something was *very* wrong. She looked casual in a white T-shirt and blue jeans, but her light khaki jacket looked like travel gear. "What did your mother say?"

"I told her we were married." As Chloë spoke, her face never changed expression. The lovely, animated woman was still, stiff, and cold. "She said my father had set it up."

"Yes, well . . . you knew he was matchmaking." Eli was feeling his way through a minefield.

"But I didn't know my exact value. Now I do. Four hundred and fifty million dollars."

That was the exact amount Conte had given Eli as a bailout.

His heart stopped. *She knew.*

"I'm impressed," she said. "I never imagined I was worth so much."

"Chloë . . ." He started toward her.

She lifted some papers off the counter and, as if to ward him off, she waved them at him. "Better not come too close. I snooped into your file. You know how angry that makes you."

He recognized those pages. She'd found the bank transfer from Conte's bank to his.

"I picked the lock on your desk."

He should have moved the documents. What a fool he'd been—but it had never occurred to him that this author was handy enough to break into his desk.

She added reflectively, "Actually, after I saw the papers and realized what they meant, I slammed the drawer shut so hard it broke. . . . Sorry."

She could not have sounded less sorry.

Right now, his violated privacy and his broken desk meant nothing. She'd gotten suspicious, she'd sought the truth, and she'd found it. Now he had no choice—he had to make her understand why he'd done what he'd done. "Chloë, let me explain."

"Explain what? It's easy enough." Her voice rose. "You set me up every inch of the way."

"I didn't. I didn't want to take your father's money, but—"

"You had no choice. I know. Something to do with your beloved winery?" She smiled like a shark, with all her teeth.

"My accountant embezzled everything." Lame. That sounded lame.

"I guessed right!" She threw back her head and laughed, a full-bodied, painful laugh. "So Di Luca Wines was in trouble, my father found you and made you a deal you couldn't refuse, and you took it."

"It wasn't that easy."

"Of course not. I'm sure you suffered every time you pulled me farther in. Looking back, I'm in awe of your strategy." She took a step toward him. "Pretend to dislike me, offer me a mystery to solve complete with a body—did you know Massimo was there when you took me up to see the still?"

"No."

She laughed again, quietly, chillingly. "I don't even know why I'm asking. You've lied in every way possible. Why would you tell me the truth about this?"

"I'm not lying."

"You introduced me to your grandmother and allowed her to charm me." She swallowed. "Please tell me your grandmother isn't in on this."

"No! After we were married, she guessed." And

Nonna had been right. The whole debacle had hurt Chloë badly. *He* had hurt Chloë badly.

"She's very perceptive."

"She was angry."

"I'll bet she was." Chloë took a breath and launched back into her tirade. "You used your connections with the police department to get more info about Massimo's murder; you claimed someone broke into the cottage so that I had to live with you. . . . No one ever did break in, did they?"

"No."

"And once I was here, you produced an absolutely *heartrending* version of your childhood." Sarcasm etched every word with acid. "I must have had 'sucker' written across my forehead."

She wasn't being fair now, but he supposed he got what he deserved. "It wasn't like that."

"The sex was great, but then, boo-hoo, I had to marry you because seducing me hurt your already wounded soul and made you afraid you were like your mother's relatives. We couldn't have that, could we?" She closed her eyes. "And when we came back from Reno, you couldn't sleep with me for fear you'd hurt me. . . ." She opened her eyes, and they were hot with rage. "No, wait. That was the cover story. You couldn't sleep with me because you had a dowry to collect. Most men have sex on their wedding night. You were busy cashing a check."

"It wasn't like that," he repeated.

She slapped her palm on the counter. "It was *exactly* like that. You had a party for us to announce our wedding—you wanted to make it hard for me to leave. You gave me these rings"—she picked them up, walked to him, put them in his hand, and curled his fingers around them—"bought with my father's money."

He caught her wrist and held her in place. "I didn't mean to hurt you."

"Hurt me? But that's not what's important here, is it? As long as *you're* not hurt, everything's okay." She yanked at his grip, yanked so hard he was afraid she would bruise herself.

He let her go. "Give me a chance to prove myself to you. Chloë, please."

"What's the matter? Is the deal null and void if we're not married a certain length of time?"

"The length of the marriage isn't specified by the contract."

She bit her lower lip hard enough to make it turn white. "A contract," she whispered. "Of course. It was a business transaction. There had to be a contract." Clearly she hadn't expected that, and somehow, knowing that had made it worse for her.

"Please believe me," he said. "It started out as a necessary evil and became so much more. I admire you so much. Stay with me."

"You admire me. Thanks loads. Why would I take a chance on you? If I ever hurt you, you would never forgive me." Color blotched her cheeks and her chin, and she observed him as if he were some kind of vermin. "After all, look at the way you're treating your maternal grandmother, an old and ailing woman who reached out to you. Our marriage could never work."

"Don't leave me. Chloë, *please*. When I gave you the ring, I meant everything I said. We can be married forever. We can have a wonderful life together. We can make our home here, raise a family—"

"Do you love me?"

He froze, stared at her like a deer in the headlights.

"That's what I thought." She covered her eyes as if she couldn't stand the sight of him. "With all the other lies you told, not even you can tell that one." She walked toward her suitcase, picked it up as if it weighed nothing. "You said you hated Abuela for using you without affection, for making you a thing of value rather than a person. So tell me—how did you justify treating me as badly?"

He couldn't. Of course he couldn't. "Where are you going?"

"Home. Texas." She held his gaze, contempt in every line of her body. "Where I belong." She nodded toward the grinning skull. "I'm leaving you my inspiration. I don't need it anymore. I don't need anything to remind me of the horror that lies within the human brain, or to recall the treachery of the human spirit. I've got it all figured out now."

No. He had to keep her here. If she left, he didn't have a chance. If she left . . . he might never see her again. "It's going to get dark. You shouldn't drive, not while you're so hurt."

"I'm not hurt." She clipped off the words. "I'm in a rage."

"Of course. I know you are." He thought rage was keeping her on her feet. "For tonight, stay in the cottage. You can be alone. I promise I won't bother you."

"So the cottage is safe?" she mocked.

"Perfectly safe," he answered.

She stood, breathing hard, then nodded. "I need to plan the trip. Decide what I'm going to do. And you're right—I shouldn't be driving. All right. I'll stay in the cottage tonight, and leave in the morning." She started for the exit. "Don't bother to hang around to see me off."

He looked down at her diamond wedding band, at the pure and glorious engagement ring. "I have my savings. It wasn't enough to save the winery. But I promise you, I paid for your rings myself."

She stopped in the doorway, looked back at him. "I'm impressed. Too bad I don't want those diamonds anymore."

Chapter 39

Three and a half hours later, Eli finished the book, *her* book, *Die Trying*. He put it down on the table, turned down the stereo, leaned forward, and tiredly rubbed his eyes.

The book was about death and murder, yes, and who did it and why, but more than that, it was about people, about overcoming adversity, about love and trust. He had heard Chloë's voice in every line, and saw her soul in her belief in the goodness of mankind.

She said she'd rather be a fool than be like her mother, distrustful and cynical.

He had personally proved Chloë was a fool for believing in him based on nothing more than her love for him.

He stood.

He had to go out to her. He had to talk to her, explain . . . something.

But how? He had no excuse for what he'd done. Nonna said so. Noah said so. Eli knew it. He'd always known it.

He had thought he would die of shame and loss if he lost the winery. The winery had been better than any living human being because the winery was a thing that could not die.

Never had he realized that it couldn't love him back. It couldn't laugh with him or tease him or wrench his guts with its sorrow.

If he had to crawl on his knees, he would bring Chloë back. And when he got her back, he would crawl every day if she demanded it.

Because reading her story, hearing her words, had shown him one unalterable truth—he did love her.

He simply hadn't recognized the emotion.

Picking up the book, he flipped through it again, seeking inspiration or maybe courage. He got his keys, because he knew she wasn't going to let him in the door. Still holding the book, he walked downstairs and out the door.

The cottage was right across the yard, the windows lit by the warm glow that signified that Chloë was within.

His heart pounded as he walked along the path, and he wished he could do everything over again.

He wished he could go back to being the man he was before, without feelings or needs.

He wished he didn't ache like this, didn't want to fix things with Chloë so desperately he could think of nothing else.

The cottage loomed before him.

He wished he weren't in love.

And he exalted in the knowledge that he had fallen for the one woman he could love forever.

As he approached the porch, he fumbled with the keys, finding the right one by the feel of its teeth.

He still didn't know what he was going to say, what he was going to do. He knew only that he had to make Chloë understand that—

Boom!

The explosion rocked the ground, lifted him off his feet, threw him twenty feet, and slammed him onto the pavement.

A fireball rose thirty feet in the air.

Heat singed his face, his hair, sucked the oxygen from his lungs.

He blacked out. Fought his way back to consciousness.

Then he was up, running toward the cottage.

The heat drove him back. He could hear screaming; it was his.

Chloë. Chloë! She was in there.

No. Pieces of the roof, of the walls, were scattered around, burning in small imitations of the massive fire at the cottage.

Chloë wasn't in there. She was gone, blown to pieces.

The flames roared and laughed.

Eli found himself staring at the fire, so bright that it burned itself onto his retinas. He was clutching the book again. Still.

He knew he had done this. He'd lied to Chloë. He'd told her someone had sabotaged the cottage to lure her into the house with him.

It had come true.

Somehow, this was his fault.

He heard screaming again, but it wasn't him this time. Sirens. It was sirens.

Red lights flashed. The fire engine whipped by him, got so close to the cottage he thought the engine would ignite. Firemen leaped out, hooked onto the hydrant, and started spraying the area. Not the cottage. The cottage was a loss. They wanted to contain the flames, not let them spread to the vines, because . . . because the winery was important to the local economy. Because they thought he cared.

More sirens behind him. And blue and red lights.

Someone, a man, shouted in Eli's ear, "Come over here. The EMTs want to check you out."

Eli didn't really hear. He couldn't comprehend . . . this.

"Eli Di Luca!" A man spoke his name in a firm tone. "You don't have any eyebrows left. Come over to the ambulance. They think you need oxygen."

Eli turned his head and looked at Wyatt Vincent.

"Come on, man. You're in the way." Wyatt gestured toward the cottage.

It was already burning with less intensity. Most of the flammable material had been blasted away.

"Let me do my investigation," Wyatt said. "You're going to want to know who did this thing."

Eli touched his forehead. The skin felt parched. Wyatt was right; Eli had no eyebrows, and the first inch of his hair broke off in seared, brittle chunks. With a nod, he walked to the ambulance. The other EMTs had fanned out over his yard. One female remained.

She told him to sit down.

He sat.

She handed him a mask.

He put it on. He coughed as oxygen drove the smoke from his lungs, and remained motionless while she bandaged his ear. Apparently it was bleeding from a cut.

She checked his head and put an ice pack on the bump forming on the back of his head. She spoke to him, waved a flashlight in his eyes, asked him his name.

Eli looked at the light, answered the questions.

A heavy hand fell on his shoulder. DuPey asked, "Was someone in there?"

Eli nodded.

DuPey's hand tightened. "Chloë?"

Eli flipped the book over in his hand. He looked at her photo. He nodded.

"Jesus have mercy." DuPey crossed himself, then turned away and started shouting at his men. "Where's

Wyatt? Get him over here. He said he was going to do the investigation. Get him over here!"

Uniformed figures appeared silhouetted against the flames. Terry. Finnegan. Some others. Nameless, faceless shapes moving and shouting . . . while Chloë was no more.

No. It wasn't true. It could not be true. If she was gone, Eli should know.

Police drove up the driveway.

Police drove down the driveway.

The firemen put out hot spots around the yard. They sprayed the cottage itself.

Eli sat numb and blank, unthinking, unfeeling, waiting for some great bleak wave to break over him.

Then something . . . something caught his attention.

Something was wrong. Something was off. Something didn't make sense here.

He started examining the vehicles in the drive.

Where . . . ? Where was the blue Ford Focus? Where was Chloë's car? Where . . . ?

Who had taken Chloë's car?

In his pocket against his leg, his phone vibrated. And vibrated.

He didn't care.

Where was her car? Had it burned, too? Had the firemen pushed it out of the way?

. No, and no.

Where was Chloë's car?

The cell phone's vibration stopped, and started again.

He stood, searching the area for a visual, and as he did, he pulled out his phone and glanced at the caller ID.

Chloë Robinson.

Chloë was phoning him.

He answered, barely catching the call before it went to voice mail. "Chloë?"

"Eli. Listen, Eli." It was her voice. Her voice, high-pitched and frightened. "He's trying to drive me off the road."

"Who?" For the first time since the explosion, his brain clicked on.

Someone had blown up the cottage. Someone had tried to kill Chloë. Who?

"I don't know. Big pickup. Big tires. Behind me." She sounded frantic. "It's dark out here, totally black, but he tried to pass on an inside corner and push me off the road."

Someone realized she was still alive. Someone was chasing her.

Eli cupped his hand over the phone, spoke quietly and rapidly. "If you see a spot that looks safe, drive off fast into the bushes, jump out and—"

"Here he comes again!" she shrieked.

The connection went dead.

"Chloë!" he yelled.

The EMT took his arm. "Mr. Di Luca, I understand you just got married, but she's gone. I'm sorry for your loss."

Eli glanced at the woman, and with a jolt realized he had to shut up, get away quietly, save Chloë. Because . . .

She was alive. Chloë was alive.

Where? Where was she?

The EMT tried to move him. "Mr. Di Luca, you've had a shock. You should sit down again."

He had to think. How could he find Chloë?

This woman really looked concerned about him.

He needed a distraction. "Is that one of the firemen who's hurt?" Eli pointed toward the vineyard, toward a place where no one stood.

"What?" She looked around.

"Yes. I saw him go down. No one's close. I'm fine, really." He sat down again. "You should go and check on him."

With a glance at him, she picked up her bag and hurried away.

Eli surveyed the area.

The firemen were busy.

DuPey was directing the investigation. Policemen were scouring the grounds. He recognized Terry's patrol car, but he couldn't see Terry anywhere.

Exactly what he needed.

Standing, he strolled over, projecting confidence with every stride. Opening the door, he slid inside.

GPS. GPS. All he had to do was locate the GPS for Chloë's phone.

Picking up the mike, he called Patricia. Terry wasn't

hard to imitate; Eli lowered his voice and spoke with Terry's deadpan delivery. "Can you get me a location on a cell phone?"

"You bet, Terry. What's the number?"

Eli recited each numeral slowly and clearly, the way Terry would, then sat waiting, mouth dry, heart pounding, until Patricia came back and said, "Current location is Browena Road almost at the summit. You at the fire? What happe—"

Eli clicked off. He slid out of the car, looked down at his hands.

The book was gone. He must have left it by the ambulance.

He patted his pockets. His keys were gone.

He'd had them when he came out. He needed them now. He had to get his truck out of here. He had to go after Chloë.

He ran inside. Got his spare keys. Ran back out. He climbed in his truck, maneuvered it around. "Hey!" he shouted at one of the young patrolmen. "Move your car. You're blocking my way!"

The boy looked at Eli. Recognized him. Said, "Now, Mr. Di Luca, I can't do that. You're in no shape to drive."

Eli looked around.

DuPey was headed in his direction.

The EMT was running toward him.

This was why Eli owned this truck. With a shrug, he put it in gear, turned toward the vineyard, and drove over the Di Luca family's 1974 planting of zinfandel grapes, his grille and bumper knocking over the trellises, his huge tires crunching the vines as he headed for the main road, leaving the fire and the grief and the chaos behind.

He was going to rescue Chloë.

Chapter 40

Chloë drove the night-ridden, winding mountain road in a frenzy of fear, taking the corners too fast. Trees and road signs flashed past. Her tires skidded on the dry pavement. She heard the roar of a powerful pickup as the driver accelerated for another shot at her, and in her rearview mirror, the wide-set headlights blinded her.

On the left, the mountain climbed. On her right, a precipice dropped into darkness. She had no idea how far or how fast it descended. She knew only that she was near the top of the mountain leading out of Bella Valley, and if the truck behind shoved her over the edge, she would roll and roll. And die.

She held the steering wheel too tightly, her palms

sweaty. She accelerated, prayed for a clear road, and drove the white line, blocking him, keeping him back.

But her puny engine was no match for his. He caught her on an outside curve, moved into place beside her. She caught the flash of looming steel; then metal crunched as he slammed his pickup into the side of her car, driving her toward the edge. Her tires dropped off the pavement onto the shoulder. She shrieked. She was going over—

Headlights flashed toward them. *Oncoming car.*

Beside her, brakes screamed. The truck disappeared from the edge of her vision, moved back behind her, and the car drove past them, flashing its headlights.

This was her chance. She put her foot to the accelerator, shot ahead of the pickup, used her car's smaller size and her own skill to drive the curves, pulling in tight, then racing ahead.

On a straight stretch, he caught her again. She braced for him to race up beside her. Instead he tailgated her, so close and tall his headlights shone through chrome bars and over the top of her car. If he didn't back off, he was going to hit—

He slammed into her from behind, his souped-up vehicle pushing her Focus ahead of him like the high school bully shoving the class shrimp.

Chloë tried to outrun him.

But he had the bigger engine. He had control.

She was locked with him, sobbing, terrified, as they took corners too fast, as he wove from side to side, pushing her, tormenting her. Laughing at her. Here and there a metal barrier flashed past, a mockery of safety. The pickup backed off for a moment; then his engine roared again, and he came up for the kill.

In the dark, she saw the flash of a country road, maybe a driveway.

She didn't hesitate.

This was her only chance.

She turned the wheel fast and hard. Skidded sideways. Saw the truck's lights headed right for her door panel. Her tires caught; she hit the gas—and was airborne.

The road was nothing but a turnout that dropped straight off into nothingness.

She screamed, "Eli!"

The car flew through the air, branches smacking the windshield. It hit the ground, the impact knocking the breath out of her. She slid frontward, then sideways, then backward. Trees battered the fenders, the bumpers. One headlight shattered. The seat belt bruised her. The air bag inflated in her face. The car flipped, then flipped again and hit a tree—and stopped. Stopped hard. Stopped fast.

No motion around her.

But she was still alive. Still alive.

She was right side up on a slope so steep only the seat belt held her in place.

The motor was racing.

Her head hurt.

Her heart was pounding.

The killer was still up there.

Get out. Hide.

She shoved the deflating air bag aside, killed the motor and the lights.

The silence was immediate, black, oppressive . . . dangerous.

High above, she heard the distinctive roar of that massive truck.

In a panic, she fought her way out of her car. Her shoulder ached. Beneath her, pine needles slipped and slid on the precipitous incline. She got the door shut—if he could see the car, she didn't want him to know she had escaped—and headed downhill, feeling her way through a forest so dark and deep she thought she had fallen into another century. She moved as fast as she dared on the steep incline, groping through underbrush, running into trees, panic moving her.

Far above, a searchlight flashed on.

She froze, ducked, crept behind the trunk of a tree. And watched.

The wide searchlight scoured the folds of the earth, looking for her. It touched on her car, lingered there, splashed into a stream, and headed for the tree where she hid. She crouched, pulled her feet in tight, pressing her back against the trunk, praying that he couldn't see her.

He couldn't. Could he?

Not unless he came down here. Or unless she panicked and ran.

She wouldn't do that. He'd tried to murder her. If he saw her now . . . Did he have a gun? Would he shoot her, leave her body for the animals to consume? If she died here, would Eli ever find her? Would he search? Would he even care?

She muffled a hysterical laugh.

Of course he would search. He was searching now. No matter what, he would find her, save her, and if that wasn't possible, if she died tonight, he would get his vengeance on the man who had killed her.

Knowing that made her feel better. Not a lot better. But better.

The light clicked off.

She lifted her head and listened.

The pickup door slammed. The engine started, rumbling low and deep. He made a three-point turn. She heard it: backward, forward, backward, onto the road.

And he was gone.

She leaned back against the trunk, exhausted, trembling, still afraid to move for fear he'd left someone at the top of the turnout to wait her out.

She was pretty sure that wasn't the case. He had seen nothing when he flashed her car except a crumpled mass of metal.

Against all odds, she had survived.

But the night was so thick it pressed on her eyeballs. Sounds rustled in the brush. And she was still so frightened her teeth were chattering.

Her heroines would never be so cowardly. But she was cold, scared, hurt in ways she'd never imagined she could be hurt, broken in body and soul.

Eli. She had been going to stay in the cottage. She

really meant to. Yet she couldn't stand being so close to him, knowing he was waiting until morning to talk to her again. Knowing her love for him made her weak. She wanted to forgive him. She wanted to forget he'd used her. But her mother taught her to think logically, and Chloë knew that when a man based a whole relationship on one gigantic lie, she could never trust him again.

So she'd run from him, wanting to get away from his betrayal.

And someone had tried to kill her.

Why? Was it some guy on a drug-fueled rampage, out to kill any person he saw?

Or was he after her?

Why would anyone be after *her*?

Because he hated her father? Because he'd found out about the pink diamond?

Because he didn't like her book?

The idea wasn't as stupid as it sounded. Some of the e-mails she'd received were nothing short of crazy.

She could stay here, try to sleep, wait until morning . . . but what if that guy *was* after her? He would come back in his pickup and come down to make sure he'd finished the job.

Oh, God. Oh, God. What had she done to deserve this? She was a writer, someone who imagined adventures, not someone who lived them.

She had to get up. She had to get away, go downhill, hope she found shelter or . . . No, wait.

She could call Eli. Or 911. Or . . .

Where was her phone?

It was in the car.

But she had to get her phone. The phone was her only chance to live through this night . . . because on her own, she would never be able to escape alive.

She stood. She stepped around the tree. She looked up.

She couldn't see anything. Not *anything*. There was no moon. The meek starlight could not pierce the branches to reach the floor of the forest.

But this was stupid. The car was somewhere in the inky dark, close enough for her to find. She climbed, using branches and brush to pull herself up, and found the fast downhill trip meant a tough uphill grind. She thought she was close to her car. Then she found herself at the bottom of a rock cliff that extended as high as she could reach, that she couldn't find a way around . . . and she still couldn't see anything.

The trees creaked in the breeze. The scents of pine and cool dirt swirled in the air.

She stood there, her hand resting on the cold, hard stone, and realized—she was absolutely, totally alone.

Her car had disappeared. Her cell phone was gone. She couldn't go up. She couldn't stay here. She had to go down.

She sniffled, wiped her nose on her sleeve, and sniffled again.

She started limping downhill.

She wasn't as afraid of the killer now.

She was afraid of the wilderness.

She was a city girl who had flunked out of Girl Scouts.

She didn't know how to tie a knot or start a fire.

There were probably wolves out here.

The night was so dark. The stars wheeled across the sky. Every time something brushed her face, she softly screamed and flapped her arms hard enough to take wing. Once she flapped so hard she slipped and fell.

Bats. Or bugs. Or both.

Every inch of this mountain was steep.

Her sneakers were not made for this kind of descent. They were boat shoes. They had little nautical flags on the heels. They were *cute*. They weren't made to walk for hours and hours. And hours and hours. And hours.

Stupid California. No civilized place would have mountains so steep she had to sit on her butt and slide. And slide. And slide faster and faster until she slid right off an embankment and landed in the soft dirt that wasn't soft enough.

The impact knocked the breath out of her and made her feel her bruises—her side and her shoulder—and her right cheek felt as if she'd punched herself with her fist. Which, during the car's tumble, she very possibly had.

She rested there because . . . because she was tired. She wanted to give up. She wanted to curl up and die.

This was Eli's fault. Why wasn't he here instead of her? He was the big primitive mountain man. He'd survived in the mighty Andes in the middle of winter. He'd probably laugh at her fears, pick her up, and carry her to safety.

And to hell with her pride, she'd let him.

Damn him. Where was he? She was not moving from this spot until he found her.

Tears sprang to her eyes. She'd been walking for so long. She needed to sleep, but it was too chilly and—

A charley horse brought her to her feet. "No. No! Not now!" She hopped down the slope, trying to ease the cramping. "Owie, owie!"

Her heroines never got charley horses, especially not on a mountainside in a pitch-black night, and they never said, "Owie!" which was stupid and juvenile and didn't help one bit.

But somehow it did make her feel better, even when she stepped into the stream she could hear but not locate.

The cold water cured her charley horse *right now*. She cursed, stepped out, knelt, put her face right in the water, and got a drink. She splashed her face and felt sweat, grime, and fear wash away. She took off her shoe, poured out the water, wrung out her sock, put them back on, stood, and kept walking.

And realized with a shock that she could see shapes. The dark wasn't so dark. The sky wasn't so black.

Night was ending.

She rested and waited as the sky turned gray, then faintly blue. It must have been five or six in the morning. She looked up the slope, and couldn't believe she'd come down that perilous incline. She looked ahead and couldn't believe the mountain could still fall away at her feet.

Was there no level ground left in the world?

But light made the descent easier. She went around the precipices instead of falling off them, around trees instead of bumping into them. As the sun rose and cast glorious light across the land, she stepped out of the forest and into a valley . . . and there she found herself in a vineyard, overgrown and untended.

She was back in Bella Valley.

All she had to do now was find her way home without getting killed.

And she could really use some breakfast.

Chapter 41

For two hours, Eli drove Browena Road in the dark, searching for a sign of Chloë, and found it near the summit in a trail of broken plastic and glass from taillights. He followed the red shards into a turnout that ended in nothingness. Getting out of his truck, he shone his spotlight along the trail of wreckage to the shattered Ford Focus.

Had she survived?

He made the descent too fast, skidding and sliding on the slick pine needles, and discovered . . . Chloë was gone.

He found her cell phone in the back window, smashed and unusable.

Using his flashlight, he looked around, found her trail, and then, at last, he could breathe again.

She wasn't safe. He wasn't stupid enough to think that. She might have broken bones. She was probably in shock. But no one had forced her out of the car; she had left on her own. She hadn't been kidnapped, and there wasn't a blood trail. She had a determined spirit, and she would survive.

For two hundred yards, he tracked her descent. He found the place where she had crouched behind a tree. He saw where she tried to climb up and realized she was lost. There, he hesitated. He wanted to go down after her. When he thought of the drop-offs and the dangers of navigating that mountain in the dark, he remembered his own ordeals in the Andes. Because of those months he spent alone, barely surviving, hunting his food and dodging his pursuers, he knew how to track Chloë . . . in the light. For the first time, he was glad of that ordeal, for it had trained him well. He knew that in this bleak darkness, he might miss her. That would be disastrous. And if she was hurt, he'd be unable to bring her up to his truck across such steep, rugged terrain.

No. He knew every inch of Bella Valley. He knew her likely path of descent: In the dark, without any idea where she should go, he knew where this part of the mountain would take her. He would drive down, and if she hadn't made it to the bottom, he would hike up to find her.

Her computer case was still in the car, leaning against the downhill front door. He reached in the broken window and grabbed it. The computer was probably smashed, too, but someone might be able to retrieve her data off the hard drive, and right now, that might mean something in their search for whoever wanted her dead.

He knew, too, that she cherished her computer and the book she kept there, and his effort was now more about renewing his courtship than seeking evidence. He was a selfish ass, an excellent strategist, and . . . and he would do anything, sacrifice anything, including his life, for her.

In the cool predawn where morning was merely a hint and a promise, he rushed back to his truck, then headed down the road toward the bottom of the mountain. As soon as he got back in the valley and within cell phone range, his phone rang. He glanced at it.

Rafe. Undoubtedly inquiring what he was doing, where he was going, whether he had gone mad with grief.

Eli ignored it.

The sun peeked over the horizon.

Ringing again. He glanced at it.

DuPey. Undoubtedly ordering him to return and seek immediate care.

He turned off the phone and pulled the battery.

He didn't need the distraction of trying to soothe Nonna or convince his brothers he was okay. More important, he didn't need the police tracing his GPS as he had traced Chloë's.

He drove the highway, then the side road; then at the broken-down sign reading, INTERESTING WINES, he turned into the unpaved driveway. This winery had been one of two dozen in Bella Valley that had fallen victim to the recession, and if Chloë had made it down the mountain, she was here: isolated and alone, hungry and cold.

He stopped to open the gate and examined the tracks in the dirt. No one else had driven this road lately, and that meant she was safe from her killer, whoever he was.

Eli drove past the tumbledown farmhouse, looking for any sign that Chloë had been there, then turned off into the gently sloping vineyard planted with a tangle of chardonnay grapes. Putting the truck in a low gear, he chugged through the long grass beside the end row, searching for one small, lone figure.

He saw no one.

Rolling down the window, he called Chloë's name.

Nothing answered but the gently warming breeze.

He reached the end of the row. Here the mountain rose abruptly from the earth, and Eli knew that far above, Browena Road curved its way toward the summit. The mountain's natural drainage channels should have led Chloë here, so he parked the truck and walked along the tree line, looking for proof that Chloë had descended to this place. If she hadn't, he'd go up that mountain after her. He would find her no matter where she had gone.

But there: footprints beside a stream, turning, trekking along the edge of the forest toward whatever she could find in this abandoned winery. Breathless with relief and anticipation, he got back in the truck and drove along between the forest and the ends of the rows, watching for her footprints to trail off into the tall grass.

He found them, a straight line leading right to a fig tree, ripe with fruit. Some had been plucked and eaten. "Good girl," he said. *Good survival instincts.*

After that, it was easy. He drove through the remnants of a small orchard of plums and straight toward the vineyard's sagging wine-making shack.

She was there, stretched out on canvas bags on a broken bench on the broken porch, asleep.

He parked the truck, walked toward her. Tears prickled his eyes as he approached.

He'd found her. Thank God, he'd found her, and now . . . how could he ever let her go again?

Softly he called her name.

For a moment she didn't stir, so deeply asleep was she.

Then she was on her feet, her face bruised and fierce, a broken two-by-four held in her hand, ready to swing.

"Whoa!" He held up his hands.

For one long moment she stared blankly. Then she recognized him. Her eyes kindled with gladness. She flung the makeshift club aside, jumped off the porch, and ran to him.

Gently, he caught her in his arms and held her, and as he petted her head, she said over and over, "I knew you'd find me, Eli. I knew you would."

She might not like him anymore, but she did have

faith in him, and that was a start back in the right direction.

Tilting her face up to his, he examined the bruise on her cheek and under one eye, and cuts scattered across her forehead and neck caused by flying glass. "Where else are you hurt?"

"My shoulder aches, and I'm still jarred by the impact."

"Anything broken?" He didn't wait for an answer, but slid her jacket off her shoulders and lifted her T-shirt.

Her left side was bruised.

"Can you raise your arm?" he asked. "Can we get this off of you?"

"I don't think so." She grimaced and flexed her shoulder. "At least, I don't want to try."

"I'll get you out." Pulling out his pocketknife, he sliced her T-shirt from the neckline to the end of the sleeve in both directions, then sliced it down to the hem and pulled the rags away from her.

"Eli!" She half laughed.

But he was not amused. The sun too clearly illuminated bruises caused by the seat belt across her collarbone and between her breasts. Her shoulder showed no damage, but he never doubted she had smacked it hard. "Anything below the waist?"

She stepped back. "No, and I like these jeans, so put that knife away."

"Darling, cutting off your clothes is the best thing

we could do for them. They're ruined." But he shut the knife and put it away.

She looked down at herself. As if for the first time, she realized how much dirt caked her, how badly the wreck and the descent had frayed the cloth of every garment she wore. She sighed unhappily. "I really did love these jeans."

He pulled out the knife again.

Hastily she said, "Nothing's broken. Considering the shape of my car, I came off lightly. But what happened to *you*?" She touched the place where his eyebrows had been.

"I've got a first-aid kit in the truck." He helped her back into her jacket. "Let's get you an ice pack and some painkiller and move to another location, and I'll tell you the whole story."

He got her settled in the truck. He turned on the heated seat for her, gave her an emergency ice pack and two aspirin washed down with a partial bottle of water he'd found rolling around in the backseat. After putting a blanket over her lap, he drove as swiftly as he dared back toward the highway.

"Why are we moving?" she asked.

"If whoever forced you off the road knows the area, he'll know where you came down off the mountain and arrive soon."

"Like you did."

"Yes. If that happens, I want you away from there."

She shifted the ice pack from her cheek to her ribs.

"I've been thinking. It was probably some kind of random road rage."

"I don't think so," he said, and told her about the cottage.

When he finished speaking, a quick glance in her direction showed her staring out the window, her eyes wide and frightened. She shuddered in tiny paroxysms of chill and distress. Tugging the blanket up to her neck, she huddled into it and whispered, "Someone's trying to kill me. Why would someone try to kill me?"

He couldn't stand it. As soon as he could, he pulled into an isolated side road and through the gate of another abandoned vineyard. He shut it behind them, pulled a chain and lock from his tool kit, and secured the gate from any but the most determined intruders.

Driving to the farthest vineyard on the place, he turned once more and drove along the row to the end.

He stopped the truck, then came around and gathered Chloë into his arms. Tucking the blanket close around her, he carried her onto a grassy knoll. There the wind blew softly and the sun shone, and he sat and cradled her, rocking her in anguish and relief.

This comfort went both ways.

He'd almost lost her, and not merely as his wife. He had almost lost her forever. When he remembered his horror at the explosion of the cottage, and his frantic fear at her phone call . . . when he remembered that someone had driven her off one of the most treacherous roads going out of Bella Valley . . . all he could do was hold her in gratitude and in love.

She was alive.

And the shell that had for so long protected him from pain lay shattered in a million pieces. No matter what, he would never be the man he was before.

That was her fault.

She deserved all the credit.

Putting her arm around his neck, she buried her face in his chest. By increments her shivering stopped and she relaxed against him.

"I don't know who's doing this, but I intend to find out," he told her.

"I know you will." She stroked his head, found the goose egg from his impact with the pavement, touched it lightly with her fingers. "My God, Eli, do you have a concussion?"

"It's okay. I landed on my head. Hardest part of me."

She laughed a little dolefully. But she laughed.

He kissed the bruise on her cheek.

She turned her face up to the sunlight and to him, and let him press his lips to her forehead, her ear, her mouth.

Then . . . he was kissing her, really kissing her, his control crumpling under the twin onslaughts of an upwelling of overwhelming relief and desperate love.

He'd almost lost her. If she hadn't left the cottage when she did . . . If she'd been forced off the road in a different spot . . .

She wrapped both arms around him. Her lips opened under his.

And he tasted the salt of her tears. Lifting his head, he said, "I've hurt you."

"No." She shook her head. "I didn't think I would ever see you again. Then I was cold and afraid, and you found me."

Then she said the sweetest words Eli had ever heard.

"Eli, please . . . make love to me. Make me know I'm truly alive again."

Chapter 42

Eli spread the blanket on the grass, and tilted Chloë back until she rested on rough wool. The green scent of crushed grass enveloped her. The cool earth supported her. The blue sky collected wisps of clouds and sent them on a lazy journey from horizon to horizon.

And Eli leaned over her, his eyes hot, his face taut with passion. With need. For her. Yet his hands were gentle as he removed her jeans, and he winced at the bruise on her thigh, the scrape on her knee, as if her pain were his.

"I'm going to be sore tomorrow." It could have been so much worse, she meant.

"So sore and stiff. I'll take care of you." He slid her

panties off, kissed her hip, her belly. "Relax and let me take care of you."

She closed her eyes against the bright sunshine and let him ease her clothes away until she was naked in this isolated place, alone with him. She felt new, like Eve cast back into the Garden of Eden and given everything she ever desired: sunshine, a faint breeze that stirred the warm air, the mingled scents of leaves and pine and Eli.

As he removed his own clothes, as he caressed her with a barely restrained eagerness, she was reminded of that first night when he had embodied all things forbidden, sinful, and sexy, when he rode her and she rode him and they were impetuous together. She wondered, as he stroked the sensitive cup of her palms, what would happen if she commanded him to stop.

As he came up to string kisses like pearls along her throat, she opened her eyes and looked into his—and saw a flame that would consume them both.

She couldn't change her mind; it was far too late for that. He might be the epitome of a tender lover who treated her bruises with loving care, but he definitely intended to claim her.

Truthfully, she wanted him to blot the last twenty-four hours from her mind as if they had never been. As he kissed his way down her body, she knew she could depend on him to do just that.

He used his fingers in long, slow, firm strokes from her shoulders down her arms to her fingertips, then again from her chest down to her belly. He lingered over the bruises that marked her in splotches of blue and purple, and lifted her thighs and kissed her lightly between her legs. She caressed his hair, brittle and broken from the heat of the explosion, and sighed with the twin pleasures of the heat of the sun and the heat of desire.

Lifting her, he turned her onto her belly and stroked her shoulders again, pressing and kneading them until the tension she hadn't even recognized dissipated. He massaged her lower back, strung kisses along her spine, nuzzled a bruise on her hip and one on her ankle.

She lay with her cheek pressed to the blanket, at peace, yet alive with passion, knowing nothing so wonderful could ever happen again, wanting to hold each moment even as it slipped away.

He touched, caressed, loved every inch of her body, then turned her again, and while she was relaxed and quiescent, he opened her, entered her, took her in gradual increments.

Even as the rhythm increased, tranquility clung to her, wrapping her in a golden daze of light and bliss.

Then he shifted, rose on his knees, and lifted her with him, and like a magician he whipped away her tranquility and revealed the hunger that beat like a drum in her veins.

She strained against him time and again, seeking . . . seeking. Every time she got close to climax, every time she shuddered and coiled her legs around him, he slowed, brought her back to the beginning. But never the same beginning. Each time she started a little higher, a little faster, with a little more desperation and a lot more need.

At last he leaned close to her, chest to chest, and pressed deep, so deep. Orgasm swept her, starting in the center of her being and spreading along each nerve, a climax composed of sky and earth, of memories and the moment, of Eli and Chloë.

Holding his body in her arms, she whimpered with joy as her spirit soared with his.

She had asked him to make her feel alive again.

He had fulfilled his promise.

As the motion slowed at last, as the two of them ceased to be one and once more became Eli and Chloë, separate and complete, tears rose in her eyes again.

He noticed at once. "What's wrong?" he whispered as he wiped them away.

The same thing that was wrong yesterday. You betrayed me in every way possible, and I'm leaving you.

But now wasn't the time, so she shook her head. "I'm exhausted, I'm hurt, and I'm in shock."

"We shouldn't have—"

"Yes, we should." Of that she was firmly convinced. "It was sweet and good, and now I've got a memory to . . ." She really was tired, because she'd said too much.

"A memory to cherish when we're no longer together?" He was no fool. His eyes grew sharp. "You should be more careful, Chloë."

"Careful . . . because I'm thoughtless?"

"Careful because your thoughtlessness could cost you everything. Think, Chloë. The cottage blew up after I predicted it would. A big truck like mine chased you off the road." His voice was reasonable, but his eyes were angry. "There's nobody you should be more suspicious of than me. And here we are, alone in the middle of an abandoned vineyard miles from where I found you. If I wanted to kill you, I could do it here and now and no one would ever find your body."

"Don't be ridiculous, Eli. I could never be afraid of you." She smoothed his short, burned hair off his forehead, and she ached with sorrow. "I trust you with my life. I just don't trust you with my heart."

Chapter 43

It was early afternoon as Eli and Chloë drove toward
his house. The silence sat between them like a living
thing, giving weight to the air, making it difficult for
Chloë to breathe.

Not that they didn't speak. They did, but politely,
like strangers recently introduced.

He asked if she thought she should go to the hospital.

She said no, she was sure she had no serious injuries, and she completely understood that it would be
better if everyone, including her potential killer, believed she was dead.

He told her he had rescued her computer from her
car.

She graciously thanked him, more pleased than she could say but restrained by this awful awkwardness between them from going into raptures.

He apologized for not getting her clothes out of the trunk, but explained that he had feared to spend the time prying her trunk open.

She agreed, and said she'd make do somehow.

"There's a country store ahead," he said. "I'd like to stop and get us something to drink. You're no doubt dehydrated, and I'm . . . dehydrated, too."

"That would be pleasant," she said, and winced. *That would be pleasant?* What was wrong with, *Yeah, thanks?*

"I realize it's an unusual request, but would you duck down? With that hair and the publicity you've had, I'm afraid you're pretty recognizable."

"Good plan." There. That sounded a little more natural.

He glanced at her as he turned into the In and Out Gas and Food.

Pulling the blanket over her head, she slid to the floor.

"I'll be right back," he said.

He was, with bottles of water, two iced teas, and two sandwiches in a plastic bag—and a gray T-shirt.

As he drove away, he handed her the shirt.

"Thank you." She held it up. It said, In and Out Gas and Food, across the chest.

"It seemed the least I could do after cutting off the other one. I got a ladies' small. Is that the right size?"

She usually bought a medium, but he sounded anxious, so she said, "Sure." Her stomach growled. She slid back onto the seat, tucked the shirt into the door pocket, and said, "It's been so long since I've eaten I'm probably an extra-small."

"Really?" He glanced at her worriedly.

"No. This will be perfect. Thank you." Right now, she didn't care about the T-shirt. Picking up a sandwich, she unwrapped it.

"I got turkey and ham," he said. "I didn't know which one you'd prefer—"

"I don't care." She took a bite.

He pulled into the almost empty parking lot of a dilapidated bar, and stopped. Opening the other sandwich, he took half and left half between them on the seat.

They both stared straight ahead through the windshield, and that oppressive silence returned until every time she chewed she could hear it in her ears. She placed the sandwich—it was ham—on the paper, careful not to make too much noise. "How long do you think I have to play dead?"

"Let me talk to Rafe. He's the expert. He's probably freaking out anyway." Eli replaced the battery in his cell phone and turned it on, glancing at the call list. "Yeah, I've received about a hundred calls, and he's ten of them." The phone started to ring, and Eli flipped off the sound. "He's going to ask questions. Tell me, when you went to the cottage, was the alarm set?"

"Yes. I remember deactivating it. I was so angry I

had trouble hitting the right buttons, and it took me three times. I was afraid the alarm would go off and you'd come and I . . ."

"Didn't want to see me again. I know." As he opened it, the cap on his iced tea popped loudly. "Did you set it when you went in?"

"Oh, yes." Because she'd wanted warning if he tried to visit her. "And I set it when I left." Because she hadn't wanted to give him any reason to complain when he discovered she was gone.

"As soon as we get back to the house, I'll have Rafe send out someone to guard the place and check security at the house. If I know my brother, he's already looked over the blast site."

Wistfully, she thought it must be nice to automatically have that aid, and knew she was turning her back on her chance to be part of exactly the kind of family who gave that support. "What are you hoping he found?"

"Something that pinpoints the villain: who he is, where he stood, how he pulled this off." Eli's face was cold and distant, thoughtful as he concentrated on figuring out what had happened and how. "What bothers me is that everyone in Bella Valley knows we're married. They should have assumed we were both in the house. I don't understand how our killer knew you were back in the cottage."

"Maybe it's not me he's after."

Eli looked at her.

Remembering the chase up that dark road the night

before, she broke into a sweat. "I know. Wishful thinking."

"Someone's watching the house. Or watching you."

Now that they were talking, she could eat again. She took another bite of the sandwich and followed it with a long drink of peach tea. "How did he know he didn't kill me in the explosion?"

"Why did you leave?"

"I decided I couldn't stand to stay." Well, he had asked.

"You did it quickly, on a whim, without calling anybody or letting anyone know?"

"Yes."

"So if the guy who planted the bomb didn't see you go—"

A thought hit her. "Could it have been a gas explosion?"

He shook his head. "Sorry. The cottage is all electric."

"Damn."

"So if the guy who planted the bomb didn't see you go," he repeated, "he would have blown it with the assumption that you were in there. What time did you leave?"

"About eight, eight thirty."

"I came out about nine." Eli was reconstructing the time line while she listened. "Where did you go when you left the house? Tell me every place you stopped."

"I drove past the art-glass shop downtown to see if it was open. I wanted to get something for my mom, a peace offering for ignoring her advice. It wasn't open. I hadn't eaten all day, so I was starved." That reminded her that she was still starved, and she took another bite, and chewed and swallowed. "I swung through the drive-through window at Boomers and got a burger. I stopped at the gas station and filled up the tank."

"People in Bella Terra saw you?"

"Definitely. No one I recognized, though."

"Do you figure you got on the highway about the time the cottage blew up?"

"Actually . . . no, after." As she realized the truth, she blinked at him. "I saw the fire engines go shrieking past while I was gassing up. It never occurred to me they were going to your house."

Eli's brown eyes narrowed as he thought. "The question is, did someone follow you out of town to try to run you off the road, or did someone come up to the fire with the police, figure out you weren't there, and go after you then? You called me between ten and ten thirty, so the time line works either way."

That didn't make sense to her. "If it was someone who arrived with the police, how would they know where I was going?"

"The same way I did: by using the GPS on your phone to locate you. And that would probably make him someone in law enforcement. Not necessarily."

"But probably. I get it. This sucks so much." She pushed the sandwich away. "I'll never feel safe again."

"Try the turkey. It's good." He nudged his second

341

half closer to her. "We've got to get this thing solved. I can't love you if you're not alive."

Love you. He knew she'd left him. And she'd made it clear she didn't intend to return for the long run. So how was she supposed to reply to that?

"Let me talk to DuPey," he said.

"Do you trust him?" Eli was right. The turkey was good, on wheat-berry bread.

"Right now, I don't trust anybody, but I don't intend to tell him you're alive, and I do intend to intimidate him into giving up whatever information he gleaned last night at the explosion." Eli faced her. "Meanwhile, when you feel up to it, I'd like you to search the Internet for anything concerning you."

"Have the authorities announced my death?" Which would have made it a little easier for her to hide . . . but a lot tougher to get another book contract.

"Probably. Ignore that and look for threats posted before."

"As an author, I've had some pretty scary e-mails. I turned them over to the cyber unit of the FBI."

"Good for you." He sounded surprised and pleased. "Did they come up with anything?"

"This woman in an asylum in Michigan was writing them all." She put down the sandwich. "But you know what? I don't think that's it. What I'll look for first is information on Massimo and the pink diamonds. If someone is searching for the pink diamonds, my ring—"

He caught his breath.

"—was a clue. Don't freak, Eli. How were we to know that someone in Bella Valley would make that connection?"

"That is our best evidence." Opening the console, he dug out an envelope, flipped it over, and found a pen. "Who was at the dinner?"

"Your family. I think we can acquit them."

"I don't know. Nonna can be a pretty tough character." He didn't look as if he were joking.

"Bao. Olivia. Tom Chan. Victor saw the ring. We saw Wyatt Vincent's party, and that included Police Chief DuPey, his wife, Finnegan Balfour, Terry Gonzales, Wyatt himself."

Eli jotted down the names.

Chloë continued. "Francesca and Brooke were admiring it in the ladies' room, and DuPey's wife and her friends joined in."

That brought his head up. "In the *bathroom*?"

"What do you think we do in there when we go in together?"

"Talk about men?"

Chloë smirked. "Don't flatter yourself. We talk about things that are important to us."

"The news of that ring would have spread all over town in seconds."

"Not a doubt. It's a great ring." She smiled without amusement. "Most of the people who looked at it assumed, like Mrs. DuPey, that it was a pink sapphire. I didn't correct them—the whole speculation was tacky. But the killer knows it wasn't a pink sapphire, because

343

to him, the symbolism of your choice of a pink diamond as my engagement ring is all too obvious. So I believe our suspicions should at least start with the people who actually saw the ring that night."

"Agreed." Leaning forward, he kissed her on the forehead. "We'll get this figured out. Between the two of us, that bastard hasn't got a chance."

She finished her iced tea, then crumpled up the garbage and put it in the plastic bag. "What did you go out for?"

"What?"

"Why did you go out to the cottage?" Her question was really nothing but idle curiosity. He'd come out to check on his investment, of course.

"To tell you that I loved your book, and I love you." He said it so casually, as if it were a fact she already knew.

He took her breath away.

"Then the cottage exploded and I thought I was too late. I thought I'd never see you again." His voice quavered, and, picking up her hand, he squeezed it as if he needed that brief moment of contact.

For the first time, she realized the truth. "If you'd come out a few minutes earlier, you'd have been in there. As it was, you've got no eyebrows, a hairline that's suddenly receding, and a bump on the back of your head." He could have been dead. At the thought, her chest grew tight and her heart hurt.

"Good thing you didn't make your book a few pages shorter." He smiled.

She did not. "Eli, if I were the cause of your death, I would never forgive myself."

"I'm fine, and you're fine, and we're going to stay fine. I was wondering"—he gestured toward the sign that announced the name of this seedy bar—"do you want me to get you a T-shirt here, too?"

She glanced at the sign.

The Beaver Inn.

"No," she said. "Thank you."

Chapter 44

The washboard gravel road on the driveway to Eli's house jarred Chloë awake, and for the first time since they had made love, she spoke without thinking. "I know you're antisocial, but this is stupid. You need to get this fixed."

"All right," he said.

She frowned. Maybe she was still dreaming, because Eli sounded so . . . agreeable. Turning, she studied him, noted his drawn cheeks, the bags under his eyes.

Agreeable? No, he was merely tired—and still so damned handsome, with a quiet charisma that made her want to forget his betrayal and live with him forever . . . or until he betrayed her again.

No, she couldn't stay with him. But at least she could look at him and enjoy the view.

The truck reached the paved area, the ride smoothed out, and she looked out at the vineyard and in horror asked, "Eli! What happened to your grapes?"

He glanced out where twenty trellised rows had been knocked over, ground into the dirt and destroyed. "I had fire trucks and police cars and the ambulance here last night. Somebody was blocked in and they wanted out."

"I hope you plan to sue them!" She'd been hanging around Eli long enough to mourn the destruction of his beloved vines.

"Shit happens."

Obviously the last twenty-four hours had made Eli run mad. The Eli she knew would never so casually dismiss the death of so many aged vines.

They reached the parking area, and the cottage—or lack of it—came into view.

Chloë gasped. "Oh, no. Oh, no." The blast had dug a blackened crater deep in the ground, burned the lawn around it, and thrown debris into the vineyard, the bushes, and onto the house. "I know you said . . . but I didn't expect . . . It looks like an F-five tornado wiped out the cottage."

"I know." He stopped the truck and looked at the destruction. "But at least I didn't lose what is important to me—" Stopping midsentence, he gestured toward the two vehicles parked by the house. "Do you recognize the cars?"

"No. But I don't like the looks of that one." She pointed at the Mercedes CL600.

Eli looked at her as if she were crazy. "It's a great car."

"It's a car my father would drive."

Eli's enthusiasm died. "That would explain the very bodyguard-looking guy lingering beside the door."

Chloë noted the motionless stranger standing up on the deck watching them. "You're right. That's Arvid Dijkstra. He's my father's main bodyguard." She waved at him.

He raised a hand back.

"Now I wonder if the other car isn't"—Chloë took a breath—"my mother."

Eli turned to her in concern. "Do you think they were notified that you were killed?"

"Oh, God." Chloë was out of the car and running toward the house, injuries forgotten in the rush to reassure her parents.

Eli followed close on her heels.

They stampeded up the outside stairs.

Eli used his key to open the door.

As they stood in the doorway unnoticed, a blast of shouting blew past their heads.

"Did he kill her?" Her mother, tall, slim, and strong, faced off with Tamosso Conte.

Tamosso, short, stocky, defiant, and more than her match, stood toe-to-toe with her. "Don't be ridiculous, woman! He didn't kill her."

"You saw the cottage where you so cleverly said she

should stay." Lauren Robinson's eyes filled with tears, and her voice wobbled. "If Chloë has died . . ."

"No, Lauren. No. Eli is a good man. He would never allow Chloë to be hurt." Papa stepped forward to stand beside her mother. He put his arm around her and said, "Trust me, *cara*; Chloë is fine."

Chloë stepped forward. "Papa. Mom." She opened her arms. "I'm so glad you're here!"

For the space of three heartbeats, her parents looked at her in awe.

Rushing at her, they embraced her, holding her in a way that made her realize how very worried they both had been.

Chloë winced as they hugged a little too tightly, and laughed when Lauren said, "Your . . . hair!"

"I cut it."

"You certainly did!"

"*Ti sta bene il nuovo taglio di capelli!*" Her father beamed, and ruffled her hair.

"*Grazie*, Papa," Chloë said.

"It's very pretty, dear. Very . . . impish." Lauren studied her, and her voice gentled. "Your face concerns me, though. What happened? I thought that you . . ." Her eyes filled with tears.

"It's okay, Mom." Chloë pulled her back and hugged her gingerly. "I wasn't here for the explosion, and Eli has protected me from the trouble."

"What trouble?" Tamosso gestured toward the cottage. "What trouble are you having?"

"We're getting it figured out," Eli said, "and I'll fill you in when we have more time. I have to ask—how did you get in?"

Chloë hadn't thought of that, and she looked between her parents, startled and wary.

"I called your grandmother and she came down to let us in. A lovely woman." Tamosso kissed his fingertips. *"La più gentile."*

"She welcomed us very kindly," Lauren said primly.

Chloë found herself swaying a little.

Eli's gaze zeroed in on her. "As you can see, Chloë wrecked her car. She's suffered a trying ordeal, and she needs her rest."

Tamosso caressed her chin. *"Cara,* I'll call my personal physician in from San Francisco."

"Really, Papa. It's not necessary." Now that Chloë's initial alarm had eased, she yawned mightily.

Eli pulled her close. "She's been up all night. I brought her back to the house so she could sleep. If you'll excuse us . . ."

Lauren got her stubborn look. "I came here because, after I heard about this highly irregular wedding, I knew my daughter needed me."

"I came because *you* went insane about the marriage," Tamosso said to her.

Suddenly, for Chloë, it was all too much: Eli's betrayal, the drive up the treacherous road at night, the terrible crash, the terrifying descent down the mountain, the hunger, the cold, the pain, the knowledge that someone was trying to kill her . . . the knowledge that the man she loved could have been killed in her place. . . . "I'm glad to see you both, but I'm going to bed." Chloë leaned into Eli's supportive arms. "As Eli said, I need to sleep."

Both parents sprang forward.

Eli swept her into his arms.

"What's wrong with her?" Tamosso trembled as he stared at Chloë's limp body.

"Exhaustion and shock," Eli told him patiently. "She was almost killed last night. She needs rest."

"If you'll carry her into the bedroom, I'll take care of her." Lauren Robinson was a vibrant woman with an air of command that all too clearly told Eli she was used to being obeyed.

She would not command him. Not in this matter. Looking her in the eyes, he said, "Chloë is my wife. I'll care for her."

Lauren stepped back, offended.

Without opening her eyes, Chloë mumbled, "I'm okay, Mom; I swear. Let me get a nap and I'll be my old self."

"As you wish, darling." Lauren caressed Chloë's hair off her forehead, then pressed a kiss there, and smoothed her hair again.

Eli relaxed infinitesimally. Chloë had told him she and her mother had a good relationship, but he had needed to see the evidence. He needed to know Chloë was safe in her mother's love.

He told her parents, "The spare bedrooms are downstairs. If you'd like to wait, I'll show you where they are, but, please, I hope you'll both make yourselves comfortable in our home." He projected a little sarcasm, since Chloë's parents were already relaxed enough to be fighting.

Lauren understood.

Tamosso was oblivious. "Ah. Good." He picked up the two suitcases sitting by the door. "I've been living in a hotel in San Francisco, waiting for your reports. It's good to stay with family instead. Come, Lauren. Now that you know Chloë's alive, let's leave the children alone."

Lauren hesitated.

Tamosso's voice snapped like a whip. "Come, Lauren." He started for the stairs.

Lauren followed.

Chloë peeked from beneath her eyelids. "No one bosses my mom around. I had no idea he could pull that off."

Eli started toward their bedroom. "He started with nothing and made a fortune. It's no accident he can make himself heard."

"I suppose. But I never see that side of him, and believe me, I've never seen a man call my mother to heel."

Eli placed her on the bed.

She moaned. "Feels so good."

He leaned over her. "Did you fake that collapse out there?"

She peeked at him through lowered lashes. "Maybe a little."

"Good strategy," he said. "Now rest. I'll take care of you. You're safe here."

"I know." She snuggled into the pillows.

Yeah. *Because she trusted him with her body, but not her heart.* A condemnation that left him both flattered and broken.

He gave her more painkillers, removed her clothes, slid one of his shirts around her shoulders, and tucked her in, fighting the urge to climb in bed with her, hold her while she slept, be with her when she woke, and make love to her again. He wanted to show her he could be trusted in every way, that the man who stood here now was not the man she'd so blindly married.

But she was sound asleep, exhausted by yesterday's events and her ordeal last night.

And he had things to do. His politically incorrect biological imperative commanded that he keep his woman safe, and that took priority over his needs.

Leaning over her, he stroked the bruise on her cheek, and his cold rush of anger felt strong and familiar. When he found the bastard who had tried to kill her and finished with him, then Chloë would discover the kind of good, kind, *persistent* man Eli could be.

He looked at her . . . and looked at her. Driven by an invincible compulsion, he straightened and went to his jewelry box. There, a dangerous pink diamond bordered by two white diamonds blinked brightly, and a platinum wedding band set with white diamonds separated by platinum crosses shone with more subdued elegance.

Taking the wedding band, he went to his unconscious wife and slipped it on her finger.

He wasn't that good a man.

Now . . . to get the bastard who had hurt his wife.

Chapter 45

Pulling the bedroom door shut behind him, Eli walked toward the stairway that led down to the bottom level to check on his new in-laws.

Another round of shouting echoed along the corridor downstairs.

On second thought, he wasn't getting involved in *that*.

Turning away, he headed for the phone, dialed, and when Rafe answered, he said, "I'm okay. Chloë's okay."

"You're an ass, Eli." Rafe's shout blasted across the airwaves. "You couldn't answer your phone?"

"I turned it off. I didn't want to risk the GPS locators finding me while I went after Chloë. And I did find her."

A pause. A sigh of relief. "Good. All right," Rafe

said. "I figured it was something like that. Nonna said you were both alive."

"One of her gut feelings?" Eli asked.

"No. When I told her you'd driven through the vineyard and crushed the vines, she said you were going after Chloë. Brooke agreed. Who am I to argue with those two women?"

Eli cackled and walked to the window to look out over Bella Valley, his view obstructed only by Arvid Dijkstra's tall figure and broad shoulders. Tamosso's bodyguard was a giant.

"What the hell happened?" Rafe asked.

"Have you been up here?"

"Last night after you got out."

"Then you tell *me* what happened. You're the security expert." In fact, thank God Rafe was on Eli's team.

"Someone who really knows his way around explosives turned your cottage to kindling."

"That's stating the obvious." Eli watched Dijkstra slowly pace the length of the deck. "How did he know Chloë had moved out there? Everyone in town had heard we'd gotten married. She should have been inside with me."

"You two have a fight?" Rafe asked laconically.

"More of a battle. She won. She left."

"When you fight, you have to do what I do. Admit you're wrong even when you know you're right." Manly advice from a guy who'd been married barely more than a month.

"I did admit I was wrong," Eli said in irritation. "She didn't care."

"She must have found out about the dowry you received?"

Eli hissed in annoyance. "Who told you? Noah or Nonna?"

"Neither one," Rafe said smugly. "When you popped up married, Brooke speculated something like that had happened, and I checked into it. You're an *idiot* to think you could get away with such a stupid scheme."

"I know that now." Trust Rafe to figure it out.

"But I'm impressed you managed to seduce her in such a short time period." Rafe laughed. "You must have hidden talents."

"My hidden talents are none of your business." Eli reined in his irritation. "Can we get back to the matter at hand? I've got this sense of a ticking clock. . . ."

Rafe sobered. "Okay. First—you're sure the explosion was aimed at killing Chloë?"

"Someone ran her off Browena Road last night."

"She has definitely pissed someone off." Rafe sighed. "We have some possibilities here. Maybe the explosive was set before the news of your marriage got around."

"The cottage has a security system, and when Chloë went in, she activated it. It was only by the grace of God and her damned temper that she left before the whole place blew sky-high." Thinking about how close it had been, Eli broke into a cold sweat.

"Look, Eli. Your standard home security system is adequate to keep your run-of-the-mill break-and-enter burglar from getting your stuff. But it's no match for someone who knows the business. I could break into your house in less than a minute."

Eli wheeled around, looked over his living room. Nothing felt safe anymore. Nothing. "Should we be checking for a bomb here?"

"I did last night. It's clean, and I spruced up your security. It's not perfect, but it's better, and it'll do until I get one of my real experts out to you."

"Thank you." Eli's relief was profound.

"The thing is, the bomb in the cottage was placed by a professional, and without examining the debris, my guess is . . . the timer was activated by the security system. As in, when the security system was set, that's what started the timer for the bomb."

Made sense. "Because if the guy had been watching for his chance to activate the bomb, he would have seen Chloë leave and stopped the timer."

"Right," Rafe said.

"But why such a long delay between the time she set the security code and when the bomb went off?"

"It was a malfunction, either mechanical or human. My guess is the perp was in a hurry and set it for one hundred and fifty minutes instead of fifteen."

"We got *lucky*?" Eli could hardly conceive of that.

"Considering how many times lately we've been unlucky, it's time we won one, wouldn't you say?" Rafe sounded exasperated. "Now . . . *why* is someone after Chloë? Because I have to tell you, Eli, that bomb shows all the markings of someone who is seriously pissed off and bent on obliterating her from the face of the earth."

"We're pretty sure it has to do with the lost pink diamonds." Eli filled Rafe in on the details of Massimo's story.

When he finished, Rafe made the right conclusion. "You set her up with the engagement ring."

"I'm an all-around great guy. She wants to divorce me because I took her father's money, and I tried to get her killed with my romantic gesture gone sour."

"She could have international jewel thieves after her. They're not nice guys." Rafe sounded as if he'd met a few. "Eli, this means they're after you, too."

"Besides some hair crisping and a bump on my head, I don't have a scratch on me."

"*Yet,*" Rafe said ominously. "Any foreigners hanging around?"

"My father-in-law."

"He into jewel robbery?"

"No." Eli thought about Conte, his wealth, and his claim to be a leather merchant from Milan. "Maybe so— I don't know what he really does for a living—but he would never hurt his darling daughter." Of that Eli was sure.

"I'm getting a guard on your house ASAP—"

"I've got one. Tamosso Conte came with a guy named Arvid something-or-other."

Rafe knew the name right away. "Arvid Dijkstra. I know him. Impeccable credentials. I couldn't do better for you than him. Does he have backup?"

"I'll ask him." Eli walked to the deck, looked around, and found Arvid pacing around the house. "Do you have backup?" he called.

"There's a replacement every eight hours." Arvid produced words slowly and with a Swedish accent. "He is on his way in from San Francisco right now."

"That's good," Rafe said. "Tell him we're expecting trouble. Does he have people he can call in as additional personnel, or should I send in one of my people?"

Eli repeated the question.

Arvid glanced at the blackened hole where the cottage had stood, and looked up at Eli. "I'll stay when my replacement arrives. Is that sufficient for the moment? If there is a problem, I can do more."

"Give him my name," Rafe said. "He knows me. Tell him we've no reason for immediate alarm, but we're uncomfortable and I'm sending someone over."

Eli repeated the message.

Arvid nodded stiffly, probably because it was hard to nod when he had no neck.

Eli remained on the deck looking out over Bella Valley. His valley, his home, so gloriously peaceful. "I will miss this place," he muttered.

"What?" Rafe's voice sharpened. "What did you say?"

"Nothing. Just that if Chloë insists on leaving me, I'll have to go after her."

"Eli, she's an author. She can live anywhere!" Rafe was clearly incredulous. "You've got a job here. A job you love. A job you do well. A job that's making me money as a shareholder of the family winery!"

"If Chloë wants to go to Texas or Italy, there are wineries in both places. I can always get a job as a vintner."

"Don't be ridiculous, Eli. You don't even go on vacation!"

"Rafe, she's my wife, and I want it to stay that way. She's mad at me, and you said yourself that I was a fool for thinking I could seduce her and take a dowry for marrying her. So what am I going to do?" Although Rafe couldn't see him, Eli lifted his hand hopelessly. "I love her."

"Wow." Rafe sounded stunned. "I never thought I'd hear you say that. Wow. Wait until I tell Brooke."

"I've got to keep Chloë alive." Eli transferred his attention to the crater in his yard, and the rows of broken vines, and said, "She and I both suspect someone in the police department."

"Security expertise, bomb expertise, access, and trust. I agree. That's a good place to start. Anybody in particular?"

"Wyatt Vincent. Mason Watson. Finnegan Balfour. Terry." Eli hesitated. "DuPey."

"Looking them up," Rafe said.

Surprised, Eli said, "You didn't balk at Terry or DuPey, and we've known them both forever."

"We knew both the people involved in the attack on Nonna and the destruction of the wine bar. We didn't catch either one of them until the harm was done and Brooke had almost been killed." Rafe's voice grew ugly with memories. "I don't acquit anyone when it comes to this stuff. You don't know what motivates a man—or a woman—especially when it comes to priceless gems. And sometimes, it pays to go with your gut. Any of these guys in particular your gut doesn't like?"

"I don't like Mason," Eli admitted. "He's too damned jolly about the corpses."

Rafe typed. "No record. He looks clean. Which is not to say you're not right, only that he hasn't been caught."

"I don't like Finnegan, either. He's DuPey's wife's nephew from Kansas. Terry says he's got some kind of record. DuPey seems to dislike him." Eli felt stupid, but he had to add, "And he's got a crush on Chloë."

Rafe laughed. "That last is damning evidence." He typed, and crowed, "I'd say you have a winner!"

Eli leaned forward. "Tell me."

"A member of the police force in Keddington, Kansas. Got into huge trouble, apparently opening a safe in the department and stealing something pretty valuable." Eli heard the creak of a chair as Rafe moved restlessly. "This is hearsay, because the records are expunged. I'll have to get my hacker to dig them out."

"Did Finnegan use explosives to open the safe?"

"I can't tell, but I do know breaking a safe without harming the contents requires either a lot of knowledge of some kind of small explosive or a real ability to get around a security system. Finnegan is fitting the profile." Rafe sounded very satisfied. "And . . . hmm."

"What does 'hmm' mean?" Eli wanted to jump through the phone and drag the words from Rafe's mouth.

"There were rumors Finnegan was sleeping with the mayor's wife *and* the wife of a county commissioner *and*—"

Eli wheeled around and headed into the house. "I'm going down to the police department."

"Wait. It's getting interesting. The mayor's wife ended up dead."

Eli rocked back on his heels. *"What?"*

"Motive uncertain. They questioned the mayor and Finnegan. Both were suspects. Finnegan was caught with her pearl earrings in his possession. He went to trial and was acquitted for lack of evidence. That was reported in the newspaper and online."

"Holy shit!"

"Don't get excited. I don't think he's guilty." Rafe's voice was grim. "It looks to me like he was railroaded."

"And if he wasn't?"

"Either way, he's our prime suspect," Rafe admitted. "Want me to come down to the station with you?"

"I'll call you if I need you. I'd like you to keep looking at anybody and everybody . . . in case we're wrong."

"I am looking. Keep in contact. When we heard about the explosion, it wasn't clear who was involved and . . ." For the first time, Eli heard the echo of worry in Rafe's voice. "Keep in contact, okay? Answer your damned phone when I call."

"I will. I am not going to get myself killed now." Not when Chloë needed him.

Chapter 46

Eli walked into the Bella Terra Police Department, leaned over the counter, smiled toothily at Terry, and asked, "Is DuPey in?"

Deadpan as ever, Terry said, "For you, he is. Now, if you were a reporter, he'd be out on a call." Terry picked up the phone, punched a number. "Hey, Chief, guess who showed up at the front desk? Our wandering hero. That's right. Eli Di Luca." He hung up. "He's on his way up."

Eli straightened.

Terry took his turn to lean across the counter. "There's speculation going around town that your new wife didn't die in that blast."

Who started these rumors? How did Bella Terra

know this stuff? Did Julia down at the beauty parlor have a microphone hidden in Eli's bedroom? After all that had happened, he wouldn't doubt it a bit. "What do you think?"

"I don't know. I know we didn't find any trace of her at the cottage, not that I thought we could have, after the way that thing blew." Terry eyed him warily. "Plus I can't tell if you're pissed or sad or both."

"Hint: I may be sad, but I am definitely pissed." Eli improvised with a little dab of the truth. "I married that woman for her father's money, and we weren't married very long."

Terry's eyes got huge and his dimples quivered. "Not long enough to collect? Uh-oh." He scratched behind his ear. "But if she's dead, where the hell did you disappear to last night?"

"I remembered I was out of milk for my cereal and hightailed it to the grocery store."

"That's what I figured." Terry nodded solemnly. "Glad to have that cleared up."

DuPey yanked open the door to the secure area behind the desk. "Come back, Eli. I want to talk to you."

"Funny. I want to talk to you, too." Eli walked with DuPey to his office.

DuPey seated himself behind his desk, doing his best to project authority. "Shut the—"

Eli shut the door, turned, put his knuckles on the desk, leaned forward, and said, "Tell me Finnegan is under arrest for suspicion of setting that bomb in the cottage."

"Finnegan?" DuPey blinked, alarmed and confused. "No! Why would I—"

"He broke into a safe at his police department in Kansas."

"Yes, but that's hardly—"

"He went to trial for murdering the mayor's wife."

"He was acqu—"

"He set the bomb to kill my wife."

DuPey leaned aggressively back toward Eli. "Was your wife killed in that blast? I'm not the right kind of investigator, but I don't think so."

Eli ignored him. "Where is Finnegan now?"

"Probably at his desk." DuPey got to his feet. His saggy eyes looked grave and his weary voice was earnest. "Look, I wouldn't put an officer on the force, no matter how I'm related to him, if I thought he was a danger to anyone. Finnegan's not a killer. He's an idiot when it comes to women, sleeps with all of them, and when there's trouble, he tries to help them. The mayor's wife . . . The mayor was beating the shit out of her every night, and Finnegan tried to help her get away. She went back for her stuff and the mayor killed her."

"Finnegan had her earrings in his possession." It felt good to let DuPey realize how much Eli knew.

DuPey hesitated, then picked his words with great care. "That is a bit of a problem."

"Serial killers keep souvenirs."

"He's not a serial killer!" DuPey rubbed his face in his patented weary way. "*Serial killer.* No. Finnegan developed a bad habit of collecting bits and pieces from crime scenes he visits and selling them on eBay. As soon as he got here, I put a stop to it, told him he could live with us and work here, but no more shoplifting."

DuPey might say he wouldn't allow a dangerous relative on the force, but Eli knew what families were like, and more important, he knew that in their whole married life, DuPey had never won a fight with his wife. If she told him he was hiring Finnegan, he would hire Finnegan.

But he knew DuPey, too, had for years, and DuPey wouldn't look the other way if he thought Finnegan was a killer. So what was going on? "Let's go talk to your wife's nephew and see what we can rattle out of him."

DuPey led the way past the private offices and into the patrolmen's room. "There." He pointed out the most dilapidated of all the dilapidated desks in there. "That's Finnegan's."

"Where is he?" Eli asked.

"Probably in the men's room." DuPey turned to the officer at the next desk. "Right?"

The furiously typing Robin Webster never lifted her brown head. "He hasn't been in all morning. I've had to file last night's reports by myself."

"Damn it." DuPey picked up the phone. "I'm going to kill that boy."

"*You're* going to kill him?" Robin bared her teeth.

Eli walked around Finnegan's desk and rattled the drawers.

They were locked.

"Give me your key," he said to Robin.

"It doesn't open his desk," she said.

"Then give me your sledgehammer."

She grinned. "If I had one, I'd use it on his head."

DuPey hung up. "Karina hasn't seen him all morning." As Eli lifted his leg and prepared to kick the desk, DuPey caught his arm. "Give me a minute and I'll find a key."

"I don't have a minute." Eli slammed the heel of his boot into the belly drawer.

The cheap old wood splintered. The contents splashed all over the floor. Grocery store receipts, pens, a staple remover, three staplers, lip balm, scissors, a flashlight, and a legal-size pad with one sheet of yellow paper.

"There's my stapler." Robin leaned over and snatched it up. "I asked if he had it, and he said no. The jerk."

DuPey scowled. "Damn it, Eli, you broke a desk. The police department doesn't even have money for toilet paper, and you go around breaking the . . ."

Eli knelt among the scattered jumble and stuck his arm into the desk, into the space where the drawer had been. From the back, he pulled out a folder stuffed full of papers, car keys, a pipe connection used on Massimo's still, and a blackened remnant of the cottage.

DuPey's voice trailed off. ". . . furniture."

"I'll buy the department a new desk." Eli opened the folder and flipped over photo after photo of Chloë in the cottage, in his house, outside at his grandmother's, taken with a telephoto lens. Opening one of the side drawers, he found books: *The Greatest Crimes of the Twentieth Century*, *The Greatest Unsolved Crimes in History*, *Explosives and Structure*, *Stalking Runs*, and, of course, a well-thumbed copy of Chloë's *Die Trying*. Eli's rage grew ice-cold, and he spoke with quiet intensity. "Does Finnegan have access to a truck?"

"He's been borrowing the department's four-wheeler on a regular basis." Robin had changed from a disgruntled woman to an officer on the verge of action.

Eli shot a glance at DuPey.

The police chief was still shaking his head in disbelief.

Now was the time for Eli to tell the truth. "That might explain how last night someone ran Chloë off the road in a big truck. She survived, but it was a close call." When Eli pulled out a copy of Chloë's publicity picture with a bull's-eye drawn on it in pink Magic Marker, he showed it to DuPey. "What do you say about your wife's nephew now?"

"I don't," DuPey said. "I don't understand it, but I *swear* that kid is innocent of anything but souvenir shopping."

Eli stood, folder in hand. "We've got to find him before he does any more damage." Pulling out his cell phone, he said, "I'll tell Chloë to keep an eye out. He's obviously been doing his research. He apparently has unexpected, deadly skills."

Eli called his home phone. It rang, but no one answered. He left a message on the answering machine.

He called Chloë's cell. Same thing.

Terry appeared in the doorway, no longer deadpan but grim and angry. "We've got a call in from the Marinos' Sweet Dreams Hotel out on the highway. A maid found Finnegan in one of the guest rooms. He's been beaten up and shot. He's unconscious, and the EMTs are giving him less than a fifty percent chance of recovery."

"He's got an accomplice"—Eli kept leafing through the photos—"and the accomplice turned on him."

"No. I'm right about him." DuPey turned to Terry. "Who checked into the room?"

Terry checked the paper in his hand. "Some guy named Proctor N. Gamble . . . Oh, shit. Fake name."

"What a surprise," Robin said.

"Description?" DuPey snapped.

"White. Tall. Well built. Blond hair, blue eyes, light tan."

"Sounds like a million guys in Bella Valley," Robin said.

"I know him," Terry said. "Sounds like—"

"Wyatt Vincent," Eli said—and held out a photo of Wyatt inside the cottage, setting the explosive he intended for Chloë.

Chapter 47

When Chloë woke up, she was in their bed—no, Eli's bed—still heavy with exhaustion and sore as hell, but awake and aware, last night's ordeal almost a dream, or more correctly, completely a nightmare.

By the look of the sun, it was afternoon. The clock said four o'clock. She was pretty sure it was the same day.

She rubbed her eyes and noticed . . . the wedding band.

The platinum circled her finger. The diamonds glittered seductively.

When had Eli placed that on her finger . . . for a second time? Did he really think she was going to wear it as if nothing had happened?

He'd placed the pink diamond engagement ring on the nightstand, where she'd be sure to notice it. *Blink. Blink. Blink.* It sparkled at her insistently, using all its allure to degrade her resolve.

No. She was not wearing those rings. She was taking her wedding band off *right now*.

But first, she needed to figure out what was happening in the house.

She swung her legs off the bed. She was wearing Eli's shirt and her panties. Her jeans were off. Eli had done that, she supposed, too.

Cocky bastard.

He had also left a note on the end table.

Gone to the police station to talk to DuPey. If you wake up, go back to sleep. If you can't and want to avoid your parents, you can do research in my office. Or maybe when you come out, they will have stopped fighting. That seems unlikely. Security alarm is set. Don't show yourself outside. Don't open the door to anybody. E.

He was so bossy. He irritated her like a bad rash.

Then she noticed she was holding the note to her heart like a Victorian maiden. Fiercely, she crumpled it up and tossed it in the trash.

She headed into the bathroom, turned, and marched back to the trash. She dug out the note, smoothed it out, carried it into the bathroom with her, and propped it tenderly up against the backsplash. The wedding band on her finger caught her attention again. She smoothed it, marveling at the silky platinum and flashes of pure color deep in the white diamond.

As soon as she got finished in here, she was putting it back with the engagement ring, but for right now . . . she'd had a tough couple of days. If she wanted to be a Victorian maiden, then by God, she would be a Victorian maiden.

Stripping off her clothes, she climbed into the shower.

As spare as Eli's bedroom was, his bathroom was the opposite, a Roman bacchanal of warm browns and ambers accented by copper sinks and copper accent tiles shining with subtle beauty. His shower slid from a gentle rainlike downpour to a pounding massage, easing the worst of the pain in her muscles, and she stood there, working her shoulders, examining the bruises she couldn't recall getting, enjoying the luxury of endless warm water and scented steam. As she washed away the grime, Eli's soap smelled so very much like him that she was both aroused and irked.

She was leaving this guy. Would she never be able to smell warm spices, cool citrus, and that deep, dark, sexual scent without remembering him?

That thought got her out of the shower in a hurry.

When she knew she was going to leave Eli, she had packed everything—her clothes, her books, her computer, her backup for her book—and stowed them in her car. Except for her computer, which Eli had rescued—she refused to be overly grateful—her belongings were still up there on the mountain, which would make dressing herself a challenge.

But she dried herself on a towel, found one of Eli's button-down shirts in the closet, put it on, rolled up the sleeves, stuck his note in the pocket over her heart, and went looking for some kind of pants.

She found them draped over a chair in the bedroom: a pair of jeans that looked like they belonged to her mother.

She tried them on and decided she was right—they were too high in the waist and she had to roll up the legs. Definitely her mother's.

The new In and Out Gas and Food T-shirt awaited Chloë, too, but with her shoulder ache, she could never get it over her head. Eli's shirt might be too big, but she would stick with it. Besides . . . there was that pocket where she could keep his note.

Obviously, she wasn't finished being a Victorian maiden yet.

She glanced at the pink diamond ring on the night-stand, sparkling enticingly. *Blink. Blink. Blink.*

Gorgeous ring.

Stupid ring.

Stupid Chloë for wanting to put it on. Her trembling fingers hovered over it. That ring, and the one on her finger, were symbols of Eli's betrayal, and she was *not* going to give in to temptation and wear them.

Pulling her hand back, she worked the wedding band off and firmly placed it beside the engagement ring. She took the note out of her pocket and slapped it down beside them.

There. She was free.

Her tennis shoes rested on the floor.

She stared down at them. Someone had washed them, but one had a huge slice through the vinyl at the toe, and the other one was no longer gray, but camouflage or some other color that couldn't be described in polite society. "I am not wearing those," she muttered. So she wandered barefoot through the house in search of her parents.

They weren't hard to find. As Eli had predicted, they were still fighting, although they'd moved to the lower level.

Chloë tiptoed down the stairs and peeked into a bedroom—her father's, from the look of the shaving kit Tamosso was getting out of the suitcase.

Her mother blocked his way. "Chloë is too young to be married."

"Chloë *is* married," her father said smugly, and walked around Lauren and into the bathroom. "To a good man," he called.

Lauren followed him and stood in the bathroom door. "It will never last. She's an intelligent woman, not someone to be taken in by some money-grubber you've dug out of your pocket."

Ugliness. Chloë backed away and walked toward the stairway.

"You give me no credit at all. He's not a money-grubber. He didn't want to take the money. He didn't want to marry my darling Chloë."

Chloë stopped. She didn't want to hear this, yet suddenly she couldn't tear herself away.

Papa said, "But Eli was a man desperate to save his winery, so he had no choice."

Chloë nodded and grimaced. She had that one figured out.

"What kind of husband did you think he would be when you had to blackmail him into marriage?" Lauren asked indignantly.

"A good one. He's driven away demons I don't understand to protect his family above all else."

Unable to resist the lure of the real story as told by her father, Chloë slowly eased her aching body down onto a step and cupped her chin in her hand.

Papa's booming voice continued. "Once my darling Chloë was part of his family, I knew he would give his life for her."

Chloë knew that, too.

"He doesn't love her," her mother said flatly.

"No. He doesn't love her." Tamosso sounded angry. "He will never love her."

Yesterday, Chloë would have agreed. Today . . . She didn't know what to think about that casually thrown-out comment in the truck. *I loved your book and I love you.* Really? Since when?

"A man in love is weak," Tamosso said. "I know that better than anyone. But I have faith in Eli Di Luca. He'll make Chloë happy. It's too bad you didn't have the same faith in me."

Oh. Chloë leaned forward. Now it was getting good.

"I left Italy to avoid the restrictions your money brings, like your bodyguard out there." Chloë could almost see her mother waving a well-manicured hand. "More than that, I left to avoid your manipulations."

"I do not manipulate."

Chloë snorted, then covered her mouth. She didn't want to interrupt this conversation.

"You tried to manipulate me all the time," Lauren said, "just the way you manipulate Chloë. If I hadn't left you, I wouldn't have had a life to call my own."

"If you hadn't left me, I wouldn't have lost the chance to be a father to my only child." Papa's voice was low and deep and angry. "You destroyed our lives because you didn't love or trust me enough to stay."

"I did love you. I never married, but I'm proud that I realized you would never remain faithful."

"I was always faithful to you," Papa said fiercely.

"Through five marriages?" Lauren mocked.

"I am not Eli Di Luca. I *am* weak. I do love. I fell in love with you the first time I saw you, and I never faltered." Papa's Italian accent grew strong and proud. "If you had stayed with me, I would have never betrayed you."

"I don't believe you."

"I know. Your great fault is your cynicism. You wrap yourself in it to protect yourself from hurt, and you never live. You only exist."

Chloë totally agreed with that.

He continued. "You took my child, the child you cradled in your womb. You hid her from me, and you left me alone. I assuaged my loneliness with women, but none of them meant anything. Every one of them looked like you. Every night in bed, I turned off the light and loved them, and pretended they were you. But the sun always rose, and I saw them, and they weren't you." Papa's avowal brought tears to Chloë's eyes. "I would have married you," he concluded.

"I know, but what makes you think our marriage would have lasted? You have a wandering eye, Tamosso." In her way, Lauren sounded as hurt as Papa. "I saw you looking at other women."

"Looking? What is looking? I'm a man. As long as I still live, I will look. But why would I shop for a wallet in Venice when the finest leather goods are in my home in Milan? Why would I drink cheap wine in a tavern when I have champagne in my own cellar?" His voice grew deep with yearning. "Why, *bella mia*, would I taste another woman when I have you?"

"Tamosso . . ." Her mother's voice ached with longing.

Chloë waited to hear what would happen next.

And waited.

And waited.

Finally she held the handrail to help her to her feet, tiptoed forward, and peeked in the door.

She leaped back.

Oh, no. She should never have seen her parents doing *that*.

As quietly as she could, she hurried upstairs—not that they were going to hear her, as involved as they were—and turned on Eli's stereo. Grabbing a Coca-

Cola out of the refrigerator, she took a drink, hoping to block out those images seared on her retinas.

Her parents. Together again. Locked in a passionate embrace.

Chloë took another swig of Coke.

Her mother was only forty-two.

Chloë hoped they used protection.

She was *not* going back downstairs.

Going over to the stereo, she turned it up. Louder. She didn't want to hear *anything* from downstairs.

As a distraction, she collected her battered computer case from the master bedroom.

Those two broke her heart.

There was a lesson there, but right now, she didn't want to think about it too deeply.

She flung the strap from the case over her shoulder, turned—and there on the nightstand, the two rings blinked insistently, as if they were speaking to her.

If her parents had stayed together, they might have been miserable . . . but for sure they were miserable apart.

What could Chloë learn from them?

To take a chance? To believe Eli when he said he loved her?

She paced over and stared at her rings, the rings he had given her.

Eli's avowal was *so* conveniently timed, and yet she couldn't imagine that that man, who had been terrorized and isolated as a youth, could look at her with clear eyes and show her his emotions . . . unless he was telling the truth.

She couldn't kid herself. If she put the rings on, when Eli returned, she would have to put aside her grief and hurt. The two of them would have to talk, and she'd have to make a decision—believe him and forgive him, or walk away and never look back. And live alone for the rest of her life.

Maybe she was a fool . . . but she was a fool for love, and Eli was worth taking a chance for.

Picking up the rings one by one, she slipped them on her finger.

Feeling unsteady and uncertain as she faced a new day, a new world, a new life, she climbed the stairs.

A breeze blew down to greet her. Eli must have opened the doors onto the deck.

She stepped into his office.

A man, dressed in a tan business suit and a powder blue tie, sat at the desk, holding the skull and touching the pink diamond placed between its front teeth. He looked up and smiled, his blue eyes amused. "I'm sure there's symbolism in a gem of this value in such an unusual setting," Wyatt Vincent said. "Why don't you come in and tell me all about it?"

Chapter 48

Chloë took a step back.

Wyatt Vincent.

Former FBI. Specialist in all kinds of crime. From a law enforcement family who had lived in the area for years.

Another step back.

Wyatt Vincent.

Skillful enough to set explosives. Present at the party after Eli announced their marriage. Smart enough to realize the significance of Chloë's engagement ring.

Wyatt Vincent.

She'd bet he was the owner of a large, tough truck with Ford Focus blue smeared on its chrome bumper.

Wyatt flung the skull aside. It shattered against the wall.

Chloë turned and fled from the room.

Like a bull, he charged after her.

She bounded down the first six steps.

He seized her by the arm.

She turned and smacked him in the chest with her computer case.

He gasped, lost his grip, stumbled backward.

The music swelled from below.

She dropped the computer and ran.

He caught her before she reached the bottom, twisted her aching shoulder, and slammed her down on the steps.

She shrieked as she landed, banging her elbow, smacking her ribs.

Still holding her arm, he dragged her back up into the office and kicked the door shut.

Black and red dots clouded her vision as she fought her way out of the deep well of pain.

"No one can hear you," he said. "The two lovebirds are all the way downstairs, and when your bodyguard asked me if I worked for Rafe Di Luca, I shot him."

He'd wrenched her shoulder backward. Her ribs made it hard to breathe. She fought to speak. "What do you want?"

"I want those diamonds."

"I don't know what you're talking about."

He kicked her between her breasts.

Pain drove like a knife into her lungs. She screamed. She threw up on Eli's Oriental carpet, gasped in agony, then threw up again.

Wyatt waited without a shred of compassion, and when she lay gasping on the rug, he said, "Let's talk reason. Do you know what I heard about you, over and over, every time I turned around? I heard how smart you are. How you were a writer and could solve any mystery. You proved it to me when you so succinctly summed up the facts about Massimo's murder. So when I saw that pink diamond on your finger, I knew it was true. I knew you'd figured it out."

"Figured what out?"

He lifted his foot again.

She rolled into a ball and cowered.

"That's better. Let's get you away from the vomit. That's gross." Grabbing her by the right arm, he pulled her toward the middle of the room, twisting her shoulder out of its socket.

She screamed and screamed in an agony so intense she wanted to die.

"Don't throw up again," he warned, and pulled the wheeled desk chair close to her head and sat down. He waited until the worst of her pain had subsided and she was sobbing softly. Then, in a conversational tone, he said, "My family's been after those jewels ever since my great-grandfather—he was a cop—got a report from the FBI to apprehend Massimo because he had stolen a valuable cache of pink diamonds, including one called the Beating Heart. My family's always had an eye to a good deal—they did really well here in Bella Valley during Prohibition, what with blackmail and all—so Great-grandpa and his brother did what they were told and apprehended Massimo up in his water tower."

"And tortured him to death," she said hoarsely.

"Yes. Unfortunately, the valiant little Italian didn't crack. Great-grandpa told my grandfather about it and, when I was a kid, my grandfather told me. Grandpa said he searched that water tower himself, looking for the diamonds. He said we had a right to those gems, since we were the revenuers who took Massimo out. We deserved our rightful pay." Wyatt lingered over his excuse, so fond of it he polished it like gold. Then his voice hardened. "But my dad, he was one of those cops who was all about liberty and justice for all, and he didn't agree. He wanted to put our past behind us. Grandpa died before he could tell me which water tower Massimo was in, and my father *wouldn't* tell me."

"Good guy." Every twitch, every motion, was a misery. Yet she had to breathe.

"Dumb guy." Wyatt couldn't have made it clearer—he despised his father. "When I was thirteen he died, a cop on the beat, killed by a drug dealer. He left my mother and me to make it on our own. She died, but I did well with the FBI, and I've made a fortune as a law consultant."

"I'm glad for you." Every time she took a breath, tears trickled from her eyes.

"It's good for children who are the products of a single parent to do well for themselves. It speaks well of the parent."

She nodded. Wyatt was crazy. Or ruthless. Or both.

And she was afraid.

Where was Eli? Would he rescue her in time?

"I've spent years visiting Bella Valley and climbing water towers, trying to find Massimo's body so I could look him over. Then you find him by chance. What a pile of shit." Leaning down, Wyatt grabbed her by the cheeks and turned her face to his. "You found the diamonds, too, didn't you?"

She bit back a groan. "Only the one tiny one."

"The one in the skull." He laughed softly. "How symbolic for you that you put it there."

"Eli put it there."

"He's going to be unhappy when he gets back and you're dead." He smiled with a ghastly simulation of kindness. "But if I place the bomb right, you'll be together soon enough."

"No." She shook her head. He was going to bomb Eli's house, too.

"Come on. You know I can't leave you alive." Wyatt made it sound like the most reasonable thing in the world.

"Don't kill him." Stupid to beg. Stupid to tremble and cry. She knew it would do no good, yet she had to try. She had to save Eli.

"Once I kill you, I can't leave him alive." Wyatt scowled. "He'd come after me, and I don't need a love-crazed wop after me."

"He wouldn't come after you. He doesn't love me."

"Nice try." Wyatt applauded twice, mockingly. "But it's all over town that he drove through his vineyard to rescue you."

"What?" *Eli* was the one who drove through the vineyard? *Eli* destroyed his vines? For *her*?

"I know. That stunned me, too. I sat there in a tearoom today and heard two ladies gush about how that meant true love for sure. I could almost hear little birds twittering around their heads." Wyatt wiggled his fingers. "But one thing I learned a long time ago about this town: The gossip's good and almost always correct."

Chloë tried to comprehend the truth. Eli had destroyed his vines. *For her.*

"I couldn't believe it when I showed up to watch you burn in the cottage and your car was gone. I really couldn't believe it when you survived that wreck. I admire you. You are gutsy; that's for sure."

He seemed to expect a response, so she said, "Thank you."

"I figured I could get a motel room and lie low, listen to the gossip, and I'd know when you showed up again. Worked out pretty good." He frowned. "Except for that little shit Finnegan."

"Finnegan?" She had no idea what Wyatt was talking about.

"I finished him off and got his camera, but goddamn. There's no telling if he had backup."

She didn't dare interrupt. She was in such pain, she didn't think she could defend herself, but . . . Eli had driven through his vineyard for her.

He *did* love her.

"I need those big diamonds so I can get out of here and get far away"—Wyatt leaned close again, his breath hot on her face—"and you know I can make you confess where they are."

Maybe she could buy herself a little time by telling him. Time for Eli to get here. Time for her to figure out a way to warn him about Wyatt. "I don't know for sure." She spoke slowly, as if thinking about every word. "But I have suspicions that they're in the last bottle of wine Massimo made."

Wyatt looked into her eyes, and as she watched, his eyes kindled with rage.

She flinched.

Dropping her face, he stood and kicked the chair out of the way.

It bounced hard against the shelves, rattled the books.

"In the wine. That bastard. In the wine." Wyatt paced the length of the office from door to door. "No wonder the word went out that some old fart would pay anything for a bottle of Massimo's wine. Massimo—that little wop thought he was *so* clever."

Chloë refrained from pointing out that since no one had ever suspected the location of the diamonds before, then yes, that made Massimo *so* clever.

But staying still and quiet couldn't distract him for long. Dropping to his knees beside her, Wyatt demanded, "Where's the bottle?"

"No one knows."

"Bullshit. He gave the bottle to Anthony Di Luca. See? I know the story."

"Yes." Regrettably, he did.

"The Di Lucas aren't going to misplace a priceless

bottle of wine, even if they think it contains only wine." He had studied his prey.

"If you know the whole story, then you know Anthony had dementia before he died. He hid the bottle; no one knows where."

Wyatt acted as if she hadn't even spoken. "Where's the bottle?" he asked again.

"I don't have it." He was going to kill her.

"You know where it is." He smelled sour, as if he'd slept in his suit too many times, and sweated with desire for these diamonds.

"No, I don't. If I did, I would have given it to the Di Lucas." He was going to kill her before Eli could arrive.

Wyatt grabbed her again, but not her cheeks this time. This time he grabbed her throat. He squeezed enough for her to feel the constriction, enough that she comprehended the threat, enough that she could see the method of her death. "See, there you go again, thinking you're smarter than me. If you had the bottle, you would have kept it for yourself."

"Why would I do that?" She shook with pain, fear, anguish. "I don't need diamonds. My father's rich."

Wyatt's blue eyes developed a maniacal gleam. "Everyone wants a gem like the Beating Heart. Do you know how many people would kill to own it?"

"Yes." Her heart beat against his strangling grip. "I know *you* would."

"I have. And I'll do it again." That mad gleam grew brighter. "You want me to go to the old lady's house and take it apart? You know I will."

"Sarah? Sarah Di Luca? She doesn't have the bottle." What had Chloë done? In her effort to distract Wyatt and keep him busy, she'd set him on Sarah. He would kill Sarah.

"Then where is it?"

Where was it? If this was one of Chloë's mysteries, where would she have hidden the bottle? She had to think. . . .

And the solution popped into her mind. "It's in my car."

"What?"

"In my car, in my suitcase. The Di Lucas said the bottle was gone, but they were lying, trying to keep everyone away until the furor died down and they could find a dealer for the diamonds." Chloë was spinning a story now. "When I visited Sarah, I went down in her cellar"—she concentrated hard on the part of her story that was the truth—"and I found it stuck in a cubbyhole in the wall. I went back and stole it. Why do you think I left Eli? I needed to get away before he found out I'd robbed them of Massimo's last bottle of wine."

Wyatt believed her. He believed she was as greedy and vile as he was. In awe, he said, "You've got balls."

She relaxed. For the moment, Sarah was safe.

Then he said, "Thanks for the information. And now"—his hands tightened around her throat—"it's time for you to say good-bye."

Chapter 49

Eli could hear the sirens in the distance, but police cars had to take the roads. They couldn't turn off the highway, like he had, and cut across country like he was. He drove on tiny roads, yes, but when he got the chance he put his truck in low gear and climbed up a hill so steep no vines would thrive. He chugged through a stream, knocked over his neighbor's fence; he would pay dearly for that. He made a straight line for his house—and Chloë.

If she was dead . . . No. He wouldn't allow it.

Her father's bodyguard was there to protect her. Rafe was sending someone over, too. Both her father and her mother would die for her.

But this guy, this Wyatt—he was lethal, he was intelligent, and he had fooled everybody.

Eli's hands tightened on the steering wheel. Chloë wouldn't open the door to Wyatt . . . would she?

No, she was so smart. So intelligent. He'd said it over and over. He'd believed it. He reveled in it. He loved their conversations, loved knowing she was in the world, bright and beautiful. . . .

But Wyatt had proved to be an expert in all matters of security. Did he even need Chloë to let him in? Could he somehow sneak inside anyway?

Eli was on his own land now, driving the access roads beside the vineyards. Looking up, he could see his house perched at the top of Gunfighter Ridge.

Hang on, Chloë. I'm coming.

He made the final push, driving past the rows of olive trees and through the vineyards at speeds that made the F-250 clear the ground. In normal circumstances, such speed would make him swear.

Now he cursed because he couldn't go faster.

He reached the ridge, drove straight up the forbidding angle of the slope, his deep tread tires biting into the dirt, throwing stones behind him in a fury. He gunned it at the top. The truck flew high, landed hard in the parking area. He skidded to a stop.

One glance showed him Arvid's bloody, motionless body.

Wyatt was here.

Eli vaulted from the truck and up the stairs, punched in the security code, and opened the door.

The red light started blinking; Wyatt had tinkered with the system. In thirty seconds, the alarm would go off.

Eli had thirty seconds to find Chloë. It was his only chance to catch Wyatt by surprise.

He glanced around, weighing the possibilities.

The music was playing. Loud.

No one could hear her scream.

The door to his office was closed.

Chloë never closed it.

Eli sprinted across the living room and up the stairs. He turned the knob; it opened under his hand. He flung open the door.

Wyatt was crouched over the struggling Chloë, his hands around her throat. Seeing Eli, he reached into his coat and pulled a gun.

Eli leaped at him.

Chloë hit Wyatt in the face with her fist.

Blood welled from a cut below his eye where her pink diamond had sliced deep. "Goddammit!" His face glowed a ruddy, angry color.

And the alarm went off.

It blared in a rhythmic, earsplitting, nauseating cacophony, blocking the sound of the shot that went awry and Wyatt's shout when Eli kicked the gun out of his hand.

Eli kicked again, intending to connect with Wyatt's head and take him out.

Wyatt caught his foot and pulled.

Eli landed on his back.

In a split second, he saw Chloë on the floor, desperately hurt, crawling away, dragging her right arm limp and useless at her side.

Then he was on his feet again, facing Wyatt.

Eli couldn't hear him shout. He couldn't hear anything; the alarm rocked the house.

But Wyatt was laughing in delight and assurance, gesturing for Eli to come at him.

Wyatt was a former FBI agent. The son of a bitch knew martial arts, and that took the fight to a whole different level.

Good thing Eli was four inches taller with a longer reach. Good thing his cousins in Chile had taught him street fighting.

Good thing he didn't fight fair.

Wyatt aimed a kick at Eli's groin. Eli jumped into the air toward Wyatt and took him down, punching the top of his shoulder, knocking him into the corner of the desk.

Wyatt's head wobbled on his neck.

He recovered fast, grabbed Eli's arm, and twisted it behind his back.

Eli felt the bones in his wrist splinter.

He shrieked in agony.

The alarm kept going off, loud, insistent.

Eli punched Wyatt in the face with the fist of his other hand.

Wyatt's nose broke.

Eli took fiendish delight in the crunch of the bone, the gush of the blood.

Wyatt must have seen Eli's satisfaction, because he

came at Eli in a blitz of karate movements, chopping him at the throat, lifting him by the windpipe, and flinging him into the bookshelves.

Behind Eli, two of the adjustable shelves tilted and fell. Books rattled to the floor.

Eli gagged, clawing at his throat. Through the pain, he saw Wyatt move in for the kill.

From the floor, he kicked upward and connected right between Wyatt's legs.

Wyatt collapsed, gasping, holding his 'nads, the shriek of the alarm a satisfying accompaniment to his suffering.

Eli started toward Wyatt to finish him off—and in a move he never saw coming, Wyatt put him on the floor and wrenched his broken wrist sideways. As Eli gasped, Wyatt leaned over him and lifted the flat of his hand to break every bone in his face. . . .

Through a haze of pain, Eli saw a large, pale, oblong stone object lift high above them. It smashed down on the back of Wyatt's head.

Wyatt fell like a lightning-struck tree, landing hard on the carpet.

Chloë stood there, holding the marble figurine of Bacchus in her good hand, a fierce expression on her face, ready to hit Wyatt again.

The alarm ceased, the silence so abrupt and startling that Eli wanted to embrace it.

He staggered to his feet. More pain. Sometime during the fight, he had cracked his ankle. Damn it. He was a mess.

But not as much of a mess as Chloë.

She stood listing to one side, her shoulder at an odd angle. A purple string of bruises circled her neck. She was breathing hard, but she held the marble figurine cocked, ready to deliver the next blow if necessary.

Wyatt had almost murdered her. He had bombed the cottage. He had driven her off the road into an abyss. And today he had tortured her, kicked her, pulled her arm from its socket, and throttled her with the intent to kill.

She had survived.

She'd saved Eli's life.

He looked down at the body at his feet: Wyatt Vincent, a big, fast, nasty, brutal cockroach with blood welling from the wound on his head.

No matter what happened, no matter whether Wyatt was sent to prison, he would never stop. He would be back to find those diamonds, to destroy Eli's family, and to kill Chloë for this humiliating defeat.

Eli looked into her angry, fragile, bruised, and vulnerable face, and he knew what he had to do. What *they* had to do.

Taking the figurine out of her shaking hand, Eli put it down on the floor. Showing her his broken wrist, he asked, "Can you help me pick up the trash and throw it out?"

She understood him immediately. Her voice rasped in her swollen throat, but she nodded, and she said, "Yes."

Pride swelled in him. She was strong, stronger than

any woman he'd ever known, coming back from near death to take that murderous bastard down.

She swallowed. Swallowed again. In a voice that quavered in and out, she said, "He threatened your grandmother . . . *our* grandmother. He threatened Sarah."

Wyatt threatened everything Eli loved.

With his good hand, he grabbed Wyatt by the back of his collar. With dogged determination and a lot of sweat and agony, he dragged him over to the open door and across the deck. Bracing himself against the railing, he looked into her pale, bruised face. "Are you sure you can do this?"

She jutted her chin. "I *will* do this."

"Okay, now, with your good hand—grab his belt and heave!"

Together they threw him three stories to the ground.

It wasn't justice.

But they could only kill him once.

Chapter 50

"Tell me again how Wyatt fell out that window." DuPey tapped his notebook with his pen and looked accusingly at Eli and Chloë as they reclined, side by side, in their bed, in their bedroom, together and home at last after two surgeries and five days in the hospital.

"We already told you all this stuff," Eli said.

"Tell me again," DuPey answered.

"I was hitting him. He was beating the shit out of me. Exhibit A." Eli raised the arm with the cast that went over his elbow. "And B." He lifted the leg with the cast around his ankle. "Did I mention I had to have surgery to have the bones in my wrist repaired? I've got stainless-steel pins in there, DuPey. I'll never breeze through airport security again."

"I know." DuPey sounded weary. "I know."

"Wyatt was about to do some fancy martial-arts turning kick, and while he was in the air, Chloë hit him with the marble statue thing Nonna gave me. Didn't you, honey?" Eli turned to Chloë.

She nodded, touched her throat where the bruises left by Wyatt's fingers shone black and yellow and ugly, and indicated she couldn't speak.

"I got that part," DuPey said. "But how did he go out the window?"

"He lost his balance," Eli explained, "stumbled backward, and went over the rail."

"A six-foot-tall man over a forty-two-inch-high rail?" DuPey asked.

"That's the way I remember it. Isn't that right, honey?" Eli turned to Chloë again.

Chloë nodded again, then closed her eyes as if the questioning had exhausted her.

Eli touched her blond fuzz of hair with gentle fingers. "DuPey, I'm sorry, but I'm going to have to ask you to leave. With Chloë's dislocated shoulder and her broken breastbone, and, of course, the damage to her throat where Wyatt strangled her, she's still weak. The doctor recommended plenty of bed rest."

"Hm. Yes." DuPey might have wanted to argue, but with the evidence before his eyes, he didn't have much to say. "You two were pretty banged up by the time we got here."

"At least they were alive by the time you got here." Eli's new mother-in-law stood in the doorway looking authoritative and disapproving. "If Eli hadn't driven like a maniac, Chloë would have been killed while her father and I were downstairs all unknowing."

"I've forgotten what you said—why didn't you hear her scream?" DuPey asked.

Lauren blushed and fussed on the side table with the bouquet of wildflowers that Rafe and Brooke had sent. "She had turned on some horrid rock music. I've always told her not to play her songs so loudly."

Chloë blushed, too, and whimpered wordlessly.

Eli looked at her in surprise. Obviously he'd missed something.

"We—Tamosso and I—wasted time trying to get the alarm to turn off. It wasn't until Tamosso found his bodyguard dead, murdered where he stood"—Lauren's voice choked with emotion—"that we realized what was happening. When I ran up the stairs and saw that dreadful man fall over the railing—"

"You saw him fall over?" DuPey asked.

"Yes. I saw him fall over the railing." Lauren stalked to the dresser. She plucked a wilting yellow rose from the bouquet Noah had sent and threw it in the trash. "Then I saw Chloë, collapsing in Eli's arms, and him holding her when he could scarcely stand—"

All of Eli's questions about Lauren had been answered at that moment in his office when she came charging in, eyes aflame, shouting for Tamosso. She had administered first aid to them both, and when the police arrived, she harangued DuPey until he abandoned his questioning and allowed Eli and

Chloë to rest, gather their forces . . . and get their story straight.

That day, Lauren had been a godsend, and she was a godsend now. In her professorial voice, she said, "Police Chief DuPey, it is time for my patients' medications to be administered. They're just home from the hospital, and it's time for them to sleep. When I think how badly battered they were . . ." She choked and covered her eyes with her palm.

"Mom, it's okay," Chloë said, her voice a rasping wisp.

DuPey shut his notebook and stuffed it in his pocket. With fine-tuned irony, he said, "I'll move along then."

Chloë waved a restraining hand and croaked. "Finnegan?"

"He's going to live, but he won't be collecting any souvenirs for a while." DuPey stood. "There'll be months of rehab, and that includes counseling, which I hope helps with his collection habit."

Chloë rolled her good arm, encouraging him to keep talking.

DuPey sighed. "He targeted you because he has a true-crime novel he wants to publish—"

Chloë made a noise somewhere between a giggle and a groan.

"—and he thought if he knew everything about you, he could successfully convince you to help him. I'm sorry; I know it was unethical, and the book probably sucks rocks, and I can't believe he went to Wyatt Vincent to interview him about his background."

"Why did he do that?" Eli asked.

DuPey quivered with irritation and worry. "Apparently, he thought he could cleverly ask questions about Vincent's motivations without Vincent catching on."

"For his true crime story?" Chloë's voice was a squeak of dismay.

"I guess," DuPey said. "Of course, Vincent was one of the brightest agents the FBI ever had. Right away, he figured out Finnegan had seen something Vincent couldn't have revealed. He tortured Finnegan just like he tortured you, Chloë, until Finnegan told him the truth about the photos. Then he shot him."

"Didn't Finnegan fight?" Eli asked.

"He went there without any weapon at all," DuPey said.

Eli was incredulous. "You are kidding. He'd seen the guy blow up the cottage. Why wouldn't he go armed?"

"According to what he's managed to tell me, he thought arriving dressed in civilian clothes would put Vincent at ease, make him easier to interrogate." DuPey looked at Chloë. "How he thinks he can be a writer when he has no idea how people think, I don't know."

She gave a bewildered shrug, then whispered, "He played into Vincent's hands. Vincent loved to hurt the people who couldn't hurt him back."

"Apparently, Vincent never worried about playing fair. I've talked to the FBI in the area, and I'll tell you this—he's not the most beloved of their former agents. In fact, his retirement from the FBI may have been less cordial than he indicated." DuPey looked grimly disgruntled.

"That I can believe," Eli said.

"In the end, Finnegan's photos of Vincent provided us with the evidence we needed to convince the legal system not to put you two in prison to await trial. We law enforcement agencies get cranky about former colleagues 'falling out the window.'" DuPey did a terse air quote.

"All right, then." Eli leaned back against the pillows and relaxed.

No doubt there would be more questioning, but not from DuPey.

Lauren took the bouquet of calla lilies from Francesca into the bathroom.

"Tell Finnegan"—Chloë spoke quietly—"that I'll recommend my agent read his manuscript. After that, he's on his own."

"I'll tell him. That'll make him feel better." DuPey nodded. "Thank you."

Lauren came back with the vase full of freshwater and a forbidding expression on her face. She cleared her throat. "If you don't mind, Police Chief DuPey?"

With a dip of the head, DuPey left them.

When Eli heard the front door close behind him, he said to Lauren, "Thank you."

"Of course. Anything for the newlyweds. Can I get you something?" Lauren hurried to Chloë's side. "Sweetheart, do you need help going to the lavatory?"

"I wish I could say no." Chloë tried to lift herself off the bed.

Eli slid his good hand behind her back.

Together Lauren and Eli helped Chloë sit up, and Lauren walked with her to the bathroom.

The broken breastbone had had to be stapled. Pain limited Chloë's movements and made every breath laborious, and when Eli saw that, he wanted to throw Wyatt off the balcony all over again.

A few minutes later she was back in bed, her grumpy face slightly damp. "I'd kill for a shower." Her voice was still scratchy, but not nearly as bad as they'd pretended to DuPey.

"You can have a shower when they let you out of all these bandages." Lauren fussed with the covers and worriedly gazed at her daughter.

"She does look like an extra on the set of *The Mummy*," Eli said.

Chloë laughed, then held her chest. "Don't. It hurts."

Would she ever laugh as freely again? Would the memory of her pain and fear ever completely leave her? Would the recollection of Wyatt kicking her, choking her, always drift through her nightmares?

Eli stroked his fingers along her jaw. He couldn't stop touching her. Somehow he would bring the sunshine back into her face. When he thought how close he'd come to losing her . . .

Tamosso appeared in the doorway. "Eli! I wanted to talk to you." He waved an expressive hand toward the bed. "I give my darling child into your care, and look what happens."

Chloë groaned. "Papa . . ."

"I intend to do better in the future," Eli promised.

"Good, because Lauren and I will have to leave you soon to go on our honeymoon." Tamosso boomed his news, and beamed.

Eli almost choked in surprise.

"Good thing," Chloë muttered.

Lauren's eyes narrowed on Tamosso. "I was going to present the news more tactfully than that."

"What? Tactful? Our marriage is not a thing to be tactful of!" Tamosso flung out his arms. "It's a joyous occasion."

"Perhaps we should ask Chloë what she thinks," Lauren said primly.

"How many parents ask their daughter what she thinks before they get married for the first time?" Tamosso's eyes twinkled, and he looked like a mad child born of a mischievous elf and the Godfather.

"I think it's about time you did get married," Chloë said, her voice almost normal.

"See?" Tamosso bustled to her side, kissed both her cheeks, and smiled. "She approves."

"Do you really, darling?" Lauren pushed him aside and leaned over the bed. "Once we got together here, we worked out some of our issues—"

"I know, Mom. Really." Chloë held up her hand to stop Lauren from talking. "Go get married before I have a little sister on the way."

Eli kept a straight face.

Lauren's eyes went wide with horror.

"That would be nice, eh?" Tamosso put his arm

around Lauren. "We should at least try. We don't want Chloë to be an only child. Only children are so lonely."

Lauren transferred her horror to him. "Are you *kidding*?"

"No." He led her from the room. "I like children. We should have more before we're too old."

Eli burst into laughter.

Chloë stared at him forbiddingly, then smiled, and finally chuckled. "Honestly. It's not funny. You wouldn't believe what I saw them doing."

"I've got a pretty good idea."

"I'm scarred for life."

Eli cackled. "Why do you think they were always shouting at each other? They were fighting the attraction."

"I thought they hated each other." Chloë stroked the fingers that stuck out from his cast. "I guess they hate each other like I hate you."

He turned on his side and smiled at her. "Do you hate me?"

She sighed. "I couldn't even hate you when I found out Papa had had to bribe you to marry me."

He dragged his broken foot a little closer to her, got up on one elbow and leaned on his cast, and tried to mend the difficulties between them. All he had were words, and the truth, and so much love he only hoped that somehow she'd hear it in his voice. "I did court you with the cold intention of marrying you for the money. I promised myself I'd be a good husband. And once I got to know you a little, I realized that wouldn't be too hard."

"There's a compliment to treasure." Chloë sounded sarcastic. She looked amused.

"But I swear to you, that night—"

"That night?" she mocked.

"The night when you found Abuela's letter. *That* night."

She nodded. "I remember some things about that night."

"That night, I wasn't thinking of your father's money. I wasn't thinking at all. You'd dug around inside me and turned me inside out. You brought all the ugliness to the surface, and once it was out, I didn't know what to do. I was so frantic . . . and then there you were, so fresh, so beautiful"—he stroked her cheek—"a living, breathing miracle. So I grabbed you and took you. I was like a stupid, clumsy adolescent."

A wicked smile curved one side of her mouth. "It's one of my favorite memories."

"I don't know why." When he remembered that impetuous outburst of lust and emotion, he was still embarrassed. And humiliated. And horny.

"Are you kidding? I liked you before, but you had such a stick up your rear. I figured you ate sawdust and drank control-ade. But that night." She took a long, worshipful breath; her eyes glowed like stars, and color rose in her cheeks. "You were passionate. You were real. No man has ever shared himself like that. No man has ever wanted me like that. I remember every minute. I always will." She put her hand to her chest as if to contain her delight. "After that night, I knew you, Eli Di Luca. Why else do you think I agreed to marry you?"

"Because you love me."

"I do. I know you, and I like what I know." She smirked. "Even better, I know you love me."

He scooted a little closer. His heart beat a little faster. "Do you believe that?"

"If you like, you can take the time to convince me yourself, but actually . . ." She drew out the suspense. "Wyatt told me."

"Wyatt?" Eli drew back in surprise.

"That monster was good for one thing." She watched him as if weighing his reaction. "He told me you drove through the vineyard to rescue me."

"Oh. That." Eli shrugged and dismissed it. "The emergency vehicles had me blocked in. I had no choice."

"You're taking it well." A smile played around her mouth. "How many rows did you take out?"

"Twenty."

"Twenty rows exactly." The smile took a firmer hold. "The trellises are connected, so you didn't merely destroy the part you drove over. You pulled other vines and wires and stakes out of the ground all the way down the rows. How many feet went down?"

"Thirty feet per row, more or less."

"How many vines gone?"

"One hundred and twenty."

"A hundred and twenty grapevines planted in . . . what year?"

"Nineteen seventy-four."

"So a hundred and twenty vines planted in 1974, years of grape maturity you can never get back, and you drove over them with your big tires"—she wiggled her fingers as she described the scene—"crunching them, uprooting them, obliterating them—"

"All right. All right." He put his hand on his chest. "Stop!" She was killing him.

She settled back with a silent laugh. "Don't tell me it didn't mean anything. That's not a stick you've got up your rear; that's a grapevine."

"You think you're so funny. I ought to teach you a lesson." He leaned down to her, his lips hovering over hers, her breath on his mouth . . . and someone tapped on the door.

Chapter 51

Chloë saw a ferocious impatience settle over Eli. "Who is it?" he snapped.

"It's Nonna!" Sarah chirped.

"How can you be annoyed with Nonna?" Chloë whispered.

"I'm not annoyed with Nonna," he said between his teeth. "I'm annoyed at the interruption."

Chloë shared his exasperation, but she flattered herself she was a little more practical. She touched the cut under his chin, and his black eye, and said, "I'm only available for a kiss, anyway. You have to keep your foot elevated. I can't move without hurting my chest or my shoulder. And we're both still on pain medication."

"I know. I know. But . . ." He writhed with frustration as he flung himself back on his pillows and called out, "Come in, Nonna."

Nonna walked in carrying a vase of daffodils and tulips. "The girls got these out of my yard. I thought they would cheer you." Her gaze swept the arrangements that decorated the room. "Although, Eli, it seems someone else thought your austere bedroom needed some brightening."

"I have everything I need to brighten my bedroom right here in bed with me." He smiled hopefully at Chloë.

Chloë patted his arm and pretended to sympathize with his dilemma, but the poor guy was fighting a losing battle. Somehow Nonna's lace shawl and Chloë's collection of glass perfume bottles had already found their way onto the chest of drawers. His stark masculine bedroom was a thing of the past.

Maybe if she got a new skull for the end table, the place would feel cozier. . . .

"Thank you, Nonna." Chloë indicated the bathroom. "Those flowers will look glorious on the counter."

"They will, won't they? With all the browns and golds in there, they'll be just right." She took them in and returned, and seated herself in the chair DuPey had vacated, the one beside the bed. "How are you two doing?"

"We're better," Eli said.

"Of course you are, dear, or I wouldn't be interrupting your kissing. I always seem to be doing that." Nonna was ostensibly talking to them both, but she was scrutinizing Eli. "Dear boy, you look so different, so . . ."

"Bruised?" he suggested.

"Happy. Ever since you returned from Chile, I have been so afraid I would never meet that strong, loving little man you had been when you were eight. I feared I would never see the day when I could look into your face and view real emotions. And now . . . here you are, in love with Chloë and willing to show the world. I called you out for marrying her for such a wicked reason as money." Nonna turned to Chloë. "I truly did, dear. I was angry with him. I don't want you to think otherwise."

"I know, Nonna," Chloë said soothingly. "And I appreciate that."

Nonna turned back to Eli. "You're a whole person now, Eli. I am so proud of you for facing your pain, taking the chance, and becoming the man I always knew you could be."

He held out his good arm to her.

She leaned in and hugged him.

Tears prickled at Chloë's eyes. She loved Nonna. And she loved Eli. And she'd never imagined a day when the two of them could get closer and be more devoted—and yet, here they were.

She had a hand in that. She was proud of them all.

Nonna straightened. "While you were in the hospital, Eli, I found out just how far you'd come on your return to the human race. I got a phone call and . . . well. I brought you a little surprise." She walked over to the door and stood beside it.

An elderly woman stepped into the room.

"Here we are," Nonna said. "Your surprise visitor.

She was such a pleasure for me to meet. I hope you're glad to see her, too." ·

Eli sat straight up, his spine vertical, his shoulders rigid, and the expression on his face . . .

Chloë worked herself into a sitting position and examined their caller.

The woman was small, barely five feet, and old, with a brown face wrinkled by the sun. Her long, dark, gray-streaked hair was pulled back into a tight bun, and she wore black from head to toe: black skirt, black shirt, black stockings, black shoes. She carried a large black purse, and if Chloë had seen her on the street, she would have thought she was a nun. Except there was a look about her, one that reminded Chloë of Eli. Oh, my God. It was . . .

"Abuela," he said.

"Eli," the old woman replied.

The brief conversation came to a halt as they examined each other.

He inclined his head. "Welcome to my home. *Mi casa es tu casa.*"

At his words of hospitality, Chloë let out a breath she didn't realize she was holding.

Nonna met her eyes and nodded, and tiptoed out of the room.

"Thank you." Abuela's voice was heavy with a Spanish accent and rough with years of smoking. "Your home is beautiful."

"Thank you. Please sit down." He indicated the chair that had seen so many visitors this morning.

She came to the bed, smelling of cigars, and sat

stiffly, with an unbending spine that never touched the back of the chair.

Chloë helped Eli pull his pillows into an upright position.

Another pause.

"You tried to call me," Abuela said.

Chloë jerked her head around so hard to look at Eli that she hurt her shoulder.

"I did," he admitted.

"The connection must have been bad. We weren't able to speak."

Chloë interpreted Abuela's words; Eli had made the attempt to call and changed his mind.

"So I traveled here," Abuela said, "many thousands of miles, leaving my country for the first time in my long life, to speak with my most beloved grandson."

"I am honored," he replied, and with his cast, he gestured to Chloë. "Please allow me to introduce you to my adored *esposa*, Chloë Di Luca."

Abuela's gaze moved to her, and although Chloë knew she'd always been aware of her, she gave her the same extensive examination she'd given Eli. "Welcome to my family."

"Thank you. It's an honor to be Eli's wife and your granddaughter." Everything about this conversation was stilted, but Chloë recognized what was going on under the surface. Much was being said, all without words.

Only Abuela's eyes moved as she looked again at Eli. "Many months ago, I wrote you a letter."

"I received it." Obviously, he wasn't going to apologize for not answering.

"The doctors say next spring the grass will turn green over my grave." When Chloë would have spoken her sympathy, Abuela waved her to silence. "I've had a long life. There have been struggles and hardships, but there have been moments of great joy, too. This is one of those moments of joy."

Clearly, Abuela did not show emotion.

So that was where Eli had learned that trick.

Abuela continued. "But before I leave this life, I want to make amends where needed. Your family in Chile, Eli, are doing well. Your cousins send their greetings."

"I remember them in return," Eli said.

Obviously, whatever newfound forgiveness he felt for Abuela did not extend to his cousins.

"Of course, my will gives all to them. They have stayed with me all these years"—a reproach, skillfully delivered—"and one, young Salazar, is almost as talented as you when it comes to blending the wines."

"I've heard of him as a winemaker," Eli said. "He is very good."

Another surprise. Eli was full of them today.

Something that passed for a smile crossed Abuela's face. "Yes. I am proud of the boy. Yet when I heard the doctor's verdict, I looked for a way to give *you* something as a remembrance of me." She leaned down and picked up her purse.

Chloë expected her to pull out a knickknack or a

piece of jewelry or something etched with the Silva family escutcheon.

She underestimated Abuela.

"It came to my attention that Owen Slovak, your accountant and friend, stole your fortune and the wealth of your winery and fled to South America." Those dark, expressionless eyes grew icy. "I don't like thieves, especially not thieves who steal from my grandson and, by extension, from me."

So many revelations for Chloë. Eli had gotten a *lot* of his traits from his maternal grandmother, including this stiff-necked protectiveness about his possessions and his family.

"As you know," Abuela continued, "I have some influence with the authorities."

"I'm aware of that." Eli's face was as impassive as Abuela's.

Yet in the way he held himself, Chloë could see his wariness.

"Under my direction"—Abuela's voice grew proud—"the authorities discovered a reason to arrest this traitor to my grandson. Apparently he had moved on to a new career—selling drugs."

"Owen?" Eli was clearly surprised.

"Perhaps he was framed." Abuela shrugged indifferently. "I don't know. I don't care. I only know Owen Slovak was quite surprised to discover drug lords are nasty when someone moves into their territory, and our justice system is not quite as . . . indulgent . . . as the one in America."

"I can imagine with so many threats, he was frightened." Eli's gaze never left Abuela's.

"I believe he was," Abuela conceded. "A day of being intimidated by our drug lords, a few weeks in a foreign prison . . . they convinced him he would like to return your fortune." She held up one gnarled finger. "With interest."

"Wow," Chloë whispered. Now, *that* was influence.

Abuela pulled a folder from her purse. "I have papers here, made up by my lawyers. I'll leave them with you to peruse, and if they are written to your satisfaction, the fortune will be transferred back into your account and you'll be a wealthy man once more." She placed the folder on the table beside Eli.

"Thank you, Abuela." Eli was pale with shock. "I am most grateful for your gift."

She stood. "I'm tired from my trip, so I will go."

"Wait!" Eli said. "What's happened to Owen?"

"He's living in Chile. He has no money. His reputation as a thief is well-known. No one will hire him as an accountant." Abuela appeared to think. "I believe . . . Owen Slovak is working as a farmhand for Del Toro Wines."

Chloë's eyes widened. She would never want to anger this woman. "Abuela, we have room if you wish to stay here."

Once again Abuela's gaze examined her, and her eyes warmed ever so slightly. "Thank you, but I'm staying with Sarah. She is lovely. You are most fortunate, Eli, in your grandmother."

"In both my grandmothers." Taking her gnarled hand, he kissed it. "Thank you, Abuela. Thank you for coming to visit me. Welcome to the United States. I look forward to seeing you again soon."

Abuela squeezed his hand, and for the first time, Chloë saw a glimpse of the woman who loved her grandson enough to make these restitutions to him.

Turning slowly, she made her way to the door and into the living room, leaving a shocked silence behind.

Finally Chloë asked, "How old is she?"

"About a million." Eli moved restlessly on the bed. "I remembered her as being a giant, but she's so short."

"And feeble."

"I should have finished that call. I should have gone to her." He turned to Chloë. "*Please* don't say, 'I told you so.'"

Chloë shut her mouth. Then she opened it again. "Okay, but can I say—if you'd written Abuela back when she first contacted you, do you realize this never would have happened? You would have never been in the position for my father to blackmail you. You would never have had to get married. You'd be single, heart-whole, and with no broken bones."

"Thank God you didn't say, 'I told you so,'" he said with fine-tuned insincerity.

"Of course not," she said righteously. "That would be mean."

"If I had written her back and been saved from my financial difficulties . . . I wouldn't have you." Eli smiled at her, a sweet smile the likes of which she had never thought she would see from this austere man. "So everything is right with the world."

"That's true." She lifted her hand and showed him her rings, glinting merrily. "Because if I didn't have you, I wouldn't know the joy of wearing your wedding band on my finger."

He grew serious. "Chloë, I don't need your father's money now."

"He won't like that," Chloë warned.

"If he were smart, he would make me pay him for the privilege of having his daughter as my wife."

She laughed. "I want to hear that conversation."

"I'll return your father's money, but I will never return your heart, and I'll never let you return mine. Because all I need in this life . . . is you." He kissed her hand with the rings. "Will you stay with me forever?"

This was the wedding proposal she had never imagined she would hear. "Yes," she whispered. "Yes."

"I will show you every day of our lives how much I love you, and when we're old, you'll look back on our lives together and you'll really know what it means to be cherished."

His face swam before her eyes, and she had to swallow back the tears before she could whisper, "I look forward to a long life with you. There is no one else who makes me feel so happy, so passionate, so angry . . . and so alive."

He kissed her, and it was as if all the kisses that went before were insignificant, because this kiss was a pledge.

And they made it together.

Chapter 52

Sarah Di Luca had always told Anthony their grand-sons got their intelligence from her.

She was joking, of course. Anthony was brilliant, good at construction and wiring and better than her at reasoning his way through intricate problems.

But for years she did the accounting for the vine-yard and the resort, dealt with the wine vendors, hired the staff.

In fact, she and Anthony had been the perfect team.

He'd been gone for ten years, yet in the deepest recesses of the night, she still missed him. She missed his warm body, those nights when he held her close and made love to her. She even missed his sonorous snoring.

In those first few months after he had passed away, the silence was what kept her awake.

She always thought of him at night.

Last night, especially.

Because last night had been different.

Since Anthony had died, Sarah had lived alone. She'd grown used to the sounds of the house, creaking in the wind. . . . Then, after the attack, the girls had come to live with her.

Bao Le, strong and fit. She watched, constantly on guard, her gaze fixed outside, anticipating another attack. She was almost frightening in her focus. As long as Bao was on the job, Sarah knew she was safe.

Olivia Kelly, soft and sweet. In only one way was she fierce: when she guarded Sarah's well-being. She was a wonderful nurse, so dedicated to her patient's care.

She and the girls had been home from the hospital almost a month now, and Sarah had grown used to the noises they made in the night. When Sarah got up to use the bathroom, Bao would check the house. After Sarah went back to bed, Olivia would drift past and look in to make sure she didn't need anything.

The girls seldom needed to use the bathroom at night.

Oh, to be so young again!

Last night had been different from those other nights. . . .

Last night, Sarah had slept hard, but her dreams had been like waking nightmares.

She had dreamed she was awake, but not awake,

419

watching through closed eyes as someone crept into her dark bedroom. Someone came over and petted her head and murmured words Sarah didn't quite catch, in a voice Sarah couldn't quite recognize.

Sarah didn't respond. Couldn't. Although she tried. She tried so hard, but she was frozen in place, unable to move, to lift her eyelids, to speak.

It was truly a nightmare, and no matter how hard Sarah struggled, she couldn't break the bonds that held her in place.

A small light flicked on. Sarah could see it through her eyelids. And through the hours that followed, she could hear someone searching her room. The drawers in her dresser. All the boxes stored in the closet. The ones under the bed. The bookcase.

The girl moved the furniture and looked behind it. She searched the headboard while Sarah lay unmoving on the mattress. Sometimes Sarah drifted off, coming back to that truncated consciousness to find the light at a different place in the room, and the searching always sounded a little more frantic.

Sarah's mind had concluded two simple facts: she was drugged, and one of the girls had done it so she could search the room.

Finally Sarah drifted off once more, and when she came back, she was alone as the morning sun shone through the window. Alone, able to move, and crying with disappointment.

One of the girls, her girls, the girls she had welcomed into her home and her family . . . one of them had searched Sarah's room for Anthony's bottle of wine.

Slowly, stiff from lying in one position, Sarah sat up in bed. Gripping the bedpost in one hand, she waited for the room to quit spinning.

Had Bao hooked an inconspicuous microphone to Sarah's clothing and heard about the diamonds, and gone looking for them?

Had Olivia overheard a conversation between Eli and Chloë?

Which one was it?

Olivia was the most likely suspect, of course. She'd been trained in the use of drugs.

But Bao was efficient in everything she did, a woman who could, and undoubtedly had, killed in many different ways. If she needed to drug Sarah, she'd figure out how to do it.

And how had the deed been done?

Last evening, Sarah had fallen asleep in front of the television. But she always did. Was the drug in the coffee she drank after dinner?

Bao had made the coffee.

Or was it mixed in the pills Olivia gave her before bedtime?

Lately she hadn't been using the walker much, but Sarah needed it today. Pulling it close, she got unsteadily to her feet.

Her mouth tasted like a garbage dump. A side effect, she supposed. She pulled on her robe, headed down the hall to the bathroom, brushed her teeth and splashed water on her face. She proceeded to the kitchen, giving fair warning of her arrival with the squeaking of the wheels on the carpet.

Olivia and Bao sat at the table, drinking coffee and looking tired. Because they'd both searched her room? Because one of them had searched and one had been drugged? The scenarios paraded across Sarah's mind in a fearful frenzy.

As soon as she walked in, Olivia got to her feet. "Do you not feel well this morning?" She was eyeing the walker.

"A little unsteady. Don't fuss, Olivia." That came out a little sharper than Sarah had intended, and she shot Olivia an apologetic smile.

"What do you want for breakfast?" Olivia's pale complexion clearly showed the rings under her eyes.

"Just cereal." Sarah seated herself. "How did you girls sleep?"

"Lousy," Olivia said. "I had the weirdest dreams."

"I slept well." Bao spoke stiffly and bowed her head as if thanking Sarah for asking.

Sarah thought she looked guilty, but right now Sarah was too distrustful to have faith in her own instincts. "I had bad dreams, too. Very odd dreams."

"That's it," Olivia announced in her best nurse's voice. "We're not drinking caffeinated coffee after dinner anymore."

"Probably a good idea," Sarah agreed.

Breakfast was quiet, the clink of the spoons against the china bowls a little too loud for comfort.

By the time she was done, Sarah had decided what to do. "It's a beautiful day. I think I'll shower and go out to the garden and do some weeding."

"We can do the weeding," Olivia and Bao said together.

"I like to weed." Sarah got her walker. Stopping by the coatrack on the wall, she picked up her purse—she wanted her cell phone—and walked down the hallway to her bedroom. She shut her door and loudly flipped the lock.

That should have echoed down the hallway to the kitchen.

Was there a camera in her bedroom? A microphone? She hated being suspicious of everyone and everything, having her sense of safety stripped away and replaced with the brokenhearted knowledge that one of the girls she adored—maybe both—was plotting to rob her.

But she had to put her pain aside and concentrate on her scheme. And if there were a camera and microphone in place, that made the plan all the easier.

Putting the walker aside, she went to the closet.

Just because she didn't know where Anthony had hidden Massimo's wine didn't mean she didn't know the hiding places Uncle Leonardo Di Luca had constructed during Prohibition for their family wines and brandies.

Going to her closet, she took the wide, white-painted wooden trim and opened it as she would a cupboard door. The hinges squeaked. The scent of cedar wafted out. Shelves lined the narrow space in the wall.

She kept concealed in here the best memories of her life with Anthony: the love letters he had written her while they were courting, the photo he had taken of her during their trip to Cuba on the beach in her bikini, the naughty poem he'd written her from Italy . . . and the wine they had created together.

She smiled fondly as she examined the tall ruby red glass bottle and the red wax seal they had so carefully crafted to fit over the cork. They'd been sure that this wine would launch the premium wine market.

And it might have, too, except for two things: they were ten years too early . . . and Anthony had used grapes planted by his grandfather, a varietal no one recognized, and the wine had been a spectacular failure. They'd been disappointed, of course, but as with everything in their marriage, they'd picked up and soldiered on.

Anthony had dumped most of the wine, but she'd kept one bottle as a memento and now . . . now she was going to sacrifice it on this terrible ongoing feud with Joseph Bianchin.

Taking it out of the cubbyhole, she carried it to her dresser and placed it there.

The mirror reflected it back into the room. The red glass glowed like a ruby.

She frowned. Too obvious?

No matter. She was a recently concussed elderly woman. She could get away with what appeared to be a senior moment.

Plucking her phone from her purse, she made a display of punching a number, but she never pressed CALL. This was for show only, for the spy who might be watching her. Speaking into the phone in fond tones, she said, "Hello, dear. I think you're right. I'm getting uneasy about the safety of Massimo's wine, so would you come by and take it home with you? Your security is so much better than mine." She made a pretense of listening, then chuckled. "Really, you can't complain. I have kept it safe so far. Come when you can. Thank you, dear!" The pretense of hanging up, and she was done.

She kept her expression determinedly bland as she gathered her clothes for the day and laid them out on the bed, but she couldn't help being startled when someone knocked.

"Mrs. Di Luca? I wish you wouldn't lock your door. If you fell, I couldn't get to you." It was Olivia.

Olivia. Was it concern that had brought her to the door or greed?

Using her walker, Sarah made her way to the door and opened it a crack. She could have won an Academy Award for her backward glance at the bottle on the dresser and the worry and guilt on her face. "I'm ready for my shower, but you don't need to check on me. I'll be out in a half hour."

Olivia nodded, her wide eyes guileless.

Sarah started to shut the door, then opened it again, wide enough for Olivia to actually see the bottle. "Oh, and, dear, Rafe is coming by to pick something up for me. If he shows up before I'm out, make him comfortable, won't you?"

"Yes. I will."

This time Sarah noted a definite shade of worry in Olivia's eyes.

Because she had always been uncomfortable around domineering men like Rafe? Or she wanted to grab the bottle and get out before he arrived?

Sarah felt sick to her stomach with misgiving . . . and maybe from the drug hangover, too.

She waited until she heard Olivia walk away, then walked down the hall to the bathroom. She shut the door—and that newly acquired paranoia made her quietly turn the lock.

She might not know which girl had searched for Anthony's bottle of wine, but she knew she didn't want her to step in while Sarah was naked and defenseless.

She turned on the water—that would block any sounds from the hall—got ready and showered as she would have on any morning, except perhaps she took a little longer than normal.

If one of the girls was going to steal the bottle off the dresser in her bedroom, Sarah didn't want to catch her.

When she finished, she pulled on her robe and tied it tightly, as if the strength of the knot would give her the fortitude she needed to face these challenges. She listened at the door, straining to hear any movement in the hallway.

There was nothing.

Cautiously she opened the door.

It was quiet. Had both the girls left?

She walked down the hall to the front of the house, to her bedroom.

The door was open.

The bottle was gone.

Tears welled in her eyes.

She had wanted to be wrong so badly.

The front door was open, and she could hear a murmur of voices outside. A man. And a woman.

Rafe. Rafe was here.

Had *he* taken the bottle?

She hurried out onto the front porch.

He stood facing Bao, frowning heavily. At Sarah's appearance he turned to face her. "Nonna, I—"

"Do you have the wine?" she asked.

"What?" His eyes narrowed on her.

No. Obviously he knew nothing. "Why are you here?"

Bao stepped forward. She was still pale and strained and still so guilty-looking Sarah didn't know whether to call her a thief or embrace her and tell her everything would be all right. "I called him, Mrs. Di Luca," Bao said. "I have to retire from my position here."

"Retire?" Sarah hadn't expected that.

"Yes. I must." Bao's eyes shifted away from Sarah, and she twisted her hands. "Last night I . . . I slept through the night. I never stirred. I never heard anything. Someone could have come in and killed you, and I wouldn't have known, so—"

"Ah. I see. Where's Olivia?" Sarah asked.

Bao blinked in confusion. "She said she had some errands to run. Why?"

"What's wrong, Nonna? You look . . . upset." Rafe's frown deepened.

Sarah said, "I was drugged last night so someone could search my room."

Rafe and Bao viewed her in astonishment and alarm.

Sarah looked at Bao. "Could you have been drugged, too?"

Bao whirled to face the driveway. "Damn her! Olivia? I never suspected that insipid little twit of having the guts to—"

"*What wine?*" Rafe asked.

"I pulled a bottle of wine out of the hiding place in my bedroom. Not Anthony's wine," Sarah assured him. "I left it on the dresser while I showered. It's gone."

"I'll check your room for monitoring devices," Bao said.

"I'll send law enforcement after Olivia's car," Rafe said.

The two shot into action.

Sarah seated herself on the porch swing and rubbed her aching head.

Olivia. It was Olivia who had drugged her. Olivia who had searched her room.

But Rafe had investigated her. Olivia had no record. She had no family, either: no mother or father or grand-parent who loved her and would keep her from going astray. Someone had offered Olivia money either before she came to Bella Terra or after she came to work in Sarah's house, and she had taken the bribe.

With her innocent eyes and shy way, she had never given a hint of the avarice that drove her. But neither had she ever uttered a word about her past, or her goals, or anything personal. Sarah should have had doubts. Instead, she had respected Olivia's privacy.

Noah drove up on his motorcycle. As he parked it, Rafe went out to meet him.

The two boys stood hunched together, talking.

And Noah . . . Sarah could tell he had been interested in Olivia. Just like the other boys, he had his secrets. Unlike the other boys, Sarah didn't have a clue what mystery lurked in Noah's background, only that something had happened that year after high school when he was wandering around the world. . . . He'd come back, her youngest grandson, the boy she'd raised free from the angst that had dogged his brothers . . . and somehow the angst had found him.

He'd never fully met her eyes again.

Foolish old woman that she was, she'd had hopes that shy, sweet Olivia would heal whatever anguish dogged him.

Instead, Olivia had betrayed him . . . as she'd betrayed them all.

Bao put a cup of coffee on the table beside her.

Brooke drove up, Eli and Chloë close behind.

The family was all there, and that meant . . . that meant bad news.

They walked up onto the porch and stood around her.

Eli sat next to her on the swing. "Nonna, I'm sorry. They found Olivia's car about twenty-five miles from here on a turnout on East Summit Highway. The bottle is gone. And Olivia . . ." He shook his head.

"She's hurt? Is she going to be all right?" Sarah asked.

Eli looked around helplessly.

"No, Nonna. She's not. She's dead, shot execution-style." Noah's face was angry and drawn, and each word was as direct as the blow of a sledgehammer. "It would appear that the professionals have descended on Bella Terra." He looked around at his family, daring them to deny him the truth. "And it's not the bottle they're after, is it?"

Sarah looked around, saw the heightened anxiety on Eli's face, and Chloë's, and Rafe's, and Brooke's. She saw the way Bao had herself braced, and knew this thing was much, much worse than she'd imagined.

"They want what's hidden in the bottle. And I know what it is," Noah said. "There's no use trying to protect your younger brother from this."

"How do you know what's going on?" Chloë asked. "Eli and I barely figured it out ourselves."

"We were going to call a family conference," Eli

said, "but . . . Noah, what do you know? And how *do* you know it?"

Noah laughed, bitterly, briefly. "I know because I'm right in the middle of it. These people . . . they're ruthless, and they are going to find Massimo's pink diamonds any way they can."

New York Times bestselling author
Christina Dodd delivers a seductive series
about an ancient rivalry that lives
in the world today. Don't miss

STORM OF SHADOWS

Available now from Signet.
Read on for a special preview. . . .

"Do you ever get gut feelings?" Aaron asked.

"When I get the flu." Rosamund laughed too long at her own joke, then grew uncomfortable under his steady regard. "I used to. Sometimes. But my father said gut feelings were nothing but wishful thinking, and I might as well depend on a fortune-teller's crystal ball."

"He wanted you to stay in the real world." And why? When Aaron had come down to the library basement with antiquities that needed to be authenticated or manuscripts that required translation, Dr. Elijah Hall had been brilliant, stiff-necked, and grim, yet keenly interested in the paranormal. Most important in Aaron's mind was his sharp instinct for the genuine above the counterfeit.

Never, ever had he mentioned that he had a daughter.

Why had he so emphatically quashed Rosamund's curiosity?

Had Dr. Hall foreseen a dread prophecy for her?

"Are you familiar with the legend of the Chosen?" Aaron asked.

"The Chosen . . ." He could almost see Rosamund flipping through the encyclopedia of her mind. "Yes. The Chosen and the Others. When the world was young, a beautiful woman gave birth to twins, each marked as something set apart from average people. Repulsed, the woman took them into the darkest woods—in these fairy tales, it always is the darkest woods—and left the babies for the wild animals to devour." She looked at him inquiringly. "Is that the legend you mean?"

"That's it. Do you know the rest?"

Rosamund continued. "Those two children were the first Abandoned Ones, babies left by their parents without love or care and, to compensate, given a gift of power. The babies survived. The girl was a seer. The boy was a fire-giver. They gathered others like them and formed two gangs—one for good and one for evil—and they fought for the hearts and souls of the Abandoned Ones."

"A battle that goes on today," he finished.

"Yes." Her brow knit. "It's not a very comforting fairy tale."

"How many are?"

"Most have endings of some kind. The witch is

tipped into the oven. The evil stepmother falls from a cliff—" She caught sight of his face. "All right, not happy endings, but still, there's none of that *The battle goes on today* stuff."

"Yet it's so much more realistic to know there can never be an end, or at least not until the"—he could scarcely stand to say the words—"until the Apocalypse."

"If the legend of the Chosen Ones were true, which it's not."

Aaron wished that she was right. Unfortunately for her and her future peace of mind, she was staring right into the eyes of one of the Chosen Ones.

Read more about the Chosen Ones
on Christina Dodd's Web site at
www.christinadodd.com.

Christina Dodd

THE NOVELS OF THE CHOSEN ONES

When the world was young, twins were born. One brought light to a dark world; the other, darkness and danger. They gathered others around them, men and women destined to use their powerful gifts for good or evil. Today, their descendants walk the earth as the Chosen, and the ultimate battle is about to begin.

STORM OF VISIONS

STORM OF SHADOWS

CHAINS OF ICE

CHAINS OF FIRE

AVAILABLE NOW

"Devilishly clever, scintillatingly sexy."
—*Chicago Tribune*